Wycaan Master: Book Five

Fʀᴏᴍ Asʜᴇs Tʜᴇʏ Rᴏsᴇ

A Novel

ALON SHALEV

Tourmaline Books
Berkeley, California

FROM ASHES
THEY ROSE

From Ashes They Rose
Wycaan Master, Book 5

Tourmaline Books, Berkeley, California
http://www.tourmalinebooks.com

ISBN: 978-0-9884428-2-5
Library of Congress Control Number: 2015908774

First Edition: October 2015

Published in the United States of America

DEDICATION

I have walked down many paths, in many lands. The true constants have been the friends who helped define how I evolved and continue my journey.

To Andy Dale & Mike Kaplin – close friends for decades, men who kept me honest along the way, steady barometers in stormy weather. Happy Half Century to each of you.

To Sir Terry Pratchett 1948-2015

You were the master of the fantasy series. You made us laugh and cry. Yet you remained humble and always accessible to your fans. You used satire to highlight so much that is good and bad in this world, and had a lot of fun doing it.

"Fantasy is an exercise bicycle for the mind. It might not take you anywhere, but it tones up the muscles that can."

You fought the good fight until you could fight no more. You wrote right up until the end because, well, that's what real authors do. You even left us with the closing scene:

Death: "AT LAST, SIR TERRY, WE MUST WALK TOGETHER."
Terry took Death's arm and followed him through the doors and on to the black desert under the endless night.'

RIP Sir Terry. You are missed.

The Wycaan Master Series:

Acknowledgements

- To Monica Buntin, my editor, for once again making sense of an awful lot of words.

- To William Kenney, my book cover artist, for your amazing ability to continually transform my jumbled ideas into such beautiful pieces of art.

- To Jeny Lyn Ruelo and her team at The Fast Fingers, for the interior design and formatting, and always being willing to deal with my tech-challenged questions.

- To my good friend, Janet Frankel, who gave the manuscript one final polish and saved me a few blushes.

PROLOGUE

T here is more than one kind of elf, but history favors those fair of skin. How could it not? The fair-skinned elves won and seized power. They destroyed and conquered. And they wrote the histories. Is it not this way the world over? The stories tell of tall, thin, lithe elves, many with snow-white hair and a love for the earth. They fight with delicate swords and bows of polished wood. They honor the land, the trees, and the different races. They extol fanciful notions of equality and noble living.

But the scribes of history display a conveniently selective memory. They shy from these elves' transgressions, ignore their elitism, and forgive their crimes. When their moral values are challenged, they unsheathe their swords and wield their contempt upon all who refuse to bow down and comply.

The fair, white-haired ones recall how they sailed across the Agate Seas from the Western Isles to discover and claim Odessiya, a beautiful, unspoiled land of blue rivers, mighty mountains, lush plains, and majestic forests. They mention the massive herds of bullists, buffalo-like creatures still shaggy and fat, that crossed the Soko Desert and the Great Plains of Agnali, providing a bountiful source of food and skins. They speak of great-toothed feline hunters that stalked the herds, and of abundant precious metals and wealth in the Ardien and Bordan mountain ranges.

But the fair elves never speak of the native Ashen Elves, who had lived in Odessiya for centuries before the explorers arrived. These aboriginal elves shared the fair elves' pointed ears, but little else. They bore dark hair and gray complexions. They recounted ancient tales, handed down from generation to generation, of Ashen Elves, ancient tales of the formation of their ancestors in the bowels of the great

Ice Fire Mountains They roamed the land, following the herds and the seasons. Though they were great warriors and those who crossed their paths regretted it, they never sought out other races to subjugate. They also possessed no magic.

The fair elves never accepted the indigenous, apparently non-magical elves of Odessiya. Neither did the Ashen Elves seek to be taken in. Instead, when commanded to bend their knees, they rebelled. Bloody battles were fought, and great treachery was unleashed—magic pitted against brute force. Perhaps it was the magic that, once set free, consumed the fair elves and fueled their craving for superiority.

A powerful spell was wrought and the Ashen Elves were banished to another dimension, buried under the great Ice Fire Mountains far to the north of Odessiya. They became isolated from time and history and finally faded from legend itself.

Forgotten.

But the gray elves did not forget. They trained hard and became one with the Ice Fire Mountains that nurtured them, growing rock-solid muscles, eruptive temperaments, and the dogged tenacity of the lava flow. They became hard of body and hard of heart. They buried their fear, their shame, their elven essence deep within themselves and allowed the desire for revenge to grow.

Then one day, a white-haired stranger with round ears entered the land under the mountains and sat at their hearths. He heard their stories and understood. He showed them how to discover and refine their own dormant elven magic and promised to one day return and help them fulfill their destiny.

And so the time nears when the gray elves' magic will break the chains that restrain them. Then the true stewards of Odessiya will return, banish the usurper, and reclaim their homes and their honor. They will have their revenge. Their time approaches.

From The Chronicles of Tarth, Mage of the Ashen Elves of Ardien.

Chapter 1

The tall elf straightened and stretched. He wiped the blood from his thick broadsword by pulling it across the bloated body of the man who lay strewn before him, then glanced at his friend. The elfe crouched, her muscles tightly coiled, looking for someone else to fight. Her pale hair showed little evidence that she had just slain four men, but her green eyes glared with rage. This was the fourth time in two months they had been attacked by roving gangs or drunken sailors and fisherman. They were elves in a land unaware of the emancipation of elven slaves in Odessiya, a long way from home and moving further away with each passing day.

"Are you okay?" Rhoddan called over, seeing how Pyre stood, her body still tense.

These men had not cared about the elves' pointy ears. They were interested in the curves of the elfe's body, sharing gruesome stories of their former conquests in front of her, as if she was not even there or didn't matter. Exaggerated as they probably were, these tales were nonetheless degrading and horrific.

"Pyre. Are you okay?" Rhoddan repeated and walked over to her. "It's over. These brutes won't ever abuse a young elfe again."

He put a hand on her shoulder, and she wheeled around, glaring up at him, her green eyes ready to explode. He hesitated. Though he towered over her, Rhoddan was startled by her vehemence. Nonetheless, he didn't retreat or look away from the dark elfe.

Finally, she nodded. "I'm alright. I'm sorry. I…"

"It's okay." He offered a smile. "Come, let's go."

"Wait." Pyre went from one corpse to the next, rifling through their pockets and taking coin, jewelry, and a couple of knives.

Rhoddan frowned. "Why are you looting them? We have enough draktans."

"It's not for us," she replied, strapping a small bag, now bulging, to her saddle. "It'll go to the women and elfes at the next pleasure house. Have you noticed how many there are?"

Rhoddan nodded. He had seen the pleasure houses and the gambling joints. He had seen too many fishing villages and ports since they had left the Emperor's fortress at Grogin.

Sellia should be safely back at Wycaan Island with the twins by now, though it was clearly not as safe as once thought. But she had Montclair, the fortune sword, and a couple of Wycaans who had served the deceased Emperor. Rhoddan was uneasy about those Wycaans who could so easily swap their allegiance, but it comforted him that Ballendir's dwarf regiment would stay with Sellia until Pyre returned. They would help rebuild Wycaan Island, and there were no better builders than the dwarves.

Sellia would, no doubt, request more Wycaans from the Elves of Markwin or take the twins there to be trained. Going to Markwin made more sense to Rhoddan. Sellia had just lost her mate, and her eldest daughter now walked another path in a place no one knew save her teacher, the sorceress Sa'gola. Sellia had family in Markwin and would be welcomed by the Elves of the West. She would need their support.

He thought back to their parting. Beautiful, dark Sellia, the elfe he had secretly loved since they first met as young *calhei*. Sellia, mated to his best friend, the Wycaan Master he had so loyally served, was devastated. Rhoddan wanted to tell her that everything would be okay, that he would return with Seanchai, but held his tongue from such wild promises. He walked from the hall, leaving Sellia hugging her *calhei* and softly sobbing.

Rhoddan had little support to offer anyone. He needed his own closure. He needed to know. Was Seanchai truly dead? Sa'gola had sent her most deadly fire, the pure white, into Seanchai's chest, and he had fallen overboard, sinking into the ocean's depths.

At first, Rhoddan and Pyre were eager to search for the Wycaan Master because they knew the water might not claim him. Seanchai, in his transformation ceremony, had walked underwater in a ley lake and received his Win Dao swords. But that didn't mean he could survive the sorceress' white fire. In the first few weeks of traveling, Pyre and Rhoddan swapped theories when they stopped each night. Was it possible that the white fire had claimed him? Had he drowned because, unconscious, he had not triggered whatever Wycaan magic he needed to breathe underwater? Had his prone body been eaten by sharks or other predators or eroded by the salt?

Finally, they had ceased guessing. It offered no relief, and served only to spiral each of them into darker moods. The trail began and ended at Braithwaite. Locals confirmed that Seanchai ate and slept there before meeting the Purple Lady. A young boy was his guide and left Seanchai on a jetty with the sorceress. Neither Seanchai nor the boy was seen after that. Sa'gola recalled how they argued and she lost her self-control when Seanchai threatened to do everything he could to take his eldest, Mharina, away from her.

In the last few days, Rhoddan had begun to wonder how long they should continue this search. More importantly, what would come after? What did a life without Seanchai look like? He allowed his horse to lead the way. This brooding was becoming a daily ritual. It numbed the pain and dulled the possibilities.

The cries of merchants and traders ahead brought him from his reverie. They had entered another fishing port. He drew his hood up to hide his ears, an action that filled him with shame. He glanced over and saw Pyre's face already buried inside her cowl. They left their horses at a stable and their bags in a room at the adjacent inn. The innkeeper eyed them nervously —two heavily armed figures hidden in cloaks—but draktans spoke louder than words, and the coins were already on the counter.

"Anyone enters our room, they die," Rhoddan growled. "And then I'll come for you, and you'll wish to be dead."

The innkeeper gulped and rubbed the heavy stubble on his face. "N-no one will disturb you. Is there anything I can get for you: food, a hot tub?"

"No," Pyre said. "Just direct us to the nearest pleasure house."

The innkeeper glanced down her body. Pyre glared, prompting swift directions. They went to their room and put their bags down.

"I don't want you going to a pleasure house until just before we leave. It will invite attention and possibly some unpleasant reactions," Rhoddan said.

"Let them come," she growled.

He wheeled on her. "If you give this campaign more importance than finding Seanchai, you will do it alone and then return to Wycaan Island."

"Since when do you order me around?" Pyre snarled, her green eyes again flashing. "Does none of this disturb you?"

"I just want to find Seanchai. Nothing else is important right now."

"You are obsessed. You know this is hopeless. The sorceress said no one has ever survived—"

"No one has ever been Seanchai!" Rhoddan screamed.

"Yes, they have, only you have never known them. Seanchai is not the first Wycaan, nor will he be the last. They die, Rhoddan. In times of strife, they die first and often. Face it. He's dead. Grow up. Seanchai is—"

Rhoddan struck her across the face. Pyre's head snapped sideways, and when she turned back, her cheek was red and her eyes brimmed with tears.

"I'm so sorry," he said, taking her into his arms. "I'm so sorry."

They stood together, Rhoddan pulling the elfe to his heaving chest.

"I-I'm so sorry," he repeated.

"It's okay," she said, her voice muffled in his shirt. "I could have stopped you."

Rhoddan pulled away and stared at her. "What?"

"I'm a trained Wycaan, Rhoddan. Don't flatter yourself. You're fast, but not that fast."

"Then why?"

"I wanted to feel your pain. I'm grieving, too, but not like you. I'm just … just feeling numb." She half turned from him. "We need to talk about our next step. Could we not both best honor Seanchai's memory by taking the twins to the Forest of Markwin and seeing them fulfill their potential? Is that not what he would have wanted?"

Rhoddan fell onto the bed. He cupped his face in his hands and gently shook. He could feel Pyre staring at him. She had seen the odd tear, but not him crying. Something was breaking through, and he heard her step forward. It was her turn to hold him. She had struck a far harder blow than he.

CHAPTER 2

It would be a while before Rhoddan and Pyre left their room. Rhoddan needed to bring his emotions under control, or he would take a swing at the first man who accidentally bumped his shoulder in the street. He peered over at Pyre, who sat at the window, staring at the bustling scene outside. He could not make out her expression, but her shoulders were slumped. He didn't have the energy to cross the room and offer comfort. He was drained, empty, and utterly helpless. It was Pyre who slowly rose, stretched and let out a long sigh. She turned to him, her green eyes swollen and moist.

"I'm hungry," was all she said, and, gathering her weapons and cloak, walked out.

Rhoddan went after her. He didn't ask if his company was welcome; he was not willing to be told no. Pyre was younger and an attractive elfe. She would draw attention without trying. Perhaps this is what she wanted. He doubted there was a man in this port who could fight her, but three or four, with an accurate knife hurled from the shadows, would bring her down.

He caught up and walked slightly behind her as she made her way to the quay. Abruptly, she stopped, and Rhoddan almost walked into her. She turned her head, peering down a narrower road where merchants had laid out goods. This was the outskirts of the market, Rhoddan assumed, and he searched for what might have caught her interest. People bumped into them, but neither elf moved. Someone shouted as a cart pulled by two oxen parted the crowd. Rhoddan took Pyre's arm and guided her gently to the side.

"What, Pyre?"

"Seanchai," she whispered.

"He's here?"

"No," she replied quickly, "but I think he might ... I don't know. It's probably nothing."

She began to walk down the street, barely glancing at the sellers of housewares, spices and fish, colorful vegetables, and fruits stacked high. An entrepreneurial merchant pressed an apple into her hand.

"Shiny fruit for a beautiful woman," he declared, not seeing her hooded face and certainly not her pointed ears.

Pyre's green eyes and white hair were distinctive enough, but she had blossomed into a curvaceous elfe, her skin pale and smooth. She was built for battle, as she trained endlessly, but this in no way served to detract from her attractiveness. Rhoddan wondered for a moment why he had never felt attracted to Pyre. She had been totally devoted to her training, and her adoration of Seanchai had taken root in the Markwin Forest so long ago. It had never faltered, and her loyalty was as fierce as his. She must be as gutted as him at the prospect of giving up their search.

Pyre stopped, chewing absently on the apple as she stared around them. There was a store of iron products and two that sold weapons and armor. She walked over and stood in front of one, paused, then moved to the next. It was quite big and looked to be a sturdy structure, made of clay, with iron doors that were probably locked at night. Most other businesses were stalls and flimsy structures where the products were taken home at night.

On the ground outside the store lay shields and armor. A few swords and spears stood in two racks just outside the doorway. A big man with curly hair and a black beard stepped outside. Usually, sellers would pounce on anyone who stopped for only a moment, but this man stood with arms folded, staring at them. He was a guard and armed.

When neither Pyre nor the guard moved, Rhoddan stepped closer to the elfe.

"What is it?"

"I don't know. Let's go in."

She stepped forward, and the man moved aside to let her pass. An older man shuffled up immediately. He was bald and slightly bent, but exuded vibrancy.

"Good day, good day. What do we have here? Two warriors from the road, huh? Fortune-swords, maybe? Are your blades nicked or your knives in need of replenishment?"

Pyre removed her hood as she peered around.

"A she-elf? I—"

"An elfe." Her voice was firm and flat. "Where I come from, we take exception to 'she-elf.'"

"Oh, my, I do apologize." The man offered an apologetic bow. "We do not see many elves in these parts. I have heard that in Odessiya, things are more, um, progressive these days. The few elves here are generally slaves or—"

"I also take exception to slavery, both for labor and sex."

Rhoddan put a hand on her shoulder and felt her tense muscles relax. She turned away from the old man and examined a sword. The man turned to Rhoddan.

"How may I be of assistance, sir?"

"I think we are just looking for now, thank you."

"May I see that bow?" Pyre called over from further back in the store.

The old man was immediately next to her. He conjured a pole with an iron hook on it. "Which one, my lady?" Pyre pointed. "Oh, I fear that will hang there forever," he continued. "Pretty as it is, the bowyer apparently made it for a giant or a man with the strengths of the gods. No one has been able to draw it. If indeed made for a man, it makes you shudder to think who it was made for."

Rhoddan walked over as the salesman continued. "I originally thought it was only meant as an ornament, but it comes with a quiver and twelve beautifully flighted arrows, all lime green to match the bow.

Rhoddan's heart leapt. He had to force himself to stay calm. "It would look nice above our hearth, my dear, and maybe one day you will provide me with an heir who can shoot it."

The man had hooked the bow and was bringing it down. "Wonderful workmanship," he said as his hand ran along the shiny wood. "Not from these parts, to be sure."

"How much?" Rhoddan asked.

They bartered. Pyre helped lower the price by acting as if she did not want to waste money on such an ornament, and Rhoddan soon enough instructed the man to wrap the bow and quiver up carefully. As the man made a great show of tying the burlap sack around it, Rhoddan asked how he came by the bow.

"Usual way. There are vultures who loot empty battlegrounds, picking up anything they think can be sold once the victorious move on. Let me see if I can remember. There are three or four of these vultures who are particularly talented at this. One—his name is Simmons, I think—he picks off many items from other vultures, as he always has better-quality steel, if you know what I mean."

Rhoddan held the package at this point and turned as nonchalantly as he could to examine a dagger. "When was he last in town? I would love to hear a story about…"

The salesman put a hand on his arm. "Simmons is not—how can I say this? Well, I sometimes wonder how dead some of these people are when he takes their weapons. Do you get my drift?"

Rhoddan whirled on the man, his congenial smile vanishing into a harsh threat. The man gasped. "Where is he?" the elf hissed.

CHAPTER 3

The bar was smoky and crowded. It had taken a while to find it. Two people who directed them winced and suggested they seek a nicer neighborhood. Rhoddan wanted to go alone, fearing that Pyre might attract the wrong attention, but she was adamant they not be separated. Rhoddan was not sure if this was fear of being alone or her being pragmatic. They fought well together, with intuitive understanding as they moved among assailants. And he had to admit as he surveyed the smoke-filled bar that he was happy she was here.

When three men rose from their table and staggered out, Pyre slipped into one of their vacated seats with its back to the wall. She was hooded and, taking out a dagger, began to clean her nails. The message was clear. Rhoddan gave her the packaged bow and went to order drinks. He flashed a gold draktan at the large woman behind the bar and moved to the end of the surface, away from the noise. She followed.

"My friend and I would like an ale each. We are seated over there." He nodded in Pyre's direction. "Is there a man here called Simmons?"

"He'll be in soon, I wager. Whatcha want with him?"

Rhoddan leaned in, ignoring her question. "When he comes in, you give him a drink on me and send him over to us."

She laughed, and her body quivered. "You don't *send* Simmons anywhere. If I tell him you want to conduct business with him, would that be accurate?"

"It would," Rhoddan said. "My master waits anxiously for us, and he is not a patient man. When do you think Simmons will appear?"

"Can't promise he will, mind. He did last night and the night before, is all I'm saying. Why doesn't your master come here?"

"He is with his men somewhere else. Two dozen of them. You wouldn't want them in an establishment like this." He gave her the coin. Hopefully, this last piece of false information would keep others from their table, especially since she knew they had money.

He returned to their table. He and Seanchai had come a long way since setting out from Rhoddan's father's camp in search of a teacher to train Seanchai's mysterious powers. They had created an alliance, brought down the Emperor, and helped create a more just and equal Odessiya. But it was still a very different world beyond Odessiya's borders.

Pyre and Rhoddan sat in silence and sipped the beer. It was warm and bitter, and Rhoddan drank only to relieve the monotony. The bar filled, and standing men were pressed against each other between the tables. The noise grew louder as time passed, and the elf was ready to leave. Just as he leaned to suggest this to Pyre, a group of men parted. Some were pushed, and others shuffled out of the way. Two huge men, both with sleeveless shirts that exposed bulging muscles and thick, black tattoos, moved in front of their table and stepped sideways, sending more men scampering out of the way and leaving an empty space around the table.

Through the wake came a furtive young man, his dark hair combed over to one side. His eyes darted around, seemingly more from habit than fear. He was well dressed—not ornate, but in a functional shirt, waistcoat, and trousers, none of which seemed frayed or dirty. He put his tankard on the table and sat.

"Who am I thanking for the beer, gentlemen?" he asked, his voice flat, almost apathetic.

Rhoddan leaned forward. "My master prefers that names are not exchanged unless business is done," he said, quite proud of his opening gambit.

Simmons immediately stood. "Then I'll thank you for the drink and be on my way. I'm an honorable trader. I shake a man's hand and look him in the eye. If he can't do the same, then best not to trust him."

"Wait," Rhoddan said. "Please take a seat. You can have my name, for what it's worth. I am Greaves. I come from Grogin, where I train soldiers."

"Grogin? I've heard some disturbing stories about that place. Are they true?"

Rhoddan nodded but gave a different answer. "Wouldn't know. Haven't heard the stories."

Simmons laughed and raised his tankard. Rhoddan reciprocated, and some beer sloshed on the table at impact. Simmons glanced at Pyre.

"Your partner's quiet," Simmons said.

"My partner is a simple lad. He would be squiring in any other place, but he is good with his blades. I brought him here to help me get out if needed. For that, and that alone, he is capable. My master told him not to speak unless I tell him to, and I have no desire to hear his droll comments."

Simmons shook his head. He raised his tankard slightly to Pyre and turned back to Rhoddan. "Whatever. You want weapons?"

"No," Rhoddan answered. "Information." He unraveled part of the bow. "Do you recognize this? I bought it from one of the traders here."

"Maybe. What of it?"

"My master seeks the man who you might have procured it

from. He's a big elf, white hair and scary blue eyes. I think what he stole from my master included two curved swords."

"What is this information worth?"

"Five draktans now. Ten more after we kill or capture him."

Simmons gulped his beer and wiped his mouth on a handkerchief. Rhoddan was impressed.

"Give me five draktans now, and I will share what I've heard."

"Five draktans is a lot for rumors," Rhoddan said. It was an absurd amount.

"No problem," Simmons said congenially and began to rise. "Thank you again for the beer."

Rhoddan put three gold coins on the table. They were the only things that glimmered here, and it created an almost hypnotic attraction. The noise level dropped abruptly and then rose again. Simmons' hand darted out, and he swept up the coins. "Do you have a death wish? You fool. Most of these men will not see that in a year."

But as Simmons made to pocket the money, he realized the silent boy was grasping his hand. Rhoddan was sure from Simmons' expression that he had not seen the boy move and that his grip was like steel. He glared at Pyre, and Rhoddan slowly put his hand on the elfe's. But Pyre didn't let go.

"Please sit," Rhoddan said. "What have you heard?"

Simmons sat slowly. With his free hand, he took a drink, but did not say anything. Rhoddan moved his own hand away and nodded at Pyre, who released her hold on Simmons.

"A woman?" Simmons said, suddenly looking at her chest. He rubbed his wrist. "Damn strong grip."

"You see those two swords on her back?" Rhoddan murmured. "She is very effective with them."

Simmons glanced at the protruding hilts and then back at Rhoddan. He took another sip of beer and this time wiped his mouth on his cuff. He leaned forward.

"You know the bow is strung for a god, right? I picked this up in the Kyber region near the sea. A kid on the beach found it. I ended up paying too much because the whole village saw it as a sign from their stupid sea god. See, even though the bow was in seawater, the salt had no effect on it. The bowstring was like new, the arrow feathers perfect. Even though it had been swept about, the quiver was full.

"Sounds crazy, right? In the inn there, I heard from a peddler that a giant had walked out of the ocean and was working in a fishing village further north. His hair was long and white as snow."

Rhoddan glanced at Pyre but couldn't see her face hidden deep in her hood. Simmons continued.

"Anyway, I heard at the next village that the sea god was working as a simple fisherman for some old couple. I wouldn't normally believe any of it, but two separate sources a village or two apart? All talk of long, white hair and strength of a bull and…"

Rhoddan leaned forward. "And what?"

Simmons stared at him. When he spoke, it was only a whisper. "He has two swords, just like your woman there."

CHAPTER 4

"**L**isten," Simmons continued. "I can see this means something to you. Maybe I can help guide you there—all for a fair price, of course. These are dangerous lands. Ain't much in the way of law and order, if you get my drift. A man and his girl could find trouble. I can send a few of my lads to guard for you at night and help bring down this so-called god. It won't cost more than those other five draktans you offered."

Rhoddan did not reply. He took another gulp.

Simmons took this as hesitation. "This thief must be in a lot of trouble for your master to send you after him. Can't be just for a couple of swords and a bow. He must be important, must be valuable. Maybe he's your lord's son?"

Rhoddan shook his head.

The arms dealer leaned forward. "Listen, my friend. You're a long way from home. What if someone else captures your quarry before you? Might be a healthy ransom, I think. Could be a cut in that for you, maybe?"

"My master is not to be trifled with," Rhoddan replied, wondering how to extricate himself from the conversation.

"Your master is a businessman, I reckon. It's why he's your master and you're his lackey." Simmons' laugh deteriorated into a hacking cough.

Rhoddan rose and slapped the man on the back. Then he leaned in from behind and whispered, "This is a lot bigger than stealing swords from dead men on a battlefield. My friend and I are highly trained. We are the ones who leave the dead lying there for you. Don't follow us out. I glimpse you, and someone else will be stripping *your* corpse of weapons."

Rhoddan left the bar and was glad to be outside. The salt air revived him. "We'll walk around for a while," he said. "I don't want anyone following us to our room."

They walked down to the quay, where mist engulfed the ocean and boats. They stopped several times, as if having a conversation, so they could see if they were being followed. Three men, not making much effort to hide, trailed them, and Rhoddan thought he saw glimpses of another further behind.

"We need to face them in the open," Pyre said.

Rhoddan stopped. "You want this, don't you?"

"I hate these humans," she said. "I need to keep thinking of Shayth and Maugwen to remember they are not all like this. The street ends up ahead. Let's meet them there."

"Be careful, Pyre. I—"

"Do you think these brutes can take me?"

"Be careful of the hate that fuels you." Rhoddan's tone was even. "What would Seanchai do?"

"Seanchai is…well, he *may* be dead." There was a glimmer of hope as she spoke, something that had been missing for too long.

At the end of the street, on the cusp of darkness, they turned, moving away from each other and drawing their swords. The three men had become six, though Rhoddan was not sure the one he had spied in the shadows was among them. They spread out; their thick arms were heavily toned, and their tattoos glistened with sweat. Each held a sword or club. One twirled an axe like a toy. But they waited. Rhoddan wasn't sure why, but then a voice spoke from behind him.

"Mr. Simmons feels underappreciated and underpaid for his valuable information."

Rhoddan turned to face a man as big as him. The man was bald and playing with a bushy moustache. He held a huge broadsword in one hand and a flail in the other.

"So he sends you to die?" Rhoddan replied.

The men all laughed.

"I think Mr. Simmons had something else in mind," the man said.

"He knows we are not alone."

"Yes, you are. You're free to go once we teach you some respect, but your woman is for us to have fun with. We'll show her a good time."

Again, the men laughed. Three more had joined the bald leader. Rhoddan sighed. There was nowhere to run, but he wasn't really interested in running.

"Have it your way," Rhoddan said. "How about you and me start this off, unless you are too scared to stand alone?"

The man played with his moustache. "No," he said after a few moments. "I like the odds the way they are."

The man in the shadows watched carefully. The big elf lurched forward, feinted a high blow, and then slashed at his adversary's legs, bringing him to his knees. Skipping past his victim, the elf turned to face the leader. The bald man could fight, and he held his own against the elf, leveraging the flail to keep his distance. His wingman was creeping around behind Rhoddan and would create a serious problem. The man in the shadows drew a small trigger crossbow—an assassin's weapon—and fired a small bolt through the wingman's throat. Both the gang leader and the elf froze, but then the elf attacked.

The assassin turned his attention to the elfe. She used the same tactic, launching herself at the man at the end of the line. Her blows were true, and the assassin was impressed at her fluidity. He had seen very few who could fight with such speed and precision. The elfe kept moving as she sliced and parried, moving into an area wide enough to keep the bulk of the men between her immediate assailant and herself. Her thin blades looked so flimsy next to their thick swords. But she never tried to match their strength, instead using their momentum to fend them off. She wounded one in the calf, and he knelt as his friends moved in front of him.

One with a spear skillfully kept her away from them. He raised the spear to throw, but suddenly cried out. The spear fell by his side as blood spurted from his throat and both hands went to his neck. He crumpled to the ground.

The three remaining men stared in the direction of the nearest building, and it was a fatal mistake. The elfe leapt between them, and her swords brought two down before they even raised their blades to meet hers. The other panicked, wheeled, and ran. He tripped and fell, his sword clattering against the cobblestones. Her silver hair now released from her cowl, the elfe jumped on top of him, one sword at his throat, the other at the back of his neck.

"What would you have done to me? What?"

The man squirmed, causing shallow cuts from the elfe's swords.

"N-n-n-nothing. Just some fun, y'know."

"I have a pretty good idea," the elfe hissed, and slit his throat in earnest.

One man had fallen to a knee and was trying to stem blood flowing from his calf. Keeping one eye on him, the elfe made her way to the fallen spearman. She knelt next to him, looking off into the darkness. She had pulled the quarrel and was playing with it in her hand. The assassin wondered if she'd see him with her elfe vision—a man in black, well shrouded. But she turned back to her final quarry, away from the assassin. He was not trying to stand. He was a boy and weeping silently.

The assassin turned his attention back to the big elf and gang leader. They had moved away into the darkness as they sparred, but now they parried back on the lit road, and it seemed as though one entered the light and the other, darkness.

The man took a step back and twirled his flail above his head, creating great whooshing sounds. As he charged forward, the elf feinted to one side and crouched low, rolling under the spiked ball, which embedded itself in the stone wall next to them. The elf rose and sliced up into the man's arm. Blood spurted from the cut vein, and the man screamed in pain, the flail's handle flying into the darkness. The elf met his glance with a glare.

"Look well, my friend," the elf said. "You stand alone. Choose. Die well or return to Mr. Simmons and explain that we have concluded our business with him. If anyone—connected or not with his organization—so much as steps in our way, we will come after him."

His chest heaving and sword hanging limp, the bald man held his cut arm to his body. "I'll deliver your message," he panted.

"Take the boy with you," the elfe said.

The man walked toward the boy, lifted his sword, and, without stopping, swung. The boy's head rolled to the ground and bounced, blood spurting upward. The elfe roared with rage and advanced on the man. But he was already falling when she reached him. His eyes glazed over as he fell backward, a metal disc protruding from his forehead.

Both elves turned in the assassin's direction, but he ignored the male's cries to show himself and retreated soundlessly into the night. Now was not the time to reveal himself. But he would…soon.

Chapter 5

Mharina thought she was all cried out—that no matter how hard she tried, she would not be able to summon another tear. She yawned. She had not yet slept, sitting up late with her mother in front of the fireplace in the Great Hall of Grogin, long after the others had retired. They talked and hugged and cried.

Over the course of the evening, Mharina impressed upon her mother that she had changed since the kidnapping—that she was no longer a young *calhei*—and, when it was just the two of them and the nearby candles had been replaced, Mharina demanded Sellia speak to her as one elfe to another and not as mother to *calhei*.

"I have decided on my path, mother, and gave my word to Sa'gola. I will go with her."

"You should never have done that, Mharina. Your bond with the twins is always most important."

"And it always will be. But I have made my choice. In doing so, I saved your life and Pyre's and Riona's." She laughed, a strange sound in this place and time. "Not to mention Riona's cute fortune sword. I could not let you die when there was a way to save you. And mother, the path I have chosen is not so bad."

"Not so bad!" Sellia hissed. "That witch is taking you from your family, a *calhei* who has just lost her fa..."

Sellia couldn't say it and brought her hand to her mouth. Mharina

leaned forward and, for the first time in her fourteen cycles, took her
mother in her arms. There was something monumental here. It was
not the mutual, supportive embrace they had shared when Sellia and
the twins first learned of Seanchai's death, when all four had clutched
each other and cried. This was Sellia, the strong warrior elfe, falling,
and her daughter reaching out to catch her.

"Mother, I have learned a lot from Sa'gola, and I have so much
yet to learn. I am not Wycaan like the twins, but I have a power and
a destiny, and I must find it. Sa'gola cares for me deeply. I cannot
explain this, but there is a profound bond between us."

She pulled away slightly so that they faced each other, their curly
black hair as entangled as their love. With her sleeve, Mharina wiped
away her mother's tears.

"Look at me, mother. Really look at me. I am a *calhei* no more."

She wanted to tell her mother how she fought the evil Ithea,
how Sa'gola taught her to heal with energy and magic and wield the
sorceress' fire. There was so much she wanted to tell her mother, but she
held back. Sellia's dark brown eyes gazed into Mharina's. A log in the
fire popped, and its sparks highlighted her mother's beautiful features.
Finally, Sellia spoke, and her tone was steady and full of wonder.

"Yes, my daughter. You are a *calhei* no more. You have become an
elfe, one who will add to her father's proud legacy."

"And her mother's?" Mharina whispered. "Will she be proud of
her daughter even when they have parted?"

Sellia straightened, pulling their hair apart with great care. Staring
into her daughter's eyes, she cupped Mharina's cheeks. When she
spoke, it was as the powerful mother Mharina had always known.

"I already am," she said. "I always have been, and I always will be."

They sat in silence for what seemed like forever, watching the
fire burn down and sipping wine. Later, boots clicking on the stone
floor made them both turn to the door. Through the entrance, purple
light silhouetted a small female figure.

"We leave early, Mharina. Perhaps you should get some sleep. Dawn is a few hours off, and our journey long."

Mharina glanced at her mother. Sellia took her hands and squeezed them. "I love you, Mharina, and I will wait for your return."

They hugged, but without the intensity of before. This was a resigned embrace, and Mharina was relieved when her mother released her and allowed her to leave, her own boots leaving a lonely wake of silence.

Sa'gola entered the room and sat in the seat her apprentice had vacated. She flicked a finger to the waning fire, and it blazed to a comfortable burn, shedding light on the two of them.

"I have nothing to say to you," Sellia said, tossing her black curls back and wiping her eyes.

"You don't need to," Sa'gola said. "But I want you to know that I love Mharina deeply. I will protect, nurture and teach her to the best of my ability. And my ability, Sellia, is considerable. What would her role have been otherwise? She would have lived in Senzia's and Ilan's shadows as they became Wycaans, causing a powerful resentment that might have poured out once she discovered her potential."

"Will I ever see her again?"

There was a long pause before Sa'gola spoke. "I cannot know. I do not see the future or know what path you take. But, in time, Mharina will plot her own course. If at that point she so chooses to return to Odessiya, I will not stop her. That is the only promise I can give."

"It's all I can ask," Sellia said, and rose, but then she stopped. "My mate. Did he die well?"

Sa'gola pursed her lips. "In truth, no. I had not intended to kill him, but to bring him to the Master. I was confident in my ability to persuade him, since his entire family was here. What happened caught me off guard, and when I attacked him, he was likewise unprepared."

Sellia took a step to the fireplace, keeping her back to the sorceress. "What made you attack him with such intensity? Mharina explained the difference between the controlled fire of color and the force of the pure white. Why hit him with everything you had? Why kill him when you were not charged to do so?"

Sa'gola did not answer. She just stared into the fire. Sellia wheeled around.

"What do you hide from me? From Mharina? What?"

Again, Sa'gola did not answer, but the emotion that had surfaced on the boat when she faced Seanchai rose again. The fire in the fireplace burned brighter, roaring up through the vent. The room became unbearably hot. Sellia stood there, beads of sweat dripping down her dark skin, her eyes shifting from a plea to accusation. Still, the fire burned higher, and soon the elfe could stand it no more. She turned and fled the room.

"She has gone, Sa'gola." A woman's voice came from a dark corner of the room. "Ground your emotion and the fire. We have much to discuss."

Chapter 6

S
a'gola slowly brought her emotions under control, and the fire gradually returned to a sputter. She heard footsteps approach, and a woman about her size leaned over the fire and placed on another log. The woman sat opposite Sa'gola and poured them both some wine. She handed the Purple Lady one silver goblet.

"Thank you," Sa'gola said, and sipped the wine. She peered over the rim of her cup at the small woman with the black, spiky hair, dressed all in black. "I saw you came with the big elf warrior, but we have not been introduced."

"I am Maugwen, a healer in the prince's court."

"Well, Maugwen, please don't think me rude, but it has been a long night, and we travel at dawn." She made to rise.

"Of course," Maugwen replied pleasantly. "We can talk more when we travel. Good night."

Sa'gola froze and then sat down again. She arched an eyebrow. "When I said *we*, I was referring to Mharina and myself."

The woman just smiled, and Sa'gola felt... something. "Who are you?"

"A healer—I told you," Maugwen said. "I met Rhoddan and Prince Shayth years ago, though the prince was little more than a frustrated bully back then. Keep that between us, of course. I was thrown into jail in Galbrieth with them and Ilana, Seanchai's first mate.

"Seanchai and Sellia rescued us from the gallows, literally. But that's a story for another time. Everyone thought me a common peasant, thrown into jail because my father evaded paying taxes, preferring to squander it on life-saving herbs for his wife. Everyone but Seanchai, that is.

"He saw something else in me—something even I had not sensed. In short, I heal with energy. Seanchai tried to train me, to help me cultivate this energy through his Wycaan methods, but my energy did not respond."

Maugwen leaned forward and poured them some more wine. As she leaned back in her chair, she ruffled her hair, and the spikes stood tall and defiant.

"So here I am with something mysterious and powerful inside of me, and I do not know its full potential or how to handle it. And here you are, all magical and powerful, from what Mharina tells me, and ready to teach."

She had been smiling faintly, but as she leaned forward, her face became intense. "I can't explain it, Sa'gola, but I think my powers did not respond to Seanchai because he is male. I have a strong feeling that you can tap into and understand how to unlock the full potential inside of me. I must find out." She leaned back again. "There is an upside to this for you, as well."

Sa'gola found herself laughing for the first time in weeks. "And what, pray tell, is that?"

"However close, however bonded, you and Mharina became, you just murdered her father."

"Murdered?"

"What would you not impart to Sellia?"

Sa'gola felt her anger rise. "Why would I tell you when I would not tell her?"

"Fine; I will hazard a guess. Seanchai was standing there on the boat with you, and you shared how close you had become to Mharina.

Perhaps you told him of your intention to take her as your apprentice, and the father in him roared. Remember, I know Seanchai. I—"

"*Knew.* You *knew* Seanchai."

"Maybe." The flippancy in Maugwen's voice was eerie. "So Seanchai threatens to do everything in his considerable power to prevent you from teaching her, to tear her away from you, that you will never see her—"

The fire roared again, and Maugwen leaned forward to lay a hand on Sa'gola's knee.

"Please, enough with the fire. I think I understand." She smiled and withdrew her hand. When the fire had receded, she continued. "I don't need to tell Mharina; she will figure it out. But I can be there to help you both deal with it. She trusts me. I have known her from birth."

"But why should *I* trust you?"

"Because I need you, Sa'gola, if I'm to discover who I really am. Quite a little triangle, aren't we?"

"How do I know you have this power you say you have?"

"Did you ever meet Denalion the Dreamwalker?"

"The old elf? Yes, I did."

"Did you ever meet him in the dream world?"

Sa'gola took another sip of wine and nodded.

"Then come inside of me," Maugwen said. "Walk in my mind and see if you can identify the power of which I speak. Then you can make your decision."

Sa'gola stared at her, wondering if this was a trap. The woman looked so harmless. She wasn't pretty; her face was round and her eyes big. Her hair was a law unto itself, and, though she was thin, it seemed to Sa'gola that in more luxurious circumstances, she might be quite plump.

"Okay," Sa'gola agreed at last.

Sa'gola followed the sleeping young woman into her dream world. She watched Maugwen heal people in the capital and on the battlefield. She noted the healer's loyalty to her friends and felt a pang of regret as she witnessed interactions with the Wycaan. She saw the special affection Maugwen had for the prince and the intimacy between them. Did she harbor love for the ruler of Odessiya? If so, it was a forbidden love, to be sure.

She saw how Maugwen learned the most rudimentary energy exercises through training at a monastery, but that it was an unsuitable system. She saw that the energy was independent, almost agreeing to be summoned rather than something to be cultivated. It was a wild magic, an untamed entity not unlike the magic used by her Order, and Sa'gola was intrigued.

She saw Maugwen at the gallows and then in the dungeons of the great fortress of Galbrieth. She saw the warrior elf—then a scrawny youngster—and the young prince, wild and unpredictable. An elfe Sa'gola had never seen appeared, and Sa'gola wondered if this might have been the Wycaan's true love, a sweet but strong elfe who pulled Maugwen through those difficult days.

And then she saw a small girl, hair spiky and unkempt, dressed in stained rags and begging on the street, pleading for food for her family and coin for her mother's medicine. Sa'gola frowned as she watched three older street boys push and kick Maugwen to the ground, beating her until she relinquished the coin and torn bread. And then she saw soldiers leap onto the boys from their horses, kicking them with heavy boots and laughing. The soldiers saw the girl, and Sa'gola shuddered, as she could almost feel the military boots kicking the young girl.

And she knew at that moment that she would take Maugwen with her in the morning, because they shared more than magic. Sa'gola's body was a network of scars, especially on her back and thighs. She had learned the magic to protect herself, to build walls of power so that no man could ever beat her again. And she would teach this to Maugwen so that she, too, would never again be beaten and abused.

CHAPTER 7

Mharina adjusted the saddle on her horse and secured her bags as the dawn struggled to pierce the chilly mist. She had woken Sa'gola as soon as she felt it justifiable and begged her to leave before anyone else woke. She could endure no more goodbyes. Yesterday, Ilan cried and begged her to stay with them. He offered to negotiate with their mother to allow Sa'gola to join them, however improbable that seemed to the three children. In contrast, Senzia, ever stoic, asked whether her big sister was leaving of her own volition or as a prisoner.

"I made a bargain with Sa'gola to rescue mother and the others from Ithea and told her that, in return, I would go with her of my own free will."

"Ithea? He's the sorcerer you burned?"

"Yes." Mharina offered a weak smile. "Though apparently not well enough. I have much to learn from Sa'gola. I will return, and we shall once again be together."

Senzia shook her head. "It'll never be the same. Our paths may cross, but we'll never walk them together."

This unsettled Mharina, not least of all because of the emotionless way her sister spoke. It also sent Ilan back into hysterics. He threw pillows at his twin sister, demanding that she take her words back. Senzia allowed the pillows to hit her, silent for a while. Then she turned to Mharina.

"Are you doing this to keep Ithea away from us? He's going to come after you, isn't he?"

Mharina felt a pit form in her stomach. Images of the pale, powerful man filled her mind. His voice scratched at her insides, and she went cold with fear.

"You're doing this to protect us," Senzia said. "Sa'gola's the only one who can stand against him, and he'll want his revenge on both of you."

"But we have Rhoddan and Pyre and the Wycaan Masters," Ilan pleaded. "We'll protect you, Mharina; we all will."

He leapt into her arms, and she held him tight. But her mind reeled in fear. Ithea would come back, and she hoped he would come after Sa'gola and her seeking his revenge, because if he didn't, he just might go after her family.

Riona hugged her and offered all kinds of womanly advice that was lost on Mharina. Pyre and Rhoddan were already gone. It was unclear why, but Mharina suspected they needed to be far away from the one who had killed her father.

She turned from her reverie to find Sa'gola leading out her small, sturdy mare. They led the horses through the great stone gateways, the smooth rock sweating from the morning mist or perhaps weeping at the loss of their creator, the former Emperor of Odessiya, the Master. He had tried to kill Mharina, and she would be dead if not for Sa'gola's intervention. She wondered if he had somehow survived the fall, the great stone Anwar absorbing him as he fell. She wanted to ask, but could see that Sa'gola had no desire to talk. The sorceress was looking back at Grogin, back through the great arches of the outer gate. Was she taking one last look?

A small person, shrouded in black, appeared, also leading a horse out of the castle. Mharina looked at her teacher, but Sa'gola expressed no surprise. Mharina's heart leapt, thinking for an irrational moment that it was Senzia, and she was both relieved and surprised when Maugwen reached them with a grimace and long yawn.

"Why waste such a fine, brisk dawn in a nice, warm bed after barely closing my eyes?" she queried with a theatrical grimace.

"Dawn is a powerful hour," Sa'gola replied. "Saddle up. It will be a long time before you find a warm bed again."

"Just the encouragement I need," Maugwen said, and mounted her horse.

Mharina rode behind Sa'gola and stared at the woman she both loved and feared. Sa'gola was her teacher, mentor, protector, yes, but she also killed Mharina's *ahdahr*. It was hard to accept, and she desperately wanted to know the entire story. She believed they had fought, but could not comprehend that the woman who professed to love her so would kill her father. Who had escalated the meeting? Who had attacked first, and what had made Sa'gola feel a need to use the pure white killing fire?

She felt her chest constrict and knew this was not the time to reflect. One day, she would ask the difficult questions, but what would it accomplish? She had sworn to follow Sa'gola, to train and apprentice with her, and she knew inside she dearly wanted this. Whatever had happened on that fishing boat in Braithwaite, she needed to bury it...for now, at least.

Mharina's filly was dark gray, almost black, just like Mharina, and they settled quickly into a rhythm. She was comfortable in the saddle, her most precious memories being the times she rode out and hunted with her mother. Suddenly, the tears erupted and, try as she might, Mharina could not stop a sob from escaping.

Sa'gola reined in her horse and turned to look at her apprentice. "We are alone out here in the open. You do not need to suppress your sorrow. Cry if it helps. We will talk later, but now it is best we ride."

Mharina sniffled and nodded. She did not want to talk now, anyway. Sa'gola offered her a beautiful smile.

"You're very brave, elfe. You've survived being kidnapped by the taragusii, an ambush by the tutans, Ithea, the Master, the death of your father, leaving your family...me." She shook her head, and her black, purple-streaked locks shimmered in the pale light. "I can only imagine how distraught you feel, and crying won't diminish how brave you are and how much I admire you."

Mharina stared at her. That was Sa'gola—so strong, so empowering, and so beautiful. Mharina gave a brief nod, not daring to try to speak. Then she glanced back at Maugwen, but the healer's face was indecipherable.

Chapter 8

Sa'gola led the party in almost complete silence through a volcanic mountain range of which Grogin, tall as it had been, stood only on the periphery. The clouds and mist seemed joined as one, and they remained cold and damp over the next few days. Sa'gola knew exactly where she wanted to stop. She led them to some caves, and they tethered their horses at the entrance. The three women entered the mountain on foot. As they descended, the ground and air warmed, and on the first and third nights, they found small wading pools.

Sa'gola encouraged them to undress and wash their clothes. They did, afterward laying them out over hot pumice to dry. Then they bathed in the same pool and soothed their tight muscles. Mharina had grown to appreciate Sa'gola's love for the water, and they had shared her bathtub in her chambers at Grogin and bathed together in the great underground lakes in the adjacent mountains.

If Maugwen was embarrassed to show her nakedness, she did not let on. She followed Sa'gola's lead without comment and without hiding her body, which was a bit thick, though pleasant to Mharina's eyes. Maugwen was not muscular like Sellia or tiny like Sa'gola, though if anyone was self-conscious, it was Sa'gola, who—subconsciously, perhaps—covered the scars on her stomach, legs, and back with her hands as much as she could.

She had never told Mharina where the older scars had come

from, though the elfe knew the new ones were from Ithea. She had witnessed him beating Sa'gola, which prompted Mharina to come to the defense of the woman she so loved and admired. Whatever abuse Sa'gola endured in her past had made her tenacious in honing her own power and defense.

Little was said during this time beyond common civilities or the sharing of information. Whether Mharina felt the silence to be comfortable or tense was more a reflection of her own mood. Maugwen did not reach out to her, but Mharina felt the woman's constant stare on her.

Midway through the fourth day, Sa'gola stopped abruptly. Mharina peered around her but saw nothing. The gorge they were riding through had widened, and the steep mountain slopes were less angled. They were about to pass through two large boulders.

"Say nothing unless asked," Sa'gola murmured. "Let me do the talking."

Mharina frowned, but then one of the rocks moved slightly, and she almost gasped. Judging by Sa'gola's nod, it was a signal. They moved their horses forward slowly, and Sa'gola reached out a hand and touched one of the rocks. When she spoke, her voice projected up the mountainside.

"We honor the home of the Granite, ancient children of the mountain. We seek only to pass through your land. We will draw no flint or iron. We will not approach your offspring. May we pass?"

Nothing happened for a long time, but Sa'gola did not remove her hand. Then the stone rumbled deeply and slowly. The other responded in kind, and Mharina felt it reverberate inside her body. Sa'gola removed her hand from the first rock and laid it on the second.

She turned her head. "You will both touch the granite and allow it to feel your pulse. You will know when to relinquish."

She nudged her horse forward, then turned and waited. Mharina followed as instructed. She felt the cold, damp rock, but it was anything but inanimate. A low hum passed through her arm and chest. Then it retreated, and she leaned to the other side, receiving the same response. Moving forward, she waited as Maugwen did the same. The healer grinned and nodded at the vibration. Soon they were riding on.

"Sa'gola?" Maugwen began.

"Not 'til we pass through their territory," Sa'gola replied. "We'll make camp soon after."

It was toward the end of the day before they passed two more similarly posted Granite. Sa'gola laid her hand upon one of the rocks.

"We thank you for allowing us to pass. May your days be long and peaceful and your offspring spread upon the mountainside."

Mharina followed. Touching each of the Granite, she thanked them. The second one rumbled a different vibration, and Sa'gola laughed. "Are we not all young in your eyes? But yes, she is a *calhei*, a child of the ancient tree stewards."

When the Granite responded, she laughed again. "Even the elves are not worthy of being called ancient in your years? Very well, but an elfe she is, and I am glad it pleases you to offer her passage through your land. Thank you."

They rode on for a short while, until Sa'gola found the entryway into the mountain. They tended the horses and took their packs inside. Shedding their clothes and entering a pool, they gave themselves to the rich, warm mineral water. After a while, Maugwen asked about the Granite again.

"What do you know of mountain trolls?" Sa'gola asked.

"Only stories told around the fire, of mighty warriors of stone who fight and create earthquakes and thunder for the rest of us."

"It is true that when the Granite fight, all who are near will hear. But such activity is rare and has happened, as far as I know, only once in my lifetime."

"How old are you?" Maugwen asked, her tone casual. Mharina perked her ears up, as she had wondered this, too. Sa'gola had hinted that there was no correlation between her youthful looks and true age.

"Compared to the Granite, I am but a babe," she laughed—a beautiful sound, Mharina thought as it echoed through the cavern.

"The dwarves have had the most interaction with the Granite, and it has always been hostile. The dwarves carve out great cities in the rock and harvest precious stones and irons. It is why I promised the Granite not to touch their people or draw any blade or tool.

"The dwarves feel they have a right to the mountains and underground. They do not ask permission or worry about what harm they do. But their cities are huge and impressive, and their skill at locating fruitful places to mine is uncanny."

"Have you ever seen a dwarf city?" Mharina asked.

"I have been to Hothengold, their capital. I attempted to counsel the High King."

"Why?"

"Remember who I worked for? The dwarves had their First Decree, and so the Emperor needed a spy who could come and go without detection. You have seen how I can disappear and move quickly. The dwarves have their own mythology about me and, while it is not always flattering, I am quite proud of the stories I feature in."

"Tell me one," Mharina pleaded, her love of stories surfacing.

"I told the High King I could come and go as I like, without detection, and that he should be pleased I didn't steal something. He scoffed that a dwarf secures what is precious to him, that those with dwarf stones protect them with their lives, and I would never be able to steal them. I was up for the challenge, but warned I would take something rarer than a set of dwarf stones or diamonds."

"What did you take?" Mharina felt herself laughing in anticipation.

Sa'gola laughed with her and waded over to sit next to her. She put an arm around Mharina and kissed her cheek. "Something very precious. Something that had passed out of memory for most and eluded those who searched so hard for it—including my master, I might add. But it would not have been right to keep for myself, so I gave it away to my favorite apprentice."

Mharina frowned and leaned away, though not far enough to leave her teacher's embrace. "I thought I was your only apprentice."

Sa'gola put her hand on Mharina's throat and held up the black stone she wore. "And now we will be able to contact each other even when we are apart."

"Is that an Anwar?" Maugwen asked, incredulous.

Sa'gola jerked away from the elfe, and her face turned hard. "Yes," she hissed, "and as long as you are in my home, I forbid either of you from trying to use it." She stared at Maugwen. "I treasure my home and its secret location. If you ever try to betray my secret, I will kill you."

Mharina stared at her teacher, shocked at her sudden turn from intimacy to rage. *Yes*, she thought, *you will.*

CHAPTER 9

"I apologize," Sa'gola said after a long silence. She exited the pool and sat naked on a warm rock, her toes touching the water. "I have had a hard life, Maugwen. One with my talents mixes with the most powerful and inevitably accrues many great friends and terrible enemies. You have met two of those enemies already.

"I have used considerable magic and skill to hide my home from prying eyes. It is probably why I never took an apprentice. Bringing someone into my home is an incredible step of trust." She looked at Maugwen. "I have thought to blind you for the last part of our journey."

Maugwen nodded. "I would understand, though that would make me your prisoner, not a pupil. Would you swear to bring me back here if I were to request it?"

Sa'gola thought about this. "I think so," she said slowly. "Unless you become a danger to Mharina or me. If it is a matter of you feeling you have learned enough, I would release you."

"My calling is as a healer," Maugwen said. "I want to discover what power and potential I possess. Then I want to return to my chosen path."

"Sa'gola?" Mharina asked. "You once told me that even the Emperor didn't know where your home was."

"That's right."

Mharina shifted to look up at Sa'gola. "Does Ithea?"

"No, my *calhei*, he does not. One day, we will confront him together. But in my home, there is nothing to worry about." Mharina felt her teacher examining her. "Does this not satisfy you?"

"What if he comes after us and can't find us? What will he do?"

Sa'gola shrugged. "I don't know. Go and conquer some other fiefdom. Isn't that the call of all powerful males?"

"Not for my father," Mharina snapped, and then reddened, but she did not apologize.

Thankfully, Sa'gola laughed. "Then what worries you about Ithea?"

"What can he do to hurt you if he cannot find you?"

Sa'gola thought for a while and shrugged. "Nothing I can think of, really."

"What can he do to hurt me that would force me, and then maybe you, to reveal ourselves?"

Now it was Sa'gola's turn to frown. "Your family," she whispered after a while. The furrows on her face deepened. "Or he may try to train the twins. It is what he counseled the Master to do. He wanted to kill Seanchai and have the Master focus on untrained Wycaans."

"Why did the Emperor not heed his advice?" Maugwen asked.

"A good question," Sa'gola replied. "I cannot say for certain, but I think the Master secretly admired your father—the fact that your father bested him twice and bonded the races of Odessiya in a way that the Master could not. Perhaps it was that Seanchai was young and defiant. The Wycaans at Grogin had been defeated and cowered under the Master's command. He had no respect for them."

She turned to Mharina, and her voice became soft. "Your father remained true to his principles at all times. It cost him his soulmate, his parents and village, his teachers. The Master scorned his loyalty to his friends and scoffed that it was his weakness. But maybe, deep inside, the Master craved someone to be loyal to him out of respect and not a thirst for power. Even the Master's own son did not fulfill his need."

She slowly lowered herself back into the water and hugged Mharina, who was sobbing quietly. "I should not have talked like this. I'm sorry."

"No," Mharina said, her voice just a muffled whisper. "I want to hear about him."

"Maugwen knew him much better than I. But I want you to know something. I *do* regret what happened, not only because of the pain I caused you, but because I would have wanted to know him better."

"The world is a darker place without him," Maugwen whispered, and all that broke the silence in the cave were the rhythmic sobs of Mharina, first daughter of the Wycaan Master.

Sa'gola led them out of the volcanic mountain range and down a winding path along the edge of a narrow, shallow valley. The path was smooth, save for the deep ruts left by an endless flow of wagon wheels. It was late in the afternoon when their path joined with one wide enough for two-way traffic. Many of the wagons they passed were laden with heaps of black rocks, and others were covered. The drivers were human or dwarf; Mharina saw no elves and raised her cowl to hide herself.

Three young women on the road with no males or weapons might attract the wrong attention, she thought. While they all—Sa'gola in particular—could probably deal with any violence, it would leave tracks in ways that their horses would not.

"We'll sleep in beds tonight," Sa'gola said, "though the baths will be less impressive than what we have been used to these few days.

But the food will be hot, and we'll sit at a table with chairs. Do you remember such luxuries?"

The town was not as exciting as Mharina had hoped it would be. It was a mining center with hostels to support the men and dwarves who worked there. There were plenty of bars and places to eat and stores that supported the mining industry. Men and dwarves milled around, staring at the women as they rode through. Mharina wondered if there were any women living there at all.

Sa'gola led them to stables and negotiated shelter and food for the horses. The owner offered all kinds of services, and Sa'gola gave him coins and told him that she wanted the horses well rested, fed, brushed, and shod the next morning, not-so-subtly insinuating it would be in his best interest to follow her instructions. Then they crossed to a large hostel.

"We 'ave nothing fittin' for ladies," a young girl told them from behind a counter. "Best I can do is put a curtain up at one end of the 'alls. But you'll 'ave men on the other side and, well, you know men."

"Just tell the owner I am here," Sa'gola said.

The girl shrugged and left. Mharina noted Sa'gola had not given her name. Her teacher smiled.

"What will she describe to him, do you think?" Sa'gola asked.

"That a lady in purple waits for her room?" Mharina suggested, and saw the smug smile on her teacher's face.

Soon, they left their bags in the comfortable room that had been cleared for them and returned downstairs in search of a hot meal. It was a similar story. The bar was crowded and all tables seemed taken, but somehow a table near the fireplace became available. While they waited for their food, the young girl brought them mulled wine, compliments of the owner. When a man stumbled over and slurred that they would be happier sitting with him and his friends, Sa'gola stood and stared up at him. Moments later he retreated, red-faced, sober, and terrified. They were left alone after that.

"It's best to let them fear you. You must never waver when challenged or confronted," she said to Mharina, though Maugwen also leaned in to listen. "When Ithea struck me, I curled into a ball. It was a reflexive action from bitter experience. Do you know what I should have done?"

Mharina shook her head.

"What you did. Untainted by trauma, you struck without warning or hesitation. As soon as he drew out his whip, I should have unleashed my power…without compromise or delay."

Mharina nodded, pondering the words, and was stunned when Maugwen exploded, "And is that how you killed Seanchai?"

Sa'gola glared at her but said nothing.

CHAPTER 10

S ellia's stomach churned. The dark elfe dug her heels into her horse and rode ahead of the party. The land in front of her was familiar now, and though it had once been her home and hunting grounds, she dreaded returning to Wycaan Island. When they left, Denalion burned the bodies of the students and guards, but otherwise they had not begun to clean the school. Now she was returning to the charred remains of innocent bodies and the memories of those she had lost that day and since.

Their approach was most vividly reminding her that the leader of the school, her mate, was dead. Seanchai would no longer stride through the grounds, offering advice and encouragement to every hopeful face. This had been his dream, his vision, and now only an empty shell remained. She bore their *calhei* here. Three beautiful young elves had grown up and played in every corner of the school.

Now she returned with two, both wounded inside, if not out. Ilan cried every night for his father and sister. Senzia had retreated into her own world, speaking only when asked a direct question and watching Sellia —accusingly, maybe, though Sellia could not rationalize why. Sellia was the invincible, impervious warrior elfe. Seanchai had regaled the *calhei* with stories of their mother's bravery and tenacity, and sometimes it appeared as if she had personally brought the Elves of the West to fight for the freedom of Odessiya and led them to that crucial victory in the Cliftean Pass.

But she had failed her mate and, more atrociously, her eldest daughter, who had sacrificed her own freedom to save Sellia and the others. A *calhei*—no, an elfe now—Mharina had been forced to mature beyond her years and had not shied away from defending her family. Beautiful Mharina, almost a living image of Sellia with her dark skin; curly, black hair; and the courage Sellia had nurtured when Mharina was younger.

A female deer cautiously skirted Sellia when she halted her horse upon a hill looking down on the beautiful lake and the stone walls of the school on Wycaan Island. Instinctively, she brought her bow around and drew an arrow. The deer froze and stared at her. Sellia frowned. The expression on the doe's face was not fear, but pity. She turned her beautiful brown head, and three fawns scurried after her. Sellia did not noch the arrow. Instead, she hugged the bow to herself. It was a bonding gift from her first mate before he died. And now her second mate was gone, too.

The doe was right to look at her with pity, and Sellia felt the tears rise. She never cried in front of the twins, never revealed her pain or guilt. Hearing the others approach, she nudged her horse forward, but three horses galloped toward her.

"Sellia, stop!" Montclair called out.

She turned, readying a cutting remark about not having to wait for him, but the fortune sword had his weapon out. The blade glistened in the sun. It was a fine sword, and Montclair knew how to use it. Behind him, the Wycaan, Master Sythen, wielded a huge broadsword in his right hand. His cheeks were as red as the band around his head and contrasted with his white beard and hair, tied back in an elf style even though he was human.

Riona was there, too, her sling ready. Sellia knew the pale, black-haired human healer also carried blades, one of which had been pressed to Sellia's throat when she had threatened Denalion. Ah, dear Denalion, ancient Dreamwalker of the Elves of the West. He was

another who would never return to Wycaan Island. He had fought
Ithea, the powerful sorcerer, and held him up long enough to let the
rest of them escape.

"What is it?" Sellia snapped.

"Use your elven eyes," Sythen said, his words clipped.

Sellia considered slapping him. He was a Wycaan who had
sided with the Emperor, and should be dead instead of Seanchai.
She tolerated him for his skill and ability to protect her children
and the fact that both twins admired him and enjoyed his training.
She turned and looked again at Wycaan Island. Smoke rose in tidy
columns. Someone was already there and apparently cooking. Sellia
pursed her lips. They had ridden ahead of the dwarves, who were
the main body of their defense. The dwarves did not have horses and
were a few days behind.

"I'll go alone," she said, and nudged her horse.

Montclair was instantly in front of her. "I can't allow that. Apart
from the fact that it is thoroughly stupid and self-serving, you employ
me to keep you alive."

Sellia snorted and tried to maneuver her horse around him. But
he moved with her. "Yes," she snapped. "You work for me. Now, get
out of my way. Enough people have died because of me."

"Since I work for you, I have an interest in keeping you alive
so you can actually pay me for my loyal and thoroughly effective
service." He offered his most engaging smile.

"I don't like you, Montclair," she snapped, knowing this to be
untrue. "But I am fond of Riona, and I don't want her mate taken
away from her. I know how that feels."

Montclair sighed. "So let's compromise and send our Weapons
Master here." He nodded to Master Sythen. "He's oozing Wycaan
skill and duty."

Sellia turned to the white-haired warrior, who nodded. "Be
careful, Sythen," she said. "We're rather lacking for Wycaans right now."

Master Sythen moved his huge warhorse forward and disappeared down the trail. Montclair watched him, but spoke quietly for Sellia only.

"I never met Seanchai, but I have heard enough to know that he would prefer you to prioritize his children and friends. Put away your death wish, Sellia. When the twins are grown, it is another matter, but for now, they need you."

"DON'T EVER PRESUME TO TELL ME WHAT MY MATE WOULD..." She struggled to bring herself under control. "Seanchai was unique. There will be other Wycaans, but they'll never be his equals. Don't ever presume to tell me what he would want, and don't ever tell me I'm not to blame for his death."

"So it's true?" A voice came from their left, and the pain was raw and palpable.

CHAPTER 11

An icy shiver coursed through Sellia's body. She could not bring herself to turn and face him, to see the pain on his face. She had seen it on Rhoddan and was relieved when he had taken off. And she saw her own haunted expression every time she bent over water to drink.

"Sellia. Look at me," the voice commanded. "The rumors…they are true?"

She turned slowly and took in his spiky, black hair and toned chest, which was covered only by a sleeveless shirt straining to hold his muscles in. He held his favored bow with the black, feathered arrows. She looked anywhere and everywhere except into his eyes.

"Who are you?" Prince Shayth Shindell demanded of Montclair, who was already turning away.

"No one of consequence, my prince. I will give you privacy."

Shayth stared after the fortune sword's retreating form, and a scowl crossed his face. But then he turned back to Sellia. He sighed and maneuvered his horse in the direction he had come.

"Maintain a wide perimeter," he called. "I'll speak with my friend privately without interruption." He dismounted and moved toward her. "Come here," he commanded, and opened his arms.

Sellia melted into his embrace, and the sobs erupted without care for who heard. Her body shook as wave after wave of mourning finally found escape, and, with each shudder, Shayth held her tighter.

As the long-suppressed release abated, Sellia tried to talk, but Shayth stopped her. "Come. We will talk in the compound." Holding her with one arm, his reins in his free hand, he led her down the hill to Wycaan Island.

"The children. The others," Sellia whispered as she gathered her own horse's reins.

"Rhoddan will bring them," he replied.

She shook her head, and Shayth stopped abruptly.

"Did he fall, too? I never heard—"

"No," she replied. "Rhoddan and Pyre left the morning after we heard the news. I do not know why or where they went. I think they are trying to distance themselves from their grief."

"I have walked that path. They are on a long journey to nowhere," Shayth sighed. "That man with you is a fortune sword?"

"Yes. He's in my service. We met in Braithwaite, where he was a hired sword hunting taragusii."

Shayth nodded. "A challenging profession. Your children are all with you?"

"Not Mharina," she sniffled, and, sipping from the water skin Shayth offered, told him of Sa'gola and her apprentice.

"Who else is lost?"

"Denalion."

"The Dreamwalker? I remember him. A fine and ancient elf. I will send word to the Forest of Markwin. Sellia, do you know your next move? I will not be able to stay here for long."

She shook her head but said nothing.

"I remember you discovered family there when you and… and—"

"Seanchai," she rasped, forcing his name from her mouth.

He squeezed her hand, and she realized he had not paused for her benefit. She stopped and turned him around. His eyes were as black as ever, but around the edges glistened encroaching tears.

Shayth never cried, not since the day he had lost his parents, and he would not now.

"I…need to get used to it," he said, and took a long gulp of water. "I cannot stay here long, Sellia," he repeated. "There is a threat in the north and—"

"I thought you defeated the Emperor's northern army."

"I did, or rather, Seanchai and the pictorians did. I'll take credit in the stories and history books, but that is not the issue. The Emperor released something from even further north, beyond the Unknown Realms—something so terrifying that it uprooted a whole nation and sent them fleeing into Odessiya.

"I have sent dwarves north to help fortify defenses, but it is a vast border, and we do not know against whom we prepare."

He paused. "I'm sorry. I didn't mean to burden you with—"

"It's easier than talking about Seanchai. I don't know what I will do. I could rebuild here and dedicate my life to Seanchai's vision of a Wycaan academy."

Shayth snorted. "You hated doing that when he was alive. Besides, you need Wycaans to teach them."

"There are two in my party. Master Sythen is a Weapons Master and Master Goldspiere will teach geology and astronomy to the twins."

"I might have need of them in the north," Shayth said. "Perhaps you should consider returning to the Elves of the West for the time being. Let the twins be trained there. It might help to open bonds between our two nations."

Sellia smiled. "You truly are a leader of men, Shayth—a king. You suppress your personal grief to lead your nation."

Shayth nodded, but she knew him well enough to know it was forced. They had come to the crossing, a path that had been rein-forced and widened when Seanchai chose Lake Mhari to set up his academy. Four horsemen could gallop side-by-side across the water to the island. They paused for a few moments, and then Sellia took a deep breath and began to cross.

"I have a man wounded and in great pain," Shayth said. "We set his leg badly when he fell on the way here, and he travelled for a week in the saddle. I would have Maugwen tend him. How is she?"

"Maugwen went with Mharina and the sorceress. I cannot tell you why, as I was not consulted. She left with them at first light one morning."

Shayth frowned, and his free hand went through his hair, encouraging the already rebellious spikes. "Is she a prisoner?"

"I don't know," Sellia said. "I hope she was going in order to guide and protect my daughter, but I'm not sure that's possible."

"Because this sorceress is so powerful? Is she really?"

Sellia turned to him, and she felt him recoil at her expression. "Shayth, it was she who killed Seanchai, not the Emperor."

Shayth stared at her, his mouth open in shock.

"My lord." A man scurried toward them. "We 'ave messages. A dozen birds arrived, and we're deciphering 'em. The news might be grave, and I'm sent to request you proceed at all pace."

Chapter 12

Shayth quickened his pace and Sellia matched his stride as they entered the Wycaan Academy. Startlingly, the place looked very much the same as before. The guards and acolytes had been no match for the powerful taragusii, and the battle, if you could call it that, was short. In fact, she reflected, it was more of a massacre.

The main compound bustled with the prince's entourage: grim soldiers; flustered bureaucrats; and auxiliary staff such as cooks, cleaners, aides, and stable boys. Two red-faced boys took their horses. Sellia followed Shayth as he moved through the throng, ignoring calls of recognition, and entered the main building. He turned into Seanchai's office, a large room with a desk, a table where eight or ten could sit, and an open space that he had used for meditation and smaller lessons.

Sellia shuddered as she followed Shayth inside. He had been careful not to move more than he had to, and, against all reason, the elfe looked around in hopeless expectation for her mate. But the faces of Shayth's officers were all strange and focused on the map and messages on the table.

"What news?" Shayth demanded.

"Who is this with you?" an officer asked.

"You are addressing the mate of the Wycaan Master," Shayth snapped. "We are her guests, and she walks where she pleases."

The officer examined her and bowed his head. "My apologies,

Mistress Sellia. My manners are rough, hewn on the battlefield and unfit for court."

"No apologies needed," Sellia replied. She moved around the group as they turned to their prince. She listened, but she moved to Seanchai's chair and picked up various trinkets, mostly handiwork from their children, made as they eagerly awaited his return when he traveled. This time, no amount of gifts would bring him back. Their family was destroyed.

She realized the room had gone quiet and they were all looking at her. A younger officer filled a cup of wine and brought it to her.

"I'm so sorry, milady," she said, her voice wavering and her eyes cast down to avoid Sellia's. "I fought alongside the Wycaan at the Cliftean Pass."

Sellia stared at the soldier and frowned. The humans had been in the Emperor's army, not on Seanchai's side. Seeing Sellia's expression, she pulled back her hair to reveal pointed ears.

"I stood with the Weapons Master, Cheriuk, and Shathea at the great gathering in the Markwin Forest. It was the proudest day of my life, and I remember thinking I could never be so happy as when I rode with such company.

"But the Wycaan Master from the East proved as inspiring as any I have followed. When he asked me to join Prince Shayth's command, I did so. I will continue to serve his wish until I wield my swords no more." She brought a tightly clenched fist to her heart, but her voice cracked. "I swear it on his memory. *Ashbar.*"

"What is your name?" Sellia asked. Her own voice sounded so small among this company.

"Penwyn." She bowed her head again. "At your service."

"Thank you," Sellia replied. "When you are off duty, perhaps we can spend time together. I would welcome the company of another elfe."

"I would like that, too," Penwyn replied, and turned back to the group.

The officer who had initially challenged Sellia spoke up. He had a huge mustache and played with it as he spoke. "We all stand with you in your sorrow, milady. With your permission, I shall continue."

Sellia nodded, and he turned back to the table. "Prince Shayth. We have received several scrolls by bird, and I have been piecing them together. It is possible that some were lost, but this is what I believe has happened.

"As per your orders, the pictorians sent a small force north accompanied by rangers to try and identify the threat. The First Boar, Arad'gug, had spok—"

"What?" It was Sellia who interrupted. "What happened to Umnesilk? He was First Boar."

Shayth left his commanders and moved over to her. "Umnesilk and Seanchai persuaded the Ice Clans, the pictorians who lived and travelled with the northern foes, to change sides and join the pictorians of Odessiya." Shayth perched on the edge of the desk and forced another smile. "Seanchai was building his alliances, as always, but to seal the agreement, Umnesilk abdicated and offered First Boar rights to Arad'gug.

"He was forced to take his family into exile and, at first, ran with Seanchai. After they separated, I gave him and Narasilk land to settle their family." He turned back to his officer. "Please continue."

"Arad'gug spoke of a warring band of creatures but refused to divulge who they are. He met one by order of the Emperor, to know what threatened them.

"According to the rangers, Arad'gug's pictorians travelled north at great speed. It is not clear how long they travelled, because they outran the rangers who, while fleet-footed, are not used to such thin air.

"By the time the rangers caught up, the pictorians lay dead in a valley, clearly defeated by sword and spear. But of the enemy, there were none dead, none wounded. The rangers tried to count the foot-prints leaving the battle, but there were too many."

Shayth ran his hand through his hair. "How many pictorians?"

"Two hundred."

"Two hundred! How many of these creatures must there have been? It would take five times that amount of our troops to defeat two hundred trained boars. And I instructed him to send a scouting party."

"There is more. Both of Arad'gug's sons were among the dead."

"What?!" Shayth's face reddened. "What was he thinking? He should have sent others."

"My guess is that he was angry when you ordered him not to lead the party himself. Being told to stay behind would be perceived as undermining his position as First Boar."

"I told him to wait for my army," Shayth's face was flushed with anger.

"That is not the way of the pictorians," Sellia said, leaning on Seanchai's desk. "Their honor would never allow it. Umnesilk was forever in the middle of the fiercest fighting. And when did we ever see him dodge a challenge?"

Shayth nodded. "Send a runner to Umnesilk. I want him to meet me north of Shindellia along the road to the north where we parted last time. He is to leave immediately. Begin preparing the main force to leave tomorrow. My guard will stay here with me another day."

"My prince." Another officer with bright red hair leaned forward. "We do not have many troops with us. To split us is to weaken our forces. Can you not leave with us?"

"Not yet," Shayth replied. "I will see my friends either settled here or on their way to wherever Sellia wishes to go."

"With respect, sire, is that a priority?"

Shayth leaned on the table, his fists crumpling the map under his weight. His eyes blazed black, and his voice became a snarl. "We are talking about my friends. Those who are here, and those who will never return."

Sellia's heart quickened at the wild fury of the boy she and Seanchai saved from execution in Galbrieth all those years ago. This same untamed rage paired with the power of a wounded prince was even scarier.

Her hand went to her throat, and she felt again the knife that Riona had pressed against her. But it was the black rage in her eyes, not the blade, that she recalled, and what had bothered her ever since now crystalized. She knew where she had seen such anger before.

Shayth stared at her. "Are you alright?"

"Yes," she whispered. "There is someone you need to meet."

CHAPTER 13

S ellia decided they would eat in Seanchai's office, away from the rest of the prince's soldiers and entourage. It was going to be complicated enough. She arranged the table for herself, Shayth, the twins, the two Wycaan teachers, and Riona and Montclair, placing the latter pair opposite Shayth. It was a solemn dinner. Ilan entered, sat in the chair behind his father's desk, and cried. Master Goldspiere went to him, and Ilan sat on the Wycaan's lap and showed him various baubles. The dwarf listened intently and encouraged the *calhei* to talk. When the food was on the table, Sellia called them over, and Ilan walked to the table with considerable composure.

Prince Shayth Shindell had hosted enough state dinners, Sellia realized, to keep the conversation flowing. He focused on the twins and the Wycaans. Ilan told him how Master Goldspiere was an expert in chemistry and astrology and described many of the experiments they had done together.

Sellia watched her son become animated, appreciating the questions Shayth asked and the encouragement the Wycaan gave. Ilan would be okay. He would channel his grief into his studies, and, even if he never became a Wycaan warrior like his father, he would make his mark somewhere. Shayth told Ilan of the research happening in the capital and said he looked forward to showing Ilan the facilities.

"That would be great," Ilan responded. "Wouldn't it, Senzia?"

"One day," Senzia replied, "but you know we cannot go yet." She had been playing with her food and not giving any impression she was listening to the conversation.

Ilan nodded and slouched. Sellia frowned, surprised that they had evidently had a conversation about this without her. Losing her mate and Mharina had focused Sellia on her own grief. Ilan demanded attention through his crying fits, but Senzia was closed off.

"What are your plans, Sellia?" Shayth asked. "We don't need to discuss it now," he corrected, seeing her puzzled expression. "You are, of course, welcome to come to Shindellia at any time. My ears are round, but you are my family and always will be."

"Thank you," Sellia said. "I have not been able to think much of our next steps."

"Senzia says we are going to the Elves of the West," Ilan said. "Isn't that true, mother?"

Sellia glanced at Senzia, who was scowling at her brother. Senzia turned to her.

"I didn't plan for this to come up now," she said, her voice quiet but commanding. "Ilan and I must be Wycaan-trained, and that can best happen in the Markwin Forest." She turned to Shayth. "We are yours to command, Prince Shayth, but know that this is what our father would have wanted if he could not train us himself. It is best for Odessiya, as well. After we rescue our sister, we will help you in the north."

There was a collective shocked silence at the twelve-year-old *calhei* addressing the Prince of Odessiya with such conviction.

"Who has decided this?" Sellia inquired, instantly regretting her tone.

"We discussed it with Mharina. We had a lot of time to consider different options and scenarios."

"You might want to discuss this with your mother first," Shayth suggested.

"That had been my intention." Senzia turned to Sellia, apologetic but not cowering. "I thought it best not to lie to you or the prince."

Sellia put a hand on her daughter's arm. "It's okay. We will talk more, and I will consider what is best for our family."

Senzia leaned away. "This is bigger than family. Odessiya is vulnerable without Wycaan Masters, and maybe even with them. If we've learned anything, it's that there are other, stronger Wycaans out there. There are sorcerers like Ithea and Sa'gola." She glanced at Masters Sythen and Goldspiere. "Who knows if there are other Wycaans hiding somewhere or what threat awaits in the north."

Senzia turned to Shayth. "You need us, and you need us to be trained and ready. But know that, first, we will rescue our sister."

"Your hair is Wycaan white," Shayth replied. "I am glad to know that you understand your responsibilities to protect Odessiya. But know, as well, that I will not cross your mother's wishes if—"

Senzia rose, and her chair toppled backwards. "Your responsibility is to no one person, but to your country. My father knew his duty."

"Sit down," Shayth replied, an edge now in his voice, and she did. "The sun has not set on the day I heard of your father's demise. I will not discuss this further. But know that your father taught me many times that our friends are our mirrors and our anchors. He often risked everything for his friends, and, in doing so, defined the great elf that he was."

"I'm sorry," Sellia began, but Shayth raised a hand to stop her.

There was a heavy silence as everyone ate, each mired in his or her own thoughts. Sellia kept glancing at her daughter. She just realized that Mharina was no longer a *calhei* and would walk her own path. Now she was seeing this in Senzia, and she knew that, though Ilan was young for his age, he was inextricably linked to his twin sister. They would travel to the Elves of the West.

Shayth focused on his dinner. He regretted that he had snapped at a child, a *calhei*, who was mourning her father. He realized he was only beginning to understand what had happened. All he wanted was to mount his horse and ride, to leave Odessiya behind and go after Rhoddan and Maugwen. He had lost his parents and been adrift until Seanchai, Rhoddan, and Ilana took him in. They changed his life, helped him bury the grief and injustice he felt. He knew he must do this for the twins. That is what he owed Seanchai, at the very least.

He realized that everyone was staring at him. Dinner was finished, and it was for royalty to dismiss people. He wiped his mouth on the hand cloth without thought. Then he turned to all present.

"These are difficult times," he said, "that might not allow for us to heal. Seanchai had a vision for a just and free Odessiya, and we must all play our part to keep his vision alive."

He turned to the two Wycaan teachers. "You served my uncle, my enemy. In the morning, you will swear fealty to me in front of my army and court or leave Odessiya, unharmed but escorted, never to return.

"The hour is late. Thank you, everyone." He rose and walked around the table, taking position behind Riona. He leaned over and whispered in her ear. "Stay a while, please. I would have words with you…*sister*."

Chapter 14

Riona had to will her body to sit back down. She was in
shock that he had called her *sister*. He had ignored her
since her return to Wycaan Island, especially at the dinner
table. When she replenished her wine cup, it shook in her hand. As
the others shuffled out, two aides entered and conferred with Shayth
by Seanchai's desk. Montclair remained and tended the fireplace,
which was to Riona's back. She was relieved. It was cold, but she
needed the time to compose herself. Once his aides were dismissed,
Shayth returned to the table and filled his own goblet. He jerked his
head when Montclair stood up next to the fire.

"Thank you," the prince said. "It is indeed getting chilly. You may
leave now."

Montclair moved to Riona's side and looked to her for guidance.

"With your permission, Prince Shindell," she said, "I would
prefer him to stay."

Shayth folded his arms and raised an eyebrow. "You have my
word I will not draw my sword unless you attack me. What need,
then, do you have for a fortune sword?"

"He has become more than that," Riona answered.

Shayth turned and stared at Montclair. He knew the face, he was
sure, but he couldn't place it. He signaled with a hand for the man
to join them.

"Fill your wine cup, as well," Shayth said. "I trust that everything said here is kept between us."

"Thank you." Montclair sat and poured himself wine. "I understand."

They sat in silence. Riona stared at her wine cup as Shayth looked at her. Montclair shuffled. "Well, this is pleasant," he finally said in desperation.

"Shut up," Riona replied, but her tone was soft.

Shayth, at least, grinned. "All right, blondie," he said to Montclair. "You broke first. House rules. Who are you, and why do I have this feeling that I know you and don't like you?"

Montclair sipped from his cup and licked his lips. "I served in your father's personal guard. I was the youngest and usually on the perimeter of the team. But when he died, I felt as if I had personally failed him. When I heard you had run away, I tracked you and watched your back. When you found out, we rode together for a while, but fought because you had become a vicious pig. I lost faith in you and turned instead to track your sister. I bested you before I left, I might add.

"When Riona settled here on Wycaan Island, I asked to become one of the Wycaan's guards. He refused and sent me away. I drifted up to Braithwaite, hiring out my sword and losing myself in the wine. I walked the same path I disdained in you, only I charged good coin for it.

"Then one day, your sister walked into a bar and created a stir. Sellia hired me, no doubt for my charm, wisdom, good looks, and sword. I fought taragusii, wolfheids, and a sorcerer. Only your sister penetrated my defenses."

"Idiot," Riona hissed at him.

"But the last part, at least, is true?" Shayth asked her.

Riona nodded. "Against my better judgment."

There was a long silence, and she could feel Shayth brooding.

"Say what's on your mind, *brother*." She needed to own the word as he did *sister*.

"Why?"

"Because he is not such a scoundrel as he would have you believe, and, after all these years on the run, I guess I got lonely."

Shayth smiled. "I've got that much figured out and, if anything, I'm happy for you. I mean: why did you disappear? Why not come for me? You must have heard about the bloody wake I left. I was spiraling out of control. How could you have forgotten me?"

Riona looked at him. He had spilt a lot of blood in his lost days after he left Shindellia, but she knew he was referring to his internal moral hemorrhaging.

"As soon as you were born, I was forgotten, discarded for being a girl. We were never close when we were together, and once we were apart, I heard enough that I never desired to know you. I wandered lost, myself, but instead of killing, I learned to heal. My growing knowledge nurtured my own self-respect.

"I had no desire to be at court, to bend the knee to a brat—to you, if you ascended to power, or our uncle's son, who was no better. When I finally wanted a home, I found one here. When I sought a great leader to follow, I found Seanchai. I never needed to bend a knee to him. He sought only to raise me and everyone else higher."

Montclair put a hand on her arm.

"Yes," Shayth said after a few pregnant moments. "He was very good at that. What now?"

She hesitated. Montclair and she had never discussed this. The fire crackled and popped. "I don't know. I do not want to come to court," she said.

"Perhaps it would be best if you accompanied Sellia and the twins to the Elves of the West, or at least go as far as you can. They could use your protection and healing skills, and Sellia will have a friend."

Montclair snorted. "Your sister almost slit Sellia's throat not too long ago."

"But she didn't," Shayth replied, "and Riona is still alive to tell the tale. That says a lot. I don't know my sister very well, but Sellia is ruthless when need be. After they are safe in the Forest of Markwin, I would like you to come to the capital if I am there, or to the north if there is unrest. There will be need for a healer and a swordsman, if you are any good."

"Any good?" Montclair bristled, and Riona elbowed him.

"Is that all? Are you the practical prince now?" Riona asked.

"No," he replied, and his edginess disappeared. "I was always at my best when surrounded by friends. Seanchai is dead, and Rhoddan disappeared on some futile quest. Sellia is deeply wounded, and Maugwen a prisoner of the sorceress who killed my best friend, the most powerful elf in the land.

"I need friends around me if I am to meet the darkness that threatens Odessiya. I need family. Now, more than ever."

Chapter 15

They struck after the slavers stopped for the night and set up camp. There were six heavily armed men and two women. Their prisoners, chained and emaciated, were mainly female, about twenty in all. The attack hit, and three slavers fell from arrows through heart or throat. Then a warrior, small and wiry, attacked two who cowered. Both of her swords blurred, spraying blood with each thrust. From behind, a huge warrior with a massive broadsword engaged three men near a tent.

It took him longer to dispense with two of them, men who knew how to wield their swords, but nonetheless, they were no match for their attacker. The third man, small and sprite, grabbed an enslaved elfe and yanked her in front of him. Both she and those chained to her screamed in pain. But the man stood panting, his blade shaking from fear as he looked up at the warrior.

"I'll cut 'er, to be sure. I will. Step back or I'll kill 'er, a poor, young, innocent she-elf."

The warrior hesitated, swirling his sword in frustration. But before he could say anything, the man's eyes bulged and he dropped his sword, slowly collapsing and releasing the elfe. Rhoddan bent over and saw a small bolt in the man's neck, splitting his windpipe. He gently gathered the elfe and called to Pyre to search for the keys to the chains. She soon jangled a set.

When everyone was released, they grabbed food from their

captors' wagons and began eating and drinking. Rhoddan called to them to be quiet, though conversation was already being set aside in favor of basic survival needs.

"In the morning you should head back west into Odessiya," he said to them. "You will live as free elves there, for slavery has been outlawed." Rhoddan waited for the buzz of disbelief to subside. "A just prince now sits upon the throne in Shindellia, and all are free to choose their work, their dwellings, and their destiny. Take weapons and coin from your oppressors. We have only what we carry and nothing to spare."

A young elfe stood up. Though her hair was knotted and her face dirty, Rhoddan thought her still attractive. "We'll go with you. We can cook and care for you. We don't want to walk unguarded. We'll be captured again."

"We can't take you with us," Pyre said. "Our path leads us further from safety, and our mission cannot be delayed."

"Why are you here?" another asked.

"I can't say," Rhoddan replied.

"But you can't leave us unguarded," the same young elfe said. "I'd rather go with you. I can use a sword! Not like you, but—"

"No," Pyre interrupted. "We can give you some more coin, enough to hire fortune swords to guide you to safety. Now, finish eating and go to sleep. We will guard you this night and leave in the morning."

There was a despondent air about them. Rhoddan signaled to Pyre, and they moved away from the group to talk.

"Perhaps we—"

"No," Pyre said. "We can't start a crusade unless we're going to focus on this and forget Seanchai. You said yourse—"

"But what *would* Seanchai do? You know he wouldn't leave them defenseless."

They argued in hushed whispers for a while. The only other

sound was the crackling wood they had lit for the released elves and, in the background, the hum of crickets.

"I'm not ready to give up," Rhoddan said at last. "We have achieved so much in Odessiya, but it's fragile. If Shayth gets drawn into a war in the north, we could lose everything Seanchai built." He glanced over to the elves huddled around the fire, and when he spoke, there was more conviction in his voice. "I'm not giving up on Seanchai until I find someone who has seen his corpse."

"Then we let these elves fend for themselves?" Pyre asked, fiddling with something in her hands and effectively changing the subject.

"What's that?" Rhoddan inquired.

"Our mystery assassin's quarrel." She stared out into the darkness, and when she spoke, her voice was loud. "It might be a good time for him to show himself."

There was a heavy, anticipatory silence, and then a figure emerged. He was merely a silhouette, bathed in black, and he hovered on the edge of their light.

"May I have my quarrel back?" he asked, his tone articulate and clipped.

The voice was familiar, Rhoddan thought, but he could not place it. "We owe you," he said. "Thank you."

Pyre threw the quarrel at the shadow, and a gloved hand darted out quickly to catch it.

"I can help you with these people, as well. I will take your money into the town we just left and hire the fortune swords. We can pay them half now, and your prince can pay them the rest upon safe passage. I'm not sure two elves could procure and trust many fortune swords, especially if you are not going with them. But they will not cross me."

"How can you be so sure?" Pyre asked.

"No one, even in this barbaric outland, crosses an assassin," the man said. "At least, not twice."

Rhoddan frowned, trying to think. "I know you," he said.

"We met only briefly, Rhoddan. I doubt I would have left an impression upon you."

"Then why are you following and helping us?"

The man took a moment to consider his answer. "Because the one you seek made a considerable impression upon me. His actions brought me to the edge of insanity, but he also saved me."

Rhoddan leaned forward, and the man slowly removed his cowl. His hair was dark and matted and his face a messy stubble. He looked to be their age, perhaps slightly older, and his dark eyes were sharp and alert. This was a man who had once been someone…else. The elf searched his memory, but could not recall. Still, those eyes…

"Don't think too hard, Rhoddan," the man said. "You knew my father better, and then only as your captor. He killed the Wycaan's mate before Shayth slew him."

"I don't understand," Pyre said, but Ahad continued.

"All my life, I trained to avenge my father's death, to kill Shayth and the Wycaan. I faced the Wycaan, together with the Emperor's son, at the Battle of the Cliftean Pass, and there, he gave me a choice. Become second-in-command to the Emperor's successor, or let him set Odessiya free."

"So you chose not to fight Seanchai and let him confront the Emperor?" Pyre pieced together a story she had not participated in.

"Yes. I chose not to kill him. I could have. Your friend was more focused on persuading us than fighting us."

"Sounds like Seanchai," Rhoddan said, sorrow coursing through him. "What happened then?"

"I killed the Crown Prince, my best friend, for the elf who killed my father."

"Pyre, this is Ahad, Master Assassin, once a confidant of the

Emperor and his son." He turned back to Ahad. "Actually, it was Shayth who fought and defeated your father."

"Shayth wielded the sword, but…" Ahad's voice had become fierce, and he stopped to bring it under control. "It is history," he said. "I may not be able to forgive them for my father's death, but in order for him not to have died in vain, I must support the Wycaan's cause."

Chapter 16

Rhoddan woke as the sky was beginning to lighten. He had guarded deep into the night and then woken Pyre. Truth is, he could not have slept without a guard after knowing Ahad was among them. He remembered a boy twisted by grief, trained by the Emperor's assassins and highly dangerous.

Seanchai never told them exactly what transpired when he confronted the Crown Prince. For obvious reasons, everyone wanted to hear about the Wycaan's battle with the Emperor instead. That Ahad had killed his prince and close friend solely on the word of the elf he blamed for his father's death was scary. As much as Rhoddan admired Seanchai's ability to bind people to him, he wondered how unstable this highly trained assassin really was. This thought did not help him fall asleep, even with Pyre guarding.

The fourteen years since the battle at the Cliftean Pass had clearly not been kind to Ahad, judging by his shabby clothes and unkempt hair and beard, and especially his eyes. Their intensity left Rhoddan haunted. He thought of Shayth when they first met, and he went to sleep with those eyes piercing into him.

Rhoddan started to turn onto his back, but stopped when he rolled over on something. There was a sigh next to him. He wiggled away and turned to see the disheveled hair of the outspoken slave elfe next to him. He stifled a wave of panic. She must have joined him after he fell asleep. He peered at her face. She was not beautiful like

Sellia, but she had a distinct look. He could not see her eyes—she was still asleep—but her facial bones were well defined. Her eyebrows were narrow and her lips full.

She winced, and her forehead wrinkled. She whimpered something he could not discern and reached out with a desperate hand. He let her grasp his arm and, before he knew what he was doing, leaned over and stroked her back, whispering in her ear that she was safe. She sighed deeply and relaxed back into what he hoped would be a dreamless sleep. He extricated himself carefully and covered her with their blankets. When he stood, he saw Pyre frowning at him. He started to say something, but she turned away. He stared after her, puzzled by her expression, and then went to rekindle the fire and make some hot tea.

He offered Pyre a steaming cup when it was ready. She had her back to him and was looking out over a ridge. They could see the town in the growing light. It looked calm and peaceful from up here, but Ahad had warned them that this one was particularly rough. *I come here to test my skills,* he quipped. Rhoddan wasn't sure he was joking.

"I should wake Ahad," he said.

"He's gone," Pyre replied. "He took the guard duty from me and woke me at dawn. He doesn't seem to need much sleep and wants to hire the fortune swords early, while they're still sober."

"Sounds like a fine set of business partners."

"Do you regret your plan now?" There was a sharp edge in her voice, and she nodded toward his bedroll. "Now that things have become more complicated for you?"

"Pyre! She must have moved after I fell asleep. She surprised me, and I almost crushed her when I turned over this morning."

"Maybe. But I saw how you looked at her. It's something I've often wondered about. The stoic Rhoddan, oblivious to the advances of elfes and consumed by his loyalty to Seanchai and Prince Shayth."

"You share that obsession, that loyalty. Who are you to criticize?"

In the heavy silence that followed, they both sipped their tea. Others stirred behind them, but they paid no heed.

"I'm sorry," Pyre said at last. "It's not my business who you... you know."

"I didn't."

"But you will, and if you don't, you just deny your feelings—suppressing them, as I'm sure you're used to." Her voice was unusually sullen, almost bitter.

"This is hardly the time for me to have feelings."

"It never is, and won't be for a long time. We always postpone love for duty. Riona was so attracted to Montclair and denied it to him and herself for so long. It's a waste, Rhoddan. Isn't it enough that none of us can settle down? Why can we not find some happiness when it presents itself?"

He looked at her. A solitary tear slid down her cheek.

"What is it, Pyre?"

"You're so blind. Perhaps it's how you cope with grief and loss. Others reach out. The elfe there has been captured, abused, and hurt, and then a noble, handsome elf swoops down and offers a fleeting moment of protection. What can be so bad in that?"

"Nothing," he said, confused.

Pyre turned to him, her eyes glistening.

"What is it?" he asked again, but she just stared at him.

"Figure it out," she said at last, and stomped away.

He watched her walk to the wagon and pull out supplies. She began to assign tasks to those who were awake. The elfe who had slept next to him folded her blanket and then his. He began to walk over to her, but stopped. He wasn't sure what he wanted to say. He didn't understand elfes. About that, Pyre was right. Seanchai had always had a mate—first Ilana, and then Sellia. It had never been a topic of discussion outside of innocent ribbing. Shayth was under pressure from his court to take a mate and produce an heir to the throne but never seemed to settle down for very long.

Rhoddan sighed, recalling his and Shayth's last conversation on the journey north together to aid the pictorians. For the first and last time, he confessed his love for Sellia, untouchable as Seanchai's mate. In distant, happier times, he fantasized they would settle down as two couples: Seanchai and Ilana and Sellia and him. The fact that he blushed and stammered every time Sellia addressed him back then seemed a more formidable obstacle than anything going on around them.

But he realized now that, even if Seanchai was gone, he could never be with Sellia. They could not build a relationship based on grief. Sellia would go to the Elves of Markwin, and he would not be allowed to pass through their protective barriers. Even Seanchai, the greatest Wycaan, was barely acceptable.

He looked back to where a few elves busied themselves making breakfast. He watched the elfe who had garnered his attention give directions and offer a hug to another elfe. Suddenly, she did not look quite so vulnerable, but a leader. His eyes followed her as she went to Pyre and conversed. Pyre was nodding and responding. The other elfe's back was to Rhoddan, and when Pyre happened to glance and see him watching, her face tightened, and she turned and walked away. The elfe turned, puzzled, and met Rhoddan's gaze. Then she looked back at the retreating form of Pyre disappearing into the trees.

Chapter 17

The elfe brought two steaming bowls over to where Rhoddan stood guard. She was so thin, he thought, and grimaced. It was not a natural look, and he glanced at the others. They were all just as emaciated. He thanked her for the bowl of hot gruel and began to eat. She used her free hand to try and untangle her hair, pulling a clump behind the points of her ears, and focused her eyes on her bowl. They stood in comfortable silence for a while, and then Rhoddan ushered her to two rocks nearby that still allowed him to look down toward the town. They had given most of their purse to Ahad, and Rhoddan was worried about it.

"I'm sorry," the elfe said, breaking the silence.

Rhoddan turned to her, drawn from his thoughts. "What?"

"I'm haunted by nightmares and rarely sleep. I woke up afraid and came to bed beside you."

"That's okay," he said. "You didn't wake me."

"You turned and took me in your arms. You don't remember, because you were so fast asleep. You muttered a name—Sellia."

Rhoddan gasped and stared at her.

"I-I'm sorry," the elfe said, again trying to hook her matted hair behind her ear. "I didn't mean—"

"Did Pyre hear?"

"I don't know. I see how I create tension between you and her, as well. I didn't mean to. I…"

She began crying silently, her body shuddering. Rhoddan reached out a hand and stroked her arm.

"You have been through a terrible time. Please don't apologize. Sellia is a close friend and will never be more."

"And Pyre?"

"Pyre has faithfully served my friend and is my partner on this mission. If she has any feelings for me, I did not know until now. It is not your concern or responsibility. You have done nothing wrong."

She sniffled and wiped her eyes. "They would hit or whip us if we cried in front of them. We learned to weep silently."

"Where are you from? How did this happen?"

She took a moment to compose herself and finish her food.

"Go get some more," Rhoddan suggested.

"Are you hungry?" She was eager to serve him.

He was about to say no, but changed his mind. "Only if you get more for yourself, as well."

She smiled and took both their bowls. When she returned, however, she had only one bowl. "There was hardly any left," she said, giving it to him.

Rhoddan took a spoonful, and then passed the bowl back to her. She grinned, temporarily erasing the lines of grief and fear from her dirty face. She took a spoonful and passed it back to him. There was something strangely intimate in this ritual, and Rhoddan felt long-dormant feelings stir.

"What's your name?" he asked.

"Troja," she replied. "I'm named after a mythical town." She shrugged. "My father loved stories, and there are many about this place. I wish I'd been able to hear more, but he was taken from us when I was still small. I barely remember him."

"Where are you from?"

"A region called Callestron in the southeast corner of Odessiya."

"You're from Odessiya? But then surely you know Prince Shayth freed all races from slavery?"

Troja smiled as she handed him the bowl, now almost empty. She flicked her hair behind her ears again, and Rhoddan realized he enjoyed the movement. "Odessiya is a very big country," she said. "We hear stories all the time, some more wild than others.

"Did you hear about the white-haired elf with magical powers? They say he could bring down mountains and kings." She laughed wryly. "An elf going around and freeing our people. Now isn't that a grand tale." She stopped at the strange, alien groan that escaped Rhoddan. She touched his arm. "What is it? What did I say?"

Rhoddan stared at her. He could feel his mouth hanging open and knew he was holding back tears. Troja leaned forward and pulled him to her. Her long, thin fingers pressed into his skin, and currents shot up his arm. "Do you also dream of such a warrior, such a savior? Have I stoked hopeful embers?"

Rhoddan took the final mouthful of food. He had meant to give it to the elfe, but now he needed a moment to compose himself. He chewed with stoic determination.

"I talk too much, Rhoddan. I'm sorry. For so long I have been afraid to open my mouth for fear of abuse or ridicule. You make me feel…Please tell me why you cry."

Rhoddan set the bowl down and wiped his face on his sleeve. So much for being the great warrior, he fumed as he stared at the ground. But Troja leaned forward, her fingers pressing harder.

"Tell me why you weep. I want to know. I have nothing to give you, but I can listen. Please." Her hand moved his chin, and she gently raised his head. "Please."

"The elf you speak of lived. The stories are true. He was a Wycaan Master, a wielder of ancient magic that has both imbued and built Odessiya and brought it down. But he was special. He never sought to defeat, but to build alliances. He drew elves, men, dwarves, pictorians and others to his cause. He bound us to his vision of a free Odessiya and a just society. He gave us love and friendship and changed our lives forever."

"You served him?" Troja frowned.

"I met him when we were just *calhei*, our faces void of stubble. I was given a simple task: to take him from my father's camp to another's. It was supposed to be straightforward, and I should have been rid of the helpless pup within days.

"But I got to know him—his vulnerability and his potential— and I stayed by his side for the next fifteen years. I don't know where my path leads, Troja, but I will never be as proud, as inspired, or as happy as I was by his side."

"What happened?"

"He fell in this dark land, just a few weeks ago. The sun has not shone since and, for me, I doubt it ever will."

He was aware that Pyre had sat down on the rock next to him. Troja turned to her. "Is your story the same? Do you travel in mourning, as well?"

Pyre just nodded, the tears welling in her eyes and overflowing down her cheeks. Troja knelt in front of Pyre and took her in her arms. Pyre made no sound, but her shoulders shuddered in grief as she allowed the elfe to hold her.

"You can run forever," Troja said, her voice soft. "But the grief will always catch you. At some point, you must confront it and let it settle in a safe and honored space inside you where it will never be forgotten, but cease to prevent you from continuing with your life. The vision this Wycaan had is still alive, no? You can work to realize his dream. What would it take for you to let him go and move on?"

Rhoddan stared at her. She seemed so wise, even as she had suffered so much herself.

"What would it take for you to move on?" she repeated.

Rhoddan glanced at Pyre, who gave him a curt nod. "We do not know if he died. No one has ever survived the kind of sorceress' fire unleashed on him. Still, we must look for his body, or at least some evidence that he is dead."

"So." Troja's eyes became wide. "He might still be alive?"

"It's unlikely."

Troja stared at him and then Pyre. "This is your mission? Let me join you. I want to help if there is even a tiny sliver of hope. All my life, I dreamed of such people from the stories told in my village and by my father. And if this Wycaan has gone to our ancestors, then I will help you complete his vision for all of Odessiya. It is a beautiful dream for all races to live free."

She leaned forward and laid hands on them, one on Rhoddan and the other on Pyre. Her eyes were large, and Rhoddan felt himself being sucked in. But he turned to defer to Pyre.

Pyre was staring at the elfe, as well. Then she looked at Rhoddan, and their eyes met. She nodded. "Our journey has already proved long and dangerous. It doesn't look as if that will change. If you see safety in Rhoddan, as fine an elf as I've ever known, then you might chase an illusion, despite his best intentions to protect you. But if you want to be a part of Seanchai's legacy, then you can join us."

"Thank you," Troja said. "I'll not be a burden. I'll go and prepare."

They both watched her walk back to the camp, and Rhoddan noted a spring in her step. He turned to Pyre. "Thank you," he said. "I know this isn't easy for you."

She turned and smiled back. "Seanchai had a knack for identifying people with unique talents and binding them to him. Perhaps we are already taking on his legacy. Even I can see that she is special.

"But don't hide behind any illusions, Rhoddan. We are doing her no favors."

Chapter 18

The sun was nearing its zenith when Ahad returned with four big men. Rhoddan felt a wave of anxiety at the thought of such a rough-looking group being led by a trained and un-predictable assassin, but Ahad directed the men to the fireplace and the stew that was cooking. He then signaled for Rhoddan and Pyre to follow him. Ahad, all business, produced a scroll outlining that these men would escort the group to Shindellia. Ahad had given them Rhoddan's coin and promised an equal amount from Prince Shayth on safe delivery of the elves.

As Rhoddan read the scroll, Ahad counted the elves. "Twenty-four," he said. "Fill in the number and sign on it."

"Twenty-three," Rhoddan replied. "One comes with us." He signed and passed it to Ahad, who smirked.

"Let me guess which one."

There was a scream from the direction of the fire, and Rhoddan saw that one of the men had grabbed Troja, who struggled to break free from his grasp. He sprung to his feet, but Pyre firmly moved him behind her. By the time Rhoddan had covered the hundred paces, Pyre had the man pinned with his back to her, one Win Dao sword at his throat and the second facing the other three men, who now stood with drawn swords. Rhoddan walked up slowly and drew his long knife. Pyre had been smart to get there first. It gave him time to compose himself. He strode over and towered above the big man.

"No 'arm, no 'arm." One of the men stepped forward, trying to placate.

Rhoddan swung his knife toward the man, who stopped in his tracks and raised his hands.

"Just a she-elf," the man who Pyre held whined. He screamed as Pyre hissed and brought her outstretched blade to his crotch. "Didn't mean…didn't mean nuffin'."

"This contract is clear," Ahad said, his voice firm, but quiet. "You touch none of the elves and deliver them unharmed. Do you not understand?"

"She ain't going wiv the group," the man protested.

"Shut up, Finks," the man facing Rhoddan snapped, and then addressed Rhoddan. "'e's an idiot, but good in a scrap. I'll keep 'im in line. Let 'im go."

Rhoddan turned to the one Pyre had pinned. "Stay away from her," he hissed. "Stay away from all of them, or I will find you and make you sorry you ever laid eyes on an elfe."

Pyre released the man, who staggered forward. He looked at Troja and smirked. Troja punched him, jerking his face to the side. The second man grabbed his friend and dragged him behind him. Then he turned to Rhoddan.

"My apologies. We ain't used to elves like you. Ain't seen such a big one like you." He offered a hand of reconciliation.

"Shake," Ahad murmured to Rhoddan. "Let him be the leader when we've gone."

Rhoddan extended his hand, and they shook. Just as he released, a third man spoke up.

"We 'ave seen a big elf, Ryles. Remember the 'uge dumb one who works for the old fisherman in Crysea? Don't talk, but strong as an ox. 'ad white 'air and swords like the she-elf does."

"Elfe," Pyre hissed at him, but the man just frowned, not understanding that he had insulted her. Then she registered the rest of what he'd said. "When did you see this elf?"

The two men looked at each other.

"A few moon cycles ago, as I remember," Ryles said. "We 'ad a job 'unting taragusii. There was more than there was 'posed to be, and we quit. Ain't good to fight them bloody lizards if theys more than you. Villagers said them lizards were searching for an elf, too. We fink of the dumb one, but 'e's kinda lost it up 'ere." The man tapped his head. "Know wot I mean?"

Ahad pulled Rhoddan close and whispered in his ear. "Enough. You got your information. We don't want them thinking this is important."

Rhoddan turned back to the leader and gave him the scroll. "You are being well rewarded. Do not abuse my generosity. This should be an easy job, and you can drink yourselves into oblivion or make lives for yourselves with the money you'll earn. Understand?"

"We ain't gonna mess wiv the likes of you," Ryles said, carefully rolling up the scroll.

Rhoddan realized the man had not read it and wondered if he even could. He turned to Ahad, Pyre, and Troja. "Saddle up. We ride west."

He met both Ahad and Pyre's eyes. He knew they meant to continue east, but he didn't want to leave a trail when unnecessary. Neither showed any reaction.

They left on the three horses. Troja rode with Pyre, the lightest combination to spare the horses. Rhoddan would have preferred the elfe behind him, but it made sense this way for the horses. He could not believe the fortune swords' account of Seanchai, but the white hair and Win Dao swords sounded just like him. His heart was still racing at the news. No one knew where Crysea was, but they would soon find out. If something was wrong with Seanchai—if his head was wounded and there was a pack of taragusii tracking him, he was in terrible danger. But at least he might be alive.

They rode out of the camp and made a wide circle to continue east. No one spoke until they stopped for the night. After caring for the horses, they laid their packs down and gathered wood. They had ascended into hills, and it would get cold once the sun set. Ahad went to hunt, and Troja focused on making food from the supplies they had. Rhoddan checked the horses' hooves, and Pyre made a small pile of twigs and wood and took out her flint. It took only three attempts to create the spark that caught. She looked over at Troja.

"We all share in all the tasks," she said. "You don't have to always—"

"I don't mind cooking," Troja replied and offered a smile.

"It's a principle we live by," Pyre explained. "Many of us grew up where all elves fought, studied, and shared the tasks. We have no servants or underlings."

Troja smiled. "Sounds strange, but nice. This feels good… normal…I cook for you because I want to, not because I'm being forced to. Anyway, I don't know how to fight like you."

"Oh, I thought you packed a solid punch back there."

"Keep a secret?" Troja was grinning, and Pyre nodded. "I really enjoyed doing that."

They both laughed, but Rhoddan scowled as he joined them. "You need weapons. From the taragusii I've seen, if you punch one, you'll break the bones in your hand. At the next town, we will pick you up a sword."

"I prefer a staff," Troja replied. "One with blade tips. It's easier to keep them away from me."

There was a haunted look on her face, and Rhoddan didn't need to ask more.

"We'll get you whatever you want," he replied, "and Pyre and I will help you practice."

Ahad returned at that moment, holding two grouse, both promisingly plump. He looked rather proud of himself. Pyre frowned.

"How did you catch those? You don't have a bow."

"I flushed them by accident and took them down with blades."

"Throwing knives? You killed two birds at the same time with knives?"

"He's an assassin," Rhoddan said, as if it was nothing. Still, he, too, was in awe.

Ahad frowned at him. "*Master* Assassin, if you don't mind."

Chapter 19

M harina woke early, unaccustomed to the noise of a town. She dressed and quietly went downstairs. The tavern part of the inn was being cleaned, so she sat outside on the porch. It was chilly, and she raised her hood as she watched the early merchants pass by. A serving girl brought her a goblet of mulled wine, unbidden.

"Thank you," Mharina said, and smiled.

The girl, slightly older, bowed her head. "Always an honor when the Purple Lady stays."

"What do you think of her?" Mharina asked, and the girl's smile vanished immediately, replaced by fear. The elfe regretted asking, but now the damage had been done. "The Purple Lady and I are only recently joined. I'm her apprentice and curious."

The girl swallowed and looked quickly to either side. Then she leaned in. "Tell you what I like about 'er. She's kind and 'elps women, but ain't afraid of no man. I wanna be like that. I wanna heal people and be able to protect meself."

She straightened and peeked back inside the inn. Then she leaned forward again. "Can you protect yourself?"

Mharina nodded. "Not as well as the Purple Lady, but I'm learning."

"Good," the girl said. "I'm glad you can 'ave both. I 'ope you'll 'elp people, too. Now, drink your wine 'fore it gets cold."

The girl ducked back inside, and Mharina drank the wine and pondered. As she did, she watched a young man with a wide-brimmed hat and thick staff. He wore a wicker basket on his back, and whatever was packed inside was threatening to overflow. Several people stopped to greet him, and a group of children followed, peppering him with questions. Whatever he replied had them squealing with laughter. Without realizing what she was doing, Mharina found herself on her feet, trailing behind the group. She stayed back a few paces, anxious not to be noticed. When he stopped to talk to one of the merchants setting up his stand, she feigned interest in a fat, purple onion at a nearby table.

Then he stopped at a small stand and took the basket off his back. An old man bustled forward and hugged him. The old man turned and shouted something—a name, perhaps—and a portly woman came out and hugged the young man, too. Then the young man began to empty his basket, removing produce with what Mharina thought to be considerable reverence.

The three leaned over as he unwrapped packages covered in burlap. Moving forward cautiously, Mharina saw a variety of mushrooms, and the old couple seemed very excited. Then the young man hugged them again and, taking a small package from the woman, left them with the wicker basket. With the children following, he made his way to a small square with a well in the middle. It was away from the noise of the marketplace. He filled his water skin and splashed the children, who shrieked with laughter. It seemed strange to Mharina how, in this tough little mining town, he elicited smiles and laughter all around. He sat on steps near a stage. It was a small amphitheater, she realized—probably where public meetings took place.

The man opened his package and pulled out a sandwich. The children groaned as he took a bite and exaggerated how tasty it was. Then he feigned surprise as he took out another wrapped package, and the children clapped and cheered.

"Would you pass these out?" he asked. "I think there are only enough for half a cookie each."

It took a moment before Mharina realized that he was speaking to her. A sea of young, expectant eyes stared at her, though she knew they were far more interested in the cookies.

"Do you know what I found in the forest this past week?" the man asked the children, who were clearly waiting for a story to accompany their cookies. "I found a golden trumpet."

"Really?" a child asked as others gasped.

"Well," he replied, "it is a mushroom, but it's far more valuable than gold. Shall I tell you why it is so valuable and called the golden trumpet?"

The children all nodded, except one. "Are there any cookies left?" he asked, crumbs and cream on his top lip.

Mharina checked. "There are two more," she said.

"One for the lady, and one for me," the Mushroom Man said, and flashed a beautiful smile.

"She gets a whole one?" the boy protested.

"She's bigger than you," the man replied, raising an eyebrow. "And she worked awfully hard handing them out. That's a big responsibility."

The boy seemed to accept this, but Mharina, feeling self-conscious, took only half. The man laughed at this, and when he took the remainder back, she saw he had sparkling, light blue eyes. He took the other half of her cookie and began to speak.

"Once upon a time, there was a wealthy king who was very sad because his queen was dying. Something was eating her up from inside, and all the healers of the land could not save her. He would sit next to her bed and weep, and he became increasingly angry with his people.

"One day, for no apparent reason, the king fired his minstrel, casting him out onto the street and confiscating a trumpet that the minstrel's father had passed down to him, a heirloom that had been in the poor man's family for many generations. The king told the poor man that he could only have the trumpet back if he found a cure for the king's wife.

"The minstrel knew nothing of healing, and besides, all the great healers of the land had already tried. He wandered from village to village, scraping together enough money from shows to eat and find shelter while he searched for a cure. Once, during a storm, an innkeeper refused to let an old woman under his roof. There were no empty rooms, and he said only men could sleep on the floor by the fire.

"The minstrel stepped forward, offered the old woman his room, and paid to sleep on the inn's floor. The innkeeper didn't like this, but the minstrel filled the tavern with his show and the innkeeper was making good money.

"The next morning, the minstrel bought the old woman breakfast and told her his story. 'What would ye do if ye found a cure?' she asked. 'Ye have three choices: Would ye sell it for all the coin ye need for the rest of ye life? Would ye take it to the king, that it might save the queen with its magical properties? Or would ye try to sell it to the king for all the gold in the land?'

"The man didn't think twice. In fact, he didn't even hesitate. 'I love my king,' he told the old woman. 'He didn't mean to hurt me so. He is desperate for a cure for the queen, and I would give it to him if there was but the smallest chance it would save her, for she is a kind and gentle soul.'

"The old woman stared at him a while, and then cackled. 'Would that I could help ye, young man. Where do ye go from here?' He told her of the next village on his journey, and she asked him what route he would take. Finally, she offered him three gifts for his kindness. One was an old mushroom knife, its hilt carved and worn with time, but its blade sharp. It had bristles on the end of the hilt and sat in a nice leather scabbard. Her second gift was a burlap sack—which he took so as not to offend her—and the third an apple, which she made him promise to eat when he broke for lunch.

"The man soon left and walked until midday. He sat on a fallen log in the forest and took out the apple. He smiled as he thought of the old woman, but as he went to eat the apple, it fell and rolled down behind the log. There, in a sea of greens and grays, he found a bright yellow mushroom. He felt a wave of excitement."

Mharina stopped listening to the story at this point, vaguely hearing that the minstrel took the mushroom to the king, who was able to save his queen, and they all lived happily ever after. She barely noticed that the Mushroom Man had dismissed the children and was standing in front of her, smiling.

"I have no golden trumpet, but I have enough coin to buy you breakfast. May I?"

Mharina stared into his deep, blue-grey eyes and simply nodded.

Chapter 20

The Mushroom Man led her across the square to another tavern. There were a few people sitting at tables, eating a late breakfast. The miners had long gone to work, and the place was quiet. Instead of ale, he ordered breakfast with milk to drink. Then he took off his straw hat and sat down. He was older than her, and his fair skin was reddened by sun. He had not shaved for some time, and she could see the shadow of a beard and a scar or burn on his right cheek. It was different shades of purple, and this made Mharina remember that Sa'gola would probably be looking for her. She really didn't want to leave him, and now he had ordered food; it would appear rude.

"So," he began, "what did you think of my humble story?"

"Somewhat predictable, but adequate given your audience," she replied with a smile.

"Ouch!" He pretended to have been hit in the heart.

She laughed and pulled her cowl back. She saw the man's eyes go to her ears, and she bristled. "I am an elfe," she said. "Do you still want to buy me breakfast?"

He nodded. "You misinterpret. I have just never seen an elfe with dark skin. I was surprised. If anything, it makes you even more intriguing. So, what brings you to this fair town?"

"Just passing through," Mharina replied. "I serve a lady who is on her way home."

"And where's that home?"

"I don't know. I've never been there."

The man nodded as a platter was brought to the table. There were steaming eggs, bread and cheese, and a large pickled onion.

"You're probably used to richer fair than this, but meat and fish here are expensive."

"This is lovely," Mharina said. "I came for the company, but I'm actually quite hungry, despite half a delicious cookie." He laughed, and she made a point to fill her plate.

When she leaned back, she saw Sa'gola standing near the door. The diminutive woman wore her hood over her head, and Mharina could not see her face. She began to rise, but the sorceress raised a hand and signaled for her to remain where she was.

"What is it?" The Mushroom Man asked, turning to look. Sa'gola was gone.

"Nothing. My lady came, but signaled me to stay. She is very benevolent. Tell me about yourself."

The man had to finish and swallow what was in his mouth. He washed it down with milk before speaking. "You probably have seen everything. I'm a mushroom hunter. I have a talent for reading the land and knowing where to find different species during the correct season."

He smiled. "I know my mushrooms. I know which ones are good to eat, which ones can heal different illnesses, and which can help you escape the world for a while. I do a good business, and I am free to roam. I wander the land, and I prefer it to being in a town. Not that I don't appreciate hot food and beautiful company when I can find it."

Mharina blushed. "Sir, I am glad at least the food satisfies your needs."

His cheeks were also red, bright against his pale skin.

"Who were those people you gave your mushrooms to in the market?" she asked.

"I call them my grandparents, but I don't know if they truly are. I grew up without parents, and they looked after me. It was difficult for them to have another mouth to feed, but they always told me this is what family does. We never speak of my parents. Once, I was told a sorceress killed them when they refused to help her in some evil deed, but then I began having nightmares and they said it wasn't true.

"I finally began to believe that there was no such thing as a sorceress, and then I actually met one. I must confess that I wasn't very nice to her. She sought a certain mushroom, and at first I refused to look for it, though she offered an absurd amount of coin. That's when I got this souvenir."

He fingered the scar, and Mharina felt a shiver go through her. The man continued. "You know, the ironic part of this tale is that she wanted it to save a life. There was once an old ruler who got usurped by his nephew or something. I would make it into a story if it wasn't so painful."

"Did you help her in the end?"

"Oh, yes. I might not be the most handsome man in the world, but I don't want to look like some scarred pirate. And she paid me less than her first offer as punishment."

He laughed, but Mharina scowled. "That's not fair. She offered you a certain amount and should have kept to it."

The man shrugged. "Since then, she has always paid me well. Once, when my grandma was sick, I asked the sorceress for help. She came and healed her. When I offered coin, she refused. That was appreciated. Still, I wouldn't go looking for her company. What about you? What's your name?"

"Mharina."

He frowned. "I once found a lake named something similar."

"Lake Mhari."

"That's right. Beautiful land. There were elves there, but I remember them to be fair-skinned. Is that where you're from?"

"I was born there, but my mother comes from a land far in the west. I would rather not talk of my family. It is a difficult subject."

The man frowned. "Are you employed by this lady or in servitude?"

Mharina thought about it. "I'm not sure. She is good to me and teaches me, but though I came with her willingly, I had little choice. Let's change the subject. What's your name?"

"Most refer to me as the Mushroom Man. Tell me what you dream of, beautiful dark elfe."

Mharina thought about this, and the man smiled.

"What's so funny?" she asked.

"You screw up your nose when you think. It's cute. Tell me what you dream of."

"I don't know," she replied. "Life has moved so fast for me. I want to be…I want to find…" she sighed, startled at how difficult this was. "I want to be a fearsome warrior like my mother and a wise leader like my father. I want to be reunited with my brother and sister and live a life as…"

He leaned forward. "You want to be free."

"Yes," she whispered. "I guess I do."

It was a heavy realization. The woman she loved was her captor, and all the love in the world would not overcome that. Mharina realized that, though she would faithfully serve her apprenticeship, her future was not with Sa'gola. The question rose unbidden in her mind: would Sa'gola let her go free when the time came?

"I didn't mean to bring such heavy thoughts upon you, Mharina. Do you know that woman standing by the door? Is she your mistress?"

Mharina turned and saw Maugwen waiting.

"I should go. Thank you for breakfast, mysterious Mushroom Man."

He stood and quickly wrapped some bread and cheese, which he put in her hands, gently squeezing.

"Look for me among the trees, rocks, and swamps," he said. "Wherever there are mushrooms, there might be a mushroom man nearby. I hope we meet again soon, Mharina, beautiful dark elfe.

He leaned forward and planted a light kiss to her hand. "Thank you," she mumbled, stunned. Outside, she lightly brushed the back of her hand against her cheek. She could still feel his kiss.

Chapter 21

They rode from the mining town in silence, and Mharina felt relieved to be back in nature. Sa'gola led them into a thick forest, and the temperature dropped quickly. The trees had dark, gnarled trunks, often covered in moss. There were fallen trunks almost completely swallowed up by thick vines; delicate ferns; and plants with thick, rubbery leaves. They halted at a stream and dismounted. The horses immediately set about drinking, and Mharina moved a few paces upstream and filled her water skin. She gasped at how cold the water was and peered up, as if expecting to see a glacier.

"Looking for mushrooms?" Sa'gola asked, making her jump.

Mharina turned slowly, wondering how to respond. "Thank you for allowing me to have breakfast with him. I enjoyed it."

"What did you learn?" Sa'gola asked.

"What do you mean?"

"I didn't just want you to eat a hot meal or enjoy a lingering kiss on your hand. I want to know what you felt, how you perceived him."

Mharina glared at Maugwen for tattling, but she was oblivious and tending the horses. "W-what do you mean?"

"Tell me what you think of the Mushroom Man. Be honest."

"Well," Mharina wiped her hands on her breeches. "I found him attractive and mysteriously interesting. I loved the way he embraced his grandparents and told stories to the children. He seems to be liked by everyone."

"Did you enjoy his attention, his parting kiss?"

Mharina felt a wave of anger. "I did. Why is this important? I didn't tell him who I was, who you were, or where we were going. It was harmless. Are you jealous?"

Sa'gola slapped her cheek. It was not hard, but it stung, nonetheless. Mharina's eyes welled up.

"Don't be impudent," Sa'gola said. "Did he tell you how he got his scar?"

"You gave it to him. You left your signature around the edges. He said you forced him to seek out a rare mushroom for you."

"Really?" Sa'gola arched an eyebrow. "Do you believe him?"

Mharina hesitated. "Yes. I think I do. He doesn't know of our connection."

"Fair enough. You will, no doubt, have further encounters with him. I know men like that. He won't give up, and he knows how to track. But you will have to meet him outside the boundaries of my home. Do you understand? He will not enter, even to find his exotic dark elfe."

"He will? He won't? I mean…I don't know what I'm saying."

Sa'gola laughed and took the confused elfe in her arms. "Oh, my poor, sweet thing. I have no doubt he is besotted with you, but even that will not be enough to give him the courage to cross the boundary of my home. He did so once before, and I taught him a lesson he will never forget. I punished him by seducing him to do my will."

Mharina pulled away. "Really?"

Sa'gola laughed cynically. "Now who's jealous?"

They mounted and continued through the forest for the rest of the day, camping deep within its shadows. No fire was lit and no guard set. Sa'gola moved around them, chanting and moving her hands. When she returned to the others, Maugwen asked why they were not setting guard.

"No one will see us here," Sa'gola said, her voice quiet. "If any should pass, they will feel a need to circle this area. We are protected from sight, but not sound or smell. This is why we light no fire and why we will go straight to sleep. No one will disturb us."

Mharina soon fell asleep to images of mushrooms and having her hand kissed. In her dream, her Mushroom Man was charming and happy. But abruptly, he stopped laughing and began glancing around, pushing her to hide.

What is it? She asked.

Fighting lizards, he replied. *Hide yourself. You can't imagine what evil they are.* She heard a familiar hissing all around her, and then the rattling laughter.

Suddenly, he vanished, and Mharina was awake, her skin crawling. She heard the low hisses and knew she was not dreaming this. She slowly turned onto her back, her hand on the hilt of her knife. Sitting up with great care, she peered into the dawn light. She heard nothing but the sounds. Mharina picked up a seedpod and shook it gently, but it did not rattle. She turned her body enough to throw it at Sa'gola's head, but missed. Thankfully, there were plenty of other seedpods, and she finally landed one on the sorceress's nose.

Sa'gola twitched, then her eyes snapped open. Slowly, she sat up and looked carefully all around. At that moment, Maugwen let out a snore—not a big one, but enough to silence the hissing. Without a sound, Sa'gola moved on top of Maugwen and put a hand over her mouth. Then she leaned in and blew in her ear. Maugwen opened her eyes and gave a small nod, and Sa'gola moved her hand away. They both sat up. The sorceress put a finger to her lips and stared first at Maugwen and then Mharina. Both nodded. The footsteps came closer.

"Can sssmell sssomething," one growled.

"Sssilent," another hissed back. "No one move."

Mharina could make out their silhouettes as the huge taragusii stood frozen, their tongues darting out to lick their noses while they strained to hear and smell. She could hear her own heart pumping and was scared they would hear it, too.

"Horsssesss," the first hissed.

Mharina glanced at Sa'gola, who was frowning. They had made a mistake. They couldn't be seen, but the pungent odor of horsemeat was as clear to the taragusii as if the horses stood in front of them in broad daylight.

One taragus approached them, sniffing more excitedly. He stood about where Sa'gola had created their barrier. He was seven feet tall, and his scaled head seemed to shimmer. His antennae were extended, almost caressing the barrier, as his forked tongue flickered in anticipation and then wet his nose.

"We are clossse," he said, and stared right at Mharina. "Very clossse."

Chapter 22

Mharina sat motionless. She was too scared of making a sound to even draw her long knife. Not that it would help against the powerful taragusii. She had seen them fight against the tutan, and they were far too strong and quick for her. A second taragus joined the first, standing just several feet from them. He was taller and reminded her of a younger Third Scale, the leader of the group who had attacked Wycaan Island and kidnapped her and the twins. His nose was also twitching, and his tongue darted to wet it several times. He looked around rather than fixing his expression on her as the first was doing. He turned and barked something.

A third taragus approached, bigger than the other two, and Mharina felt a wave of fear course through her as she recognized Third Scale. He looked so much older, and his shoulders were no longer as erect as before. There was something in his eyes that showed he had been through much since bringing the *calhei* to Grogin. He hissed an order, and the two others retreated. He kept looking ahead, extending his tendrils to feel the boundary that Sa'gola had set. Retracting them slightly, he turned to see that he was now alone.

"Missstresss," he whispered. "How good that you are alive, and the brave, young Mharina, too."

"Thank you, noble Third Scale." Sa'gola's threw her voice so it came from behind him, and he turned, momentarily confused. But then he returned to looking somewhere between the sorceress and Mharina.

"Many yearsss have I ssserved the Massster through you. I alwaysss had the greatessst ressspect. But now, we are sssent to capture or kill you. I cannot disssobey."

"Was that young one a *banta* of yours?" Sa'gola projected her voice from behind him on the other side, and he glanced reflexively in that direction.

"Why play with me, Missstresss? You know my sssensses are good. Yesss, he is my oldessst sssurviving ssson."

"Who orders you to action? The Master or Ithea?"

The taragus licked his nose. "I may not sssay. Only that I have my ordersss."

"Do you see me? No. So return and say as much."

"The othersss alssso sssenssssed your presence."

"I do not want to kill you, Third Scale, or your *banta*."

"And I would not want to sssee him die. Better you kill me firssst."

"Is there no other way?" Sa'gola's voice was hard, but Mharina sensed her regret.

The taragus remained standing, hissing quietly to himself. His tongue darted out several times, and then he smiled. "To die at the hands of the Massster or his minionsss isss to die a ssslave. To die in combat at the handsss of a ressspected friend isss to die free."

Mharina shook her head. "You can't," she whispered to herself. "You have family. You have honor."

"And honor is the path I choossse, brave little elfe."

"Die well, then, Third Scale," Sa'gola said as she rose to her feet. "Die free."

The walls of their protection seemed to melt as Third Scale staggered slightly forward. He drew his huge axe, bowed to the small woman, and charged. Sa'gola's purple flames flew into him, and he roared with pain. But, though he was buffeted from the force, he pushed forward. Sa'gola took a step back and sent more purple fire into him. Four other taragusii ran back toward them. Mharina stepped in front of Maugwen and crouched, ready to protect her.

"What are you doing?" Maugwen exclaimed.

"Stay behind me," she replied, going inside herself to bring forth the energy.

Since killing Ithea, when she had seen the sorcerer beating Sa'gola and pure rage had summoned the fire, she had never used it to fight. She had practiced, but knew instinctively this was different. The elfe felt a tingle in her fingers.

The first taragus was only twenty feet from her when she unleashed the fire…or tried to. Nothing happened, and he sprung at her, a huge axe above his head. It blazed as the blade caught a sliver of sunlight that pierced through the tree cover above. Mharina screamed and closed her eyes. But a bright purple blaze penetrated her eyelids from without, and she opened them to see the huge warrior twitching at her feet. She looked up. Third Scale was on his knees now, his face screwed up in agony, and Sa'gola stood in front of Mharina.

"How many, Third Scale?" her voice was eerily calm. He did not answer. "Just this once, my friend. I know you are bound by orders, but in telling me, you will truly die free of your shackles."

It was not clear whether Third Scale struggled more with pain or his honor. Finally, as the first of the three advancing taragusii was almost upon them, he hissed, "One will ssstay back and ride."

Sa'gola moved to one side and sent a sweeping wave of fire that pushed all three attacking taragusii into the rocks on their right.

"Go, Mharina. Find the messenger and do not hesitate."

Mharina sprinted forward in search of the one scout who would return for more help and send news of their direction. She must stop him, she repeated to herself over and over again. It was not hard to track the taragus' path, and when she came across their strange, lizard-like, black-scaled horses, she already saw a taragus already mounted and scampering back through the brush.

Without hesitation, she mounted a horse, as well. She felt it adjust its spiked back to enclose her, and then she cried out, "Go, bearer of Third Scale!"

She did not know if the creature understood, but it allowed her to direct it after the fleeing taragus. They galloped with difficulty through the thick brush, but so did the one they chased. He looked over his shoulder several times to see her progress, and Mharina felt a sinking feeling, convinced that it was the *banta*, eldest son of Third Scale.

She ducked at the last second to avoid a low branch and felt her clothes being ripped by lesser branches that her creature was ignoring. One branch scratched across her face, and she yelped in pain. Abruptly, they exited the forest, and the sun blinded Mharina. Then she realized the taragus was behind her, not in front. She wheeled her creature round, and its sharp turn almost threw her.

"You are not the Purple Lady. Doesss ssshe ssso look down on usss that ssshe sssends a child to face a proud taragusss?"

"Sa'gola respects you more than the Emperor or Ithea do. They incarcerate and bend you to their will with threats and punishments." Mharina shouted.

"Not me. Not my father." The taragus unsheathed his axe.

"Your father, too. Third Scale never lost his desire to be free, and he will die now as a free and proud taragus."

"Then he isss weak. I know my place. You will die with the honor of being sssstruck down by me. I will become Firssst Ssscale and ssstand taller than my father. Your life has been ssshort and insss-significant. Die well if you can, weak she-elf."

Mharina raised her arms, but the taragus only smiled.

"I sssaw you back there. You could not bring forth the fire. You are not the Purple Lady. You are weak and pathetic like all elvesss—like your father, the peace bringer." He hissed cynical laughter as he approached, axe held high. "He wasss a weak elf and a fool. We all make fun of him in our ssstoriesss around the...aaaagh!"

The fire was bright orange, eclipsing even the morning sun. It flowed from her hands, pummeling the taragus, who wheeled around, his axe flying, suspended in air for a few moments before crashing to the ground. His lifeless body smoldered even after the twitching stopped.

Mharina, panting from exertion and exhilaration, stepped forward and stood over the corpse. Her nostrils flared, and she threw back her head. From deep inside, the words roared out. "I AM MHARINA, DAUGHTER OF THE WYCAAN MASTER. HE LIVES ON IN ME."

A hand touched her shoulder, and she wheeled around. Maugwen backed away from her, staring up in awe. Behind her, at the forest's border, stood a disheveled Sa'gola, holding the reins to a dark beast.

"Yes," Maugwen said, her voice quiet, but steady. "You are his daughter, and, Wycaan or not, I know Seanchai would be so proud of you."

And the fierce elfe warrior and sorceress' apprentice fell into the small healer's arms, crying.

Chapter 23

"I'm going back," Sa'gola said, and, turning briskly, mounted the lizard creature she had commandeered and returned to where their camp was.

"Is Third Scale dead?" Mharina asked Maugwen.

"He wasn't when we left, but he had little time left."

Mharina stared after Sa'gola's wake. Something was bothering her. Why would Sa'gola rush off like that if Third Scale was already nearly dead? They mounted the second lizard horse, Mharina in front and Maugwen grasping her hips from behind. Suddenly, it hit Mharina why Sa'gola was in such a hurry. She called over her shoulder. "Did Third Scale tell her who he was serving?"

"No." Maugwen's breath was hot in her ear, but that was not why she shuddered.

The elfe urged her beast on, and they galloped back through the forest. When they reached the camp, Sa'gola already stood over the fallen taragus, though he was so big that even on his knees, she was only slightly taller.

"What is she doing?" Maugwen peered around Mharina.

"She's torturing him." Mharina's voice rose with her fury. "After all they have been through together. He's the one taragus who seems to understand they're little more than slaves."

She jumped from the mount and stormed over. Third Scale was panting, and there were beads of sweat pouring down his massive head.

"Your loyalty is irrelevant," Sa'gola was saying. "You have this one chance to set yourself free."

"But…free from what? If I do not have honor, what isss left?"

"Damn you, Third Scale, I need to know."

The big taragus shook horribly from whatever invisible power streamed from her to him. He let out a deep sigh, but never cried or screamed. It was too powerful, and Mharina grabbed Sa'gola's arm.

"What are you—"

The elfe was flung back as torrents of intense heat burned through her whole arm. Sa'gola stared at her with eyes blazing. "Stay back, apprentice."

Mharina steadied herself and, holding her arm, walked forward again.

"This isn't right," she whispered, and put her hand deliberately back on Sa'gola's. Instantly, the hot currents went through her, and she gasped again, but this time she held on, channeling all her strength to hold on to Sa'gola.

Mharina was shaking now. She could dimly hear Maugwen calling out. Her vision blurred, and she vomited. Still, she kept her grip. She could barely make out Third Scale, who was also shaking and fighting just to breathe. Mharina fell to one knee but maintained her grip. Finally, Sa'gola stopped, and both taragus and elfe toppled over.

"Very well," Sa'gola panted. "You'll have your wish for Third Scale to die quickly. But you'll kill him yourself."

Mharina watched her walk away and then struggled to rise. Her whole body still shook, and Maugwen had to help her up. She stared at Sa'gola as the woman grabbed her bedroll and pack and clumsily mounted her horse.

"Catch me up," she snapped, "and do your duty properly."

She rode off, and Mharina turned to Third Scale. He was smiling, though there was spittle dripping from one side of his mouth.

"Help me up, brave elfe. Let me die ssstanding, not on my back."

Mharina and Maugwen both helped him rise, but he soon swayed and sunk to his knees. He was using considerable effort, but still held his head high. He licked his nose twice and nodded.

"How did my ssson die?"

Mharina almost denied his death, but it seemed wrong to lie, almost disrespectful. "He died well," she lied, "with honor and dignity."

Third Scale stared at her, and she feared he could see through her lies.

"I-I need to…" Mharina stammered.

"Yesss, you do. Your missstresss has commanded you." His voice was barely more than a whisper.

"I-I wouldn't, but I…"

"…mussst," he completed.

"Thank you, Third Scale," she said, tears in her eyes.

He frowned. "For what?"

"For looking out for the twins and me. For caring." Her voice broke. "For being a friend."

"Even in sssuch circumsssstancesss?"

"Yes. W-we part as f-f-friends." Tears ran down her face.

He managed a smile, but it quickly became a grimace. "Asss friendsss, then. I thank you. Now, finisssh it. I do not like to sssee you in sssuch misssery. Come. Let me die ssseeing you sssmile."

Mharina shook her head as she raised her hands. But then, as their eyes met, she forced herself to smile, and he nodded slightly. The fire was hot and furious. The elfe wanted only to finish him as quickly and painlessly as possible. She sent the orange flames into his massive chest and, when she stopped, the great taragus warrior Third Scale fell slowly forward, one final time.

Mharina took her time catching up to Sa'gola. She assumed the sorceress would stop if they were leaving the path. The forest got denser and wetter. She saw mushrooms aplenty and wondered if the Mushroom Man came here to harvest. When they finally reached Sa'gola, she had set up camp. Three rabbits roasted on spits over a small fire. A thick, pungent, gray soup simmered and bubbled.

Mharina dismounted and unsaddled the bags. Then she joined the others. Maugwen asked what was being cooked, and Sa'gola spoke of two mushrooms that grew here. They ignored Mharina, and this was fine. When the food was ready, Maugwen took Mharina's bowl and filled it before her own.

They ate in silence, and then Mharina went to sleep. If they posted guard, she didn't know, but she slept all night, though her dreams were tumultuous. She fought Third Scale, his son, Ithea, and then the Emperor. Her father fought Sa'gola and, at some point, she joined in, piling fire upon Sa'gola, who curled up as she had under Ithea's whip. In her dream, Mharina couldn't stop herself, and she cried as she lashed out. She woke to a graying dawn, her hair wet with sweat, tears, and humidity. Her head was on Sa'gola's lap, the sorceress gently stroking her hair.

They soon broke camp, and the dense trees gave way to swampland. Insects buzzed everywhere, and their clothes clung to their bodies. As they progressed, fog began to rise around them. It hugged the horses' hooves and then their feet and legs.

"Stay exactly behind me," Sa'gola called back to them.

A bird screeched, and they all turned in the direction of the sound, but Sa'gola led them on. The fog rose and thickened. They could not see their boots or stirrups. Mharina sweated profusely now, and she tried to wipe her forehead on her sleeve, but it was just as wet. The fog was soon up to their saddles, and then they could no longer see their waists. Mharina felt a wave of panic, as though this was water and she would drown. The fog was cold and clammy as it pressed in on her chest and then her throat.

"Sa'gola?" she called, and her voice sounded small and far away.

"Still trust me?" Sa'gola called back.

"Yes."

"Remember that, and embrace the fog. It is my creation and follows my command."

Mharina gulped as the fog rose above her head, and now there was nothing to see except the rump of the horse in front of her. It was getting colder, and she was shivering, her teeth chattering.

Then they stopped. "No one can pass this point except those who are invited," Sa'gola said. "It is a wall of ice for all others."

It felt as though the ice receded only enough for them to pass, and Mharina, who was riding last, felt it close behind her. Her horse whinnied in discomfort, but they were through. Almost instantly, the temperature rose and the fog receded. The trees were scattered now, but it was still swampland. The sun pierced through light clouds, and they heard waterfowl fly over a lake. Occasionally, they crossed bridges. Men with black skins moved around furtively.

"Do not fear them," Sa'gola said. "They live here and pay homage to me. I protect them and help heal their sick and bring their babies into the world. They think me a spirit and are scared enough to only come close when I beckon or they have need."

She turned her horse and faced Mharina.

"It is a good arrangement, and we live here in serenity. This is my home, my sanctuary. I hope it will, in time, become yours, as well."

Chapter 24

Shayth rode out of Wycaan Island before dawn. He led a long column that swelled as more soldiers camping on the shores of Lake Mhari joined them. Yet, though more than a thousand followed him and he had reunited with his only living relative, he felt so alone, and it dragged his thoughts back to the dark times before he joined Seanchai, Ilana, and Rhoddan.

He did not look back, and his immediate guard, sensing the growing broodiness, kept a discreet distance. Soon, when he was sure his entire entourage was behind him and the supply wagons were advancing, he would break with his chosen soldiers and speed to the capital.

There was a serious threat in the north, so powerful that an entire nation had migrated into Odessiya. Shayth and Seanchai had answered the call of the pictorians and gone to their defense, but the defeat of the Emperor and those from lands further north of Odessiya had solved only part of the problem. Arad'gug had been vague about what the Ice Tribes fled from. The Master had taken him to see for himself, but the pictorian would not speak of it. Rumors told of mighty warriors, as big and strong as the pictorians, but armed with other powers.

Whatever they were, these creatures had struck repeatedly, sending all in flight. The pictorians tripled their nation as the Ice Tribes joined the Northern Tribes, but their new First Boar, Arad'gug, was not impressed with Shayth and had not followed his orders to hold his troops. Now many of his nation lay dead, and Shayth would have to reassert his authority. The prince shuddered at the thought of what could fell an army of two hundred pictorians. But he had time to consider his course. He would return to Shindellia, collect intelligence, and leave these troops in the capital, leading fresh forces north. He had left a large battalion of soldiers in the capital, and the dwarves had sent soldiers and builders to reinforce and create defensible positions in the north.

Still, he travelled alone. Sellia was heading west and Rhoddan east, both outside the borders of Odessiya. Maugwen was…he had to think hard about this. Was she a prisoner? Had she gone of her own will? If so, was it to protect Mharina? Or was there another reason?

Maugwen and he, shorn of their friends and families, had stayed close friends. He often wondered whether something deeper could have flourished had he not been the prince. His advisors often viewed her suspiciously, aware of the intimacy borne from such difficult shared experiences, and were clear that Shayth was to marry a noblewoman and create a dynasty. He knew they were right and that Odessiya needed stability and normalcy. A royal wedding and birth would be a welcome gift…to all but him.

And then there was Seanchai. He was having trouble grasping that the Wycaan was dead. He had not asked for details. Having defeated the Emperor twice, Seanchai seemed invincible. And yet, how many times had he showed himself to be naïve? He could imagine Seanchai trying to turn the powerful sorceress who had, by all accounts, turned Seanchai's eldest daughter. After all these years, he knew his best friend was capable of endangering himself to find the good in a person. Had Seanchai finally come up against someone who could not be turned?

He shook his head as he felt the tears rising. The Wycaan had seen the dying embers of good buried deep in Shayth's soul. He had taken the violent, half-crazed killer and turned him into a prince. He had made Shayth a better man.

Shayth's thoughts went to Montclair. He fleetingly recollected a swordsman who had tracked and fought him. Driven by loyalty to the Shindell family, he had both saved Shayth and walked away in disgust. Shayth did not question why the man had left him or why he still evidently held such disdain for his prince, but deep inside, Shayth became aware of a need to convince Montclair that he was a different man. Perhaps he wanted to convince himself, as well.

His horse stopped as two men galloped toward him. They were men from the advance, but nonetheless, his guard moved swiftly forward in front of him, and Shayth, accustomed to danger, moved a hand to the hilt of his massive broadsword.

"Prince Shindell," one called, obstructed by Shayth's guard. "I bring a report from the rangers."

"Let him through," Shayth instructed.

The man led his horse in a slow trot, flanked by two bodyguards. His colleague stayed back.

"Sir. There is a battalion of dwarf infantry camped ahead. You will reach them by nightfall. They are heavily armed and seem quite happy to be on the march. There's a lot of singing and pipe smoke."

Shayth laughed. "You do not know dwarves, my man. Dwarf armies are always infantry. They hate riding anything, and they take their pipes and quaffing as seriously as their fighting. What are they doing here?"

"They have been sent by the High King in Hothengold to aid you in the north. They are led by a curious fellow named Ballendir."

"Curious?" Shayth was still grinning.

"He is apparently their officer, though he drinks and smokes more than the rest of them…and tells many stories. Fanciful stuff, from what I heard. He tells tales of fighting alongside you and the Wycaan Master. I almost cut out his tongue."

"Oh, I'm glad you didn't try," Shayth said. "I would hate to have seen you come to harm, especially for claiming a man lies when he tells the truth."

"He does?"

"Ballendir fought by my side in all the great dwarf wars. He led us to Hothengold and devised the strategy that brought us victory. When no other dwarf dared, he stood up to challenge their very history. He defied The First Decree and led his people out from the darkness. You heard stories from a hero, my man. Next time, raise a tankard of ale with him, by order of your prince."

"Yes, sir. Gladly. This Master Ballendir gave me a message for you, sir."

"What?"

"He said that his soldiers come in the name of the High King of Hothengold, but he comes to ride once more alongside a friend. He said that friends should never ride into battle alone."

Shayth pursed his lips and nodded. He dismissed the scout and rode forward. Once again, his guard settled around him while still giving him the space he needed. And he needed it. Shayth's eyes filled with tears. He pulled his hood up, disappeared deep into his cowl, and wept.

I am alone, Ballendir, old friend, and you are most welcome.

CHAPTER 25

S hayth knew they were close to the dwarf camp long before he saw it. A thick, pungent smell of fire permeated the air, enriched by pipe smoke and cooking meat. A short while later, voices carried on the breeze, rounds of laughter and raucousness that abruptly stopped as a deep horn was blown. Shayth led his convoy up a dusty path that crested onto a plateau, half of which was covered with tents and fireplaces. Dwarves sparred with axe, spear and sword in a clearing. Further along stood targets for archery. A dwarf bow was short and very tightly strung. Few dwarves could master it, but those who did were equal to even the elves in this skill.

At the sound of the horn, the dwarves left their toils and ran to stand in formation. Three platoons stood in clearly defined ranks, while an honor guard formed two rows wide enough for Shayth and his guard to pass between. All stood to attention, their axes and battle ornaments—fine objects wrought of steel and bronze—glimmering in the sun. Shayth knew this was orchestrated to send a message. For all their frivolity, this was an army, and they would demand the respect of all. He rode through the columns and toward the officers who awaited him. Three broad dwarves stood in a row, each rigid and stern of face.

In front of them, however, almost hopping from one foot to the other, was Ballendir. His red beard and hair were as wild as ever. His face was paler than Shayth remembered, but he lived his life

now largely underground. Shayth dismounted thirty paces from his
friend, and a young dwarf scampered over to take his reins. Then
he walked half the remaining distance; Ballendir joined him in the
middle. Though considerably shorter, Ballendir swept the human up
in his broad arms.

"Bless mah axe, Shayth. It's good to see yeh, old friend."

"You too, Ballendir. Thank you. One needs the light of a true
friend in these dark days."

"Aye, they do, laddie. Come. Break bread with mah in the
command tent. Let yeh men set themselves up, and we will feed yeh
all tonight. Should make for an interesting introduction. We have
meat and beer aplenty to get us to Shindellia."

Shayth nodded and turned. But a dwarf officer was already
directing Shayth's officers, so the prince signaled with an arm for
Ballendir to lead him away. They entered a tall tent with a big table in
the middle scattered with several open maps. Later in the campaign,
perhaps, there would be an assortment of models, showing terrain
and fortifications. To one side, another table bore wine flagons; beer
barrels; and an assortment of bread, cheese, and pickles. Ballendir
piled up a plate with food and filled two tankards with beer. He and
Shayth moved to a small table in the corner, little more than a cube
of wood with cushions around it.

"No one will disturb us," Ballendir said, taking a swig and filling
his bread with cheese and pickles.

There was a commotion outside and Ballendir began to rise, but
Shayth motioned for him to wait.

"Our guards must become allies. Let them work it out together."

"Aye, makes sense. Yeh become a wise king, then?" There was
sparkle in Ballendir's eyes. "No, I see yeh hate it as much now as back
then. Back then, eh? What happened, Shayth? Tell mah straight and
have done with it."

Shayth spoke softly, recounting Seanchai's fall at the hands of a sorceress, of her taking Mharina. He told how Sellia would go back to her people and request the twins be trained, and of Rhoddan wandering in the lands far to the east. He left out Riona and Montclair for the time being. Ballendir listened carefully, chewed slowly and washed his palate with beer. He nodded and sighed and shook his head.

"What is Rhoddan looking for?"

"I don't know. I thought to send someone to summon him, but he was always Seanchai's closest friend. They were together from the start. I can't imagine the grief he is feeling."

"Can't yeh? Yeh was pretty close to him, yerself. He…he helped yeh a lot."

"No question about that. Perhaps I am lucky to have all this prince stuff to distract me."

Ballendir harrumphed, skeptical. "I have no idea how to comfort yeh. I would find it helpful if there were a few heads we could chop off, but I guess we'll have to wait fer that."

Shayth shook his head. "I have used violence as a way of mourning before. It doesn't work, Ballendir. It just makes the world a little darker and me a little emptier."

"Well, there is always beer and wine and some good pipe weed."

He pulled out a huge red pipe and began to pack it. "Would yeh like me to fetch yeh one? It might—"

Shayth laughed. "I have never wanted to. Do you remember teaching Seanchai to smoke the dwarf pipe? He almost choked himself that first time."

They both laughed at the memory, which led into how Seanchai had tried to hide that he had never ridden a horse and how he had been so intimidated by Ilana, and especially Sellia. The stories poured out, and their laughter grew louder. First the guards, then other men and dwarves entered the tent in large numbers and gathered around. There was something different, something foreign in the stories, the laughter. The men watched their leaders slap their legs and gasp for breath while tears streamed from their eyes. Suddenly, Ballendir noticed them watching and realized what was happening. Shayth sensed it, too, and fell silent. Then Ballendir rose and stepped onto the cube table.

"Every one of you must fill a tankard. That is mah order."

All rushed to the table, and dwarves filled and passed tankards and goblets. They stood then, no one drinking, staring at the great dwarf leader and the ruler of Odessiya—both flushed, but not from drink, both with wet cheeks, but not from sweat.

Ballendir took a sip, perhaps to calm his emotions. "This great land of Odessiya was once ruled by an evil emperor. Men were pawns to his whims, dwarves hid underground, and elves were little more and often treated worse than slaves. Then one day, a frightened young elf from Morthian Wood ran away, determined to stay free rather than serve as fodder on the Emperor's battlefield.

"He conquered the hearts of the people, forging us into an alliance, and studied the ways of the great Wycaan Masters. He was not brave. He was not confident or commanding, but he imbued a love that yeh could not help but answer. He formed alliances between races and bonds between friends that no axe could break. Friendship was his secret weapon. Not his Win Dao swords or magical bow. Not armies or muscle. He bound us with love to a cause. He had a vision that all races would live free and together as one people."

He paused, not sure what to say, and stared into the pewter tankard he held. Shayth rose. With Ballendir on the table, they were almost the same height. Shayth put an arm around Ballendir.

"He changed our lives, all of us," Shayth said. "But those who were closest to him, like Ballendir and myself, he transformed into leaders. He is gone now, slain in a land to the east of Odessiya. But we will not forget him. We will not forget his lessons and his vision. There is a threat in the north. I cannot tell you what we face yet, but it is powerful and it is scary. But it will never destroy the freedom we have built."

He paused as cheers broke out along with nods of agreement.

"We will continue to expand the alliances that Seanchai created. Today, the finest soldiers of men and dwarves will join together as one. We will be joined by elves and pictorians, and we will fight to protect our homes, our mates, our young."

The cheering grew with each pronouncement. Shayth heard his own voice rise with his adrenaline. "We will fight, many races as one people, with one will, to keep Odessiya free and the dream of Seanchai the Wycaan Master alive. To Seanchai!"

Men and dwarves raised their tankards as one. Beer sloshed everywhere as they thrust them repeatedly into the air.

"*Seanchai!*"

"*Seanchai!*"

"*Seanchai!*"

Chapter 26

The news that awaited the prince in Shindellia changed everything. He had already sent messages ahead to prepare men and supplies to leave, but had not anticipated that the pictorians were already engaged in battle. He ordered his men to prepare to march north. A ranger appeared from the north just hours after Shayth had entered the capital. "My prince. It is very confusing in the north. May I speak frankly?"

Shayth nodded.

"Arad'gug did not appreciate the High King in Hothengold sending builders. He screamed at the dwarf officer, claiming the notion that pictorians, particularly those from the Ice Clans, would cower behind walls was insulting. He then announced that he would take the pictorian army north to confront the enemy and leave the dwarves there to build what they want, where they want.

"One of the dwarf designers was threatened, and your advisor to the pictorians told Arad'gug that all the dwarves served under your authority and protection. He also relayed your message that Arad'gug was not to send more than scouting parties beyond the borders of Odessiya until you arrived. He laughed and asked whether you even knew where the borders were. He mocked you, saying only a non-pictorian would hide behind borders and they would live however they want."

Shayth sent another message, reiterating that the pictorians should not advance until he arrived. Arad'gug did not respond, which prompted Shayth to leave Shindellia and head north. Acting upon advice from Ballendir, he did not send further communication to the First Boar. Instead, he sent a message to Umnesilk to meet with him when the army passed near where the pictorian had settled his family. When they arrived at the designated place, Umnesilk was already waiting. But he had not come alone. Shayth recognized two others—one, the young nephew, Narasilk, who Seanchai had been so impressed with. The second was Umnesilk's mate, Onywei, who tended an impressive fire with a huge, skinned bison roasting over it.

Shayth approached with his guards near and the battalions rumbling a short way behind. He saw Onywei turn to her towering mate, gesturing in animated fashion. Umnesilk just shrugged and folded his massive arms across his chest. Shayth dismounted and left his horse with a guard. The former First Boar stepped forward and grabbed Shayth up in his arms as the prince extended a hand, squeezing Shayth until the prince wheezed. When he was released, Shayth saw the pictorian's face was grim.

"Well met, Prince Shindell," he said in his deep voice. "We at your service."

"Thank you," Shayth replied. He noticed that Onywei was now talking excitedly to Narasilk. "What's wrong?"

"Onywei say the bison Narasilk hunted not enough for all army. She think you come with guard and so prepare food for all. Now enough for one bite of bison and carrot each. Hope men not hungry."

Both Narasilk and Umnesilk laughed, but Onywei, though she did not understand the Odessiyan language, cuffed her nephew for good measure. Shayth stepped in front of her.

"Please tell Onywei that I bring important guests. With her permission, I would like them to experience the warm tradition of pictorian hospitality."

Onywei smiled and bowed when Shayth's message was translated. She said something, but Umnesilk cut her off sharply. She looked

momentarily hurt, but continued speaking. Narasilk looked help-
lessly between his aunt and uncle, not sure what to do.

"Please tell me, Umnesilk," Shayth said.

"Best not."

"Is it condolences for my friends? Tell me, and let's get it over
with."

"Yes. She say we sorry for death of Wycaan and split of his family.
Family is everything to pictorian. We meet mate of Wycaan, and she
and Onywei talk of elf pictorye and that dark elfe want family. Now
family not together and mate dead."

Onywei stood by Umnesilk's side, and they nuzzled. Shayth
turned to one of his guards. "Have the men set up camp. The officers
will dine here. Ask Ballendir to bring his senior officers, too. We eat
as one army."

When he turned back, Umnesilk was facing him again. Shayth
took a deep breath.

"I mourn him, too, my friend, as do his wife, their children, and
our friends. All who were close to Seanchai have suffered a great loss.
But we must move on. As cruel as it sounds, this is not the time to
mourn. I head north and need your advice."

Umnesilk gestured that they sit on a circle of trunks that had been
laid in a crude square. Onywei brought them each a large tankard of
hot broth, and when Ballendir joined them, he was introduced and
greeted formally. There was little love lost between dwarves and pictorians, the latter having been used to put down the rebellions of
the former. Shayth told Umnesilk what he knew from the messages
he had received. Umnesilk turned to Narasilk, who shuffled with
discomfort.

"Tell," Umnesilk commanded.

"What I tell you," Narasilk began, his tone deliberate, "must be
kept secret."

"He your prince," Umnesilk growled.

"Please," Narasilk said. "I tell you, but ask that you not reveal secret. Have dear ones still in pictorian city. See them secretly. If found, they exiled or worse. Yes?"

"I understand," Shayth said. "What do you know?"

"Northern Tribes not happy with First Boar. Already many challenges, but he win and noble boars die. He have Emperor's axe that Wycaan gave him. Already mighty before then. Now not sure even Umnesilk could win."

Umnesilk growled, and Shayth was quick to bring them back to focus. "What else, Narasilk?"

"First Boar send pictorians to…to find out?"

"Scouts?"

"Yes, excuse. He send four or five, and them not return. One time they wake to heads of scouts on spears outside city. This very worrying because strong boars defeated and no guard lines outside city see enemy pass. Even footprints in snow not there."

"Not possible," Ballendir interrupted. "Yeh telling me they're ghosts?"

"Not saying ghosts. Saying what been told by boars I trust," Narasilk replied without showing anger. Shayth was impressed. The young boar turned back to Shayth. "Last time they put three heads on spears in front of home of First Boar."

"Not possible," Umnesilk shook his mane.

"I tell you," Narasilk responded, and it was clear they had already discussed this. "Walk through guards and walls without signs." He turned back to Shayth. "Need to say something not good."

"Go on."

"First Boar then send party of one hundred boars led by sons. Not return."

"I heard two hundred," Shayth replied.

"Not know exactly. Mainly from Ice Clans who know land better. Was stupid to—" He stopped and stared at Umnesilk as his uncle growled. "Not okay to speak bad about First Boar. But though Arad'gug strong and understand to hold power, he not smart like last First Boar."

Umnesilk was clearly seething. Ballendir turned to him.

"I think the lad just paid yeh a compliment."

"Not speak bad about First Boar," Umnesilk snapped. "Not good in front of not-pictorian, especially not prince."

"Umnesilk, my good friend," Shayth replied, keeping his voice calm. "Never think I do not hold the pictorian nation in high regard, but not every boar is perfect; neither is every elf, human, or dwarf."

Ballendir, who sipped from a small flask he had produced, let out a burp. "Right yeh are," he said by way of apology.

Narasilk stood slowly. "I ride back with you. I challenge Arad'gug for First Boar and get back axe Wycaan gave me to guard for him. Plan to give to Umnesilk, I think. Wycaan not want bad First Boar. Cannot have bad leader now with such danger. I will hold axe again."

Umnesilk stood, his chest heaving. "Blood of noble pictorians run in nephew. But he still young and without enough experience. If he fight, noble blood will run out of body."

Umnesilk turned and walked into the gathering darkness. Shayth stared after him.

"Uncle finest First Boar ever. He take us into Emperor's army and gather great glory. He take us out when see as mistake. He win friendship of Wycaan and lead us well. But honor everything for him. He gave up First Boar for nation. I think he prefer to be executed as tradition demanded."

"Why wasn't he?" Ballendir asked, but quickly answered it himself. "Let mah guess. Our white-haired friend wouldn't turn his back on his friend." He turned to Shayth. "Play the honor card, Shayth. He will not refuse yeh, his prince."

"Seanchai took his honor away when he intervened," Shayth replied. "I won't do it again."

"Then yeh no leader, Shayth. Be the king, not the young pretender." When Shayth turned on him, Ballendir met his gaze. "A king will demand whatever is needed to protect his kingdom and his people. Yeh need a wise leader in the north. Order him back. Order him to take the axe and become First Boar once again, not for him or you, but for the pictorian nation and for Odessiya."

Shayth was shaking his head, but Ballendir was not going to stand down. He rose to his feet, his face flushed.

"Then we lack more than a First Boar, my friend. We face a scary enemy without a Wycaan and without a leader. Stop feeling sorry for yehself, boy, and be the king."

The fist flew into Ballendir's face and took him on the chin. The stout dwarf whirled round and, his back to Shayth, bent slightly and spat out some blood. Then he straightened and turned back. When Shayth, breathing heavily and riding the familiar rage, looked into Ballendir's face, all he saw was a grin, and his rage disappeared.

"Good," the dwarf said. "I think yeh got mah point."

Chapter 27

The giant pictorian stood alone, staring out into the night, guarding his family and his prince. Behind him, the fires were burned down and an army slept. Shayth watched him long enough to see a full moon rise to present the former First Boar in a noble silhouette, his great horns distinct and his huge axe gleaming. They had been through a lot together. The one who had run from his royal birthright now ruled. The one who had fought to lead his people and guided them wisely now stood exiled and disgraced.

This was going to be a tough conversation. Shayth flexed his sore fist. Damn that dwarf and his rock-like chin. The rage had coursed through Shayth so fast, he was more stunned by its sudden appearance than anything else. He was no king, as Ballendir thought, but the same enraged, violent boy who had rampaged through Odessiya seeking vengeance on anyone who crossed his path.

He watched Umnesilk swing his axe with slow, elegant fluency. If Seanchai were here, he would be having this discussion with the pictorian, binding Umnesilk so that he would join Seanchai out of friendship and defy the code of honor he lived by. But Shayth was no Seanchai; both he and Ballendir knew that. Shayth wanted to retreat into his pain, feel sorry for himself at the loss of Seanchai, but Ballendir urged him to step up.

It was what made Ballendir such a great leader. Shayth sighed.

He lacked leadership ability without guidance from his friends. He thought of Ilana and Seanchai and Mhari and all their friends who had fallen along the way. He took a deep breath. He would not fail them. He would answer the call as they would have. He took a deep breath and stepped forward, standing side-by-side with the towering boar.

"Wondering if prince fall asleep on feet back there," Umnesilk said. "Have such heavy thoughts that mean not sleep?"

"The same that weigh you down, my friend: family, honor, duty, leadership."

Umnesilk nodded slowly. "I know. But you be good king. I know."

"How do you know?"

"Good king gather wise leaders around him, but still know when to punch them on chin."

Shayth looked up and saw the pictorian smiling. "You heard about that, huh?"

"Yes. Whole camp hear. Dwarf leader very proud. Like him. Make you almost pictorian. Maybe *you* become First Boar." Umnesilk chuckled roughly; it was a good sound to hear.

"You must be proud of Narasilk, no?"

"Yes. Pictorian blood strong in him, I say already. But sad if he die because my fail. He good warrior with heart of pictorian, may be great warrior one day. But Arad'gug mighty warrior now. He already defeat boars who would test me."

"Test you, yes, but not defeat you."

"I not go back. I gave word. It not honorable that I even live. Mate worry I kill myself, now Wycaan dead and me free from his bonds, but it not pictorian way. I die fighting. Only way."

They stood awhile in close silence, then Shayth took a deep breath.

"When Seanchai bound you to him, did he not also bind you to his vision? Can the pictorian nation be strong if they are not free? What good will it do if whatever we are facing slaughters your people because Arad'gug can fight but doesn't think like a leader?

"Let me bind you as Seanchai once did. I share his vision, and I pledge my life to ensure that Odessiya and all its races, including the pictorians, live free and prosper. But I cannot do this alone. I have lost too many of my friends, people who made me who I am today. I cannot stand alone, and Ballendir, for all his wisdom, is not enough." He turned to the pictorian, and his voice hardened. "Face me, Umnesilk."

Though a shoulder and head above even Shayth, Umnesilk obeyed the order. "You address me as prince, and maybe one day as king. I ask you to bind yourself to me. If not for me, then to honor Seanchai and his vision. I ask you to put aside the honor code of the pictorian nation and to take on the larger need for your people and all the races.

"I ask you as a free and brave warrior. Become the leader that Seanchai saw in you. Even if you never stand as First Boar of your people, you can yet serve them by serving me. In doing so, you become greater even than what you aspired for, because you will no longer need a title to justify your actions; you will act with a higher purpose.

"Will you serve me, Umnesilk, as you served the Wycaan Master? Will you swear to keep all the races free, to fight for their right to live in peace and thrive? Will you stand by my side and offer me your experience, your wisdom and your great battle axe? For the races of Odessiya, will you swear the allegiance you offered the Wycaan, now to me," he took a deep breath and shook as he said the next words for the first time ever, "the future king of Odessiya?"

Umnesilk stared at him. His eyes grew big, and his mouth dropped. Shayth had never called himself a king before. Slowly, the mighty pictorian dropped to one knee and held his huge axe above his bowed head.

"Learn few elf words from noble Wycaan," he said as Shayth drew his sword and laid it upon the pictorian's great axe. Then Umnesilk looked up. "In memory of Seanchai, greatest of leaders: *Ashbar.*"

Chapter 28

Troja grunted from exertion as she weaved her thin body with grace, fighting off the double sword attack. Her staff whirled with precision, and she matched Pyre's strength even if she could not match her speed. She retreated step by step, and sweat trickled down her angular face. Finally, Pyre feigned with one sword to Troja's left and jabbed the other through the center while Troja's attention was occupied, stopping with the tip touching the elfe's chest.

"That was good," Pyre said as they both reached for the water skins. "You have discipline and technique, but we need to work out the best way to protect your center with the staff."

Rhoddan watched from a rock nearby, sharpening his already finely honed sword. The wet stone slid rhythmically up the length of the blade. He had sparred with Troja earlier, and his overwhelming strength had made short work of her. It seemed as soon as Troja faced a male, her countenance changed and she lost her poise. They would need to work on that, too, but Rhoddan was apprehensive to talk to her about it.

Troja had been with them for three days now. She was constantly on edge, and if anyone nonchalantly touched her arm or walked up without announcing themselves, she would whirl around, wide eyed and ready to defend herself with the knife Ahad had given her, the knife that never left her belt. She always apologized, and once, after she took a swipe at Rhoddan, she burst out crying. Yesterday, Ahad had taken her into the nearby port to buy supplies, and she returned with a staff on her back. It was thin and supple, which made Rhoddan wonder about its effectiveness. But Ahad had been with her, and the elf had to admit, the assassin—*Master* Assassin—knew his weapons. Troja proudly showed them some moves her father taught her. They were stiff and awkward at first, but she soon overcame that.

Rhoddan sharpened the small, retractable blades on each end of her staff, and that night, Troja fell asleep hugging it. For the first time, she did not wake in the night from bad dreams. Rhoddan was loath to wake her to replace him on guard duty, but he knew she would be insulted if he treated her differently. He had quickly discovered that she harbored a fierce pride. Still, he never asked her about what had happened when she had been enslaved.

"You again," Troja pointed her staff toward Rhoddan. "Unless you're too tired."

Rhoddan grinned. She was the one breathing heavily, and the sweat glistened on her amber skin. Her shirt was soaked and clung to her.

"Sure you don't need a breather?" he suggested.

"Oh, I think the mighty warrior is scared."

Pyre let out a loud laugh. "Don't pull the wolfheid's tail," she said.

"What's a wolfheid?"

"You don't want to know," Pyre said. "Come on, great warrior. Show her what you've got."

Rhoddan rose and drew his heavy broadsword slowly and somewhat theatrically, to make it as ominous as possible. Pyre smiled, and Troja yawned just as dramatically.

"You make him playful," Pyre said. "I've never seen that. Good job."

Rhoddan glanced at her inscrutable face. He really couldn't be sure if she was happy for him or not. But then, he wasn't sure what he was feeling. He began to spar with the thin elfe, immediately putting her on the back foot. Pyre stopped them.

"Don't try and compete with his strength, Troja. Chances are you will never face anyone weaker than you. Use his strength against him."

Pyre rose, put up one of her Win Dao swords, and signaled for Rhoddan to strike a high blow. As he did, she met his blade and allowed it to follow the momentum down, guiding it away from her.

"As you move him away, try and unbalance him. See if you can get him to overstretch because of his own momentum. Watch."

Rhoddan made the same move and she feigned, but this time moved slightly to one side. When he repeated the movement, he had to lean in, and Pyre flicked him down, making him stagger, then whipped her sword to his throat. Rhoddan pretended to choke and fall dramatically to the ground.

Troja laughed, but Pyre frowned.

"What is it?" Rhoddan asked.

"You're changing," she replied. "I've never seen you like this."

"Like what?" Troja asked.

"He's…having fun," Pyre replied, and there was wonder in her voice. "Enough games. Get up and let Troja practice."

They sparred for a long time, with Pyre constantly coaching Troja. Her improvement was fast and impressive. When they stopped after Troja had unbalanced Rhoddan twice, she turned and hugged Pyre.

"Thank you," she said into Pyre's ear, and when they disengaged, Pyre was smiling.

"Not bad," Ahad said from where he'd been observing. "Of course, the opposition wasn't much, but you should take what you can."

"How about you, then, assassin?" Troja rose.

"*Master* Assassin," Ahad chided.

"What's the difference?"

"The difference?" He arched an eyebrow. "I'll show you."

He drew his thin sword and sparred with her, cutting inside her guard with ease and sending her sprawling. She rose and dusted herself off.

"Okay," she said. "Not bad…for an assassin."

Ahad pulled a scarf from his bag and turned to Pyre. "Please tie this over my eyes and make sure I cannot see." Once she had, he asked, "Troja, would you like to check?"

"No," she said, and there was nervousness in her voice. "How fast should I go?"

Ahad shrugged. "Start slow and speed up until you defeat me."

Troja began slowly, creeping around him, but he turned with her as she struck. She stopped trying to confuse him and attacked again. Whether from up high or down low, from right or left, he met her, blade to blade. Rhoddan watched with wonder. Troja's face screwed up as she focused and went faster. She attacked quicker now than she had sparring with Rhoddan, and still he blocked her.

"Rhoddan," Ahad called. "What are you waiting for? I can feel you straining at the bit."

Rhoddan moved to Ahad's other side and joined the fray. Ahad's movements became a blur, and beads of sweat became flowing rivers. Finally, he feinted, sending Troja sprawling. But Rhoddan moved left, then abruptly right, inside of Ahad's defense, and had his sword at the assassin's chest when the human turned.

"Got me," Ahad conceded, and tore off the blindfold.

"That was…" Troja didn't finish the sentence, but Rhoddan did. His voice expressed the awe he felt.

"…the difference between an assassin and a Master Assassin."

Chapter 29

"We're being followed," Ahad said the next day as he moved his horse next to Rhoddan's.

"Any idea who?"

"No. They're good."

"Apparently not good enough." There was a smirk on Rhoddan's face.

"I'm going to ride ahead and circle around. Be prepared while I'm gone. You look a lot more vulnerable without me protecting you."

Fond as he was of Rhoddan, Ahad enjoyed wiping the elf's grin off his face. He pushed his horse forward and galloped ahead, weaving through the hilly terrain until he found a small spring with grass growing on its banks. Ahead, the stream exited a gorge, and he tethered his horse there, allowing enough slack for the stallion to drink and graze.

He climbed one of the hills and let his mind wander back to his promising childhood in Shindellia, privileged son of the army's most feared and celebrated general. He thought of his friendship with the Crown Prince and the Emperor. He had clearly been destined to walk a different path. He had wasted over a decade. After his father died, he had gone in search of his mother. Though he never found her body, her entire family had been wiped out, he knew inside that she was dead. From there, he travelled a dark and destructive path but never stopped training and honing his considerable skills. An assassin never went for long without work, and he had money stashed all over Odessiya.

He fell flat on the ground. There were voices on the other side of the hill, maybe thirty feet from him—the distinct hissing of taragusii. He looked around for cover, but there was none. He was out in the open without even his horse.

An assassin is never careless, at least not twice. He chided himself for letting his mind wander. Once he thought it safe, he crawled to the ridge and peeked over. A patrol of four taragusii had passed, but in the valley below were at least a hundred more. He gulped. This was not a raiding party. He watched as small groups rode in and out of the main body in all directions. They were searching and Ahad instinctively knew the Wycaan was their quarry. He retreated, first crawling and then walking briskly. When he reached the bottom of the hill, he immediately saw tracks from taragusii mounts. He edged nearer until he heard their rasping voices.

"But if we go back now, we'll have to ssshare the horssse. If we cook it here, then only we eat it."

"We need to report back," another replied. "Fourth Ssscale is impatient. Where isss itsss rider?"

"Impatient, yesss, but Fourth Scale doesssn't know we're here. He doesssn't expect us until tomorrow, at leassst. Fresssh meat. The rider hasss probably run off, afraid."

"Collect sssome firewood, then, but let'sss be quick."

Ahad brought out his small crossbow but was not sure where the scales ended and the flesh began. He leaned around the rock and found himself face-to-face with a taragus holding bracken. The taragus began to alert his friends, and Ahad shot a quarrel straight into his mouth. No scales there. As the taragus staggered backward and fell, Ahad sprung out. Another taragus to his right turned immediately. Ahad flicked his arm, sending a deadly shuriken spinning into his opponent's throat. The taragus staggered forward and brought a hand up to pull the blade out. Ahad leapt at him, kicking out with a straight leg and jamming the blade deeper. The taragus crumpled.

But the other two were now alerted. One called to the second, who mounted one of their black creatures and turned to charge. Ahad didn't think the taragus was trying to kill him, but to get past. He loaded his crossbow again. The rider crouched, a mass of scales, and Ahad searched for a target. Finding none, he lowered his crossbow to the mount and shot between the creature's chest scales. It was no horse, but the whinny of pain as the creature fell was familiar enough. The taragus rolled and sprung to its feet, a thick, serrated broadsword already drawn.

The final taragus approached cautiously, slowly whirling its sword. Ahad drew his own sword, which looked flimsy in comparison. But it was built of old elven steel, and having it shatter was the least of his worries. He dropped the crossbow and drew a second shuriken. Both opponents raised their blades, ready to deflect a thrown knife.

Ahad, who could not allow himself to be cornered against the rock face, made the first move. He advanced on one taragus and then swept in on the second. It was a good trick for street fighters, but these determined and trained warriors did not let their guards down. The taragus he attacked parried two, three blows, and though the creature was on the back foot, it prevented Ahad from making a thrust count. He turned on the second and pushed the taragus back with a flurry of strokes, trying to get both taragusii in front of him.

But the first taragus sprung before Ahad could position them where he wanted. The taragus hissed in surprise as Ahad parried blow after blow without ever turning round. The taragus changed his rhythm, feigning a blow, but then, as both taragusii struck together, Ahad rolled from under them, and their own blades clashed.

Ahad pivoted while he crouched, and one blade sliced the first taragus' calves. Then the assassin changed direction in one fluid movement and slashed the second with his knife. Riding his momentum, he rose and jumped above the first taragus. The blow from Ahad's sword sent the taragus' blade deflecting from his own head. But Ahad's knife followed and pierced the taragus between the eyes.

As he turned to face the second taragus, he heard hooves galloping. Both man and taragus turned, but the figure who came through rode a horse and struck with two Win Dao swords. The taragus wheeled around from the blow, blood spraying all around.

Pyre turned her horse as it slowed and came to a stop in front of Ahad.

"Couldn't let me have all the fun?" he smirked, wiping his blades and then retrieving his crossbow. But when he turned, he saw that Pyre's face was pale and full of fear. "What happened?"

CHAPTER 30

"Where are the others, Pyre?"

The elfe stared at him. She dismounted and wiped her face on her shirt. Ahad took her arm and guided her to a rock, where she half leaned, half sat. He tethered her horse by his own before bringing her a water skin. She drank it dry, gulping so loud it seemed to echo. He refilled it in the stream and gave it back to her. She drank only a little this time, wiping her mouth again on her sleeve.

"We were jumped by other taragusii patrols. We fought them off and mounted, but only Rhoddan and I got away. Troja was pulled out of her saddle by what I first thought to be a lasso rope, but what was actually a very long whip.

"We rode back to help her, but there were several captors holding her. She was screaming so terribly, and then Ithea was standing in front of her facing us, his whip crackling. He is still using Denalion's body, which is strange, but he was the same as I saw him last time. Rhoddan turned to me and ordered me to go. I thought he would come with me, but he dismounted. I hesitated, and he again ordered me to leave. He drew his sword as I left."

"Who is this Ithea?"

"He is...was...second only to the Emperor, a dark sorcerer. He almost killed Sa'gola."

"Who?"

"The sorceress who killed Seanchai. That's how powerful he is. He killed Denalion because he needed his body, and…" She trailed off, seeing that Ahad was getting lost. "Rhoddan has no chance against him," she finished.

"Does Rhoddan know this?"

"Yes, but I'm sure all he heard was Troja's screams. I don't think they were hurting her. Taragusii might eat you, but they don't torture. It was the trauma from being held prisoner again, I'm sure. I should never have left. I should not have listened to Rhoddan."

Ahad put his hands on her shoulders. "You did the right thing. You would have faced this Ithea and all his taragusii and died."

"But Rhoddan…"

Suddenly, she was in his arms, and he held her close as she cried. "I'm supposed to be a Wycaan," she sniffed. "I'm supposed to be his equal. Seanchai would have…"

Her voice trailed off, and he stroked her long hair while his thoughts flew to different scenarios. After a few minutes, she pulled away and looked at him, expecting, he feared, a plan.

"Okay." He leaned back next to her, resting his head on the rock. "We go back. I'll go into their camp at night. I can probably get in and out, unless…"

"Unless what?"

"Unless this Ithea is really on the Emperor's level. He might sense me. I'll see if I can find Rhoddan, too. If he's alive, I will try to get them both out. If he's badly wounded or I can't find one of them easily, I may only be able to save one."

"We can't just leave him…or her."

"No, but if it is too much for me, or if this Ithea stands in our way, then we go on and find Seanchai. Then he can face this Ithea, and we'll have more of a chance to rescue them."

"What if we don't find Seanchai? What if we do and he is not who he was?"

Ahad put his arm around the elfe and stroked her shoulder. "There are many flaws to my plan and many options that we can change and adapt. We don't even know if Ithea plans to keep them alive. Will they make attractive enough bait for Seanchai if he is alive, or for Mharina? One of the secrets to people like you and me staying alive is recognizing when we cannot win. Getting ourselves killed will not help Seanchai, Rhoddan, or Troja."

Pyre turned to him. "I made a promise to Troja. I promised that if she was ever caught again and I couldn't save her, I would kill her. If Rhoddan is dead…"

"Being captive to the taragusii is not the same as being captive to the slave traders. The latter are sadistic and evil; the taragusii will not torture or abuse her—you said so yourself. You do not kill her… for now, at least."

Rhoddan woke to a pounding head and Troja's whimpering. He tried to open his eyes, but one was swollen closed. She was tending his wounds with a salve. Her legs were chained together with enough room to walk, and her hands were loosely constrained. Nonetheless, they were chained, and she was again bound and terrified. He was propped against a tree trunk, rope binding his arms, body, and legs in place. His chest burned, and he could feel lacerations all over his body.

"Troja. Are you harmed?" he whispered. He could see her shake her head. "It's okay to be scared, but do not fear them the way you feared the slave traders. These captors are different and disciplined. Do you understand?"

She nodded, but was biting her lips to keep control.

"It's different this time. You aren't being held as a slave, and you have me. I'm in great shape to protect you." He tried a laugh, but it swiftly became a grimace. "What did they do to me?"

"The leader, a red-faced old elf, kept whipping you, calling out to Pyre to give herself up. At first, you shouted for her to leave, but he kept striking you until you lost consciousness."

A silhouette appeared behind her. "You put up quite a resistance, my friend," Ithea said, his voice deep and warm. "I was very impressed. Don't stop," he instructed Troja. "He must heal. I provided the salve, Rhoddan warrior. I have no desire to kill or torture either of you. I want the Wycaan, if the rumors that he is still alive are true. If he isn't, I want the young elfe that rides with you. She will make fine bait, as well."

"Bait?" Rhoddan asked.

"Yes," Ithea laughed. "It is so poetic, isn't it? We kidnapped his children to lure him to Grogin, and now he will become bait for his daughter and the purple whore."

"So the Emperor is still alive?" Rhoddan asked.

"No. You might wish he was, though, when you get to know me. And if you create problems, then you *will* get to know me."

He stood and laughed. It was not maniacal or sarcastic. It was measured and controlled and exuded power.

Chapter 31

The taragusii posed a challenge that Ahad was not accustomed to. They possessed a strong sense of smell. He realized this after two failed attempts to pass the outer sentries. They did not see him. No one ever did. But their twitching noses and annoying tongues gave him ample warning, and he gave up.

The following morning, he led Pyre back to the taragusii they had killed. When he explained what he planned to do, she left him to his own devices. He slathered the creatures' blood and sweat over his clothes, hands, neck, and face. The expression on Pyre's face when she returned confirmed that he had succeeded in his objective. They spent the rest of the day resting, and Ahad slept for several hours in the afternoon.

That night, he returned to the main camp. The outer ring of guards was easy to pass. They were spread out and did not expect to be attacked. Anything less than an army went out of its way to give taragusii a wide berth, and such a mass of people would never get this close without warning. There was an inner ring of sentries, and they stood close enough to talk to each other, pacing back and forth about a hundred steps each way. Eventually, Ahad found what he was looking for: a rock tall enough to hide him from one guard while the other had his back to him.

Once past the inner line of guards, it became easier. Almost everyone was sleeping, and those who weren't were tired and felt safely protected. One tent was different than the ones the taragusii slept in, and two guards stood outside. Either it housed the prisoners or the sorcerer. He decided not to take chances and continued in the opposite direction. It proved a wise decision, as he found Rhoddan and Troja tied to a tree. There were no guards near them, but two taragusii sat not far away. They could be feigning disinterest.

Ahad crept around to the other side of the tree and came up behind the two. Rhoddan snored softly, and his exhalations seemed forced, perhaps painful. Close up, Ahad saw the elf was pretty beaten up. He had deep, burned lesions all over, some scabbed, but many still open. Ahad looked at the elfe. She did not seem wounded, but from her almost manic stare, he feared for whatever mental turmoil she endured. She was tough, but fragile.

He wanted to wake Rhoddan and talk with him, but didn't trust the elfe's heightened nerves. He moved carefully closer to her. Then he quickly clamped one hand on her mouth and the other on her chest, pushing her down. Her whole body tensed as she went to scream. He pushed again with his hand, and virtually no sound escaped. He whispered into her ear.

"I am Ahad. I am a friend of Rhoddan's. You are Troja—we sparred together. I am Ahad, a friend of Rhoddan. You are Troja—we sparred together. I'm Ahad…"

Her chest had been jerking up and down in fright. He felt sweat on her face and continued whispering his name and then hers. Finally, her panting subsided, but he kept his mouth by her ear.

"When you are in control and I can remove my hand, I want you to nod slowly. Nod three times."

She nodded once but shuddered on the second, and he clamped his hand harder.

"You're doing great, Troja. It's okay you feel this way— it's to be expected. Take your time and nod again when you are ready."

She succeeded on the third attempt, and he released his hand.

She turned awkwardly, not wanting to wake Rhoddan or alert the guards.

"I'm sorry," she whispered.

"Don't be. After all I imagine you've been through, you are one of the bravest elfes I have ever known."

"How many elfes have you known?"

"Not many. Actually, just you and Pyre, so you're either in first or second place—that's pretty high on my list."

She smiled, and he tried to disguise a sigh of relief.

"Are you hurt? Are you treated okay?"

She nodded.

"Do you know what they want with you?"

"Us in exchange for Pyre or the Wycaan Master."

"What happened to Rhoddan? Did you see it?"

She whimpered, and he was ready to clamp his hand back on her mouth.

"Water," she whispered, and Ahad offered a small water skin. She sipped a bit and nodded. He quickly secured the skin back in its pocket while she continued. "The leader, Ithea, has a whip that is more than just a whip. It sizzles with energy. He used it to bring Rhoddan down, but Rhoddan continued to fight to get to me. If he hadn't lost consciousness, he would have died. He wouldn't give in, even though I tried to call to him."

Ahad wiped tears from her face.

"Can he move? Can he run if need be?"

Troja shook her head.

"Where are they taking you?"

"We are staying here for a while and then returning to their fortress. He thinks if he can capture the one you call Seanchai, then the Wycaan's daughter and Pyre will come to rescue him. Ithea wants Pyre for himself, but will kill the elf's eldest *calhei*."

Ahad nodded. "Listen to me carefully, Troja, for I must go. Pyre and I will look for the Wycaan and, one way or another, come to rescue you both. But it will take some time, and we need Rhoddan to heal. Tell him I said that he must not fight them or try to escape. He must only focus on getting better."

Troja looked at the sleeping elf. "Will he listen?"

"To you, he will. He has strong feelings for you. I see it. Pyre sees it. If need be, tell him that any escape will endanger you. Now I have another question. Can you hold yourself together?"

She nodded.

"The taragusii won't hurt you if you obey orders. They won't taunt you. Cooperate with this Ithea. He is far more powerful than you, and you have Rhoddan to look after. If he were alone, he would die trying to escape, but now he has you, and you can keep him alive. We will come as soon as we can."

"Promise?" Her voice sounded so quiet, so fragile.

Ahad stroked her arm. "I promise."

Rhoddan muttered something in his sleep, and Troja leaned over to hush him. When she turned back to Ahad, he was gone.

Chapter 32

Mharina panted. Sweat dripped from her forehead, and she wished she could wipe her stinging eyes. But she had no sleeve; her black, sleeveless shirt stuck to her body. Perhaps this was part of the training. Maybe Sa'gola had an obscure reason for it. But for now, all Mharina could do was blink.

The elfe stood on a rock in a cave above a pool of bubbling water. This was no soothing bath; the water would scald the skin off her body. But she embraced the dormant fire underneath it, reaching down and channeling it up through her entire body and into the palms of her hands. She held a ball of fire, which shimmered and spat. It was not quite round, and she focused on keeping it consistent and settled. Then she molded two balls that hovered above her palms.

"Good. Show me tall, thin columns," Sa'gola called.

Mharina frowned as she focused on slowly stretching the fireball into the desired shape and splitting it into two. She turned her attention to each and smiled to herself as both responded. But as soon as the second stretched out, the first returned to the hovering ball.

Mharina harrumphed, eliciting a laugh from her teacher. The elfe did not respond, but focused again, first on one and then the second, with the same results. Frustrated, she combined the balls into a single globe of energy and lashed out with an elegant set of hand movements, sending the energy swirling forward like a thin rope and responding to every movement of her arms. She switched between hands, swirling and snapping the fire strand. She loved this movement and often played with it, relaxing in the fluid motion that flowed out of her.

"Try it moving both hands separately," Sa'gola suggested, and Mharina obeyed, dancing with the fire. She felt her entire body sway in a rhythm that consumed her.

Then she felt it, the bond, fire and elfe no longer separate entities. It responded to her intention. She was *leading* it. The realization hit her as she focused on her body and the fire responded, an extension of her very self. The heat, the sweat, and the tension left her, all but forgotten. There was nothing left in the world but her and the fire. They were one and moved together, responding to each other's every nuance.

She did not want to stop—did not want to lose the feeling, the vibrancy, the exhilaration. Through this wave of ecstasy, she heard Sa'gola calling as if from miles away. But her teacher's voice pierced through, her tone increasingly insistent. Finally, Mharina sensed the urgency and ground the energy. She turned and walked toward her teacher, now aware that her hair was soaked and matted, her shirt clung to her body, and her chest heaved for breath.

She felt the heat recede from her fingertips, replaced by a humming vibration of vitality. She began to share her exhilaration with Sa'gola. Crack! The slap across her cheek was hard and sharp, and the sound echoed back to her. She raised her hand to her cheek, which stung from the force of the blow. Sa'gola turned and walked away. Mharina was stunned. She stood for a moment, blinking back tears. She raised the hem of her shirt and wiped her face, sweat and tears intermingled.

She followed Sa'gola through the portal and out into the field near the sorceress' house. Sa'gola did not turn around, but walked toward the lake. At the edge, she stopped and raised an arm.

"Keep walking," she ordered, and Mharina passed her and entered the lake.

It was freezing, especially after the hot cavern. She hesitated as the water began to numb her toes, feet, and ankles.

"Keep walking," Sa'gola hissed.

Mharina went to strip her shirt off, but again Sa'gola spoke, her voice harsh and sharp. "Keep your clothes on."

Now her thin trousers stuck to her in a different way. Her legs were so cold, and she let out a small cry as her waist and stomach submerged. She gasped as her chest constricted against the assault, and then, as her neck went underwater, she took a deep breath and kept walking. She was completely submerged. The silence was deafening, the pressure of cold water absolute. She kept walking until the air had almost escaped her. With no choice, she kicked off the bottom and swam to the surface. She turned, treading water.

"Come out," Sa'gola called.

When the elfe reached the shore, Sa'gola was sitting on one of a pair of rocks where they had sat before to talk. It was not cold, but light cloud cover denied the warming sun from reaching her. When she sat, a small breeze made her hug her wet body. She shivered, but Sa'gola ignored it. Mharina tried to stop herself by biting her lips. She would like to discard her wet clothes but knew if she started to, she would be stopped.

"You are very talented, Mharina—extremely so. But you are young, impulsive, and naive. The fire is not your friend. Dance with it, but keep it at arm's length. It seeks to consume you, not because it is evil, but because that is its nature. It burns, it consumes, and it destroys.

"What would have happened if you had kept walking into the lake without breath?" Her student's chattering teeth were the only response, and Sa'gola continued. "You would have drowned. The elements are not your friends. Maybe the Wycaans think they are at one with the elements, but they are foolish romantics. The elements do not love or hate, do not make friends and enemies. The elements are not good or bad, they just are, nothing else. Never deceive yourself that you ride with the elements. You do not. You control them. At all times, you must be in control. Do you understand?"

"Y-y-y-esss," Mharina managed.

"Take your clothes off." Sa'gola said, and disappeared, returning moments later with a blanket from her cottage. She took Mharina's clothes and laid them on a rock.

Mharina still shivered, despite the thick woolen fleece. She stared at her teacher.

"Go on," Sa'gola said, her voice soft now. "Use the fire to warm yourself."

"I-I-I d-d-d-d-don't want to," Mharina chattered, fearing the control the fire had over her back in the cave.

"Use it," Sa'gola ordered. "It is yours to command. That is the essence of our power!"

Almost effortlessly, Mharina ignited the fire in her stomach and warmed herself. The action demanded almost nothing of her physically, but was one of the hardest things she had ever done.

Chapter 33

After a tense meal, Mharina went for a walk by herself. She needed the space to process what had happened. Sa'gola would understand. These were intense times, the three of them in a small cottage, and sometimes the young elfe just needed to be alone. The cottage sat on a wide patch of pasture facing the water. A river fed the lake, and Mharina followed it upstream. Occasionally, she met a man or two leading mule-drawn wagons laden with produce or hay.

When they first arrived, Mharina wondered whether the native inhabitants even saw them. But she knew that Sa'gola defended the people when they were threatened, helped heal their sick, and delivered their babies. No, they knew of her presence, but the rules were very clear. They passed her with eyes staring firmly ahead and gave her ample space.

She turned from the road to a path they had followed when they first came through the mist. The trees closed in around her, vines hanging from their branches, and the earth on either side of the path gave way to puddles that turned into swamp. Mharina had been intrigued with the swamp since she first saw it: its thick, bubbly, potent broth; the elusive animals slithering in and out of its murky waters; strange birds that squawked from tree to tree; and the relentless, wispy fog that had initially intimidated her. Now she enjoyed the privacy and the chance to think.

Her training was going very well. Her control of the elements was growing daily, and she was a conscientious student. She also sat in on all the healing lessons Sa'gola gave Maugwen. However, she was not invited to Sa'gola and Maugwen's private meetings, though she knew whatever Sa'gola was trying to teach Maugwen wasn't going well. Neither was it ever discussed. Maugwen would offer her a rueful smile or shrug, and Sa'gola told her it was none of her business.

Under different circumstances, Mharina could have been happy here. She loved her teacher and embraced the serene environment and the craft she was learning. But every time she achieved something, she imagined sharing it with her father. Seanchai loved celebrating his students' successes, and she had often followed—pathetically, she now admitted—as he walked the training grounds of the Wycaan Academy. When she excelled in Denalion's lessons, she would run to tell her father…if he was actually on Wycaan Island for once. She sighed. It was more than just that he died. She felt as though she had simply never had the opportunity to get to know him, and now she never would.

She snapped a spindly branch, unsheathed her knife, and began to strip the branch's bark as she walked. Her thoughts went to the lesson today, to her exhilaration with the fire and the reprimand Sa'gola had meted out. Her cheek still stung and was slightly swollen. The sorceress was petite, but she packed a powerful slap. This was not the first time Mharina went too far in her training and needed to be pulled back. Sa'gola feared she had too much of her mother inside her, but wanted Mharina to be tougher than her father. This annoyed Mharina, who snapped harshly at Sa'gola. The Purple Lady sat through it with a huge grin across her face.

Now, Mharina felt the anger rise again and threw the stick with all her strength. It spun through the air but, just as it reached the top of its arc, it stopped and fell straight down. Mharina stared. She had reached Sa'gola's protective boundary. She stood still for a moment, captivated by what she couldn't see. When they came through on their way in, she wondered how her teacher could construct something so complex and effective. Now, a few months on, she realized Sa'gola used her control of water to create the fog and of air to create that dense, effective, solid wall. Was this also how she was able to disappear?

Mharina was under no illusions that she could do it, herself, but she felt good about understanding the theory behind it. She sheathed her knife and began weaving her hands in front of her. She would have to learn total control over water and air to truly disappear or protect herself in a similar way. For now, she contented herself folding the air and, as she added water, she produced a small ball of mist.

She continued to fold air and water, and the mist became fog. The fog was clumsy, erratic, and non-uniform, but she was thrilled. She weaved animal shapes and birds that she set free and laughed. Laughed out loud. Forgetting everything, she was momentarily so happy, a carefree *calhei*. Self-conscious of her frivolity, she glanced around. No one had followed her. The people here kept away from the mysterious women and the ominous fog. But as she turned to the boundary, she saw him.

It was merely a silhouette, but the round straw hat and the wicker basket left little to discern. There could, of course, be other mushroom hunters gathering in these parts, but her instincts cried out, and she was sure. He was crouched and looking in her direction. Now he rose and carefully stepped toward her. He pushed back his hat, uncovering a few blond curls and his arresting blue eyes. There was no mistake.

He looked cautiously in her direction, but it seemed pretty clear that he could not see her. Still, he wore a look of earnest hope. Was it for her? She looked harder. He wasn't perfectly defined, either, the fog adding a blurry shimmer around him. He took a few paces forward and was prevented from advancing. Cautiously, he raised a hand and palmed the barrier, cocking his head to listen. Mharina realized she was not breathing. Slowly, she released the last bit of oxygen in her chest and inhaled. She stared as he tried to comprehend what was in front of him.

After a few minutes, he released the straps on his wicker basket and put it on the ground. He knelt and rummaged around inside for a small burlap sack, which he laid reverently on the ground. Then he rose, returned the basket to his back and looked just to Mharina's left shoulder.

"For your apprentice, milady. But if she wants to share them with you, I suppose that is her right."

Then he laughed and turned away.

Chapter 34

"You did what?" Sa'gola was furious.

"I waited until he left before I took the sack. I made sure. I knew you wouldn't want me to contact him without your permission, so I didn't. Why are you so angry?"

"And you brought the mushrooms here?"

"Yes. I fried them. We'll eat them with the soup I've prep—"

She stopped, because the glare Sa'gola was giving her was serious. She knew her teacher well enough to know when something was badly wrong.

"What have I done?" she asked, her voice suddenly an uncertain teenager's.

"He'll come back and see they're gone. He'll discern footprints. He'll know where we are."

"But he can't get in, and he will know only that someone took them."

"Oh, he can't get in, you say? How well do you know this handsome young man? Tell me, what have you discerned from his children's stories and shared breakfast?"

Maugwen interjected from the corner. "Sa'gola. She did what she did. Shouting at her is not going to—"

"I didn't ask you!" Sa'gola snarled. "Do you remember what I told you I would do if you ever gave away my home?"

"Kill me," Maugwen said without hesitation. "But what she did was an honest mistake of…"

"…of a besotted girl!"

"…of *your young* apprentice who *you* chose. It was an honest mistake, and we will put it right."

"How? He's as good as your rangers, and I have a hard time out-witting them in your land."

"The natives here. Are there similar tribes on the other side of the boundary?"

"Yes. What's that got to—"

"And he will know them?"

"Yes."

"That doll you showed me—the one with the multi-colored coat—that you told me is a religious talisman…"

"What are you getting at, Maugwen?"

Maugwen would not be hassled. "Do they have those talismans on the other side?"

Sa'gola stopped and stared at her. Then she nodded. "We leave one of those in the sack, a thank you from the person who took it, and lead a trail off in another direction, toward the villages there. Good. Thank you, Maugwen. I'm glad I brought one sensible person here, at least."

Sa'gola had returned to her calmer tone.

"I am sorry, Sa'gola," Mharina said, feeling wretched. "I really am."

Sa'gola hugged her. "I know you are. I know you're young and that you'll make the mistakes of youth, especially in the field of love. Anyway, it isn't like he has found his way through my boundary this time."

She laughed as they disentangled. Then they all froze at a sharp rap on the front door.

Sa'gola walked to the door. Mharina could see her summoning power, and the pit in the elfe's stomach got harder. Had she just led the Mushroom Man to his death? She began to rise, but Maugwen caught her attention and shook her head sharply. When Sa'gola opened the door, no one was there. Mharina tried to peek around the sorceress, but could not see anyone. Still, she sensed a presence—a powerful one—and could see her teacher remained visibly tense.

"We cannot find you," a shrill, feminine voice said, "but we are near you, no?"

"Aye, these be fine protective wards, Sa'gola," a second, huskier voice added. "Very impressive."

"And you will respect them by not trying to penetrate," Sa'gola snapped.

"Same old Sa'gola," the first laughed. "You have taken an apprentice or two. We have felt the awakening and the new, concentrated powers forming around you. Why has the elusive Purple Lady, after decades of solitude, suddenly decided to train others?"

"Sometimes the student chooses the teacher, not the other way round. I had not anticipated this before I went on my last mission."

"Your last mission, yes," the bodiless voice continued. "How is your Emperor? We felt major shifts there, as well. A great battle has taken place, one of great and powerful magic."

"The Emperor is dead, but Ithea still lives and is, perhaps, even more powerful than before."

"Ithea," the second voice spat. "Why have we allowed him to live so long?"

"Allowed?" Sa'gola snorted. There was a tense, ensuing silence until Sa'gola broke it. "What do you want with me?"

"Bring the girl to meet us."

"But she has barely started."

"You be one of the most powerful of our Order, Sa'gola. It be only right that we ensure that…that she be suitable."

"Suitable? Since when…"

"We be a bit cautious these past few decades, my dear, and with good reason. Our Order becomes more involved as the world slides into havoc, as the humans ascend. The balance has been disturbed, and the way be not as clear as when you and I were young apprentices."

"She has scarcely begun her training," Sa'gola repeated, and Mharina sensed fear in her strained tone. "She will not be ready for the Testing."

"I do not expect we will test her in the traditional sense. That would be a waste of a life if she be truly not ready. But we be wanting to get to know her. She is an elfe with an interesting lineage, which makes it all the more worrying."

"She's no Wycaan," Sa'gola said, rather too quickly.

"How can you be so sure? She might not be natural-born, but—"

"I know," Sa'gola said. "I have been around Wycaans more than anyone. I met her parents and siblings. I know."

Again, there was a pregnant silence.

"Very well," the first voice said. "Bring her to the conclave. We look forward to seeing you both."

Mharina sensed they were gone, but Sa'gola stood there, staring out the doorway, for a long time. Finally, she turned and stared at Mharina.

"I need to tell you about our Order," she said. "But first, let's eat your mushrooms. They are, for now, the least of our problems."

Chapter 35

S a'gola didn't speak that night. She retreated to her private chamber and closed the door. In the morning, Mharina woke to a flurry of activity coming from the kitchen. The elfe was usually the first up and, being the youngest, saw it as her role to prepare hot water and food to break the fast. She slept in an alcove off the kitchen and sat up now to observe her teacher. Sa'gola could do anything quietly, and this was anything but. She seemed flustered, and her face flushed. As she turned, she saw Mharina observing her.

"Do you plan to sleep in all day? Shall I bring you breakfast in bed?"

Mharina kicked the blanket off and got up quickly. She had no desire to endure Sa'gola's sarcasm. Once dressed, she came to the kitchen to help. Sa'gola ignored her, preparing food in packages.

"Are you okay, Sa'gola? What's wrong?"

"Go wake your friend," the sorceress snapped. "We leave soon."

They left the cottage and quickly crossed through the barrier, heading further north without discussion or explanation. At first, Mharina wondered if they were going straight to this conclave, and a pit formed in her stomach. But by midday, they settled in a small cave. The mountain stood alone, a day's walk from the nearest range. The rock was porous, suggesting dormant volcanic activity, and Mharina was not surprised when Sa'gola led them to a small mineral pool. Without a word, they all shed their dusty clothes and entered the pool. Sa'gola sighed and closed her eyes. Mharina washed her clothes and then Sa'gola's. She stepped out of the pool and spread the clothes on the warm pumice rocks.

"Thank you." They were the first calm words Sa'gola said. She punctuated them with a long sigh, her eyes still closed.

As Mharina eased herself back into the water, Sa'gola got out and perched on the smooth, warm rocks. She held her knees to her chest and gently stroked her scars.

"Sa'gola," Mharina swallowed hard. "I am your apprentice. I followed you, despite all that has befallen my family. Isn't it time I know?"

Sa'gola looked down at her, but her expression was not angry, just conflicted. Mharina had not seen her so vulnerable since the fight with Ithea.

"Would you prefer me to leave you two?" Maugwen asked, and Mharina realized she had forgotten her friend was even present.

"No," Sa'gola said. "You will come, too. They have sensed your power, as well."

"Well, I'm glad someone has. All *I'm* sensing is frustration."

She received a wry smile, but then Sa'gola took another deep breath and began speaking. "The World of Faded Memory that everyone speaks about so nostalgically was not as perfect as we are led to believe. Then, as now, good fought evil, evil fought good, and most who participated ended up dead.

"It is said that the elves ruled, though I suspect that is because the elves wrote the histories. There were a number of kingdoms with different rulers. Some had benevolent leaders, while others suffered greatly. The dwarves, giants, pictorians, and humans all maintained a measure of semi-autonomy.

"What really kept the status quo was the magic. The Wycaans leveraged it and continually scouted potential young from all races. While it was a racially diverse order, the Wycaans were all male. In many kingdoms, females were terribly exploited. Even in kingdoms where they weren't, they never held power or learned to fight. But there was an aspect of the magic that the Wycaans were unaware of. You have talked with your siblings about them being natural-born Wycaans, but this was not a known phenomenon then. Many who were born with magic went through their life oppressed, without knowing they were special.

"There was an elfe called Shadona. She was a princess married off to a tyrannical prince from a neighboring kingdom. An old, wise Wycaan advisor served the throne, and the king instructed the disdainful prince to listen to the Wycaan's teaching and advice. One day, when Shadona's husband was being particularly cruel to her, the teacher tried to intervene. The enraged prince attacked the old elf. He could have defended himself with his Wycaan magic, but the fool instead tried to talk to the prince until it was too late.

"In much the same way you sprung to my defense against Ithea, the princess unleashed fire from her palms and killed her husband. Not knowing where the fire came from and fearing that the Wycaan would be blamed, the princess destroyed the body, suggesting a terrible accidental fire had burned their chamber. The old Wycaan secretly taught her the Wycaan way and showed her how to sense magic in the natural-born. When the king sent another son to marry the princess, the Wycaan left, but continued to teach her through dreamwalking.

"She took two loyal maids, and they prepared a secret place where she stowed coin, jewelry, and clothes. When her new husband became abusive, too, she dispensed with him, feigning an attack that also suggested she was kidnapped. The king grieved his two sons, but did not send anyone after the princess. Shadona lived in her hideout, refining her magic, imbuing it with the feminine element, strengthening and improving it.

"She began to move through the lands, punishing cruel men

and identifying natural-born female Wycaans. A legend spread of a shadow that haunted the lands. Shadona allowed this, as it took attention away from those who left to learn and follow her. She took them back to her secret cave. When their numbers grew too large, she moved into an underground city that had been gutted and largely forgotten, its people massacred. They built strong wards to protect their city, and it became a thriving home for powerful females."

"That sounds great," Maugwen said. "Why aren't they more prominent in the world now?"

"Because," Sa'gola said, "in the real world, there are rarely any happy endings. Let's sit by the fire and continue."

CHAPTER 36

T hey left the pool and returned to the cave. Sa'gola lit a fire with her magic, and a purple hue illuminated the walls. They divided the food she had prepared, and a skin of wine was passed around while she continued.

"The magic we use is similar to that of the Wycaans, but it is an inherently feminine energy. Its power is different, and the ways it is worked and countered are not similar. This is why we are so effective against Wycaans and other organic magis. Because it is feminine energy, Shadona decreed that no male be allowed to learn it, that if a sorceress bore a male child, it would be killed."

"Killed?" Maugwen's eyes were bursting, and she received a glare from Sa'gola. "I have delivered many babies," the healer continued, "and it is the ultimate magic."

"No doubt," Sa'gola replied, "but there were good reasons behind this. If a male mastered our magic, he could use it to subjugate us. Almost every woman in the Order had known male domination and was not willing to risk returning to it. But more importantly, there was the possibility that a male birth could harness both Wycaan and Shadona's magic. This is called the *Iyzun*—the balance—and it would make someone more powerful than anyone in either order. It had not been seen since the ancients. So members of the Order rarely took mates as others did. Neither did the Wycaans, by the way. Your father was a rare exception, and perhaps it was his downfall."

Mharina tensed, but Sa'gola moved on.

"Of course, they did occasionally seek relations, and children were born. The females were kept and trained. But most of our Order is still selected according to their natural potential, like what I sensed in you. We all go out and search for such potential. For some, it is their job in life. Others, like myself, just keep our eyes open. We are expected to train at least one apprentice to pass the Testing in order to perpetuate our Order.

She broke to eat and drink. Mharina did the same, and Maugwen excused herself, returning a few minutes later.

"Every few decades, a sorceress disobeyed the edict and kept her son. It always had a bloody end, with more than just the boy's life sacrificed. We lived with the fear that one sorceress would disobey and allow her son to grow. This is why, even though we are scattered now, we keep an eye on each other. Some can travel by folding time. That is what you saw. They sensed your growing power and came to check.

"There was also a period of great strife when the Wycaans and kings got wind of our Order. They captured a sorceress and tortured her. She died before revealing her art, but they pieced together enough to know that she was not an anomaly. A horrible dark age ensured, in which many women were tortured and burned at the stake. Men purged themselves of troublesome wives or mothers-in-law, ugly or deformed girls, or to take revenge on women who spurned them."

"Following Shadona's instruction, we went into hiding, showing ourselves only when there was great need. Shadona herself disappeared completely, and many eventually thought her dead. It was a period of great suspicion within the Order, as many fought to take leadership. Some groups broke away; others rebelled—though I cannot tell you against whom or why."

"Were you involved in this?" Mharina asked.

"I was a little girl, not born in the Order; I began my apprenticeship in the middle of all this, but not before I saw my mother and grandmother burned. I was attacked and scorned, a little lost waif, begging on the street.

"One sorceress bore a boy and trained him extensively in our arts. No one knew who his father was, but it was assumed he also had powers, for the boy was born with a strange physical appearance and unpredictable disposition. He was a young man before anyone sensed his presence. He and his mother had learned how to mask his prints, and he travelled far and wide to learn from many great leaders. He left a trail of fear, and yet intrigued the gifted teachers who gave their secrets freely.

"He learned not only from sorceresses, but also from Wycaans and other male magicals. He built up the female and the male magic inside of him with equal respect because he yearned for the *Iyzun*, the mastery of both male and female magic." She reached a hand out to Mharina. "I felt the *Iyzun* in your father."

Mharina pulled back and sighed. When she spoke, her voice was quiet. "Please continue."

"The sorcerer's mother was Shadona, the mightiest of us all. She had disappeared because she couldn't bring herself to do what she had made so many do before. She was tracked down and captured. Some say she gave herself up because she realized the danger she had set in motion. Shadona was brought to stand trial.

"Her son heard of the trial and somehow evaded our wards, even though Shadona swore she never told him. He killed many of our Order until Shadona volunteered to lead a select group against him. My cohort of young sorceresses and I were taken along, the hope being that the arts we had learned would defend us against him if his mother could not stop him.

"He killed the entire group, including our two teachers, some of the most accomplished sorceresses ever. He dueled with Shadona and me for hours, but she would not kill him. Then, just as it seemed he was weakening, he created a massive, burning lash of fire.

"Some of its strands broke through my wards and wrapped themselves around me. You have seen the scars. I let the pain burn through me but held my defenses up to protect not only myself, but also Shadona. When she saw I was hurt, she challenged her son to finish it by killing her. I didn't believe he would, but, without hesitation, he sent the white fire through her. I fell to the ground, and he came and stood over me. I was the last one alive.

"He straddled me, staring down with his blood-red eyes, and lashed me repeatedly with his fire. Before I lost consciousness, he stopped and said, 'I will let you live, little witch. I want the rest of them to know what I did and who I am, so that they will always live in fear of my presence. Tell them who did this and how. Tell them you, the most accomplished of their order, live only because Ithea decided it would be so.'"

Chapter 37

Sellia considered it apt that their party rode out from Wycaan Island in the rain and wind. Everyone was wrapped in cloaks with no desire to look back. It was just as well, she thought. None would return here, at least not in her lifetime. She didn't know why she felt this so strongly.

Though she led the party, she was really following her *calhei*, as it was the twins who decided where they would go. She realized she didn't really care, as long as she was with them. Would this be her destiny now, to endlessly follow her children? Their plan was to train at the Forest of Markwin and then somehow rescue Mharina before going to help the prince. It was the plan of children, she knew. Training would probably take years, and then there was considerable traveling. Not to mention they didn't have the first clue where Mharina was.

She wondered how Mharina was faring. Her eldest was tough, she knew. They had clashed because...because they were so similar. She tried to imagine how she would react in the same situation. She had lost her parents at young age and been brought up by Uncle, Ilana's father. But she had been stoic, throwing herself into her training. She was deadly with her bow, could stalk any animal or person, and... well, she was younger then. But she had not lost her skills or spirit. Even losing Seanchai had not extinguished her desire to excel.

Mharina would throw herself into her training, Sellia knew. She would bury the pain and grow a hard shell around it. She would become the best she could, and then…and then what? There had been something between Mharina and the sorceress. Perhaps that was what hurt Sellia the most. There was an intimacy, a deep trust and understanding. Sellia would usually be happy for one of her *calhei* to form a profound bond with a teacher, but the woman who murdered Mharina's father? What terrible, conflicting emotions churned inside the young elfe? How could she ever deal with them in the constant presence of Sa'gola? Worse than that, what if Sa'gola found a way to heal the pain and cement their relationship? Senzia and Ilan planned to find and rescue their sister. Sellia would accompany them and mete revenge on her husband's murderer.

But Mharina had sworn in the ancient language to defend Sa'gola. It was payment for Sa'gola rescuing Sellia and the others from Ithea. When Rhoddan drew his sword to slay the sorceress, Mharina stood in his way. And Sellia remembered how confidently Sa'gola sat with the huge elf warrior about to attack her. She knew Mharina would fulfill her oath.

"Sellia! We should break," Master Sythen called out.

It was no longer raining, and she had lost herself in her thoughts. They had been following a river that fed Lake Mhari and were beginning to climb uphill. The ascent protected them from the wind, but she knew the old Wycaan was correct. She raised an arm, and the caravan ground to a halt. She led her horse to drink and gazed around. Montclair guarded from a tall rock. Riona, Sythen, and Ilan were taking food from one of the packs. Master Goldspiere, the dwarf Wycaan, was examining the local rocks and minerals. Ilan had revealed a propensity for such study, as well, and they had formed a fierce bond.

Where was Senzia? Sellia peered around, panic rising.

"I am right behind you," Senzia said, her tone light.

Sellia jumped and brushed aside her momentary annoyance.

Senzia sat on a rock, her feet dangling down. Her fair skin and white hair were constant reminders of Seanchai.

"You stalking me?" Sellia asked, keeping her own voice light.

"I think you don't want to be alone, but neither do you want to talk," Senzia replied.

Sellia smiled and moved to sit beside her daughter. Senzia shuffled to make room, and Sellia put her arm around her.

"When did you get so wise?" she asked, and forced a laugh. Senzia joined with an obliging chuckle, but the silence soon returned. "How are you doing, little one? You can be honest."

"I miss Mharina so much. She might be bossy and annoying, but I love her and fear that when we find her, she will be different."

"I share that fear," Sellia said. "It will be quite some time until we find her. Maybe years."

"But we won't stop, right?"

Sellia squeezed her. "Right. Family first."

The others were getting ready to ride. Senzia jumped down from the rock to join them.

"Senzia," Sellia called. "You never mentioned your *ahdahr*. It's okay to mourn him." Senzia turned slowly with a strange glint in her eyes. "What is it, my dear? I'll tell them to ride on, and we can catch them up."

"No, we should stay together."

"Then what are you afraid to say?"

"*Ahdahr*
. He's not dead."

Sellia froze and felt tears welling. It was the innocent certainty in her daughter's voice that wrenched her so—Senzia's juvenile denial. "Oh, my dear little *calhei*. Don't you believe the sorceress?"

"I believe she believes what she saw."

"And Mharina saw it in the Anwar."

"I believe the fight happened and *Ahdahr* went overboard."

Sellia walked to her, knelt, and hugged her fiercely. "It's natural to hold on to such hopes, Senzia, but that's all they are. I'm sorry. I so want him to be alive and put all this right. But I heard—"

Sellia stroked her back and murmured that it would be all right. Then Senzia pulled away. When she spoke, her tone was sharp. "No. You don't understand. When I said I know, I mean *I know.* I'm a natural-born Wycaan, the daughter of a natural-born Wycaan. I would *know* if he was dead."

Someone called to them, and Senzia turned to walk to her horse. Sellia shook her head, feeling the pain and loss her daughter felt. Youth had given her the chance to numb grief with wild hope. Perhaps it was better for now.

Then Senzia turned around. "Ilan feels the same. He brought it up first."

With that, she joined the others.

CHAPTER 38

The rain held off for the next two days, but the brooding cloud cover threatened to open at any moment. They had left behind the valley and entered the ominous Bordan Mountain range, where Seanchai first met Ballendir and his clan. Seanchai hadn't known that General Tarlach's army followed on his trail, and a huge battle had ensued. Though they had escaped and inflicted heavy losses upon Tarlach's forces, it had been a tragic fight, with many dying. To save the clan, the elders had evacuated everyone though tunnels, then allowed the army to enter their underground caverns before collapsing the mountain upon themselves and the army.

Until then, the dwarves believed the Emperor did not know of their existence and protected themselves by implementing The First Decree—that no non-dwarf could enter underground. But Seanchai's bravery and leadership led the dwarves to enter his alliance and renounce the decree. The subsequent ballads coined this as the birthplace of the alliance, but Sellia felt only sadness as the mountains stared impassively down on her.

Her thoughts went to Senzia's earnest face. Was she a cruel mother to deny her daughter's fantastical notion? Senzia had not wanted to tell her, because she knew Sellia would not believe her. And Sellia had indeed discarded it. At night, she allowed herself to imagine that her children were correct. They were Wycaan, after all, though scarcely trained. Could there be a connection between Wycaans that she wasn't aware of? She wished Pyre was with her. Maybe she could provide some insight, but Pyre had fled with Rhoddan. If not for her *calhei*, Sellia would have gladly joined them.

The party had stopped. Montclair and Riona had gone ahead, but now they galloped back. Master Sythen rode up next to Sellia, his hand already on the hilt of his massive broadsword.

"Taragusii tracks ahead," Montclair shouted.

"How many?" Master Sythen was all business.

"Hard to tell. They march in regiment, so you can never be too sure."

"Any ideas what they might be doing here?" Sellia asked. "The dwarves never returned, right?"

"That's what's worrying," Montclair said.

There was a collective silence, and then Riona spoke. "Could they be after us? Who do they follow now that the Emperor's dead?"

"That's an excellent question, my young healer," an icy voice said from a rock nearby.

There was a collective gasp. It was Ithea, his body healed, his skin still pale and taut around his face. His egg-shaped head bore no hair, and his eyes seemed a lighter shade of red. He was even taller than Sellia recalled.

"Are you really here?" Montclair asked, his sword already drawn.

"No, but I could be soon. And please, do not throw a rock through me again. It was most insulting the last time."

"What do you want with us?" Sellia inched her horse forward, anger rising.

"Oh, beautiful, fiery elfe." Ithea's smile was quite disturbing. "I have missed you all. The gallant knight, the sultry healer, and…where is the not-quite-Wycaan elfe?"

He received no response.

"Very well. I have little interest in her, anyway. Master Sythen,

I miss our sparring. And Master Goldspiere, how did they drag you away from your experiments with dust and bones?"

He laughed and abruptly turned serious once more.

"I want you to return to Grogin—all of you. Come voluntarily, or my taragusii will drag you."

"Where are you?" Sellia asked, anxious to keep the conversation going and seeing everyone else was frozen with fear.

"East of Grogin. I have some friends of yours captured and will arrange for you to meet at the fortress. The big, burly elf warrior has behaved himself so far, but his lovely, black-haired she-elf is a bit crazy."

Sellia heard a murmur behind her and whirled around. "No one speaks," she hissed. They had all picked up that the elfe with Rhoddan was not Pyre. "Why are you holding them? What do you want with us?"

"The Master brought your children here as bait. It worked well, despite the unexpected consequences. My plan's similar."

"Who are you hoping to ensnare? My mate is dead."

"And wouldn't you like to meet the one who killed him? Maybe I'll allow you to torture her before I kill her. I plan for it to be a long and painful death. Ha! I can see in your eyes that the idea intrigues you. You may not feel quite the same way about her apprentice, but I don't need your help dispensing of the young one."

"Wait," Riona stepped forward. "Do you remember when you came to me in that world you and Sa'gola had conjured? You were burnt and in pain. The white sheet stuck to your raw skin." She continued to advance. "Do you remember that I made you healing teas and took you to the waterhole, where I slowly peeled the charred cloth away? Do you remember how I healed you with the salve and took care of you?"

"I remember," he replied. "I remember everything for almost five centuries and appreciate your loyalty to your art. I will not kill you, and I may spare your lover if he doesn't get any noble and impetuous ideas."

"I want more," Riona said. She was now very close to him. "I want you to spare Mharina. I don't care about the sorceress, but spare the elfe. She is young and acted impulsively."

"Impulsively? I thought she acted exemplary, rising to defend her teacher and battle the most powerful magical entity without hesitation or fear for her life. I could spare her life, but she must pay a price. Perhaps she can train with me after she watches me torture Sa'gola to death."

"Never," Sellia said.

"I thought not. And so she will die. You will come to Grogin, willingly or by force. My taragusii await your decision."

They all continued to stare at the rock long after Ithea vanished.

Chapter 39

The party rode in silence for another hour until they found a cave at the edge of the mountain range that Master Sythen deemed conducive to defend. Montclair reminded them that the taragusii do not see well in the dark and would not attack. They lit a fire and shared food while Master Sythen looked out from the cave, his back to the fire to preserve his night vision. With his hand on his hilt, he called gruffly to Sellia.

"What do you plan to do?" he asked.

"I'm open to suggestions," she said, and shrugged.

"If we go back," Master Goldspiere said around the food in his mouth, "Sythen and I are dead. Ithea only ever loved one person beside himself, and that was the Master. We failed to protect him. We are walking dead."

"Two great Wycaans are no match for a four-hundred-year-old sorcerer?" Montclair asked.

"We are well past our prime, young man," Sythen replied. "We are good, but not that good. Ithea is at the height of his power. With all my skill with weapons, he merely tolerated me to spar with him for the exercise."

"I don't see us having much chance at outrunning the taragusii, and we don't know how many of them are here," Master Goldspiere said. "There will be passes in the mountains where we won't be able to ride, and these old dwarf legs will not outrun a taragus."

"What did you say?" Ilan asked. "The last part."

"I said my dwarf legs are—"

"Mother," Ilan interrupted. "How did you and father escape the Emperor's army when they had the dwarf mountain surrounded?"

"We followed an underground network of passages to Hothengold. You know the st—"

"Montclair?" Ilan said, cutting her off, too. He had risen to his feet in excitement. "If the taragusii can't see at night, are they able to see underground?"

Montclair stroked his goatee and nodded slowly, contemplating. "Maybe not. Or at least it might slow them down."

"Do you know how to find these passages, mother?" Senzia asked.

Sellia shook her head. "The ones we took were destroyed when the elders brought down the mountain."

"A brave act," Master Goldspiere said. "I had friends who died there."

"Master Goldspiere," Ilan continued, unperturbed. "How can we discern an entryway under the mountain?"

"Well, we need to read the rock strata," the dwarf began. He continued for some time, long after everyone but Ilan stopped listening.

The plan sounded good in theory. In practice, it proved considerably harder. When dawn arrived, they were already up and examining every option Master Goldspiere suggested. Sometimes they met sheer rocks, and at other times began down short passages that resulted in dead ends. Hope rose when some of the passages were sealed by rock fall, suggesting possible open passages nearby. As they exited one such cave, they heard pounding feet as the taragusii passed by. But no one dared peek to count how many. Montclair listened carefully and estimated seventy.

"How accurate would you say that is?" Master Sythen asked, looking impressed.

"We can assume between fifty and a hundred," Montclair answered with considerable authority.

The others grinned when Riona rolled her eyes.

It was almost dark by the time they found a promising tunnel, though it was too narrow to lead the horses. Montclair found an area away from the main path to tether the horses where there was grass and a small spring. He ignored those who argued to just free them. They entered the tunnel but could not make much headway and, content being out of view of the main pathway, settled down to sleep. Montclair took the final shift, as he always did, and woke them when gray morning light peeked over the horizon.

By wordless consent, they forwent breakfast and made their way into a large cavern. It was unmistakably carved, and Master Goldspiere proudly pointed out the nuances of dwarf architecture, such as subtle supports in certain positions, and exhorted the skills of his people.

"When Senzia and I are with the Elves of the West, will you go back to Hothengold?" Ilan asked. He was the only one listening to his teacher's lecture.

"Oh, how I wish I could," Master Goldspiere sighed. "To see the great walls, walk in the mineral gardens, and pay homage to our gods. I have always dreamed of standing beside the High King in Hothengold as his esteemed advisor, a position fit only for a Wycaan dwarf."

"Why not go back, then?"

"Because the only time I would see him is when he swings the axe at my execution. Remember who I served when you came to Grogin?"

"Ah," was all Ilan could manage, and there followed an awkward silence. They walked on a while, and then Ilan said, "You are a super teacher, Master Goldspiere. Maybe one day when this is all over, I will find you and we can continue to study together."

He reached out and took the old dwarf's hand.

They entered another large cavern, and now it did not require Goldspiere's expertise to see the work that had been done to allow wagons and pulleys, all evidence of considerable dwarf industry. It took a long time to pass through the cavern, and its different junctions and paths meant they were no longer sure of the direction they were following—even Goldspiere.

At the end of the cavern was a cluster of stalactites and stalagmites, some already joined as complete pillars. Others would take thousands of years to complete even the short distance remaining. But just beyond that, they were confronted with a collapsed tunnel.

"I think we are close to where Ballendir's Clan Den Zu'Reising lived," Goldspiere said. "Our way is going to be laid out for us if there is a passage under the mountain."

It was hard to say how long they walked. They stopped for five meals and once to sleep, but, devoid of most light, it was impossible to know. Sellia felt a growing desire to be above ground and remembered that Seanchai had suffered in much the same way. She glanced at her children. Senzia's expression was indecipherable, while Ilan remained intrigued by the rocks and minerals. He peppered Goldspiere with questions and, though he always received answers, they were increasingly less enthusiastic.

When they found a path out of the cavern, it ascended. No one questioned whether taking it was a smart idea. They were tired and hopeless and just put one foot in front of the other. Finally, they saw a gray light. It was either dawn or dusk.

Sellia closed her eyes and took a deep breath, inhaling the fresh air. When she opened her eyes, she was facing at least a hundred taragusii.

CHAPTER 40

I n truth, the taragusii were just as surprised. It was dawn, and they had camped in what looked like a ravine leading into the tunnel entrance. Sellia sighed at their unbelievable bad luck. Those taragusii who were awake turned and hissed together, a sound that reverberated around the camp, slithering off the rock walls and alerting the others.

"Sellia." Master Sythen spoke calmly, drawing his broadsword and releasing his staff. "Take the *calhei* and your friends back inside. Do not argue. Go."

"What are you—" Ilan began.

"Go. Do as you are told," Master Goldspiere agreed, his voice impassive, two double-headed axes already whirling in his hands.

But the moment they began to retreat, the taragusii were upon them. Montclair immediately stepped forward to join the Wycaans, his blue sword a blur. Sellia hesitated, and Riona stepped in front of her.

"Go. Please."

"You only have a sling. Come with us."

Riona just nodded toward Montclair and turned, her sling already loaded. Sellia grabbed both children, and they ran back into the tunnel. The sounds of battle gave them adrenaline. Then Senzia suddenly stopped.

"What is it?" Sellia asked.

"That's the heir to Odessiya we left behind. *Ahdahr* wouldn't leave her. That's Shayth's sister."

"How do you know?" Sellia asked, but her daughter just rolled her eyes. "Another Wycaan trick? Anyway, I'm not your *ahdahr*. Perhaps if he had put his family first, he would still be alive and we would not be fleeing for our lives." Sellia flinched, regretting the words as soon as they came out. "I'm sorry."

"Go back for Riona. Ilan and I will carry on and hide if we must."

There was something in her daughter's eyes that made Sellia hesitate. Senzia was Seanchai's offspring in most ways, but Sellia recognized the determined expression, the stubbornness, as her own. Not fully understanding what she was doing, she whirled around and set off, an arrow already noched.

Riona and Montclair were backed against the rock face, blocking the passage. His sword swished elegantly, and the bodies were piling up. But where one fell, five more appeared. Sellia shot one taragus who got past, then a second, a third, and a fourth. Her bowstring sang with her fluent movements, and the fifteen arrows were soon accurately dispensed. It was but a drop in the ocean.

Montclair met Sellia's stare and pushed Riona to her. "Please," he cried.

"No!" Riona screamed back, her knife pathetically small in comparison to the battle weapons around her.

"All of you, back!" Master Sythen cried.

They retreated into the narrow confines, the Wycaan elf at the mouth fending off the four or five who currently stabbed at him. The taragusii were big, and there was not enough room for more of them to advance.

"Now, Goldspiere!" he shouted between breaths.

Sellia saw the dwarf fiddling with a small bag and what looked like twine. He stared up at her.

"Go. Leave, all three of you. You cannot help us anymore. Only the *calhei* matter!" He struck his flint erratically, trying frantically to light the fuse. "Damn! I can't! I can't!"

"Do it!" Sythen yelled, and then looked behind him to see what was happening.

It was a fatal error. The blade pierced right through him, its serrated edge dripping blood. Still, he swung his sword, though it was slow and desperate. He dropped to one knee, still preventing the hoards from passing him. But he fell, and it was only moments before he was trampled on.

The taragusii kicked Sythen's body out of the way and charged Master Goldspiere. As Sellia stepped forward to go to his aid, he turned and smiled at her. "For Ilan!" he cried, and ignited himself in bright blue flame. An ear-shattering blast sent everyone reeling backward, and Sellia turned, choking from the dust, her ears ringing. She pulled Riona with her, and the two of them and Montclair distanced themselves from the explosion as quickly as possible. Then they turned to see if anyone else made it through. No taragusii. No Master Sythen and no Master Goldspiere. They walked briskly and almost passed the *calhei*, who had hidden themselves. Ilan jumped out, grinning.

"You look like ghosts," he said. "Even you, mother."

Sellia didn't smile back. She just stared at him, ruffled his hair, and pulled him to her tightly. "I'm sorry," she whispered. "Both Master Sythen and Master Goldspiere fell protecting us. Master Goldspiere collapsed the tunnel on himself and the taragusii with an explosive."

Ilan's fingers tightened around hers, but he didn't cry as she expected him to. When he pulled away, his eyes glistened and his voice wavered. "I made those explosives with him. He wasn't very good at lighting them, though. I'm glad he died the way he wanted to."

Then he took his mother's hand and, head bowed, led the group away.

They reentered the great cavern and backtracked along the side they had not yet explored. Twice they stopped, thinking they heard noises, but nothing appeared. They found another tunnel and followed it around and down. Sellia began to wonder how smart this was. There was no food and little water down here, and their supplies would not last if they got lost. Ilan stopped them and bent over, examining a rock.

"I'm not sure this is the time for that," Sellia said as kindly as she could manage.

"I don't think we are heading west," he replied. "The rocks here are not the slate and black stone from the Bordan Mountains. We're either heading north or back east."

"How do you know?" Montclair asked, intrigued.

Ilan looked up, his face sad and puffy. "I had a very good teacher."

"Sellia. We need to decide what to do," Riona said. "I'm not sure how long we can run like this. We have no idea where we're going."

"What do you suggest?"

"Return to where we entered the mountain and take our chances above ground."

"How can you be sure there are not more taragusii waiting there?" Montclair said.

"There will be," Riona replied. "But what other choice do we have? I don't want to watch us die of hunger, exhaustion, or dehydration. Even at Grogin, we have a chance. Maybe we can escape before we reach Ithea."

"And if we don't?" Sellia heard the steel in her voice. "I don't want to go back there."

"I don't, either," Senzia spoke up. "But if we are captured, then Mharina will come, and maybe Sa'gola can beat him. She might not be as powerful as Ithea, but she outsmarted the Emperor. This was a nice idea. But we must take our chances above ground."

The *calhei*'s comment ended the debate. It took a long time to retrace their steps, though Ilan proved remarkable in his ability to recognize certain rock features as they went. They exited the mountain in the dark, very near to where they entered. Montclair insisted they keep walking until they found where the horses were tethered. But as they reached the spot, they could see the animals were gone.

"They must have escaped," Montclair said. Then he took two crunching steps and saw the mass of bones and an ashy fire pit.

"They'sss very tasssty," a voice said from the dark. "Sssorry we didn't leave you sssome. We were not expecting guesssts."

There was laughter from all around.

"We have bowsss, and you are sssurrounded. Master Ithea wantsss the elf *banta*. You'll all be left unharmed if you come quietly."

Sellia sighed and slowly took her bow from her back and dropped it to the ground. It did not make much noise but thundered in her ears nonetheless.

Chapter 41

King. *King.* Shayth rode at the head of his army, shaking his head. What had he said? Where had it come from? The word had always been so alien to him, often spat out contemptuously. He had ruled Odessiya for fourteen years without taking the crown, though others in the court of Shindellia had clamored for it. The rest of Odessiya was more concerned with food, shelter, and living their lives in peace.

He thought about what made him ready to take the next step. His kingdom was in danger from an enemy more than equal to the pictorians, who were surely the most ferocious fighters in the land, and under their new first boar, held precariously to an alliance.

His people were in danger, and without Rhoddan, Sellia, and, of course, Seanchai, it felt like he stood alone. He glanced behind him at Umnesilk, but the huge boar wore an inscrutable expression. Next to him, ever alert, was his nephew, Narasilk. Shayth's army followed the pictorians in a column of five abreast, and behind them, Ballendir led the dwarves.

Shayth recalled the first time people bowed to him. He and Rhoddan had taken three orphaned kids back to their village. Rhoddan, seeing that the villagers were not happy taking in children without their mother, told them they must, on order from the Prince of Odessiya. Shayth thought it preposterous until the entire village went down on their knees in acquiescence. He was furious with

Rhoddan, and when they left the village, he hooked his friend on the chin, knocking him out for a short while.

He grinned to himself. Rhoddan and Ballendir now belonged to an exclusive club. He glanced back again at Umnesilk and wondered what damage he would inflict on himself if he swung a fist at the former First Boar. When they camped that night, Shayth told Ballendir that Rhoddan shared the honor Shayth had bestowed on the dwarf and spun out the story around the fire. Everyone guffawed.

Ballendir spoke up from behind a cloud of pipe smoke. "I am honored to share such company. But tell mah true. Mah chin is not hurting. How's yeh hand?"

Shayth raised his hand and flexed it, exaggerating its stiffness. This was met with more laughter. The prince looked around. Ballendir had brought two other dwarves with him, and they all looked tiny compared to the looming Umnesilk and Narasilk. There were also two officers that Shayth had invited. He would need to make new friends, he realized, for the good of the realm.

"Good thing it was mah," Ballendir said, and pointed to Umnesilk. "If yeh had hit him, I think yeh'd have broken yeh hand. Is that right, mah friend?"

Umnesilk shook his head. "If prince send fist to my face, I bite off and eat."

The crowd chuckled tentatively at this, unsure if Umnesilk was joking. The image was too easy to conjure.

"Why did yeh agree to join him now?" Ballendir asked.

Umnesilk did not answer immediately, instead staring into the fire and sighing. Then he seemed to remember where he was. "Not want prince to punch me in face."

This had the dwarves laughing all the more and eased any tension the races felt with each other. More men and dwarves joined them as other stories followed, each wilder than its predecessor. Ale and wine were passed around and pipes packed and relit. Shayth stared at each

of them. He had to move on and build the same trust and loyalty he
had with Seanchai, Rhoddan, and Sellia.

New friends. New title. He could feel the crown bearing down
on his head…and he wasn't even wearing it yet.

It was another three days before they reached the snow line. Their
long caravans of wagons laden with food, wood, and extra blankets
and clothes could only advance slowly. The dwarves marched on foot,
and Shayth was loath to tire them. In addition, everyone except the
two pictorians needed to acclimate to the thinning air. They stopped
to refit their attire and bags. The horses were shod with horseshoes
that imitated the shoes the pictorians wore. The undersides had sharp
metal shards that bit into the snow and offered greater grip and
control. Whoever—or whatever—Shayth was facing, he wanted to
face them with his cavalry.

From here on, Narasilk began telling stories about the different
places they passed. On that mountain, he had slept alone for the first
time, building himself a shelter and gathering dung to make a fire.
In the forest to their left, he had joined his first hunt for the woolly
cows that migrate in herds and made his first kill. Umnesilk tried to
silence him a few times, but Shayth enjoyed it. He liked Narasilk,
who was so enthusiastic, and his stories broke the monotony. He
asked Umnesilk to let Narasilk continue.

They were above the snowline for three days before they spotted
the first pictorians. The scouts watched from afar but did not come
to greet Shayth's troops.

"Are they rangers?" Shayth asked Umnesilk.

"Have guards around rim. These follow. One go back to report."

"They'll be reporting you are with me, my friend," Shayth replied. "Are you ready for this?"

Umnesilk hesitated. Then, in a deep rumble, he replied, "No."

As dusk settled, a solitary pictorian joined them. He was old, with a wrinkled face and only a few long splays of grey-white hair. He leaned heavily on a thick, carved staff, expending energy just to stand as straight as he could. Shayth gave orders to stop and camp for the night. He approached this old pictorian with Umnesilk and Narasilk.

"He was one of our greatest warriors," Narasilk said, awe clear in his tone.

"*Is* one of greatest, nephew. You stand before legend. Warrior inside, always."

"Yes, Uncle."

When they reached him, the younger pictorians bowed. The old one came and touched foreheads with each of them. Then he bowed to Shayth before turning to Umnesilk.

"Why come back? Know laws well. You exiled. Never return to live or visit, on pain of death."

"Serve prince now," Umnesilk replied without emotion. "Go where he go."

The old pictorian stared at Shayth. "You not happy with Umnesilk? Why return him?"

"He told you," Shayth replied, hearing the stiffness in his voice. "Umnesilk is here as my advisor."

"You either cruel or stupid."

Both Umnesilk and Narasilk bristled at this.

"He your prince," Narasilk snapped.

"He far away," the old pictorian said. "I First Boar must follow."

There was an awkward silence. Then Umnesilk asked, a slight tremor in his voice. "How he as First Boar?"

The old pictorian looked from one to the other slowly. Then he asked Umnesilk something in their native tongue. Umnesilk nodded, and Narasilk leaned to Shayth's ear. "He ask if can trust you to talk in secret. Not tell other humans."

"Then we sit at fire, just four of us. Come, shelter built," the old pictorian said, and pointed the direction. "There, we talk."

Chapter 42

They moved to a way station, a rickety structure that none-theless might tip the balance between life and death in a snowstorm. The old pictorian's eyes followed Shayth's bodyguards as they secured a perimeter around the place. Inside the station was a small table surrounded by log stumps to sit on. Shayth noted a few boxes that possibly held supplies and, in the corner, a pile of thin mattresses. They settled around the table, the pictorians looking very uncomfortable on the small seats.

"This Gruenk, friend and loyal aid to First Boars before me," Umnesilk said.

"Advisor no more," Gruenk replied. "Arad'gug think me too close to you. He right. Also, I say what I know. Some leaders like, others no. Arad'gug not like."

"Are you in danger?" Shayth asked.

"No. Clan remembers my deeds. Arad'gug tough but smart. He give me space and jobs like this. If he want to kill me…" He shrugged.

"Why did he want you to come greet us, then, especially if you are close to Umnesilk?"

"Not know Umnesilk here. Sent to guide you, to say that Arad'gug fine warrior and leader. First Boar have many with him, more arrive every day. We not know how many, but I think soon Ice Clans become biggest. Lot of tension as Arad'gug put his boars on council. Sends ours to scout north when Ice Clan boars best know land."

"Tell me about the enemy," Shayth asked. "Have you seen them?"

"No, and even Ice Clan boars tell different tales. Strange. Pictorye of Arad'gug led hundred boars. All found dead. If they kill enemy, we not see bodies. Enemy take bodies, maybe. Pictorye of Arad'gug both dead, too. Make First Boar mad with you." He nodded to Shayth.

"Why Shayth?" Narasilk asked.

"Prince tell First Boar to send only scouts and Arad'gug not to go. So Arad'gug send pictorye to show his family fearless. Arad'gug want to go to prove he mighty warrior."

They paused to eat some dried meat that Gruenk produced. Shayth gnawed at it for a bit before he gave up. It was tough.

"Has no one seen this enemy?" he asked.

"Only Arad'gug," Gruenk replied. "Emperor show to make him and other northern leaders flee south. Emperor say he protect them, but only in Odessiya. He tell them, 'Go south and conquer all in your way. I guard you in rear.'"

"And even though he saw his foe," Shayth asked, "Arad'gug is still willing to confront them?"

"Arad'gug has heart of pictorian warrior," Umnesilk said. "We not run."

Gruenk and Narasilk nodded, and Shayth sighed.

"Do you have any advice for me?" Shayth asked.

Gruenk thought about this. "Try prince's way because you prince. But if not work, try pictorian way. First Boar may become angry, but all nation understand and show respect."

Pictorian way? Shayth wondered, and shuddered. *What does he mean by that?*

They rode deeper into the snow. The long caravan of supplies slowed the advance, wagon wheels constantly getting stuck in the snow. Shayth was loath to press ahead for fear of being cut off. In any case, the tough dwarves and his soldiers were still acclimating to the thin air as, of course, were the horses, which bore the brunt of the exertion.

As they ascended, trees became sparser and then disappeared altogether. Mountains rose on either side of them—huge, white monoliths that stretched up to meet the deep blue sky. Two days later, they approached Umnesilk's former village. Shayth saw the great boar's shoulders stiffen and his expression was one of resigned resolution as they came closer The big pictorian dismounted and spoke to no one, ignoring Ballendir's banter and Narasilk's endless questions. He jogged as he led his horse.

"Will you enter your village?" Shayth asked.

"You must. Dwarves build camp there. Ballendir must check and leave supplies. Show dwarves your support."

"I meant you, specifically. Are you okay? It was your home."

"*Was.* Not part of pictorian nation. Not now my home. Here to serve Prince of Odessiya."

Shayth sighed, but he was soon distracted by the camp of pictorians outside the entrance.

"Are they guarding the dwarves?" he asked Gruenk.

The old pictorian shrugged. "Some think. Arad'gug not trust dwarfs. Dwarfs not like."

"Will they stop us from entering?"

"No. You prince. Arad'gug gave order but decided before we knew Umnesilk come."

As they approached, one guard stepped forward.

"Welcome, Prince of Odessiya. Arad'gug, First Boar of pictorian nation, send appreciation that you come. You stay here. If want, we move dwarf builders out. No problem." He grinned, suggesting he would be happy to do this, and then glanced at Umnesilk and

Narasilk. "They are problem. Arad'gug say not enter. He say they go back south. First Boar can have heads for coming back, but as present to Prince, let go away."

Shayth sat up in his saddle and took a sip of water to wet his throat and consider his reply. "Thank you for relaying your First Boar's welcome. We will enter and camp together with the dwarves. They are our dear friends and close allies. All my advisors will enter, too."

The pictorian frowned. "First Boar say—"

"I understand what Arad'gug said, but I am the ruler of Odessiya, and I choose my own advisors. Tell Arad'gug that he relinquished any rights on these boars when he gave them to the Wycaan who served me. Through his gesture, they are not here as pictorians, but as part of my court."

"Not accep—"

"Enough," Shayth snapped as the pictorian huffed and twirled his battle-axe. "Either step aside or be sentenced for treason against the crown."

The boar did not move. "You pass. Not them."

Shayth nudged his horse forward. The pictorian did not even look at him, only Umnesilk, bracing himself to fight the towering boar. As Shayth passed, he drew his sword in one fluid movement and swung with all his strength, hilt first, into the back of the pictorian's head. The guard collapsed unconscious to the ground. When they had safely passed the other guards, who did step aside, Shayth turned back to Gruenk and offered a grim smile.

"Pictorian way?"

Narasilk nodded. "He, too, join noble club with Ballendir and Rhoddan. Need to know. Big honor for pictorian."

As they passed through the thin entryway into the ice bowl that had been home to Umnesilk's family, Ballendir laughed at Narasilk's comment, and Shayth and Narasilk joined in. Soon the walls rever-

berated with the cacophony of Ballendir's approval and the pictorians' laughter. Only one boar did not join the frivolity: the former
First Boar. But all laughter stopped as soon as they were through.
Where there had once been beautifully carved ice houses, there now
were only the ragged tents of the dwarves. Most of the bowl was flat
and empty.

"What happen?" Narasilk exclaimed. "Why dwarves do this?
They be warmer in homes."

"Not dwarves," Gruenk replied, his voice low and tentative.

"Arad'gug," Umnesilk growled.

"Why?" Narasilk was shocked.

"To destroy all memory of greatest First Boar in centuries,"
Gruenk said.

Shayth just stared.

Chapter 43

There was no reason to stay at Umnesilk's former home or delay the impending confrontation with Arad'gug. Gruenk had tried a second time to persuade Shayth not to take either Umnesilk or Narasilk with him.

"I have no choice now. When that guard challenged me, he did so with the authority of the First Boar. If I give in on this point, how can I assert myself with the next? It would not be...royal."

Gruenk nodded, conceding begrudgingly. "Would not be pictorian, either. Must bring him. Only hope you can take him back afterward."

The snow was too deep to ride through, so Shayth led his horse behind Umnesilk. The former First Boar had not said a word the entire time. He had not explored his former home or looked around; he just rolled out his blanket and closed his eyes. In the morning, he stood, waiting to leave, his expression rigid. When he saw that Shayth was ready, he led his own horse out ahead of them.

There had been a long discussion about who should accompany Shayth. His honor guard, of course, and Umnesilk and Narasilk, but Shayth did not want to take his army. It made sense to let them rest and acclimate rather than appear as a threatening presence. Ballendir insisted on coming. He was angry at the way the dwarf builders had been treated and wanted to "have a chat" with this Arad'gug. Shayth refused at first, but after a hushed argument, a compromise was reached. Ballendir would come but not confront the First Boar, while Shayth would make a point to introduce him as his honored friend, forcing Arad'gug to welcome him.

They climbed higher and into deeper snow. Shayth began to wonder how it was possible to fight on such terrain. His cavalry would be useless and his footmen exhausted before they even swung a sword. And what kind of enemy were they facing? Who could defeat a hundred pictorians without any sign of losses? What kind of beings could walk into the pictorian capital and leave the heads of the vanquished outside the First Boar's home without detection?

Shayth pondered whether this was even going to be a conventional war. If his enemy was something stronger, faster, better than them, it would be a very short battle. He needed a Wycaan, and he sighed—not only because of the enemy, but also Arad'gug. He needed Seanchai.

The white walls surrounding the pictorian town rose up before him, and the ice tunnel came into view. He marveled at it the first time he passed under, but now he just smiled at Ballendir's exclamation.

"Oh, Narasilk. What I wouldn't give to bring mah king and people to see such a marvel of building. We dwarves hew stone and rock, but yeh shape a fluid material. I am in awe of yeh people. Look at this perfect dome, so smooth, so glistening, like a thousand diamonds in rock bed. Do yeh hear mah words, Umnesilk?"

The former First Boar, still walking in front of Shayth, nodded curtly but did not pause or turn around. His eyes were fixed ahead of him. Gruenk shuffled up alongside Shayth.

"Pictorian tradition to meet outside and invite in. Strange, but I think not meant as slight to you." He looked again at the entrance. Nobody was there.

"It's a slight to Umnesilk?"

"Maybe. But I think just rather avoid awkward situation for

Arad'gug to meet him outside and have to invite in. Please under-stand."

"I'll accept your reason, Gruenk. If you're right, it shows diplomacy."

Gruenk didn't answer, and they passed through the tunnel into the huge bowl of ice. But this city, too, had been transformed. A huge area had been cleared to allow for the Ice Clans to take up residence. Shayth wondered if the families living there had given up their hearths voluntarily. From what he knew of pictorians, he rather doubted it. A huge square had been cleared near the meeting tent where Shayth addressed the pictorians last time he had visited. Now, the square was packed, the audience expectant, and the tension palpable.

There was a raised platform made of wood—a precious material above the snowline—with several seats, the biggest in the middle. Arad'gug and his council sat there, waiting. Shayth stopped a fair way from the platform. His entourage and guards settled around him. Arad'gug would have to shout to get his attention or step down from the stage. Shayth had no intention of looking up to a seated leader when he was the Prince of Odessiya. It had been a clumsy ploy by the First Boar. The crowd grew restless. Gruenk, realizing what was transpiring, walked to the dais and knelt before the First Boar, who glared at him. Shayth could not hear the conversation, but Umnesilk bent to him.

"Put First Boar in bad situation."

"I rather think he put himself in this position. Does he think I should stand in his shadow?"

"No. But he not come to you with me by your side. It mean accept without argument."

Shayth nodded, realizing he should have thought of this. He turned to his guards and advisors. "You all wait here, guards included," he called.

Shayth approached the council, but stopped exactly halfway. He stood there alone. Arad'gug and his council just stared at him.

"Arad'gug, First Boar of the pictorian nation," he called out, "the Prince of Odessiya stands alone, waiting to be welcomed. Only among his most trusted and honorable subjects would he allow himself to stand without guards."

There was a murmur among the crowd as Arad'gug rose and approached. When he reached Shayth, he did not bow or bend the knee but stood staring at Shayth as though fighting not to glare at Umnesilk.

"Prince Shayth Shindell," he called out after a moment for all to hear. "You welcome in pictorian land. We thank you come with army to honor alliance and oaths taken."

Then he stepped forward, and they held each other's forearms in apparent friendship. The First Boar pulled Shayth closer, almost into a hug.

"Why you bring him?" he hissed. "Why insult me?"

"I am the Prince of Odessiya, Arad'gug, my friend. I choose my council and answer to none for it. He is not here to insult you. There is no need for you to address him, and he won't speak in your presence. But I'll seek his advice whenever I need it."

"He banished."

"You banished him as a pictorian. I bring him as part of my court."

"Pictorians here not talk to him."

"That is your choice to make."

"Bad times. Not need dis…distractions."

"I think we'll all need to show a little flexibility if we are to vanquish our common enemy."

Arad'gug snorted. "Vanquish? No. We hold out a while, but they conquer pictorians and then rest of Odessiya fall. You come to save us. Ha! You come to die with us."

Chapter 44

The first meeting went well for the most part. It was a formal sharing of information. When Shayth asked if anyone had seen the enemy, no one raised their hand. He stared at Arad'gug, who looked away. Shayth was convinced his uncle had revealed who was advancing upon the Ice Clans, or such a warrior nation would not have turned tail and run. Umnesilk and Narasilk stood silently throughout and ignored the glares and muttered threats from the Ice Clan boars. But Ballendir was clearly irate about it, and Shayth cut the conversation short. He stood and addressed the tent.

"Thank you, my friends, for a constructive first meeting. My entourage will return to our tent; my guards wait outside." He turned to Arad'gug. "I'd appreciate a warm drink and a chat, just the two of us."

Without waiting for an answer, he sat down and stared at the log table. There were some arguments among Arad'gug's guards, but the First Boar had little option. One boar sat a tray of broth and thick slabs of flat bread on the table between the two leaders. Even before the servant had exited, Arad'gug took some bread and dipped it in the broth. Shayth wondered whether he knew he had done something insubordinate by not waiting for royalty to begin. But as he watched Arad'gug eat, he decided the First Boar was simply hungry.

Arad'gug looked up. "Pictorian way. Host eat first to show no poison. But not good if guest then not eat."

Shayth smiled. "I'm not educated on your people's rich customs. I hope one day to learn more." He reached forward, tore off a piece of bread, and dipped it.

The food was rich, meat with thick broth. Shayth copied Arad'gug, who cupped the bread to scoop out pieces of meat and vegetables. When they had both satiated themselves enough to continue, Shayth leaned forward.

"I'm sorry for the loss of your two pictorye."

Arad'gug's demeanor darkened. He picked up the last piece of flat bread and ripped it to bits. When he saw what he had done, he tossed the crumbs he was holding.

"Just two of us. I speak from heart now, not mind. Yes?" Arad'gug said, and when Shayth nodded, he carried on. "You wrong to not send me out. Had to show I not coward. So sent pictorye."

"It would have been wrong and impulsive to send out the First Boar," Shayth replied. "I can't afford to lose you. I think the only thing stopping them is that they are trying to understand our organization. They're not attacking random tribes or villages. If you went into battle and fell so easily, they may have overrun your people by now."

Seeing this offered little solace to Arad'gug, he changed track. "You will have your chance for revenge, my friend."

"On you?"

"What? No." Shayth noted that the Emperor's huge battle-axe was strapped to the pictorian's back. He felt himself bristle. "I did not tell you to send a party at all. I ordered you to wait. You disobeyed me."

"Need to be First Boar."

"Yes, you do. But we're in an alliance. All you have done from my perspective is deny Odessiya a hundred brave boars who will be sorely missed. Arad'gug." He leaned forward. "When we are alone, you may speak freely, and I promise I will always listen to your counsel. But in public, I am the…" He hesitated. "I am the prince."

Arad'gug stared at him. "Why not say king?"

"It isn't the time. Tell me. Who is this enemy we face? You have seen them."

The pictorian stared at him warily but didn't answer.

"An entire nation would not have fled south just because my uncle told them to. He showed you what you were facing. Tell me."

"How you know?"

Shayth leaned forward again. "Because I am a Shindell. I am of his blood. I know how he thought." He looked away. "I share such thoughts."

"Me cannot tell. Me die if tell."

"He put some kind of curse on you?"

Arad'gug nodded, and for a brief moment, the fierce mask fell. Shayth was shocked to see fear in the First Boar's face and could not take his eyes away.

"Me die by worthy opponent, not in bed by poison or magic."

"I believe you will, Arad'gug, and the one who defeats you will have to be a most formidable warrior."

A disruption outside jerked them both back to the present, and when Ballendir and a pictorian burst in, Arad'gug's expression immediately returned to normal.

"There's been a fight," Ballendir said between breaths. "Umnesilk has killed three boars and is standing at spear point facing another dozen."

Chapter 45

"What are they chanting?" Shayth asked Gruenk, staring at hundreds of angry pictorians in the arena.

"Justice. Kill. Challenge."

"Challenge?"

"Pictorians not big on trials. We fight. Some want Umnesilk head. Others want him to challenge Arad'gug."

"How did it start?"

"Some Ice Clan boars taunt. Umnesilk ignore, but Narasilk respond. When come to blows, Umnesilk enter to defend nephew. I fear Umnesilk not challenge because of honor."

"Damn!"

Umnesilk and Narasilk were chained to the side of the platform, standing with their heads held high. The pictorian council sat on the raised platform, and it felt as if everyone in the city was present, waiting and watching with great anticipation. Shayth walked toward the dais.

"Pictorian way," Arad'gug said loudly.

"I have witnesses that say your boars started this. Why do I not see them in chains, ready to answer for their lack of discipline?"

"Who start not important," said a boar next to Arad'gug. "It who left standing."

"That does not sound pictorian. I thought you would respect those who defend themselves."

"Not for prince to interfere in pictorian law," the boar replied.

"There will be no bloodshed. We are at war and need every warrior we have. I will take Umnesilk and Narasilk from here." He turned to the guards. "Unchain them."

"YOU NOT RULE HERE!" Arad'gug exploded. "Me, First Boar. Me say he die or challenge. No coward in pictorian army. If not challenge, then coward." He glared at Umnesilk, then Shayth. "You be prince in south. Not here. We answer to no small human."

Arad'gug was standing now, and the tension was palpable. Shayth turned slowly, but before he could compose a response, Narasilk screamed back.

"You not insult Prince! You not dishonor greatest First Boar. I challenge in his name. I, Narasilk, proud nephew of Umnesilk."

And for the first time, Umnesilk lost composure and winced. It was a painful sight for Shayth to see on his friend.

"No," Shayth replied, and turned to Arad'gug. When he spoke, his voice was quiet, but its authority carried far. "You insulted me and the crown of Odessiya. This boar serves me faithfully and bravely. You will apologize or leave the dais."

There were some grins from other boars on the council, but Arad'gug just stood there, frowning. He had made a huge mistake and was looking for a way out. But a round of chanting rose. Shayth strode back to Gruenk.

"Are they chanting peace, peace, peace?" he asked, grimacing.

"You have set challenge for Arad'gug. There no other way now."

"You said to use the pictorian way." Shayth shook his head. "How am I doing?"

He turned back. Arad'gug was standing and holding Seanchai's great double-headed battle-axe, the former weapon of the Emperor.

"Yeh sure about this, laddie?" Ballendir whispered.

"I have fought many pictorians," Shayth snapped, then sighed. "I never meant it to end this way."

"He's not just any pictorian. He's First Boar, and it ain't his brains that kept him as leader."

"Listen, Ballendir." He pulled the dwarf close. "If I lose, I have a sister, Riona. She is traveling with Sellia. I name her my successor. Will you make sure it happens?" When Ballendir nodded, Shayth called to two of his advisors and repeated his succession plan.

Then Shayth removed his cloak and turned, unsheathing his great broadsword, which shone in the bright sunlight. He walked into the middle of the arena and waited for Arad'gug to join him.

"That was a foolish thing to say," Shayth said. "A good leader always measures his words."

Arad'gug hesitated. "Not mean to kill you."

"But you want Umnesilk's life so badly, and that colored your judgment. I'm disappointed in you, Arad'gug. I have no desire to fight or kill you. If you abdicate, I'll give you commission over a large number of troops in the coming war. But you will not be First Boar."

Arad'gug shook his head. "Prince still not understand pictorian way. No First Boar step aside." He paused a moment. "But thank you."

"Umnesilk stepped aside."

"He fool. He weak."

Shayth bristled "I think, my friend, that it is you who does not understand pictorian ways. You are tragic."

"And you dead."

Arad'gug sprung forward and swung his axe. Shayth sidestepped the whistling blade and thrust, but his sword hit Arad'gug's armor and ricocheted. Arad'gug charged, his axe swinging left and right. He was able to change direction with amazing dexterity for such a huge boar with such a heavy weapon. Shayth backed away, deflecting the attacks with relative ease. He had to focus on the pictorian's unpredictable moves, but, while they were fast, they did not get near to penetrating Shayth's guard.

He retreated to the dais and feinted left before moving to his right. Arad'gug fell for the move, and Shayth landed his first blow, a slice that cut both the boar's non-axe hand and the side of his neck. A trail of purple blood dripped onto the churned snow.

Arad'gug just laughed. "Good move, Prince," he boomed, and many pictorians laughed with him.

Again Arad'gug sent Shayth into retreat, and this time the blows were relentless. Utilizing the double blade meant Arad'gug never had to turn the axe or make a preparatory swing. Shayth was sweating now; they both were. The human's arm began to ache. Suddenly, Shayth's sword caught in the nook under the smaller axe blade, and Arad'gug wrenched it from his grasp. It spun behind him. Roaring, Arad'gug lunged as Shayth staggered from the momentum.

Seeing his adversary's attack, Shayth slowed his stumble and, as Arad'gug swung, he fell into a roll close to the boar's body, stabbing up with the knife from his boot. He felt flesh rip where the armor met. It was luck that his slash was so accurate. He continued the roll and scampered to his sword. As he grasped it and turned, Arad'gug plowed into him, and they both rolled. The boar managed a head butt that brought tears to Shayth's eyes, but the prince managed to cling to his sword's hilt.

When he rose, his eyesight blurred and refocused just in time for him to sidestep Arad'gug. This time, Shayth advanced, raining blows that the First Boar found hard to negotiate. Pictorians, Shayth knew, were not used to retreating, and Arad'gug would be eager not to be seen retreating to a human. The blows came faster, and now Arad'gug was also panting and sweating. Shayth saw that the First Boar was looking to break his retreat, and an idea formed. He still held his boot knife.

He purposely swung wide, and Arad'gug, seeing the opportunity, struck forward with all his strength. Shayth met the blow with his sword, but did not parry. Instead, he let the pictorian's swing follow through and, riding the momentum of the staggering, off-balance boar, rolled around the pictorian's arm and swung up onto the pictorian's back. As he rolled over Arad'gug, he reached back with his boot knife. It slid along the First Boar's throat, and purple blood spurted everywhere. Arad'gug, still with Shayth on his back, collapsed. Shayth, now on his knees, looked down at the First Boar's face as he wheezed for breath. Using all his strength, Arad'gug raised a hand and beckoned Shayth to lean closer.

"Well...fought, my...prince. Gray Elves...big as Wycaan...some have...power like him. Look to your...stories. Ashen Elves...they called. Too powerful...even for...mighty prince of...pictorians."

He spluttered, and the wheezing ceased. Shayth leaned over and closed his eyes.

"Your last battle, my friend, did not end in defeat. You freed yourself from the Emperor's chains. May you feast in the halls of your ancestors."

Chapter 46

Pyre and Ahad rode in tense silence. The elfe was loath to leave Rhoddan and Troja in Ithea's hands, but Ahad had stood his ground. He was a Master Assassin, but he knew when he was facing a stronger adversary.

"If Ithea has taragusii combing the land because he, too, has heard rumors the Wycaan lives, then we must find Seanchai first. If he is the simpleton the fortune swords described, then there is something wrong with him, and a defenseless Wycaan is a terrifying concept. I know how you feel about Rhoddan, but—"

"It's not just Rhoddan. Troja must be terrified. How much abuse and captivity can an elfe take?" She paused for a moment, and then frowned at Ahad. "What do you mean, how I feel about Rhoddan? We have fought together for a long time. He is a brave warrior and a great elf."

"Ri-ii-ight."

"Right? What do you mean, 'Right?'"

"Look at you, getting so defensive. Explain it to yourself. We need to leave."

Pyre glared at the arrogant human as her horse fell into step behind his. He was right, of course, but she had spent the best part of the last few years denying it. Rhoddan either was oblivious to her feelings—which was quite possible—or not interested. He had never had a partner, and this had puzzled her. He was handsome in his own way, and charismatic when he occasionally let his guard down.

Troja brought that guard down with stunning ease. Pyre did not know if she believed in love at first sight, but there was something almost magical in how they had bonded so quickly and smoothly. If it were meant to be between Troja and Rhoddan, she would not stand in their way. She liked Troja and meant it when she said she didn't want to leave her behind. She had not gone back to their aid simply because Rhoddan ordered her to flee. She sighed.

"You did the right thing, Pyre. Rhoddan couldn't leave his elfe, but he wasn't willing to sacrifice you and lose any hope of having a Wycaan fighting on our side. They're together. They'll get each other through this and wait for our rescue."

"How can you be so sure that Troja will last?"

"She is damaged," he replied, "but she's not broken. The taragusii won't torture her, and she has someone to care about this time. Also, Ithea's plan can't work if they're killed. What I imagine she has experienced would destroy all but the hardest survivors. Troja is a survivor."

"Have you ever been in love, Ahad?"

She could see his shoulders tense. "Yes," he replied, but did not elaborate.

"What's it like? How do you know when you're in love?"

He nudged his horse to the side of the road, and Pyre brought hers to ride alongside.

"It was amazing. My heart skipped every time I saw her, every time she touched me—just unintentionally brushing my arm was enough. And I was consumed with the feeling that I couldn't live without her."

They rode in silence for a little while.

"What happened?" Pyre asked.

"There's an unbreakable code among assassins. Once a kill is brokered, the assassin who receives the assignment must carry out the kill. There's no other way."

"If you don't, do they kick you out of the Guild of Assassins?"

He laughed. "Can you imagine dozens of highly trained, rebellious assassins wandering around? No. There is only one way out. Five assassins are assigned to eliminate the traitor. If the traitor survives, then he is free to live, but can never return to the city where he failed to fulfill his vow.

"I was given an assignment to kill a wealthy merchant who had allegedly been cheating his partners for years. The merchant was my lover's father. I dispensed with him one night—I certainly knew his villa well—and the next afternoon hugged and comforted his daughter.

"She told me how her father feared being set up by his partners and carved out of their business. She explained how much she loved him and how she would never again be complete without him around. Then she cursed the cruel, heartless beast who killed him, because he took a life without trying to work out if his victim deserved it.

"She had no idea it was me; that was not the problem. The problem was that I agreed with her. I left town the next night and have never returned. My departure was seen, correctly, as a sign I was through with the guild. But this is an organization with life membership."

"Did they send assassins after you?"

"They did."

"And you defeated five assassins by yourself?"

Ahad turned his head and grimaced. "I killed ten of them. All but one were members of my class and my closest friends."

Then he dug his heels into his horse and rode forward alone, done talking. Pyre let him go. She was a Wycaan warrior and had killed her share without any remorse. It was still a task to be taken with gravity, and those she killed were enemies of Odessiya or Seanchai. She had never killed someone because she had been paid for it.

She thought about how Seanchai agonized over the deaths of so many people, both by his own swords and through his name. Setting Odessiya free was costly, and he never felt good about what he had done. She was beginning to understand him now. She looked again at Ahad, encased within his assassin's cloak. He was the same age as Seanchai and Rhoddan and just as trapped in his destiny.

"I'm sorry," she called to him.

She did not know if he heard. He never responded.

Chapter 47

They smelled the carnage long before they saw it. The stench of burning corpses made them cough, and covering their mouths and noses with handkerchiefs offered little respite. Moments later, black pillars of smoke rose prominently in the blue sky. From a ridge that looked down on the fishing village, the distant sound of fighting carried on the sea breeze.

"We should go in," Pyre said, checking the straps on her boots and weapons.

"We don't know how many there are—or who they are," Ahad replied. "We can't charge in and confront fifty taragusii."

"There are innocent people being killed, and one of them might be Seanchai."

Ahad frowned, and she knew he was conflicted. "Okay, but tread cautiously."

They negotiated the steep path at a slow, deliberate trot, not wanting to risk the horses. When the terrain flattened out, they transitioned into a gallop but slowed on the outskirts of the village. Already, a dozen people ran past them, clutching children and bundles. In the square, five taragusii lined up people against a wall and inserted their tendrils into each head. The people screamed, and many collapsed. A few were able to crawl away, but some lay still.

Pyre unsheathed her Win Dao swords and charged, her horse leaving a thick wake of dust. She severed two heads before the rest even noticed. The taragusii interrogating people tossed them to the ground and unsheathed their serrated broadswords. Three other taragusii, who had been herding more people into the square, ran over to stand with the others.

All six taragusii braced themselves as Pyre swung her horse around, preparing for another charge. Facing her meant they had their backs to Ahad, who walked through the dust cloud and shot two through their necks with his small crossbow. When Pyre charged, one taragus stepped out to meet her. He moved with amazing agility, meeting her sword with his and barging into her horse, sending it and Pyre flying. She rolled elegantly and was stable on her feet. The taragus was concussed and did not resist as one of her Win Dao swords severed his neck. Two more taragusii attacked and she fought one with each of her swords and maneuvered them so that both always faced her.

They attacked in tandem, and Pyre found herself retreating. As they tried to spread out on either side, she sidestepped to keep them in front of her. When one tried to maneuver around the other, Pyre attacked, bumping them into each other. Both stumbled, and she dispensed of them in ruthless fashion. She spun around to help Ahad with the remaining two taragusii and instead found the assassin sitting on one of the bodies and talking to some villagers. The second body lay nearby.

"Glad you could find the time to join us," he said as Pyre walked over, dripping with sweat and panting from the fight.

"You-you—how did you kill them?"

Ahad just flicked a hand. "No point in drawing it out in this heat, and these folks probably need to get back to their lives." He turned back to one of the men. "I *do* need to know what they were looking for and if there are any more."

"Like I tell yeh, six ov 'em take off when 'e mentioned Crysea.

Don't blame 'im, Mister. It 'urts so when they stick their tentacles in yeh."

"Ain't no more lizards here," another man said, "but there's many of 'em searching the region. Dunno what they's searching for."

"A bloke wiv long, white 'air," another spoke from where he lay on the ground.

"Please give the man some water; my skins are empty," Ahad said to Pyre, and walked over to him. "Tell me about the man with the white hair."

Ahad crouched next to the man, who drank copiously. Water dribbled down his chin, and he stared up at Ahad.

"How d'yeh kill 'em so easily?" another man asked.

"My friend and I are very talented."

"Not 'er. I saw 'er swords flying like the wind. But yeh—yeh just flicked an 'and an' they fell. Big, strong taragusii just crumpled at yeh feet."

"Tricks of the trade," Ahad dismissed. "Now, if you don't mind, I need information and perhaps some food. We must leave in haste."

"I'll get yeh food. Least I can do," the man replied and limped off.

Ahad turned to the man lying down. "Are you hurt?"

"Me insides feel all churned up like milk bein' set for cheese, if yeh know what I mean. Really 'urt when they stuck me. Sorry I told 'em 'bout Crysea, if that be bad. Couldn't stop meself."

"I know. Have you seen this white-haired man yourself?"

"I 'ave. Me family lives in Crysea, see, and I was visiting me sister. Saw 'im come in wiv the boats. Tall, very tall—an' strong, they say. 'e's a pointy, too. Don't talk much. Me sister says that old Kennins fished 'im out the soup and brought 'im 'ome. Man don't remember nuthin', they says. But I fink he might be a bit daft in the 'ead. I ask 'im lotsa questions, an' he don't know nuthin'. Me sister fink it 'cause 'e was under for so long. Salt water ain't good for the brain. Know what I mean?"

"So he lives in Crysea?"

"Yeah, wiv old Kennins and 'is poor wife, Moya. She suffers when it rains and can't do much. The boy does everyfing for 'em: grows the crops, feeds the animals, fixes the 'ouse. All 'e does is sleep in the barn an', when 'e ain't working, stare out to sea."

"Poor boy," a woman said as she came over to help the man sit up. "But what does them taragusii want wiv 'im?"

Pyre saw them all looking at Ahad. "I don't know," he lied. "But I must find out."

"Better 'urry, then," the man said. "A good 'alf dozen left 'ere, and them lizards can call ovvers."

"How far is it to Crysea?" Pyre asked.

"Depends." One of the men creased his brow. "Two days if yeh push yeh 'orses."

"But I hears the taragusii don't travel at night," the woman offered.

The man who had gone off for food returned now with two packages. "Ain't much, sir, but it'll keep yeh going. Some smoked fish an' veggies wrapped in seaweed."

"You gonna rescue the boy?"

"That's the plan."

"Them folk in Crysea, many are very old. They won't live if the taragusii stick 'em."

"We'll do our best," Ahad replied, mounting his horse. "Pray to your gods."

Chapter 48

"Your lad be a strange one, Kennins," the grizzled fisherman said to his friend as they sipped glasses of onza to toast a good day's fishing.

"Aye," Kennins replied, staring at the boy, who sat by the quay watching a pair of squawking seagulls. "But he be a goodun'. Strong as a bull and never tires. His swords kept them protectioneers from us, and he keeps the house clean and lets Moya rest now her bones be failing."

"Does he ever speak? By the scales of the mermaid, I don't think I've ever...is he mute?"

"Nah," Kennins replied. "He says thanks 'n please, but otherwise only cries in his sleep."

"A tortured past?"

"Aye, so it seems. I don't pry, and he don't offer. That be the way of it. He helps me fish and fixes the nets and the boat. I feed him and give him a roof over his head at night. That's about it."

"Where did you find him?"

Kennins shuffled in his seat and took another drink. But he offered no reply.

"Where did you—"

"He be a gift," Kennins snapped, and shifted in his chair. "From the sea."

Both fishermen stared at the young man, not a lad or a boy

by any means. He stood head and shoulders above everyone in the fishing port, his white hair and piercing eyes so distinct that one almost wasn't surprised to see his ears were pointed.

"He an elf?" the other fisherman asked. "Never seen no elf before."

"I think so," Kennins replied. "None of us seen a pointy before, but we have pictures in children's books, and the priest said he's one."

"The priest couldn't see a storm if the clouds broke over his head." They both laughed.

"Aye. Still, the priest be the only one who ever travelled much, an' he can read. I don't care if the lad's a pointy. I'd take a dozen of 'em and make meself rich."

"Nah. You'd sit here all day and spend your fortune on onza." They both laughed, and when they stopped, Kennins' friend asked, "From the sea, you say? Found him floating?"

"Do you remember the storm last spring? The big one that smashed Jeonkin's jetty?"

"I had just left for Braithwaite. Waste of time, that. How I thought I could get rich there, I dunno. Just got back here with me boat and me shirt. You know."

"Forgot when you left. Anyways, I got caught in the storm, and the wind pushed me into the graveyard."

"Shrykes! Them coral trees smash everything."

"Thought I's a gonna. Me boat be twisting and gonna smash on one of them upside-down trees, and I could see its sharp barbs. I patted me wheel and told the boat we be joining the graveyard. That's when he rose from the water as though he'd been climbing. Thought the gods sent him, but he looked as surprised as me."

"Climbed up?"

"Aye. Looked real scary. Thought the underworld come to claim me. He be green-like, and his skin shriveled. He held the coral wiv one hand and the big upside-down hook I have on the bow wiv his other. The boat still buffeted in the wind and rain, but he just held it steady-like for ages."

"Really? Don't sound right."

"I tell it how it is. He held it until the sea's calm, and then he climbed on board. I thought maybe he gonna eat me, but he just pointed to the sails I had crumpled in the front. I dunno what to do, so I nodded, and he lay down and went to sleep. Lad be exhausted."

"He come from under the water? Did he cough up anything like seawater or blood?"

"No." Kennins glanced again at the blond figure. "He can…he can…don't tell no one, right? Don't want the priest to hear. But I fink he can breathe underwater."

"How much onza have you been—"

"No! I-I'm sorry." Kennins shouted, and immediately regretted it. "It's kinda scary. Listen. A moon's turn ago, I dropped anchor over near Seadragon's Cove, and it be stuck. After we struggled with it, I told him to cut the line, but he shook his head, took his clothes off, and dived underwater.

"He was gone a long time—too long. I fear he be dead. Then he swum up and scrambled onto the deck. He wasn't breathing hard or nothing. Just a little cut on his hand and a few scrapes. Then he pulls up the anchor like usual. No ways he held his breath, and no ways he be coming up wivout his lungs busting. Know what I mean?"

"Hey!" the fisherman called. "Come here, lad."

The broad elf rose and walked over slowly. His expression offered neither eagerness to join them nor annoyance at being disrupted. He pulled up a rickety chair and sat down tentatively, as if afraid to put his whole weight on it.

"Name's Hawkins. I'm an old friend of Kennins."

The elf nodded.

"Um, let me get you a glass. Finest onza in the dockland." He turned to get the barman's attention.

"Just water. Thank you," the elf said to the barman, who nodded and brought both.

"Kennins here tells me you're a fine fisherman."

"Thank you."

Hawkins waited in vain for anything more, but the elf just drank his water.

"Where're you from, lad?"

"Don't know."

"You don't remember anything before Kennins here fished you out?"

"Only the silence of the ocean bed."

"What?" Hawkins tried not to glare at him, and the elf just shrugged. "Where'd you get them blades?" He nodded to the two thin, arced swords on the elf's back as the elf shook his head. "But you know how to use them, right?"

"Apparently."

Kennins looked at the young elf. The only time there was any semblance of peace on the lad's face was when he practiced with the swords. His sequence of movements was an impressive dance. He practiced at dawn and after dark when all the chores were finished. And when the extortionists came and threatened Kennins, the elf had demonstrated his dance was a deadly one.

Two children ran up to them, both boys in rags with bare feet. They hugged the elf, who smiled as he opened a muscled arm.

"Me mom gave us this," the slightly taller boy said, holding out a small block of honey. "But we only got one. Would you? Please."

"Please, please, please, please!" The smallest jumped up and down.

The elf took the honey block in his hand, maneuvered quickly, and began chewing. He opened his hand. The honey block was gone, and the boys groaned. The elf shook his head.

"Did you boys wash behind your ears?" the elf asked quietly, and they stared at him, frowning.

Then the elf leaned forward and put a hand on one of each boy's round ears. Kennins heard the elf mutter something, and he produced two honey blocks, one from each of their ears. The boys squealed with delight and turned to go.

"Hey!" the elf called out. "Forget something?"

Both boys jumped into his arms and gave him a hug. Then they ran off, whooping with joy.

"Best we go," Kennins said, and emptied his glass. "You're gonna have every kid in the quay over here before long. Evening, Hawkins."

"How'd you do that?" Hawkins asked as the elf rose.

The elf just shook his head, a pained smile on his face.

"You remember nothing of your past? Really?"

"Really," the elf replied, and his smile was gone.

"Well, I'll tell you something about yourself, lad," Hawkins said as he stood, too. "Whatever you was before Kennings fished you out the big soup, you was a father."

The elf stared at him.

"I sees it in how you act with the kids, how you needed the hug. You was someone once, lad, and you needs to find out who. There might be a family out there needing you."

The elf stared at him, and Kennins saw the pain on his face surface and disappear again quickly. The mask was back up. Kennins didn't know much about anything outside of the ocean, but he knew this was a catch he needed to set free soon.

CHAPTER 49

The elf held the reins loosely and fell into the steady rhythm of Old Jack, Kennins' horse, as it pulled the cart. The old man usually sat next to him and dozed as they returned to the hamlet just out of town. He glanced at the graying fisherman. A few times he had caught the old man just before he fell off the cart, but today he seemed quite awake. The elf stared forward again.

"You not be talking to me friend back there," Kennins said. "He be okay. Just asks a lot of questions, he does. Always has. No harm."

Silence.

"You don't talk much, to be sure, but I think I be learning your silences. This not be a good one. What troubles you, lad? Do you not see me as friend enough to share?"

Only Old Jack's trotting hooves penetrated the silence.

Kennins sighed. "You don't need to talk. You be working hard, and I be feeding you and giving you a bed. That be our agreement. Can't ask more from a hired hand."

The elf sighed, but said nothing.

"It just be that Moya and me, well, we not be so lucky with the childbearing, and it be…well, it be nice having you around and feeling how it might be with a son. I be a silly old man, eh?"

"Thank you," the elf said, his voice soft. "It's an honor that you think of me so. I have no problem with your friend back there. I ask myself the same questions every day, many times every day. What troubled me is that I think he's right about the children. It feels very familiar. And you know what that means?"

"That you need to leave?" Kennins replied.

"Yes, I do. But it also makes you a grandfather."

The old fisherman laughed, but it soon developed into a hacking cough. The elf took the reins in one hand and patted Kennins on the back with the other.

"You be the death of me," Kennins said when he had his breath under control. "That you be so. You know that I thi—"

The elf's left hand pressed on the old man's chest and then his lips. They both went quiet. The hamlet was just around the corner. The elf passed the reins to the fisherman.

"Wait a few moments," he whispered, "and then ride in slowly."

He jumped down, making no noise, and disappeared into the trees. His swords were in his hands, though he was not aware of when he'd drawn them. He welcomed the adrenaline like an old friend, stalking silently through the wood to the back of the hamlet.

The woods almost backed into Kennins' small cottage and the barn the elf slept in. He ate all his meals with the old couple and took care of the house as much as Moya would let him. Lately, he had eased the pain in her joints by sending warm energy into her body, laying hands at places he instinctively knew would elicit sighs of relief.

In front of the cottage was a small vegetable and flower garden that he had dug, sown, and weeded for them. Now as he passed by the edge, he saw much of it had been trampled. He made his way behind the cottage and peered through a back window but could see nothing. They were in the front of the small house, whoever *they* were. He carefully crept along the side, listening.

"When did you sssay they would return?" The voice was deep and metallic.

Moya spoke quietly, and the elf strained to hear. "Anytime now, but don't be hurting them. Kill me if you want. Don't hurt my—"

"Shussssh," another rasped. "I hear a cart."

"Moya," Kennins called. "Come outside and help me. That lazy elf stayed in town to drink with his friends. I be needing your help to unload."

The door squeaked as it opened. The elf, crouching at the side of the house, saw four lizard-like creatures step outside. They were as tall as or taller than him, and they walked on their hind legs. The one in the back dragged Moya behind him. Two others spread to the left and right, while one moved closer to the horse and cart. They all carried broadswords, big and glittering in the setting sun.

"Where isss he?"

"Who? The pointy? Lazy good-for-nothing. He be drinking in town. Be useless come morning. I'll drag him out of the gutter, and he'll be just sitting on the boat and heaving over the side. Know what I mean? You want him? Go get him. But leave my wife alone. She's old, and we be no threat to you."

The lizard flicked his forked tongue to wet his nose, as if considering his next step.

"Perhapsss. But you have been helping him. You ssshould be punissshed."

He took a step forward but stopped when he heard a cry. The elf had leapt at the creature holding Moya and, with a wide arc, severed his arm with his sword. Moya fell to the ground.

"Get inside," the elf cried, trying to get her on her feet with one hand as he turned to meet the attack from another lizard. "Kennins! Get out of here."

The elf turned a heavy blow aside, sending one lizard sprawling, then turned to block a second with one sword while cutting the creature's throat with the other. His movements were fluent and

familiar. He wheeled and kicked the one he had tripped as he turned
to face the leader.

This one was more skilled, and they parried. Sensing the fallen
lizard had risen and was advancing, the elf ducked under another
swing from the leader and sent both lizards crashing into each other.
Both stumbled, and one fell. As the leader regained his balance, the
elf, already in midair, stabbed him with one sword through the chest
and swung a deadly blow to the other.

Turning, he advanced on the one who had lost his arm. He had
risen, though he swayed from the effort, and, as the elf approached,
the creature attacked. But the elf feinted to the side and blocked it,
sending the lizard crashing into the plastered wall. The whole house
shook. The elf kicked the lizard's sword from his grasp and held his
swords to the lizard's throat.

"Who sent you?" the elf asked, hearing the alien chill in his own
voice.

The lizard licked his nose. "Kill me. I will have the honor that
my friendsss had."

"Oh, I will kill you, alright. The question is whether I do it
quickly or painfully."

The lizard looked up, and there was no fear in his face. "However
you want."

"Tell me, damn it, who am I?"

"Who are you?" The lizard seemed to frown, his tongue darting.
"You do not know? Really?" He tried to laugh, but it came out as
a rasping cough. "At least my death will have meaning," he said, and
stepped forward, the elf's blade piercing his throat.

The elf watched the creature fall and then turned. Kennins
remained rooted to his spot, but was now hugging his wife. They
both stared at the elf, awe and horror upon their faces.

Chapter 50

The old fisherman and his wife sat at the table in silence. The elf took the fish they had not sold and tossed it in a pot with carrots, potatoes, and water. He hung the soup on a thick metal hook over the fire and filled two mugs with strong wine and set them before the couple.

"I'll take the bodies away and let the wolves have them. I'll be back before the soup boils."

Outside, he threw the giant lizards onto the cart. He took the biggest one's boots and tried them on. They fit, so he left them on while he gathered up all their weapons. Then he rode away from the homestead and dumped the bodies away from the path. As he returned to the cottage, he thought how he fought, using well-practiced drills and martial exercises, but he couldn't remember how he learned any of it. And these creatures knew who he was. They appeared to be hunting him.

It occurred to him that he might be in danger. He stood out, and people in town would not think twice talking about him. More worrying than his own predicament was that he was endangering Kennins and Moya. They were both old and frail. He unhitched Old Jack and led the horse into the stables, giving him feed and water. He would brush him in the morning, which was unfair, but he needed to be with the couple. Inside the cottage, Kennins and Moya were drinking the soup. He looked at them, feeling a wave of apprehension. Kennins looked into his soup, but Moya offered a smile.

"Can't even trust you with the soup," she chided him. "It would have burned, and you never thought to add any herbs or salt."

She rose and picked up the third bowl, but the elf stopped her. He took the bowl and poured for himself. It smelled good and reminded him how hungry he was. He returned to the table and sat opposite them, tearing some bread off a loaf and dipping it into the broth. No one spoke until spoons scraped on empty bowls. The elf refilled everyone's bowl and, when he sat, the fisherman looked at him.

"I'm learning your silences, old man," the elf said, and was relieved when the fisherman smiled. "But I can't answer because I don't remember."

"How you be knowing something be wrong?" Kennins asked. "We not be in eyesight of the farm."

The elf smiled. That was not the question he expected. "There were no sounds coming from the animals. We were late, and I needed to feed them. They should have been complaining."

"Really?" Kennins said. "It be that simple?"

The elf nodded. "Have you ever seen such creatures before?"

"A long time ago. Them be taragusii, and they come marauding up the coast. None be able to stand against them. Was terrible times. There be stories that they ate humans. We lived out on the boats for a time. Docked only to sell our catch and take on supplies."

They went silent again, each dwelling on the possibility that they would need to do that again.

CHAPTER 51

The elf released the thick, damp rope from the moorings, his breath thick in the crisp morning air. He usually treasured these moments when the world was just waking and the fishermen were leaving for another day on the water. But today was different. They had loaded the wagon with the old couple's most treasured belongings and brought them into town to Moya's sister. The elf would return alone to the homestead after the fishing was done to gather more possessions and feed the livestock. Old Kennins would ask some of the other farmers later in the day to take his animals for a while.

The elf raised the sails, though there was little wind. Kennins sat at the rudder and watched the elf row them out to sea. It usually took two men—one each side—to use the oars, though Kennins did it himself when he had no money to hire, shuffling back and forth between oars. What they hadn't discussed was how long the couple would stay in town and how it would be after the elf left them. And leave them, he would. He faced the old man as he always did, but his back was to Moya, who had insisted on coming. She had no desire to be caught in town by the taragusii after what had happened yesterday.

He could see on the man's face that he and Moya were staring at each other, conducting a silent conversation facilitated by years of marriage. The sails buffeted as the wind strengthened away from the shore, and the small tug picked up momentum. They sailed out to Kennins' favorite spot—a rich, subaquatic forest. At the old man's command, the elf let the nets fall over the side and attached the ends securely to the tall wrench that would later help pull them back in.

Kennins maneuvered the boat around the forest, and gradually they felt the nets strain and the wrench creak. He told the elf to lower the sails and put down anchor. Then the elf pulled the lever back and forth, cogs screeching as he dragged in the bulging nets.

Sweat dripped from his face, and his muscles strained against the weight of the nets. He stripped off his shirt and panted, but the exertion felt good. Seagulls collected above, screeching their encouragement and planning their impending meal. Many tiny fish slipped through the nets as they surfaced. They were often dazed and floated to the top of the water, becoming easy pickings for the scavengers.

"Kennins," his wife called. "Can you not help him? It used to take three of you to lift a heavy net."

"He be stronger than five o' us," Kennins replied with pride. "The lad'll tell me if he be needing me, though in truth, I ain't sure I be much help."

"I…got…it," the elf panted. "Nearly up."

The boat tilted as Kennins opened a small area of the boat's side and the elf dragged the net over a tighter net, reinforced with seasoned planks that allowed the water to drain away. Once safely on board, the three of them filled barrels with the catch. Moya was fast and efficient at first, but slowed quickly.

"Leave it be, Moya. The lad and I'll quickly pack 'em. Mebbe get lunch out."

His wife looked at him, a sad expression on her face. "We used to do this together from morn 'till dusk, and then have enough energy to make out on the barrels as we returned to port."

"And we still be together and in love. But the lad can help make up for our age, and I think he be too embarrassed if we kiss 'n stuff while he be in the boat."

The elf blushed, and both humans laughed together. It was a beautiful sound, the elf thought as he rolled the full barrels to a submerged part of the boat and covered them with a wet sail. Then he joined the couple, who were laying out some bread, smoked fish, and pickles.

"I not be feeling too good 'bout you going back alone," Kennins said.

"Would you be a help if he ran into them lizards?" Moya challenged. They had clearly already discussed this.

"I would prefer to go alone," the elf addressed Kennins. "If I'm attacked, I have only myself to worry about. I can run if I need to, but won't if we get trapped together. I couldn't forgive myself if anything happened to you."

Kennins turned to his wife. "How long do yeh think we can stay at yeh sister's?"

"As long as we need to," she answered. "That house belongs to both of us. Our pa left it to share."

"I don't like it," Kennins muttered.

"I don't either," Moya replied, her voice flat. "I fear we endanger her and her husband."

Kennins stared at her. "Do you think they be coming after us in town?"

"There be nothing here for them to fear except for him, and he be leaving."

They both stared at the elf, who attacked another hunk of bread and fish.

"We ain't be kickin' you out, lad," Kennins said, and the elf felt Moya stiffen. He looked at her, and she winced.

"It's not like that," she said. "I'm scared. I know I don't have much time left, but I want to enjoy it with my husband on our little farm. Ain't much, but we built it together with stone 'n sweat 'n love. I wanna die in our house, in the bed we shared, drifting off in a painless dream."

"I understand," the elf replied. "You deserve such an end—not what I might bring upon you. Anyway, I need to find out who I am and why they're hunting me."

"You be a fine warrior, maybe a leader of men," Kennins said. "Ain't never seen no one who can do what you do."

"Maybe I'm a killer being hunted for atrocities."

Moya put her hand on his arm. "Not you, my lad. I don't know what you were, but character doesn't change that easily."

The elf rose and made his way to the bow. He closed his eyes and let the sun warm his face and the wind tousle his hair. He inhaled the sea air. He would miss all of this: the sea, the smell of salt and fish, this dear old couple who had become family. He reached back and caressed the protruding hilts of the curved swords. They felt too familiar, and he recalled the well-practiced moves he used against the taragusii. And then he thought of the delight on the last taragus's face when it discovered the elf did not know who he was.

It was clear he was somebody, and the thought terrified him.

Chapter 52

He ran most of the way back to the farm. It was not particularly far, and the exertion eased his tension. He led Old Jack, who pulled the cart and whinnied occasionally for him to slow down. Before he crested the last hill, he stopped abruptly and put a hand on the horse's neck. Old Jack twitched his ears. The elf leaned in and whispered, "Quiet, my friend. Do you smell that?"

Something was burning, and a thin smoke cloud dissipated above the house. The elf tied the horse in the brush. He drew his swords and crept around the homestead as he had the day before. He stopped and closed his eyes. He had a strong instinct that maybe he could look around without seeing. Breathing deeply, he allowed his mind to imagine the path into the farm. He saw the small vegetable plot trampled and churned up, weeds and carrots strewn on the ground and tomatoes crushed, their bushes torn out.

The barn was a charred skeleton with only the sturdiest studs standing. The house was half burned, its stone foundation and walls black, but intact. The thatched roof had collapsed and burned. He searched around with his mind, surprised at the ease and clarity with which he picked up this new, yet familiar, skill. He saw the taragusii footprints but did not sense their presence. He felt so certain of this that he stopped skirting the homestead and walked straight in.

All was as he had foreseen. He sighed as he walked through the vegetable patch. This had been such a promising crop. The potatoes and eggplants lay splattered on the topsoil. Nearer the house was a small herb garden that Moya tended so lovingly, now uprooted and splayed on the ground. She had tried to teach him how to use these herbs for cooking, but everything he made was burned, over-cooked, or raw. His only consistency was that it all tasted bad: too spicy or too plain. He sighed. He would miss Moya.

Inside, he looked around for the barrels he was supposed to retrieve. They had been smashed open, and he found clothes strewn around the front room. The iron stove that Moya so treasured stood impervious to the fire, a tribute to the woman's stoic pride. He looked around for something he could use to pack up whatever could be salvaged. Then he remembered the spare barrels stacked in the woods behind the house.

He climbed over the waist-high stone wall and walked out among the trees. Here, the air was fresher, and he inhaled, wondering how the old couple would take the wanton destruction of their home. He thought of Moya's death wish and sighed as he picked up a barrel. There were only enough possessions left to fill a few of them.

As he made his way back to the house, he heard voices. He lowered the barrel quietly and hid behind a tree, peering into the charred remains of the house. There were two humans. No, one was an elfe. They were looking around, gently kicking the wood and debris aside, searching for something.

"Are you sure this is the place?" the elfe asked. "It doesn't look like anyone lives here."

"The wood is still warm," the human replied. "It was burned today, and its inhabitants fled."

"The taragusii beat us here," she said, and kicked something in frustration. "How did they manage that? We rode all night."

"It might be different taragusii, and they could still be around. Be quick. We need to look for bodies."

"There are none. Seanchai would not let himself be caught off guard."

Seanchai? Storyteller?

"Maybe he fled before they could take him, but remember, he's probably not the same Wycaan he was."

The elfe kicked something again, and sparks flew up in front of her—the house still smoldered. "Damn! The most powerful warrior in Odessiya is wandering around and might not even know his own name."

"At least no one here will recognize him for who he is. He's killed a lot of people and made many enemies who would pay handsomely for his head or capture."

"What shall we do, then?" the elfe asked.

"Head back into Crysea, I guess. See if he or those who lived here are there."

"How will we find them?"

"Let's take the horse and cart that were tethered there with us," the male said. "Someone will recognize it. We need to know what direction he went in."

The elf—Seanchai, apparently—watched as they turned and left. He saw that the human was heavily armed and the elfe had the same swords he had. He was tempted to follow them, to try and learn more about them and see that they did not harm Moya or Kennins. But they did not seem the type to needlessly hurt people. If they were going to return Old Jack and the cart, maybe it was time for him to leave. He walked back into what remained of the house and foraged. He filled a bag with dried fish and a few vegetables. He found half a loaf of bread, burned on the outside but edible inside. He took a threadbare cloak, a blanket, and a leather belt. The old couple would not resent him these pickings. They had been family…almost.

He walked out of the house and turned to face it. These had been peaceful times. He had grown to love Moya's mothering and

Kennins' inner strength. They had accepted him and given him room. He should pray to the gods for their welfare, but he didn't know which gods or how to pray.

Now he faced a decision. Head east away from the danger, or head west straight into the danger. The former offered escape, but the latter offered answers. Heading back meant confronting his past. He had killed many, they said. He had many enemies who would want him dead. He chose east, away from the violent past that was starting to catch up to him.

Up on the hill, he glanced back at the remnants of a brief home. *Goodbye, Kennins. Goodbye, Moya. I'm sorry I couldn't be the son you dreamed of.* He thought of the little children down by the quay. Kennins' friend had declared him to be a father. There were children somewhere missing their father, perhaps a mate who loved him.

He continued to stare at the homestead and then, circling it, headed west. He would find out who he was.

Chapter 53

I n the ensuing weeks, Sa'gola pushed Mharina mercilessly. She feared the elfe's potential would be tested by the Order, even if it was not *the* Testing. They trained with fire, water, and air, and Mharina learned how to draw energy from plants, trees, and animals. She practiced combining the elements, particularly water and air, and she took more control of the mists and fog. From there, she learned how to fold distance and time. Her successes were very basic, but she privately celebrated each one. Sa'gola taught her to scry and even the basics of dreamwalking. At all times, she drove her student to fill herself with the power of the elements.

Alone, Mharina delved deeper into the fire, preparing herself to fight with the fire whips. This was her strongest element, and she embraced every new level she reached. Her training became so intense that she no longer prepared food, but rather ate what was given to her and fell asleep as soon as the evening meal was finished. Maugwen took on more responsibilities without protest, growing concern etched across her face every time their eyes met.

One day, Mharina went out into the swamp and scryed Sa'gola and Maugwen. Sa'gola felt her presence and communicated with her. Continuing into a meditative state that allowed her to see into the swamp, she dove with her mind down into the murky depths and felt the vibrancy of potent life that lived there, basic life forms that possessed the potential to become sentient beings. She was excited as she brought her mind to the surface and instinctively scryed around to see if she was alone. She was not. The Mushroom Man stood on the other side of the barrier, his basket on his back and his hat slightly askew. He stared intensely.

"Mharina? Is that you?"

Her chest constricted, and she felt dryness in her mouth.

"Go," she whispered. "You cannot cross the boundary. You'll pay for it with your life. Please go."

"I want to be part of your life," he replied. "What is so wrong with that?"

"Nothing," she said. "But I need to finish my training first, and then maybe we can try. Will you do something for me?"

"Name it."

"Do you know of Ithea?"

"Who doesn't? But I fear to get close to him."

"I understand. I worry he may attack my family, and I want to know they are safe. They went back to Wycaan Island at Lake Mhari in Odessiya. Can you find out if they are safe?"

"It's a long trek."

"I know. I ask a lot, but I'm going away, too, and it might be that we can be together after that."

"I will go for you. But if Ithea is there or near, I must retreat."

"I understand. Thank you."

He shuffled a bit, searching for something to say. "Did you enjoy my mushrooms?"

"Yes. But you got me into trouble."

His smile was beautiful. "They were worth it, no?"

"As I think are you," she said, and immediately blushed. She turned and ran back to the cottage.

They left Sa'gola's house the following day. Mharina watched the sorceress put an array of wards around the house and listened to her explain each one.

"This will prevent anyone from entering. That last one stops time, so when we return, the cottage will be clean and the food as fresh as when we left. Believe me, when you return exhausted from a long trip, you will appreciate such luxuries." She followed this with an intricate set of hand motions that necessitated a lot of concentration. "This is one I'm proud of. I will see an image of anyone who approaches the cottage."

They set off, taking six horses. Three would bear them and another three, their supplies. Mharina thought of her request to the Mushroom Man. Had she sent him to his death? She began to feel apprehensive about her impulsiveness. She guessed at least Sa'gola wouldn't see him lurking around the wards while they were gone.

"What is it, my *calhei*?" Sa'gola asked. "You're chewing your lip."

"The same thoughts plague me. What is Ithea doing? Has he tried to kill my family?"

Sa'gola nodded. "When we leave the conclave, I'll show you how to use the Anwar around your neck. I don't want you to seek Ithea, because he has the ability to sense when he is being scryed. But you can check on your family. Okay?"

"Thank you." Mharina felt a grin escape. "Can I look for anyone apart from Ithea?"

"Not if it's someone close to hi…" The sorceress arched a thin eyebrow. "Your Mushroom Man?"

Mharina's blush was enough of an answer, and Sa'gola laughed.

"If you can look without getting hurt when you find him chasing another pretty, young girl, then yes."

Mharina's blush transitioned into a huff, which elicited raucous laughter from both Sa'gola and Maugwen. They rode out of the valley in the opposite direction from where they had entered through a tunnel Sa'gola created by folding the mist that swirled around them. It would help them cover distance more quickly and provide them a means of escape if it was called for.

"How does this tunnel work?" Mharina asked.

"It's a more direct path to our destination," Sa'gola explained. "We can cover great distances, and if any pursuers follow us into it, I can collapse it behind us."

"Would that kill them?" Maugwen was staring behind her.

"I don't see how. But it *would* leave them wherever they fall."

"How close will it bring us to your Order?" Maugwen asked a while later, her stomach clenched.

"It will actually take us three days north of Shadona City. Even though we have come from the west, anyone tracking us will think we travelled from the north."

"Neat," Maugwen said.

When they exited the tunnel, it was already dusk, and the graying skies revealed little beyond the foreboding peaks of a mountainous region. Sa'gola pointed to a small cave, and they made their way over. Mharina glanced behind her. There was no tunnel, no mist, and no evidence of their arrival.

A few carefully wrapped sacks were already inside the cave. Sa'gola told them to leave them for emergencies, and they feasted instead on the bread, cheese, and pickles they brought with them. Sa'gola lit a small fire inside the cave. It glowed purple in a way that Mharina found strangely comforting, but it offered more warmth than light. Maugwen announced that she would take a walk and allow the other two to confer. Sa'gola joined Mharina by the fire as the elfe played with the Anwar stone she wore around her neck.

"You have worked with fire, water, air, and the living elements, but we have not worked with stone. This is important, as rock absorbs significant power. The dwarves know this best and work their magic through their stones. When we leave here, I want to train you to use the stones."

"And that will include the Anwar?"

"Yes."

"Do you use it often?"

"I am always on guard, forever trying to follow my enemies." Noting Mharina grimace, she continued. "It's not all about healing people and delivering babies. When we met, I told you I am no lady. When someone crosses me, I am ruthless. It's what has kept me alive."

"If I see that my family is in danger, will you let me go to save them?"

"It depends on the situation. If Ithea holds them captive to draw us there, then no, not until you complete more of your training."

"How long will it take to complete?"

"You must never stop learning. You must not. Those who are more powerful than you are in that position because they have trained more than you. Those who are less powerful than you desire to get better and become your equal or more. They train hard. I train incessantly. I never stop. You have seen this."

"How can you sustain that?"

The purple firelight illuminated Sa'gola's grim expression.

"I know that Ithea is better than me. I have the scars to remind me. I know he continually seeks to learn more of the ancient mysteries, and I know that one day I must face him again. When that happens, I must win. I'll never let him control me again."

"You will win," Mharina said, meeting her teacher's grim gaze, "because this time you won't stand alone."

She put her arm around her diminutive but powerful teacher and hugged her.

Chapter 54

The next three days passed without event. It rained continually, and Mharina could not distinguish between cloud and mountain peak. She kept her eyes fixed on the rump of Sa'gola's mare and her teacher's slouched back. They rode in silence and ate while riding, pausing only briefly when needed. Their path continued to ascend, and the mountainsides closed around them. When they stopped for the third night, the cave Sa'gola selected was a welcome sight. The sorceress lit a bigger fire than she had the previous nights, and they all stripped off their clothes and lay them out to dry. Wrapped in their sleeping blankets, they sat in silence, chewing unenthusiastically on dried meat sticks and hard bread.

"The hardest part of the journey is behind us," Sa'gola said. "We will at least escape the rain from here on."

"We will?" Mharina asked.

"Yes; now we head this way." The sorceress pointed into the cave.

"The city is underground?"

"Not quite, but you'll see. I don't want to spoil your first impression."

"Sa'gola?" Maugwen spoke up. "Why am I here? Surely no one expects to test me."

"I would hope not," Sa'gola said. The silence that followed was deafening.

"Why bring her, then?" Mharina asked. "She could be in danger."

"She *is* in danger," Sa'gola sighed. She looked at Maugwen. "Let's face it, you and I are not progressing very well. But I feel something inside of you. Others have felt it, too, and that's why they want you to come. It might be that you'll be tested enough to show your potential. Maybe another will identify how to train you and you'll be free to choose to study with her.

"But I'm far more worried about what they'll do with you, my dear," she said to Mharina. "They're fascinated with the fact that one of the most powerful and experienced of our Order is training the offspring of a Wycaan Master."

"What difference does it make if I have a Wycaan's blood inside me? We agreed I wasn't one. My *ahdahr* would have known. Or Denalion. Or the Emperor."

"No, we never agreed. I don't think you are Wycaan, but they're right not to discount it. So here I am, training you our way. Then you return to your people and suddenly transform into a Wycaan. What are we left with?"

Mharina smiled. "Someone who can match Ithea?"

"Yes, potentially a Wycaan sorceress—one who has the *Iyzun*."

"Wouldn't that be good for the Order?"

"Assuming they trust you. But what if you instead aligned yourself with Ithea?"

"After everything he's done to my family and to you?"

"Power, my dear *calhei*, is power. And you have a significant grudge against me, too. If they can't trust you, best to kill you now, no?"

"How will they know if they can trust me?"

"The Testing."

"Can you tell us what the Testing is, at least?" Maugwen said. "Give her something to prepare for."

"Yes and no. I don't know which tests will be used to check for

Iyzun. We've barely scratched the surface of her training. If she lives, she'll still have years to apprentice."

"If she lives?" Maugwen snarled back. "You took her as an apprentice, promising to train and protect her."

"And I will, as best I can. But I cannot take on the whole Order. Now, we should go to sleep and make an early start. What was that?" She looked up, a hard expression on her face.

The question was to Mharina, who had muttered something under her breath. Mharina met her gaze and repeated the words louder and slower.

"I said: *calhei* no more."

They woke early and wordlessly packed their bags, then descended into the cave. It opened into a large, round cavern. Sa'gola continued with her eyes on the ground, but Mharina gazed all around. The cave roof was carved in long, elliptical lines that swept down to the ground. Others crisscrossed in the other direction. As they approached an exit, the lines swept down as if to escort them through. Along the edge, now, Mharina could see intricate paintings.

"Was this all dwarf-made?" she asked as she identified the stone art.

"Who else has the patience and bloody-minded perseverance for such work? But they're long gone from here. We don't know why they left, but it was in a hurry. We collected many precious stones and carved rocks. We also found weapons, books, and stones."

"Stones?"

"Yes—the last thing a dwarf would leave behind, so we assumed some were killed."

They entered a long, winding corridor. The air became thicker and wetter, and they all felt the cold. Sa'gola wrapped her fleece around Maugwen. "Use your inner fire," she said to Mharina.

The corridor reached an underground lake. It was huge and swallowed up in darkness.

"Is there a boat?" Mharina asked.

"No. We must walk."

"Walk?"

"Yes. Maugwen, you, as well, I suppose. Do the breathing exercise I taught you. I will get Mharina going and come back for you."

"Is this a test?" Maugwen asked.

"For you, yes. But really, it's meant to prevent those who have not mastered the elements from crossing."

Sa'gola grabbed Mharina's arms and moved her away from Maugwen. "You know how to fold water, my dear. Do it four times and take a step. Walk across, not down; keep your weight steady and don't let it sink. Start slow, but try to find a rhythm that will allow you to walk normally. When you near the bank on the other side, stand straight and wait there."

Mharina had made water balls before—a game, really—which had not prepared her for this. Was she being watched? If so, this Testing might end pretty soon. She stood on a smooth, flat rock along the shore, breathing and focusing on the water. She entered it with her mind and slowly bound it together. When she felt she had made a path of several steps, she tentatively put a foot down and began to walk, focusing her mind always three paces ahead. The water below her felt gelatinous, rubbery and responsive…and weak.

She kept her concentration on the path ahead and folded the water into tighter density. As she continued, she fell into a rhythm, walking faster and more confidently. The bank rose in front of her, but she forced herself not to look up. She neared the other side, conscious now that she was being watched. She was only twenty paces from the shore when a woman with wings outstretched swooped above her head. Mharina fell into the water. It was not deep, and she could stand, though her hair and clothes dripped as she dragged herself out of the lake.

Bird woman landed in front of her, a smirk firmly entrenched on her face. "I am Formel," she said, and swept her wings around in a lavish bow. She was no older than Mharina but already on the elfe's bad side.

"I am wet," Mharina grumbled.

"Yeah, sorry about that. They wanted to see how strong your mastery is on water. Where is your teacher? She is a legend here. I can't wait to meet her."

"Are you going to try and make her fall, too?"

"No. It wouldn't work. What would she do to me if I did?"

"Burn all those feathers, I hope."

"Oooh!" Formel ruffled her feathers. Her dark brown hair curled around her face like a mane.

"I can do that, too, actually." Mharina stared into the girl's eyes, and Formel swallowed hard.

"But you won't, my dear," said a woman's deep voice behind her. Mharina turned and was shocked to see a tall, muscular, dark elfe. "Close your mouth. You have seen dark elfes before."

"Only my mother," was all Mharina could manage. Then she recovered herself. "I'm pleased to meet you."

"Don't be. I'm to be one of your judges."

Chapter 55

Mharina nodded as calmly as she could, which wasn't very. She turned to look back over the water, but she could not see Sa'gola or Maugwen.

"We are behind you," Sa'gola said.

"And we're quite dry," Maugwen offered.

"How did you—"

"The human girl cheated," another young woman sneered. "She couldn't get through by herself."

Sa'gola turned on her. "Mind your tongue. She came because she was ordered to by those who knew she was not ready."

"How can she be tested then?" someone else called out.

"She will not be tested, Esmet. We'll try and help her find out what she is." The voice was old and shrill, but did not lack for authority.

An old woman slowly made her way to Sa'gola, leaning on a beautifully carved staff of flowers and herbs.

"For you, my dear Dina, I gladly come," Sa'gola said, and strode over, her arms extended. They touched foreheads, and Dina put her hands on Sa'gola's cheeks. They stood there for a few moments, both with their eyes closed.

"He attacked you again, my dear. I'm so sorry."

"My apprentice came to my defense and very nearly killed him."

"Really? Interesting." Dina turned to Mharina, who was trying not to shiver in her wet clothes. "What a beautiful child." Then she glanced at Mharina's ears. "I'm sorry—a beautiful *calhei*. Come."

She held out her arms, and Mharina let herself be embraced. The old woman sent waves of warmth that swirled around her and gently touched her. She felt engulfed in a blanket of heat, and when it subsided, her clothes were dry, if stiff.

Dina stepped away and smiled. "I'm glad you fell in. It gave me the chance to hug you. We are more formal these days than we were when I was young."

"Dina was one of Shadona's first sorceresses," Sa'gola said. "She is the last of her generation and the wisest of all our Order."

"Tut tut," Dina chuckled. "You're setting this young elfe up for certain disappointment."

"If Sa'gola pays you that compliment, I am sure she's right." Mharina said.

"Formel, come here. You might earn forgiveness if you lead these young ladies to a bath and find them fresh clothes. Please escort them to their room and then to dinner." She turned to Mharina. "If she fools around, you have my permission to singe one feather. Only one, mind."

Formel pouted as she led them away.

"I really don't have time for this," she muttered, and glared at Mharina, who, as nonchalantly as possible, rubbed two fingers together to kindle a small flame.

Formel turned away quickly. "Follow me."

Sa'gola walked slowly, her arm wrapped in Dina's. They did not talk, but sent out feelers to examine each other. They climbed stone steps, and Dina leaned more and more as they progressed.

"Would you like to rest, dear one?" Sa'gola asked.

"No, we are almost there. Thank you."

"Why don't you take a house nearer the Heart? Why live out here and deal with all the stairs?"

"I have no desire to live in that hive. I would rather sit on my stoop and watch the little girls play until I pass on to our Mothers."

"So you're no longer involved in all the intrigue?" Sa'gola asked, suppressing a grin.

"I may be slow to walk, but my eyes and ears still work. When it gets important, I make sure I'm called for." Her laugh was more of a wheeze.

They entered a simple cottage with a big rocker and smaller stools. Dina flicked a finger to the fireplace, and orange light filled the room. Then she slowly maneuvered herself to the rocker.

"What about you, my dear? Your Emperor is dead. I'm sorry for you if you mourn him, but not for his legacy."

"I killed him, Dina."

"You, dear? Why?"

"He was about to attack Mharina. It just happened."

"And I hear you killed the Wycaan, too."

"That wasn't planned, either."

"Am I safe around you, Purple Lady?" She chuckled. "Why did you kill him?"

"He threatened to take my apprentice from me."

"Oh, my. I think I see a theme forming." They both laughed, but Dina stopped, puzzled. "Wasn't he her father?"

"Yes."

"And she's still willing to be your apprentice?"

Sa'gola nodded.

"And you feel comfortable teaching her, knowing that one day she might kill you?"

"I don't think she'll ever harm me," Sa'gola replied, but there was uncertainty in her voice.

Dina sighed. "You play a dangerous game, my dear."

"Remember when I was here last, and you chided me for not taking an apprentice? I said I wouldn't take just anyone and that I didn't know how to find the right one for me. Do you remember what you said?"

"That you would know it when you met her. That was how it was for me when I found you in the gutters of that miserable town. You looked such a wretched little girl, soaked and muddy, your hair matted and your body full of cuts and bruises. But I saw inside of you and knew right then you would be my greatest contribution to the Order. And I was not wrong."

Sa'gola came over, knelt, put her arms around the old woman, and rested her head on her lap as she had so often as a young apprentice. "I'm so tired, Dina. Why was I summoned?"

"You angered Ithea."

"He's always angry with me. I defy him, and my apprentice burnt him."

"Why didn't you finish him off?"

"I thought we had. We cast his body into the heart of the volcano, but he survived somehow. Now he seeks Mharina and me."

"He won't find you if you don't want him to."

"He will. He'll kill or capture Mharina's family, and she will find out."

"How? Not that you should keep it from her."

"She has an Anwar, and I promised to show her how to use it."

"Ithea senses when he is being scryed. We found that out at a very high cost."

"She doesn't need to scry him. She will look for her family."

"Then you'll let her go and face him? Alone?"

Sa'gola was silent for a while. "He defeats me, Dina, because he gets under my skin."

"He did a terrible thing to you with his fire whip."

"I'm the closest to his equal, and yet he holds this terrible advantage over me."

"But not over Mharina," Dina said. "She has completed a good amount of training, and when she takes the Testing…well, if she survives…she'll be considerably stronger and wiser."

"Who will she face?" Sa'gola asked, suddenly terrified.

Dina stroked her hair. "One of the council. One of our oldest and wisest."

"What? She won't survive. She's just a child."

"Maybe," Dina said. "But there's something special in her, I think, and you sense it, too."

"Not *that* special."

"Maybe."

"How do you know, Dina?"

"Sa'gola, you know me very well. We have a friendship that spans decades and have shared everything. But even I must keep secrets from you."

Sa'gola stared at her. "What are you saying?" she whispered.

Dina pursed her withered lips, trying to decide if she should tell or not. Finally, as only the crackle of the fire filled the room, she sighed. "If I tell you, you cannot see the girl until after the Testing. Swear it to me."

Sa'gola swore and listened to what Dina told her. The Purple Lady felt an increasingly heavy sense of foreboding.

"What if you're wrong?" she asked when her teacher had finished.

Dina grimaced. "Then she will die."

ChAPTER 56

Mharina practiced in the stone courtyard of their small house. The stones were all beige and rather crumbly to the touch. Ilan would probably be able to tell her what kind of rock it was. But Ilan and Senzia were far away, as was her mother. Mharina was nervous and frustrated. Where was Sa'gola? Surely she should be here coaching her student and offering final instruction.

The elfe whirled her two fire whips in a much-practiced form that served as much to calm her as to offer defense. But her movements were erratic, and she finally stopped. It was hot in this cave—stuffy—and she had worked up a good sheen of sweat. She wiped herself down and peeled the sticky black vest away from her skin. Then she picked up a jug and gulped the water down, allowing it to dribble down her chin and onto her chest. While she drank, she became aware that someone was watching her. She turned to see the old woman with the carved staff sitting in a chair and Maugwen serving her a drink.

"Could you get another chair, dear?" Dina asked Maugwen. When she returned, Dina thanked her and said, "Please, I need to speak with Mharina alone. Could you ensure that no one disturbs us?"

Maugwen shrugged. "There are only the two of us here. We haven't seen Sa'gola, but I suppose she might come back."

"No, she won't." Dina smiled. "I'm more worried about people outside these walls."

'You want me to stroll around outside?"

"You're new here. I don't know what Sa'gola shared about the Order, but we are a conspiring bunch of hags. Yes, please. It is very important."

"Okay," Maugwen said, and, picking up her own water skin, walked through the beige stone arch.

Mharina watched the old woman, whose eyes followed Maugwen. "Will someone be able to help her?" the young elfe asked. "She is a lovely woman and wonderful healer, but she's very frustrated."

"She is complex," Dina answered. "I honestly don't know. If Sa'gola is flummoxed, then I can't think who can help her here. But maybe someone will have an idea. I, however, must focus on you."

"Where is Sa'gola?"

"She is forbidden from seeing you before the Testing."

"Why?"

"She has unusually strong feelings for you. She might compromise your preparation."

"I don't understand."

"You don't need to. Just focus on yourself. Has Sa'gola told you how the Testing happens?"

"No."

"Why do you think the Order has deemed it necessary to test you this early in your training?"

"I have no idea."

"Think about it. You need to know."

Mharina sighed. The old woman's eyes were a deep, disarming azure color.

"Sa'gola is considered to be very powerful in the Order."

Dina nodded.

"And she might be the key to stopping Ithea. So you want to check what she has in her arsenal. Am I close?"

"No. But that's a good answer. Tell me: who trained you before Sa'gola chose you?"

"I was tutored by a dreamwalker, Denalion."

"From the Elves of the West? Goodness. He must be very old by now."

"He is dead. Ithea took his body."

"I'm sorry, child. I met the redheaded dreamwalker, and he was a kind and thoughtful elf. Ithea has killed too many good people. He killed my lover, his own mother."

"Shadona? I'm sorry," Mharina replied.

"Did your father ever train you?"

"No. He was always gone on a mission, serving Prince Shayth."

"So you weren't close to him."

"I never said that. I loved my father dearly, and…"

"And?"

"And nothing. Please change the subject."

"I cannot. I'm curious. Do you harbor desires to avenge your teacher?"

"That's ridiculous. I swore in the ancient language to protect Sa'gola and have always done so. I'm her apprentice. That means a lot."

"So it should. Sa'gola was my apprentice, and she and I remain close. Were there other Wycaans who trained you on that island or at Grogin?"

"No. They trained my brother and sister at Grogin. I have a friend, Pyre, who is Wycaan, and she showed us some things. But I'm no Wycaan, so the focus was always on the twins."

The old woman nodded. "Let me tell you about the Testing. It will be a series of challenges on your control and mastery of the elements. What you need to understand is that there is great danger involved. The tester can kill you if you refuse to follow her path and

fight back. You need to be cautious, but ruthless. Do you understand?"

Mharina felt a bead of sweat roll down her forehead and chin as
she nodded. "Why would she try to kill me?"

"You possess power, knowledge, and magic. This can be taken
from you. Have you ever entered someone's mind and soul? Do you
know what I mean?"

"Yes. Sa'gola let me once. I could feel her heart beating."

"That was both extremely trusting and extremely stupid of her.
Still, she's very fond of you, and it is a powerful way to heal. Do not
give up your essence lightly, child."

"Can I do that to the tester if the opportunity arises?"

Dina laughed. "That depends. What is your end goal?"

Mharina did not hesitate. "To kill Ithea."

Dina's smile disappeared and was replaced by a sad frown.
"Really? Sa'gola has chosen well. Then I would say yes, my dear, be
ruthless and take whatever you can. Your tester is someone with great
and powerful knowledge."

"Why did you ask me about my training? Surely my father,
Denalion, or the Emperor would have sensed if I had Wycaan abilities.
Or the Wycaans at Grogin. Do you think it's possible I harbor Wycaan
blood?"

"No, I do not. But if you do, young one, do you know what that
means?"

"The *Iyzun*."

"Yes. And if you truly possess the *Iyzun* and your goal is to face
and defeat Ithea, then you must let nothing stand in your way. Do
you understand? It is critically important for everyone in the Order
and in Odessiya. Everyone."

"Yes," Mharina said, a heavy weight pressing on her shoulders. "I
understand. Who will test me?"

"Me."

Chapter 57

A young woman with bright ginger hair and freckles came for Mharina the next morning. Her expression illustrated the gravity of the situation. In fact, she had trouble looking Mharina in the eye. She bore a bundle of clothes Sa'gola had prepared and laid it reverently on the bed.

"What is your name?" Maugwen asked.

"Talwyn," she replied. "My sister took the Testing. I never saw her again."

"Thanks for sharing that," Maugwen snapped, turning to help her friend. "You can wait outside."

"You too, Maugwen. I can dress myself."

Mharina dressed in the black, long-sleeved shirt. The wide sleeves came almost to her wrists; they would not restrict any hand flicks. She pulled up stretchy black pants that clung to her legs, yet felt like they would also not prevent her range of movement. Over all this went a plain black dress with a ball of orange fire embroidered over the heart. To this, she added her boots and, with a deep breath, went outside where Talwyn waited.

"M-my first teacher was an elfe," Talwyn said quietly. "She gave me this and told me it belonged to a powerful elfe warrior. I would like you to wear it for the Testing…if you want, that is."

She held out a thin, black, woven leather headband. A small black stone sat in the middle. It wasn't smooth, but ashen black.

"Thank you," Mharina said. "What stone is this?"

"Tourmaline," the girl replied. "It is said to attract positive energy."

She helped Mharina fix it securely and stood back to admire it. "We should go. You look ready."

"Thank you. I wish I felt ready," Mharina answered, putting on her traveling cloak and following the girl.

They stepped into the courtyard. Maugwen stared, taking Mharina in from boots to headband.

"Looking good," she said, and forced a smile.

Talwyn suddenly turned to Mharina and grabbed her arm. "This is barbaric. It shouldn't happen like this. Make sure you win, and one day we younger ones will change everything."

Then she squeezed Mharina with a hug before turning and leading them out. They wound their way through deserted streets. There were no women carrying baskets, patrolling, or strolling with loved ones. Not even any children playing. Mharina realized this was going to be a spectacle for everyone. They entered into a huge arena packed with onlookers sitting in rising rows that hugged the cavern walls.

"You must leave her here," Talwyn said to Maugwen. "There's a seat behind Sa'gola for you."

"Thank you," Maugwen replied. She turned to Mharina, her expression grim, and when she spoke, her voice was tough. "Remember what the old woman said. No mercy. None. Make your parents proud."

She gave Mharina a brief hug and walked into the crowd.

Mharina saw Dina waiting for her in the middle of the arena. She looked around for Sa'gola and found her in the front row to one side so that, sitting on one of the two chairs in the middle, she would not see her teacher without intentionally looking. She walked slowly over to Sa'gola, and the women surrounding her teacher bristled. Mharina halted and just bowed to her.

"You look good," Sa'gola said. "I believe in you."

Mharina turned and walked to Dina, who invited her to sit in an intricately carved chair. An identical one faced it, only a half dozen paces away. Mharina stood in front of her chair and waited, extending her hand to invite the old woman to sit first. It was a sign of respect and received as such.

"Thank you, young *calhei*. You look resplendent. Are you ready?"

"I am," Mharina said, sitting down but not leaning back. "Thank you for your words of guidance."

"We will begin by sparring. I will attack, and I expect you to defend yourself. I will interchange between elements, and you will match me if you can. Please stop when I tell you to. Do you understand?"

"I do," Mharina said, beginning to rise.

"Stay seated, young elfe," Dina said.

Almost immediately, Mharina's vision blurred, and she saw herself standing and facing Dina, who crouched without her staff. The battle was mental, not physical, but when the old woman sent sharp icicles at Mharina, one slashed her arm and she felt blood seeping out. She focused, adjusting to the virtual arena she now stood in. She managed to deflect the second wave of icicles but was sent sprawling by a fierce blast of wind.

She rolled back to her feet and crouched, every muscle ready, every sinew tense. Dina attacked now with fire, first balls and then a leash. Mharina retreated, but sent her own fire leashes out and fended Dina off for some time with a measure of comfort. Then Dina broke off.

Good, Dina's voice said inside her head before another attack came, this time with stone. Mharina knew stone was her weakness, so she fended off the attack by folding air and deflecting the projectiles. Dina sent ice again, and a wall of fog erupted before Mharina. One icicle got through and pierced her arm, almost in the same place the previous one had.

Rely on your other sight, Dina called inside her head, and Mharina reacted quickly, pushing aside several attempts with the fog. She twisted and swerved as the attack intensified, falling twice but recovering both times. The pace quickened, and she was soon relying on instinct to match the old woman. Faster and faster they went, and, as she felt her energy drain, Mharina unleashed her fire to burn the fog and hold the old woman at bay. Dina tried to pierce her defense, but to no avail, and then attempted to compromise her fire with water, but this was Mharina's element and she slowly began to assert control. She wasn't so much attacking as moving with such deftness that she was destabilizing Dina.

Stop! Dina commanded, and Mharina immediately grounded the energy.

She sat in her chair, panting, and saw the old woman was sweating, too. She rose and took two water skins from a nearby table and brought one first to Dina. This elicited a murmur from the crowd, and she wondered how much anyone had seen. She drank and wiped her face and neck on the hem of her dress. Then she turned to Dina, who smiled fiercely.

"You have done well, *calhei*. Now let us begin the real Testing."

Chapter 58

These words sent ice coursing through Mharina's body. She sat down stiffly and faced the old woman, who just stared at her. Then Mharina felt a tingling vibration spread throughout her body. Her periphery faded until it was, once again, only the two of them. Dina was inside her head, sifting through memories of her father, sister, and brother. She saw Denalion teaching them on Wycaan Island, walking in her dream world. There was Pyre, teaching her to hunt and use the bow. And then it was back to her father.

What are you looking for? Mharina asked telepathically.

Your essence, child, Dina replied.

I am no child, honored teacher. I am elven, and a calhei no more.

You are young and foolish to let me in.

But I want you to be inside. I need to know if I'm Wycaan.

We all do. Where would it be?

If I knew, Mharina replied, *then I would have gone there myself.*

No, you would not. They told you it never existed, and you believed them. Your own father deceived you. But I must know. Show me!

Mharina gasped as the tingling turned to daggers. Still, she did not defend herself. All those questions about her father and other Wycaans. She needed to know, once and for all, no matter the cost. She could feel Dina sifting through her mind, and, despite the excruciating pain, Mharina let her.

I can't find it, but it must be here, locked away, Dina said, panting.

How can...you be...so sure, Mharina gasped. *Why do...you...think this?*

Because it is the only chance you have to kill Ithea and save Sa'gola from a terrible death. Because you must be.

You aren't...sure...are you? You seek...out of...desperation. You are torturing...me on a...a whim. This is...crazy.

He killed my mate. He murdered his own mother, tortured my apprentice, your teacher. He will kill us all, enslave our girls, and destroy the world. Dina was screaming, her voice shrill and burning Mharina's ears. She heard herself cry out in pain.

It must be you. It could have been your father, but he was a soft fool, a dreamer. He was never fully trained, so he couldn't understand. He thought your Emperor was his enemy—two stupid Wycaan fools, two weak men driven by their own delusions while all the time, Ithea grew stronger. They were idiots, your father and his Emperor, never seeing what stood before their very eyes. Both died useless deaths that will mean the death of our Order, of my apprentice, of your teacher, of our world.

The old woman dragged Mharina to the brink of insanity. *Ahdahr,* Mharina cried out. But Dina continued pounding her, relentlessly tearing through her mind without caution.

To put our destiny in the hands of weak, stupid Wycaan males. It was...

Images of her father crying, fighting, killing filled her mind. Dina was forcing these images in front of her. There were scenes she had never seen, which had happened before her birth. She saw the fear in those he met, the anguish of those he denied help. She saw her father's first mate, Ilana, dead in a castle tower, her namesake, the Wycaan Master Mhari, dead, crushed by the great stones of the walls of Galbrieth. She moaned as she saw her mother crying, and, all the time, her *ahdahr* watched, confused, scared, and weak.

Then, for just a fleeting moment, his eyes locked with hers, and she felt a spark of his love touch her. It was enough. From deep within, even as he turned away, deep, red pain erupted into a fierce wall of bright orange fire. Mharina roared in anger. *My ahdahr! You will not tear his memory from me!*

And now she advanced, gathering new energy that consumed her body and soul, and she roared again. This was her essence. This was her living force of magic, and it burned hot and bright. She felt Dina recoil as she advanced, watched her own body glowing, felt the intensity of her rage, her power. And then Dina was outside of her head, but Mharina did not hesitate. Dina had told her to take what she needed. Now she knew what she needed, and she advanced inside of Dina. The old woman gasped and fought to stabilize herself, but Mharina interchanged between the woman's fire that Sa'gola had awakened in her and this new essence that Dina had ignited.

She pushed deeper, seeing white-haired humans, elves, dwarves, and others from a distant time. She saw Dina retreat into an underground lake with a mighty stalactite dripping water overhead. She followed and saw, for a fleeting moment, her father walking the same path.

She cried out, summoning yet more power, but turned from him to follow Dina. Her *ahdahr's* murky shadow moved aside. She submerged and the water filled her, but it could not quell her fire. She saw the weapons but took nothing, fully intent on tracking Dina. She pushed the old woman back into a huge room, its walls covered in words. Dina grabbed for the words, but Mharina claimed them for herself. The old woman screamed.

The words entered her—the lessons, the stories, the words, always the words. This was the Wycaan power, and it poured into her. She cried out in ecstasy as she felt her body expand to receive it, her chest pushing out, her mind a sponge absorbing more and more. She could not stop herself. Her muscles hardened as the words filled every sinew, and still she pushed on. At the end of the room she found Dina, backed against a pillar, her eyes wide, blood dripping from her mouth and eyes.

Mharina stopped then, panting and realizing what she was doing. *You said to show no mercy,* she screamed. *You said to take everything so that I can face him.*

Dina just stood there, gasping. Mharina continued.

I will avenge your mate. I will save your apprentice. I will give strength and new life to your Order, Dina. I will do it for you, for my father, for my family, and for all people of Odessiya. I claim the Iyzun. I bring the balance of the two magics, Dina, and I will fulfill your desire. ASHBAR!

Everything exploded in a blinding flash of brilliant white light. Mharina fell from the chair, sprawling on the ground. She gasped for breath. The stone floor was mercifully cold. She tried to rise, but her legs failed her. She pulled herself along one hand at a time, her nails digging in the gravel, toward Dina's slumped body.

When she got to the chair, Dina's small, withered body slipped to the ground. She caught the woman and cradled her head to her own chest. And suddenly, the tears erupted.

"You knew this was the risk. You warned me, prepared me." Her sobs echoed around the cavern. "You wanted this. You craved another with the *Iyzun.* You were Wycaan and you learned the feminine magic, but you could never assimilate the two. You were so close, yet you watched Shadona die and your apprentice suffer abuse and torture, and all the time it ate you up inside because you could not meld the two powers and protect them."

More sobs erupted. There was a hand on her shoulder, but she did not care. "You were so close, and yet you couldn't cross the line. But I can, and I will do it for you, and for my father and Sa'gola. I will walk your path. I didn't want to kill you. I didn't."

She bowed her head, shaking, and her hair fell over Dina's face. Her hair, sweaty and tangled...and snow white.

ChApter 59

The elf, who was called Seanchai—he must get used to the name—walked in a wide circumference to avoid the fishing port. He looked down at the small buildings cradled in a valley near a sparking sea and wondered again whether he should go back to protect Moya and Kennins. The two elves he spied were heavily armed. What if they were bounty hunters? Would they force the frail couple to talk? He descended the hill and entered the town. Near the docks, he beckoned to the two small children he had produced the honey sticks for.

"I need a favor. Do you know where Moya Kennins' sister lives?"

The older boy nodded while the smaller one picked his nose, disappointed that the funny man was not going to play a trick for them.

"There are two strangers looking for them. I want you to watch them without being seen. Can you do that?"

The older boy nodded profusely.

"If they harm either Moya or Kennins, you are to run back here to me as fast as possible. Okay? I'm going to hide on that boat there."

"We be good at that," the older boy said, and dragged his brother after him.

The elf went to Kennins' boat and settled down. He fell asleep and was met with a cacophony of strange dreams. A beautiful, dark-skinned elfe, fierce and proud; a red-haired old elf, ancient and scary; and fleeting glimpses of *calhei*.

The boy was shaking his arm, and he leapt up.

"They be gone. Ask questions and leave town. I follow them, and they be heading east. They be on horseback, too."

"Thank you. Keep an eye on old Kennins for me, will you?"

The boy nodded. "You going away?"

"Yes."

"Where?" the smaller one asked. "You be so much fun."

"I have to find my own children, little *calhei*," he replied, and then bent and hugged them both, slipping coins into their pockets. " Guard this well. Goodbye," he said, and released his grip.

He left the boat for the last time and walked down the pier, back onto the quay. Kennins waited for him with a gray mare. He gave the elf the reins.

"What is this?" Seanchai asked.

"You earned it," Kennins replied. "I rather be giving you money, but at least I can do this. Follow them. They be good for answers and good of heart, I think."

"My name is Seanchai," the elf said.

"A man should know his name. It be a good start."

"I'm sorry about the farm."

"It be too much for us without you. Before you came, we be talking about selling and moving back here. We be okay. We be having each other."

The elf hugged the old man tight.

"You were good to me, you and Moya—kind and generous."

"You be a son to us for a while. It be nice to live the dream, even for a short time. We thank you."

"If I find my *calhei*, I will try and bring them here, and you will get to be a grandfather."

"I be liking that. I be teaching 'em to fish and enjoy the seas, like you learned."

"Thank you," Seanchai swallowed hard, and climbed up on the horse.

He followed the fresh tracks of two horses riding abreast out of town. He was not sure whether approaching them would be a good idea, but Kennins seemed convinced, and he trusted the old man. The mare was not young, and he did not push her. Later in the day, he dismounted and ran alongside her. It felt good to exert himself, and the horse nickered at the idea. It was on the second day that he caught up to them.

He heard a fight going on long before he saw them. He tied his horse to a tree that was hidden from the road and carefully climbed up onto a rock ledge. Below, about forty taragusii tried to attack the two below him, who stood with their backs to the rocks.

He watched the elfe wield her two swords elegantly, darting in to kill and then retreating to the rock face. He watched the man dispense with taragusii using hidden blades. There was a small crossbow on the ground. About a dozen bodies lay strewn in front of them, and the other taragusii trod on the bodies as they tried to engage the two. Now the human had a staff with a blade at either end, and he whirled it with incredible dexterity.

Still more taragusii swamped the two fighters. The elf counted another twenty. Suddenly he heard a sound behind him and whirled around. Four taragusii had come, no doubt planning to jump down on the human and elfe. Seanchai drew his swords and let his instincts take over. He dispensed with two in quick fashion, as they underestimated his skill. The other two were more careful. As one sparred with him, the elf tripped on the rock he was standing on. The second taragusii suddenly charged. The elf recovered in time to sidestep and send the huge lizard over the edge. The second soon followed, and the elf checked to see what was happening below.

The taragusii had managed to separate the two, and now the fighting was more desperate, as each fought three or four at a time. The elf didn't hesitate. He launched himself into the throng and sent a half dozen taragusii sprawling. He rolled and sprung onto his feet, and then the fury took over.

He cut his way through the taragusii in front of him. Already, a large group had seen enough and was retreating. He glanced behind him and saw the human and elfe were now fighting a half dozen at most. He charged on, cutting down taragusii as the battle rage elevated his speed and reflexes. He fought with adrenaline and instinct, following a form that he had learned somewhere. He killed another dozen, and the rest fled. *They would be back,* he thought. *They want me.*

He turned to find that the elfe and human had killed or incapacitated the rest and now stood staring at him, both panting from exertion. The man moved between bodies, finishing off two wounded and retrieving small knives and sharp discs. He pulled bolts and quarrels from corpses. Everything disappeared into his cloak. The elfe remained standing, staring at the elf. He sheathed his swords. Though she was dark-skinned and he not, they both had bright white hair and the same weapons. He put his hand on his heart.

"My name is Seanchai, I think. There is no need to fear me."

The elfe abruptly grinned. "Oh, I know who you are, and I do not fear you. I admire and love you. Welcome back, Seanchai, Wycaan Master of Odessiya."

CHAPTER 60

"I find all this hard to believe," Seanchai said as he stared at the young, exuberant elfe.

Pyre had been enthusiastically telling him his own life story, from when he ran away to escape conscription and trained with Mhari, to his leadership in the rescue at Galbrieth, the alliance with the dwarves, and the battle of Hothengold. She spoke in great detail of his coming to the Elves of the West and how the two of them met and became friends. She spent a long time describing the trial when she, as only a young *calhei*, stood up to the council, and how the Weapons Master and a hundred warriors decided to go with Seanchai to the decisive battle at the Cliftean Pass when he had defeated the Emperor.

Seanchai saw that Ahad listened intently while he prepared food and tensed when she mentioned that Seanchai killed the Crown Prince. He stopped them so they could eat the rabbit stew, but Pyre only took a couple of mouthfuls before continuing. Seanchai became more interested when she talked about Sellia and his *calhei,* and a puzzled and then pained expression spread across his face when she told him Mharina went with Sa'gola.

"Do you remember any of this?" Ahad asked.

Seanchai stared into his stew, uneaten and getting cold. He shook his head. "No. But I have a strong feeling that I have killed many people with my swords."

"And your bow." Pyre jumped up to retrieve the carefully packaged bow and quiver.

This did nothing to ease Seanchai's feelings, and he unwrapped it slowly and with great apprehension. He stared at the elegant, lime green bow, the wood smooth and intricately carved. The few nicks it sported took nothing away from its resplendent beauty. He rose, sat his bowl down, and slowly walked about twenty paces from a tree stump, swinging the quiver onto his back. He stared at his target and felt his breathing change. He drew an arrow and noched it. He felt the taut bowstring resist as he pulled it back and settled his sights.

When he released the arrow, he let out a deep sigh. He noched a second, then a third. Soon, twelve arrows vibrated in the wood. They were not bunched very well; in fact, a couple were closer to the edge of the stump. He watched, astonished, as twelve became eleven and then ten. One by one, the arrows disappeared. His quiver became heavier as he stared at the stump. Slowly, he reached back and fingered the fletching.

"That's convenient," he said, and both Pyre and Ahad laughed. "Where did I get this gift?"

"It was a present from the Bloodwye forest, where the Elves of the West live," Pyre said. "You told me how the bowyer had set up several bows for you to try. You selected this one, but it was not a bow he had made. It was, indeed, a gift of the forest."

Seanchai stared at the bow and frowned. "How can something so beautiful be such a ruthless killing tool?"

Pyre did not answer, and the Wycaan sighed. He shot into the tree stump for a long time, and gradually, his twelve arrows began to bunch closer and closer to the middle of the stump. He sped up his shooting until the arrows barely had time to reappear in his quiver. He sweated and panted as he shot faster and faster. His shots became more erratic, and one arrow actually missed the target completely.

"Stop!" Ahad called, and everything except the elf's heaving chest froze. "That's enough. Come sit and eat."

Back at the fire, Pyre handed Seanchai his bowl of stew. He wiped his forehead with his cloak and began to eat slowly.

"What happened?" Pyre asked.

"I'm a monster. I've killed hundreds, maybe thousands. Others followed me in good faith and died fighting for me. I left tens of thousands without mates or fathers, all because I had this bloodlust. I felt it now, the exhilaration of being able to kill so ruthlessly, so efficiently. The power…it feels so good, and yet is so evil."

"You're wrong," Pyre erupted, her face red. "You led a nation to freedom. Elves were little more than slaves before you helped liberate them. The dwarf nation cowered underground, losing their identity. Many humans were exploited and forced into servitude.

"You brought a country together, helped members of many races find their dignity and self-worth. You helped Shayth become the prince he was meant to be. You will see when you return to Odessiya how revered you are, and you will take your place once again as a leader of the people."

"No." Seanchai shook his head. "I will not kill again. I will not make decisions for people or stand in judgment. I must find my family and take them far away, where we are not known."

"You can't do that!" Pyre blurted out. "Shayth has taken his army north to fight some grave threat the Emperor loosed before his death. Rhoddan and Troja are captives of Ithea, a powerful sorcerer, at Grogin. You can't just walk away from your friends, from all who depend upon you."

"Friends are not family," Seanchai muttered. "I have to keep my family safe."

"Before, you risked everything for your friends, refused to leave them in Galbrieth to face execution, and always went back to protect them. They *were* family. We *are* your family."

Seanchai stared at the tears streaming down her dark face.

"You always said your work would only end when all people are free and able to live in dignity. You built Wycaan Island to raise a generation of Wycaans trained not only in fighting, but also healing and moral leadership. You had a vision."

"And you told me I left them defenseless, to be massacred by taragusii."

"You were away, helping to face the threat in the north. It wasn't your fault."

"I left innocent youth in my care undefended. I left my family exposed. Do you not see the pattern? Wherever I go, I bring disaster and death. Even now, you told me that the taragusii are torturing innocent people who don't even know me. I leave a wake of innocent deaths wherever I go. I can feel it. I won't do it anymore."

Pyre opened her mouth to respond, but Ahad put a hand on her shoulder and shook his head. He crouched down and looked at Seanchai. When he spoke, his voice was quiet but firm.

"You have had to absorb an awful lot. Now is not the time to make decisions. You don't know where your family is, but Rhoddan and Troja are being held captive as bait. We believe Ithea hopes that your eldest daughter will come to rescue them, which makes me think he might have already captured other members of your family, or will soon. Ithea hates Mharina and her teacher, Sa'gola, and wants to kill them. Even if it is only about your family and not Rhoddan, the elf who stood by you from the very beginning, you need to come to Grogin."

Seanchai looked at him. "You want me to fight this sorcerer, but I don't think swords or a bow will help."

"You are a Wycaan. You possess the magic of your order."

Seanchai shook his head. "But I don't remember any of it."

CHAPTER 61

There were few things worse than waking up in the middle of the night in the frozen wastelands with a full bladder. Shayth cursed the wine he drank with his officers and Ballendir. At the time, matching them goblet for goblet seemed a good idea to boost the men's spirits, but not now. At least Shayth had certain privileges to temper his bad decision, including the bucket in his tent. He rose and walked over to relieve himself. As he did, a shiver coursed through his body. It was not from the cold. He started to turn and glimpsed a shadow.

"Do not turn around," a deep, rough voice rasped. "To see me means to die. You in no danger, for now, at least, not-King Shindell."

"How did you get in?" Shayth asked, trying to clear the sleepy, drunk fog from his head.

"I walk past guards at will. I walk through walls and along paths without leaving trail."

"Did you harm any of my guards?"

"There was no need."

"I thank you for that," Shayth said. "What can I do for you?"

The shadow laughed, a sound not unlike a blunt saw hacking its way through wood. "What can you do for me? Hmmm. Nothing, I think, but will consider. No, I come with message from our Mage. You must come to Horn's Point. Do you know it?"

"No. I have never ventured further north than here."

"Bring one pictorian scout with you. Scout will know place. He will leave you there and go to nearby shelter. You will allow yourself to be blindfolded and brought before Mage. I not know if she allow you to look upon her, but I to guarantee your safety."

"How am I supposed to explain to my council and guards that I'm walking alone and unarmed into the mouth of the enemy?"

"That is your concern. You are not-King. You decide. You may come armed if wish, but, should you try to fight, it be your end."

"What if I decide against coming? Why do we not parley in the open?"

"If you not come, we begin killing soldiers. We kill one on first day, two on second, three on—"

"Yeah, I get the gist," Shayth snapped.

"Then you come?"

"Yes. I'll set out the day after tomorrow. I need to settle the leadership issue for the pictorians."

"Ah, yes. You killed Arad'gug. That impressive. He worthy warrior."

Shayth pondered this show of respect. "If you understand the pictorians, then you know why it is important to keep the stability here."

"Yes. Their…unruliness…is biggest weakness. When you come to us, Mage will ask about white-haired one."

Shayth almost blurted out that Seanchai was dead, but stopped himself. Was this shadow talking about his friend or his uncle?

"Tell your Mage I look forward to meeting her, and I pledge to come in peace, to listen and talk."

The shadow lingered. "Why you not-King? You smart leader."

"I'm not as royal as you think. I have a…a regrettable past."

"Hmm. Very well. We see you in three days. We might have scouts watching when you journey to us. Do not fear. They there to protect and ensure you reach right place."

"And the pictorian who accompanies me," Shayth said. "Do you guarantee his safety?"

"Yes, as long as he goes to shelter and remains there until we bring you back to him."

"Thank you. How long should I expect to be away?"

"Hmm. It is two-day trek either way. I think week, but it for Mage to decide."

"So be it," Shayth said. "We will meet in three days."

There was no response, and Shayth sensed that the shadow had gone. A sharp breeze cut in through a corner of the tent, and he walked over and closed it. He was tempted to look outside, but knew he would see nothing.

Shayth met with the pictorian council the following morning. Just before entering, he took Umnesilk aside.

"I need a scout, one who knows the way to Horn's Point and the shelter near it. He must be patient and trustworthy."

"Why?" Umnesilk asked.

"I will tell you later. But if he disobeys my orders and does not stay where I tell him to, he will be killed. Please select well. You are not an option."

Umnesilk grunted, but before he could respond, Shayth swept past him and entered the meeting room. There was a circle of about twenty wooden chairs, solid and functional. One was more ornate and sat upon a slightly raised dais. The pictorians, who were gathered around a table with food and drink, watched him as he walked to the table, exchanging brief pleasantries as if in the court at Shindellia. This seemed only to baffle them all the more. He took a thick mug and filled it with the dark, bitter drink that pictorians appreciated. Then he turned.

"Let us sit," he called out and walked toward the dais. There was a murmur behind him, but Shayth turned just before he reached the First Boar's chair and sat in the seat next to it. The relief in the room was palpable.

Gruenk walked up to him and said loudly, "You have right to take seat. You challenged and defeated First Boar. Nowhere in our writings does it say only pictorian sit on throne of First Boar."

Again, a murmur swept around the gathering, accompanied by defiant glances. Shayth sipped his drink and waited for it to subside.

"The chair stays vacant," he decreed. "I am the Prince of all Odessiya, from the pictorians in the north to the elves in the deep south. I rule and serve all as one people. But I respect the need of the pictorian nation to name a First Boar and, though I would be honored, I do not believe I could do the role justice. I would be away in Shindellia most of the time. *Our* people deserve a better leader than that."

This time, the murmurs were more congenial.

"But I come with a request. I wish for amnesty for Umnesilk and his entire family. I want his home restored to him."

"Do you expect him to be again First Boar?" a broad pictorian with sharp horns asked.

"I have an opinion, but it is not my place to decide. I do, however, strongly advise that you choose a strong leader, one who has a strategic mind and is ready to face the danger at your gates. Choose one who understands the need to work with my commanders and me. That is all I ask. And choose quickly. Today."

Another spoke in the guttural pictorian language. Gruenk translated for Shayth. "He ask why so fast? Pictorians often take days to decide, and boars who want lead must fight."

"No fighting," Shayth snapped, but quickly recovered. "We need every boar to be ready to defend your people and our northern borders. I fear we are already outnumbered. As your prince, I insist you respect my wishes."

He looked slowly from one stunned face to the next.

"No challenges," Gruenk declared. "As oldest boar, I will preside over ceremony."

There were a few whispers, but Gruenk seemed to grow in statue. "And I nominate first candidate. I nominate Umnesilk as First Boar of Pictorians. He served us as brave and fearless leader. He close to king, and he willing to sacrifice own hearth and office for good of unity between clans. What say you?"

Shayth stood and walked out of the circle to allow the pictorians their own space. As he poured another drink, he thought to himself, *Arad'gug called me King, and I did not correct him. The Ashen Elf, if that was what it was, taunted me with the name not-King. I didn't expect that to hurt so.*

Chapter 62

Shayth followed the towering boar selected to guide him to Horn's Point. Each of the lumbering pictorian's steps was hard to keep up with, especially in the snow. Umnesilk had selected a boar from the Ice Clans who had served as one of Arad'gug's bodyguards.

"Dar'thuk not speak much. Follow orders and know land. I tell him what you order. He know to stay at shelter. He think there food for eight or ten days. He say after six, he leave, so enough food for you for two days."

Shayth nodded. "But I don't think I can find my way there or from there back here."

"Hmm. I think you wrong to go alone. Why—"

"I need to buy time. A second army has been recalled to Shindellia. They will outfit themselves and come north. But I fear if we don't know who or what we are dealing with, it won't matter how many troops we have."

"Yes," Umnesilk conceded. "Still not good prince go alone. If return alone, head south. We will patrol and watch for you. But—"

Shayth ended the conversation before his friend could persuade him not to go. Now, he walked on the snow crushed by Dar'thuk's huge boots, and his mood darkened. What was he hoping to achieve from this? He had sent word to the Elves of the West asking for assistance. They had Wycaans there, but he felt sure they would ignore his request. He was not Seanchai.

He thought of Pyre and wondered where she was. Seanchai had spoken highly of her and her potential, if they could just unlock whatever was holding her back from becoming a true Wycaan. She was wandering around, grief-stricken, with Rhoddan. He could have done with Rhoddan, as well, he thought. The stoic elf would keep him closer to the spirit of Seanchai. He was so deep in thought he almost bumped into Dar'thuk, who had stopped to stare up at a ridge.

"We not alone," he grunted.

"They said they would track us. You don't need to fear—"

"Fear? I Pictorian. Was bodyguard to Arad'gug, First Boar of Pictorians."

"You were. I apologize. Now, can we please keep moving?"

"We not alone, and I not see them."

"So how do you know they are here?"

"Always feel tingle in horn when danger close. This why I bodyguard to Arad'gug and why I live so long."

Shayth nodded, but had no desire to stand around. "We need to go."

"Why Umnesilk ask me? I rage with you."

Shayth sighed. "What? You're angry with me? Because I killed Arad'gug?"

"Yes. Why you kill him?"

"Listen. This is not the time or place. Now walk."

Dar'thuk glared at him. "Not sure why I not kill you here. No Umnesilk to—"

Shayth wheeled on the pictorian and pointed in the direction where the boar had signaled, "Because I'm the only one standing between them and the entire destruction of your people—pictorian annihilation—forever. Understand?" He took a deep breath. "Umnesilk said you don't talk much. Perhaps that's for the best."

Dar'thuk harrumphed and began to walk again. *Pictorian Way,* Gruenk had advised, and Shayth allowed himself a small smirk.

They camped in a small cave that offered little beyond shelter from the wind. Shayth slept badly, dreaming of Seanchai falling from the boat into the ocean, and then Riona, and a third time, his parents, their faces blurred. He woke at first light and nudged Dar'thuk with his boot. The boar grunted but rose quickly. They gnawed on dried buffalo meat and cheese as they walked. The land around them was hilly and pure white. There were no trees or bushes to break the white glare. Above them, an impenetrable gray cloud cover offered no encouragement.

Shayth's feet were numb when Dar'thuk stopped and pulled a long spear from several harnessed on his back. He struck down hard until only half remained aboveground. Then he turned to their left and continued. A short while later, he repeated the action with another spear. Then he moved again to the left, stopped about twenty paces away, and dug around two protruding wooden points.

"Here shelter. I come back and dig. Leave open for you. No human can open. Not strong enough. Understand? You follow pole right and then left. Nearby."

"Understood. Thank you."

"Thank Umnesilk," he said, and began to trudge back the way they came.

They reached Horn's Point in the afternoon. It looked like little more than a small mountain that curved to a point. They walked around it but saw no one and no footprints.

"Devils can still be here," Dar'thuk muttered. "They walk through walls and not leave trail."

"I guess you had better go, then. I don't want you coming into contact with them. Please go back to the shelter, mark six days, as we agreed, and then head home."

Dar'thuk stared at him, unsure.

"Go on," Shayth said, "and don't look so worried. You don't even like me."

"True," the pictorian replied without even a small smile. "For my people, then—try not to die."

Shayth watched the huge pictorian walk away. "I'll try," he said quietly, "for all our people."

He turned and walked around the base of the hill again. There was nothing new to see, and he grimaced at the thought of waiting. He yawned as he saw the sun was beginning its downward trajectory. There was probably no more than three hours of daylight left.

"Do not turn, not-King." Shayth was pretty sure it was the same Gray Elf, judging from the tone that had visited his tent. "I glad you came. Now I put scarf over eyes as agreed. Okay?"

Shayth nodded, and his eyes were soon covered, preventing him from seeing anything. The blindfold smelled of musk and age.

"Hold this with both hands."

A wooden staff was thrust into Shayth's hands. He felt along it, and in the middle, another long staff jutted out at a right angle. His companion gently pulled, and Shayth followed. He stumbled once, and the other grunted and slowed. A few minutes later, they stopped.

"Come forward and climb onto sleigh."

"Sleigh?"

"Sit on seat like horse and cart. Yes?"

Shayth made his way forward and felt an iron box. He climbed inside, unsteadily groping around, and found a plank to sit on.

"Hold on," his guide said, and then: "Hut! Hut!"

There was a snap of a whip and a series of short yips from dogs. Then Shayth felt the box being pulled forward. The wind burned his ears and, even blindfolded, he felt his eyes watering. Shayth lost track of time. He began to doze, but each time was buffeted by wind as the sleigh moved to one side or the other. He was so cold now, shivering and teeth chattering. He huddled up as best he could. They were descending now, and then it grew abruptly dark. The dogs' paws and sleigh rails echoed as they traversed from snow onto gravel. They were underground, he surmised. The dogs slowed, and one barked. It received a distant bark in reply. A firm hand took Shayth's arm.

"Step out. Be slow. Muscles cold."

Shayth did so and needed the steadying hand. The staff was again thrust into his hands.

"Can I see the dogs?" he asked.

"Why?"

"Always wanted a dog of my own. Just interested."

"Not now. Maybe if Mage agrees. Come."

And Shayth held on as he was guided deeper underground.

Chapter 63

Shayth didn't need to see to know he was in a big cavern with many eyes scrutinizing him. Here stood the Prince of Odessiya, and they could kill him without breaking a sweat. His hand closed on his sword hilt for comfort, but he quickly removed it. When he was brought to a stop, a murmur of expectation swept through the cavern. He turned his head to catch the different sounds. It was an incredibly vulnerable feeling.

"The not-King of Odessiya, Mage," the voice said from his side. "He came as he promised, alone. We not followed."

"Has he asked you any questions?" The voice, though female, was also deep and powerful.

"He wants to see dogs. I not show him."

There was a round of laughter, and Shayth swallowed hard. The Mage waited for it to subside.

"Do you have any other important questions, not-King?" she asked, and there was again laughter.

He thought a moment, composing himself. He was not a common prisoner. "I am Shayth Shindell, Prince of Odessiya. I wonder why you fear me so that you must keep me blindfolded now that I'm inside your cavern. You met my uncle. I suspect you did not blindfold him."

There was a buzz of…what was it? Respect? The Mage did not answer immediately, again waiting for silence.

"When your uncle came to us, we were in need. He helped us reach our full potential and, to answer your question, yes, he walked among us with eyes wide open. You were blindfolded to prevent you from knowing the location of our camp. Why are you still blind-folded? Because it is interesting to see how you cope with such a disadvantage."

"Oh," Shayth heard the edge in his own voice. "That's what puts me at a disadvantage? Not the hundreds or thousands of armed Gray Elves around me?"

The Mage breezed past his sarcasm. "Our dogs come from an ancient breed called Samoyed. They are beautiful, regal creatures—intelligent, loyal, and strong. The ones we breed have piercing blue eyes, as do we. And you will be allowed to see them before you leave."

There was a round of laughter. Shayth waited for it to recede. Then he looked in the direction of the Mage's voice.

"Do the Gray Elves have a ceremony of guest rites? In Odessiya, we offer our guests hospitality rights. Wine and bread, once shared, ensure the visitor's safety as long as they abide by the rules."

"No," the Mage replied. "We do not have such a ceremony. But then, we never have guests."

Again there was laughter, and Shayth listened for the echo off the roof.

"You hosted my uncle and Arad'gug."

"Your uncle made Arad'gug come to us to bring him to heel."

"*Can* you bring a pictorian to heel?" Shayth asked.

"Yes. For the survival of his people. Is it not the same with humans?"

Shayth thought for a moment. "We treasure life and desire to protect our families and clans. But we also live by values, one of which is to be free. The people rose against my uncle for this reason."

"Hmm," the Mage replied. "Bring the not-King to the council room. We will talk more there, and he can look upon us."

The staff was again placed in Shayth's hands, and he was led away. He could feel when there were no longer eyes upon him. He thought of what a blind man once told him, that when deprived of one sense, the others sharpen to compensate. Now in a smaller cave, he was gently pressed on the shoulder to sit down, and his blindfold removed. He stared around him. The small cavern was illuminated with orange light that seemed to originate from bunches of mushroom-shaped clusters. About twenty oblong rocks stood on their ends at a slight angle. On five of them sat gray elves. A vacant space between them was carved as a more conventional chair.

These elves looked very different from the ones in Odessiya. They were taller and broader, similar in size to pictorians, and their skin was a gray hue. Their hair was all straight, some black, a few gray, and one white. Most wore bands around their foreheads—simple, functional affairs. Their ears were long and pointed, but stretched back close to the sides of their heads. Their eyes, as the Mage had said, were a piercing blue.

All were armed with two axes, one long and one short, both double-headed. There was no decoration or flamboyance; unlike the dwarves, it was all made for functionality. Each wore a chain with a small metal hexagon. In the middle of many, but not all of the hexagons, was a red stone, some paler than others. Shayth thought the younger elves wore brighter stones.

"Here," said a voice he recognized as the one who brought him, and he turned.

The elf held out a stone cup with water. Shayth took it and sniffed.

"It taste metallic," the elf said, "but it safe. Just water."

"Thank you." Shayth drained the cup quickly, and the elf refilled it.

"We not eat same food as you, but after speak with Mage, then share what have."

Shayth nodded and looked around. "Where does the light come from?"

"Mushrooms."

"Those really are mushrooms? Fascinating."

"You ask strange questions—dogs, mushrooms. Are all humans so…"

"Inquisitive? No, everyone is different. Is that not the same with your people?" The elf shrugged, and Shayth's eyes were drawn to the stone around the elf's neck. "Will you tell me about the stone?"

A frown appeared on the elf's face. "You ask Mage. Not know how much I to share." He cocked his head. "She comes. Think well upon questions, not-King. Destiny of your people depends on it."

Chapter 64

The atmosphere in the room changed. The elves sat up even straighter with tension or anticipation. Shayth himself sat up, but did not turn. Two huge elves, by far bigger than any other in the room, came and stood a few paces from him, one to his left and the other to his right, not impeding his view of the council, but clearly making their presence felt. They faced him and kept hands on the hilts of short axes. Their expressions were grim and fixed.

An old elfe walked in and made her way to the chair. All elves stood and bowed their heads. Shayth stood, too, eliciting a tense reaction from the two bodyguards. He held his hands to his side, palms facing them, in Odessiya's sign of peace. They stared at his hands and frowned. It meant nothing here. The old elfe walked slowly but without weakness. It was a regal entry, Shayth thought. She wore a black dress and cloak. She eased herself into her chair and stared at Shayth.

"The Mage of Gray Elves," the elf who had brought Shayth announced. "Here stands Prince Shayth Shindell, not-King of Odessiya."

"You may all sit," the Mage said, not taking her gaze from Shayth. Her voice was slightly raspy, but she was comfortable with the human language. "You are either very brave or very stupid to come before us alone. Why did you come?"

"I have proved myself many times to be both brave and stupid,"

Shayth replied. The elves smiled, all except the Mage. "I came under your assurance of safe passage. I value the lives of my people and would prefer to solve this amicably rather than spill blood. My highest responsibility is to defend the lives of my people."

"Your uncle did not hold by such sentiments. Who is the more common ruler: him or you?"

Shayth thought about this, sifting through the history lessons he had ignored as a boy. "I suspect him. My family has never excelled as kings."

"Why are you not king?" she asked.

"It's complicated. I have not always walked a noble path. There is much in my past that shames me." He told of the death of his parents and his violent rampage.

"The not-King has a dark past. He wonders whether he is truly worthy of the throne?"

"Something like that."

"How will it be resolved?"

"Good question. In my short reign, I have been too busy helping my people to live free. I have spent considerable time creating conditions that allow humans, elves, dwarves, and pictorians to live peacefully and with enough resources to eradicate hunger and disease."

"Have you succeeded?"

"There is still much to do, but Odessiya moves forward. It is a big country with many different races and sub-races."

"Who turned you from the violent path you were taking?"

"An elf." Shayth saw them all stiffen slightly. "A visionary Wycaan Master, though he was little more than a bewildered pup when we met."

"Is this the one who killed your uncle?"

Shayth hesitated. "He bested my uncle in battle twice but never slayed him. In truth, I don't know exactly what happened at Grogin. Events transpired outside my borders, and I was already on my way here. There are many rumors in taverns and castle halls, but they are rumors, nonetheless."

"Your uncle is dead," the Mage said almost casually. "Do you mourn him?"

Shayth frowned. "How do you know?"

"He held a certain control over us. It has been severed."

"Can you tell me more?" Shayth asked.

"There was a powerful magical clash, and we felt him pass. The rumors you heard: do they say your Wycaan friend killed him?"

"I'm not sure. There are others who are also powerful. I have not encountered them."

"You are being evasive." Her deep voice took on a stern edge.

Shayth took his time. "I don't believe leaders of our level should dwell upon rumors. I don't want to mislead you."

"In not laying a path, you keep us standing in one place."

"Perhaps, but that is better than rushing forward into the swamp of uncertainty and illusion."

She smiled. "Do you know our story?"

"No. I only found out about you from Arad'gug as he died. I sent hawks to the capital asking for the scholars to research in the Great Libraries."

The Mage sighed at the inconvenience. "We will adjourn. I wish to talk with the not-King alone." She turned to Shayth as she rose. "Come."

One of her bodyguards turned to face her, though his body remained in front of Shayth. "Not with his sword, Mage."

"I promised him he would not be asked to relinquish it."

Shayth spoke up. "Give me your word that it will remain untouched until I return, and I will gladly leave my sword."

He started unbuckling it before the Mage nodded her agreement. For good measure, he also removed two dirks, one from each boot. When he looked up, the bodyguard who had spoken bowed his head to Shayth. The Mage turned and walked behind her chair to a stone corridor Shayth had not noticed before. When it was just the two of them, he spoke.

"Thank you for trusting me with a private audience."

"Thank you for trusting us to come here. I think you're very brave. But I don't believe you will achieve the end you desire."

They exited the corridor onto a high ledge inside a large cavern. About thirty gray elves painted the opposite wall. It was a huge mural with a dozen different scenes.

"This is the story of my people," the Mage said. "We were the original race of Odessiya. Our history goes far back, deep into the World of Faded Memory. We were here when the first fair-skinned elves sailed from the west.

"We lived here in a beautiful, unspoiled land of blue rivers, mighty mountains, lush plains, and majestic forests. We hunted the migratory herds of bullists. Do you know what they are?" When Shayth shook his head, she continued. "That is because they no longer exist. The fair-skinned elves hunted them into extinction. These buffalo-like creatures were shaggy and fat and provided us with food and skins. Great cats, huge and lethal, trailed them. They had long fangs and great shaggy manes, and they preyed upon the herds as we did. There was enough for all. When we hunted the big cats, it was for ceremonial reasons. We made beautiful jewelry and weapons from an abundance of precious metals. Life was good until the fair-skinned elves came."

She went silent, and Shayth tried to follow her narrative through the pictures being created.

"It is a fine piece of art," he said. "I would like to see it finished."

"No, you wouldn't," the Mage replied. "When it is completed, we will attack Odessiya."

Chapter 65

S hayth shivered. If the old elfe had said this with any malice, it might have been easier to stomach. Instead, it was with a calm finality that struck terror in him. He tried not to show it.

"You have jumped ahead somewhat," he said slowly, his eyes glued to the mural. "Can you fill in what happened between their arrival and your fanatical desire to commit genocide?"

The Mage barely cracked a wry smile. "We began to fight. At first, it was scattered skirmishes, for we were tribal and had no army. But the fair-skinned elves were organized and drove us from the plains into the mountains. They brought shieldhei with them—horses that were disciplined but never subjugated."

"I have seen them," Shayth said, and instantly regretted it. He couldn't reveal the Elves of the West.

"How?"

"A few entered Odessiya in the south. The elves there were very excited and saw it as a portent. When they approached the shieldhei, however, the animals fled. I was lucky to be traveling there at the time. One of my rangers found them first and took me. I sat watching for a long time. They are very graceful."

The Mage stared at him, clearly not believing his story. She continued anyway. "My people slaughtered them to extinction, or so we thought. One night, about fifty Ashen Elves entered their main cavalry camp…"

She didn't finish, and there followed a long silence. Finally, Shayth prompted her.

"What happened next?"

"We were strong, and in the mountains, we could use the terrain to our advantage. They pulled back for a full cycle of seasons, and we began to make our homes in caves and gorges. Then, the following spring, they returned. Not with an army, but with white-haired ones. We watched them as they set up camps, all on mountain peaks at the four corners: north, south, east, and west.

"We attacked them, but they had built invisible wards to protect themselves. It was our first encounter with magic, and we were in awe. We should have fled, but by the time we understood the danger, it was too late. They created a magical field around the entire mountain range, and we could neither leave nor attack.

"Many of our people were not yet in the mountains, so they attacked from outside. The Wycaans fought them, and our people were slaughtered. They rarely faced us to cross swords. There was no need with their magic. As their supremacy became more apparent, they became crueler. Our people were tortured, our leaders ridiculed, and, when we tried to surrender and make peace, we were spurned.

"Then, one day, we felt the weather change. Though it was summer, a thick cloud, gray and foreboding, surrounded us. We could see nothing, feel only the cold and dampness. There was no light, as the cloud totally encompassed us. There was a great shaking of the earth, as if the very mountains crumbled or a thousand volcanoes erupted.

"The loud, piercing sounds made our ears bleed, and we lost consciousness. No one knows how long we remained like that. When we woke, our world was under a mountain, and we were imprisoned there. Slowly, we were able to build a life. We could exit and walk upon the snowy tundra for a short way until an invisible barrier stopped us. The barrier, thankfully, did not stop animals from entering, so we were able to hunt. The huge caverns were damp from the melting snows, allowing mushrooms and other foods to grow.

"We lost thousands before we adapted. Only the strongest survived and were able to procreate. It created a race that was strong and fit, but we never forgot the beautiful land we lost, and our hearts hardened like the stone prison that incarcerated us. We dreamed of when the barrier would fail and we would kill every fair-skinned elf and take back our homes. But the barrier showed no sign of weakening. We needed more. We trained and cultivated our talents, but we could never pierce the barrier. That is when your uncle came and made us an offer we could not refuse.

"Even he could not break the barrier, though he could pass through it. He was the first round-eared that we had met, and he taught us of his—your—people.

"Then he confirmed something we had wondered: since the fair elves had magic, then so did the Ashen Elves. He taught us how to harness simple magic, and then, when he left, we cultivated it. He returned every season, each time teaching us a little more to cultivate. And we learned well. We used it to break the chains of our prisons, and now we are back."

"What do you want? A home?"

"We want all of Odessiya. We want revenge on those who incarcerated us."

"But this happened centuries ago. No one is left alive. You cannot punish the great-great-great-grandchildren for the sins of their ancestors."

"We can, and we must. We will never be free inside," she said, and brought a fist to her heart, "until we heal ourselves of the grave atrocities perpetrated against us."

"I'm sorry for what your people went through," Shayth replied, looking at her now. "But don't you see that if you do to us what was done to you, you remain captive within the same crime? You become the perpetrators instead of the victims. No one caught up in such terrible madness is truly free. The world has moved on. Odessiya is an alliance of many races, including elves. You can become a part of this vision. We will help your people find land—fertile land that you can live on in peace and dignity. In time, your people will become part of the government, as the other races do. Isn't that a better future?"

The Mage thought about it. "What becomes of that?" She nodded to the mural.

"It remains a powerful reminder of the injustices against your people. We will create another one in the capital for all to see and bear witness."

"But see: the last scene is almost completed."

Shayth saw the outlines of a battle and a mound of dead bodies that reached to the top of the wall.

"It can be changed," he said simply. "It must."

They stood together, staring at the mural. Finally, the Mage shook her head. "We could live beside you, not-King," she said at last. "But we kill all the fair-skinned elves and the white-haired ones. Think about it and talk with your advisors. Deliver the elves, and we will settle and live in peace."

"I cannot do that. A king swears an oath to protect all his people."

"But you are the not-King."

Shayth was blindfolded and returned to the sleigh. A sack was placed in his lap. It squirmed and yipped.

"What is it?" the prince asked.

"A puppy," the voice of the one who had brought him here said. "A present from Mage."

"That is very kind of her. I would have thanked her."

"You should not. Samoyed have same blue eyes as us. She wants you to remember, every time you look into dog's eyes, we watch you."

Shayth swallowed hard as the sleigh moved out into the ice tundra. He thought of his options as the wind whistled past him, causing his ears to tingle and his eyes to water. He stroked the pup through the bag, and it settled down and nestled in his lap. He could feel the dog's heartbeat. It was quick and constant even as it slept. Then he realized it was his own heart that was beating fast.

CHAPTER 66

The elf tossed and turned, struggling to find a comfortable spot and silence the thoughts that flooded his mind. Ever since the old man pulled him from the sea, he had slept well, exhausted from physical labor and the fresh, salty air. This was an alien feeling. But now he understood that ignorance had been his elixir. He sat up and stared at the fire's glowing embers, as if the flickering light would give him guidance. A piece of charred wood crackled, but offered nothing more.

He rose and stretched, unused to sleeping on the ground. His back protested as he rose on the balls of his feet and then his toes. Unbidden, his hands came up from his sides, palms facing the sky. They met above his head and, palms facing down, lowered slowly together. He inhaled as he stretched and exhaled as he brought his body closer to the ground.

It felt good...familiar...important. He did it again and again, taking deeper breaths, stretching higher and sinking lower. His fingertips tingled, and the sensation slowly spread up his arms and into his chest. It moved from his toes up through his legs and into his loins. He grounded—yes, he felt *grounded* was the correct word—the energy and walked over to the elfe, who was guarding. She faced outward, but had seen him.

"Do you recognize what I was doing?" he asked.

Pyre nodded. "It is the foundation of our power, of the Wycaan magic."

"Show me."

"In the morning. I'm guarding now, and you need some sleep for when you replace me."

"No. I cannot sleep. Please. I think this is important."

"Go ahead," Ahad said from his bedroll, yawning. "None of us will get much sleep with his restlessness. I'll guard."

Pyre led Seanchai to a tree, a large fir with a thick trunk. "Stand facing the tree, but do not touch it," she said. "Your feet should be shoulder-width apart and your weight spread evenly. Good. Now, bend your knees slightly."

She moved around him, tucking in the stem of his spine, lowering his shoulders, moving his arms out slightly to his side and gently arching them. She massaged his fingers, loosening them and then bending them as though they were grasping something.

"Breathe in through your nose and fill your stomach with air. Good. Now exhale again through your nose. That's right. Keep going."

She straightened his neck and tucked his chin in, then stood back to admire his pose. "Not bad for a novice," she said.

She grinned, but Seanchai just frowned. "You never did have much of a sense of humor," she sighed.

He closed his eyes and focused on the breathing exercise and his stance. It was very familiar. His body filled with vibrating energy, and it felt good. He went into deep relaxation, his mind losing itself in the calm and emptiness. He distantly felt his hands float up in front of him as though he was caressing a ball. His fingers vibrated, and he thought he could actually feel the ball sizzle. He became aware that Pyre was gently moving his hands above his forehead.

"Hold the moon," she whispered, and his fingers touched something there but not there.

Later, she moved his hands, still holding a ball, in front of him, and he felt his stomach expand into the circle in front of him. His stance became stronger as he imagined his feet burrowing down like roots of a tree searching underground for water and stability.

Pyre moved his arms to his side, elbows bent and palms facing downward.

"Imagine that you're standing in a river with your hands on top of the moving water."

He did, and the river took him.

They rode steadily the next day, mainly in silence, fatigued from the lack of sleep. For a long time, their path took them up a winding mountain. Ahad, who was in the lead, stopped a little way from the peak.

"What is it?" Pyre asked.

"We'll be seen for miles around," he said. "I don't like it. Perhaps we should traverse it at night."

"We cannot stop every time we feel exposed," Pyre countered. "There might be dozens of such peaks between us and Grogin. Rhoddan and Troja are rotting in a dungeon while we crawl along."

Ahad turned in his saddle and glared at her, but did not say anything.

"Let's dismount and walk the horses over. We might pass unnoticed," Seanchai said.

There was little rhyme or reason behind the suggestion, but it was a compromise, and they took it. On the peak, however, they saw a swarm of creatures to the south—possibly taragusii—and a lone figure watching them from a nearby hill. It was the figure that held their gaze. He was dressed in a long, dark cloak, and his hood covered his face. They slowly mounted their horses.

"Only one of him," Pyre muttered, and led the way down to the valley between them.

The figure followed suit, showing no particular hurry. His horse was a beautiful, sleek, well-groomed chestnut. He reached the valley floor before them and waited for them to approach. Pyre and Ahad rode side by side, fanning out as they neared him. But the figure was no longer looking at them. His eyes were wide, and he was staring at Seanchai.

"Who are you?" Ahad asked, keeping a safe distance in case of an ambush or other treachery.

"I am a king's messenger," the man replied, eyes remaining fixed on the Wycaan. "I serve Prince Shayth Shindell and am instructed to seek the warrior Rhoddan."

"We are his friends," Pyre replied, but Ahad held up a hand.

"Do you carry the seal?"

The man reached into his saddlebag and pulled out a scroll with a deep red seal upon it. "Do you want to break it?"

Ahad examined the seal. "No," he said. "I have seen enough. Rhoddan has been captured. We're on our way to try and free him."

"Are you the Wycaan Pyre?" the man addressed Pyre.

"I am."

"Then the message is also meant for you." He stopped and stared again at Seanchai. "Is it possible?" he asked, and bowed his head in reverence.

"Please don't," Seanchai muttered.

"You came to my village with your brother, Rhoddan, and freed our people from extortionists. Then you healed my little sister. She had the heats an' shivers, and you sat up with her all night until she rested easy. I love my sister and place myself forever in your debt."

Seanchai just stared at him, but Pyre turned in her saddle. "This was the other Seanchai, the true Wycaan," she said. "There are tens of thousands like this man who owe you so much and live in the knowledge that you demand nothing from them."

Seanchai turned his gaze on Pyre but said nothing.

Chapter 67

The messenger travelled with them for the rest of the day, though Ahad cautioned against any further discussion. He was keenly aware that there was a band of taragusii in the vicinity and wanted to put distance between them before breaking to camp. Pyre took the first watch that night, and they were all relieved to have a fourth sharing the burden. Seanchai moved to a nearby tree and began the exercises Pyre showed him the day before. When Ahad caught the man watching the Wycaan, Ahad called him over.

"Either get some rest or help me cook. I want to keep the fire brief."

"Is it really him? I can't believe it. Everyone thinks he's dead."

"Come here," Ahad said, lowering his voice. "Cut these mushrooms I found."

The man sat next to Ahad and drew his knife. Ahad leaned in.

"Listen carefully. Seanchai is both here and not here. He has gone through something horrific and isn't himself. We don't know yet the extent of the damage, but what you see right now is a pale shadow of the warrior who saved your village and healed your sister. Tread carefully around him. This will take time, and we need to move slowly."

The man frowned. "But we don't have time," he whispered, agitated. "Prince Shayth has sent rangers out throughout Odessiya. The country is in dire need. We face invasion from—"

"He needs to recover, remember who he is, and face what happened," Ahad said. "I'm not sure you should ask the Wycaan to go north."

"Are you crazy? Odessiya faces an invasion and could be overrun. You think I can go back and tell Prince Shindell that his only real weapon is trying to find himself?"

"This is a delicate situation. We need to coax the old Seanchai out from his shell, and it isn't going to be easy."

The man attacked the mushrooms with a sharpened vigor. "I don't think you understand what the prince is facing. The pictorian leader sent out a hundred boars—pictorians, I tell you—and they were slaughtered with no sign of casualties inflicted on their enemies. This is serious. How can anyone refuse the call to defend the realm?"

Ahad looked up at the Wycaan, still and focused. He shook his head. "I wish I knew."

"I am duty bound to deliver my message. I will talk to Pyre and the Wycaan."

Ahad shrugged. "Let's make this soup. Right now, I'm more concerned with extinguishing this fire before it becomes a beacon to every taragus within a half-day's ride."

When the soup was ready, Ahad called Pyre and Seanchai over. Pyre ate standing up with her back to her companions, still on guard. After he finished eating, Ahad took her place, but stayed near to listen to the conversation.

"What news, then, from the north?" Pyre asked.

The messenger wiped his mouth on his sleeve and took a swig of water. "I thank you for the food, Master Ahad," he began, and Ahad nodded in acknowledgement. "We still don't know who is attacking the pictorians. Whoever it is enters their camps undetected and kills any pictorians who venture north. They slew a hundred boars without any casualties of their own that we could see. It says everything when I tell you that even the pictorians are frightened."

"What is Arad'gug doing about it?" Pyre asked.

"Arad'gug is dead, killed by our prince."

"What?" Pyre and Ahad reacted in unison.

"It is so. I heard the prince took the exiled Umnesilk with him as advisor. A fight broke out between Umnesilk and some of the Ice Clan boars. I believe there were fatalities, and Arad'gug brought the former First Boar to trial. Prince Shayth was so incensed that he told Arad'gug in front of all his court that Umnesilk was a member of his court, so he, Prince Shayth, was responsible for disciplining Umnesilk.

"Arad'gug didn't accept this, so Shayth challenged and killed him in the way of the pictorians. It was a difficult fight, but the prince is a fearsome warrior, quick and skilled. He defeated the First Boar, and now the pictorians must decide who will replace Arad'gug."

"Umnesilk?" Seanchai mumbled, and they all looked to him. He stared up at them, perhaps not realizing he had said it out loud. "Umnesilk?" he repeated. "Who is that?"

"Umnesilk was the First Boar before Arad'gug," Pyre answered. "He led his boars for the Emperor, and you persuaded him to leave the fight at Hothengold. Later, you went and negotiated with the pictorians to enter the alliance. This is why Shayth went north to answer their call for help."

The messenger saw his opening. "This is why Prince Shayth sent messengers to all corners of Odessiya, calling all warriors to go north and answer the threat. He sent me here to seek out the elf warrior Rhoddan and the Wycaan Pyre. He said that he needed the Wycaans by his side and has sent messengers even to the Elves of the West." He looked over at Seanchai, who was staring at the glowing embers. "He talks about you. I have heard him. He says you'd have tried to negotiate to avoid bloodshed, but if you failed, you would lead our nation to victory."

"How can one elf stop an army of unstoppable enemies?" Seanchai asked.

"Because you are not just an elf. I've seen you fight when the northern men and the Ice Clan pictorians attacked the Northern Clans. You're amazing."

"And how many died by my hands during that battle?"

"Hundreds, to be sure," the man answered with ecstatic fervor. "Giants, blue men, pictorians. Anyone who tried to kill our people."

Seanchai stared at him, his eyes hard. "And how many wives did I make widows? How many children did I deny fathers to guide them as they grew up?"

The man hesitated, his cheeks reddening. "These things happen in war," he offered meekly.

"It is *the* consequence of war," Seanchai said.

"Yes. Yes it is."

"I will not turn more children into orphans, and I will not deprive women and elfes of their mates. Not anymore. Tell your prince I am Seanchai the Wycaan in name alone. Tell him that I will find my family and atone for my sins. I will take them far away, to a place that does not know of my violent past and will allow me to live in peace and heal my family and myself."

"I doubt such a place will ever exist for you if you run," Ahad said.

Before Seanchai could answer, the messenger sprung to his feet. "If you do that, you condemn tens of thousands to death with your selfishness," he shouted. "It's true there will be no widows or orphans, but that's only because they'll all be slaughtered. You betray your prince and country."

Seanchai rose slowly. "I have no prince and no country, only a past tainted with death. I must put the ones I deserted first. I will not go north. I will not fight."

CHAPTER 68

Mharina did not remember how she got to her bed or how long she slept. She was aware of someone—Maugwen she thought—waking and feeding her, spooning soup into her mouth and encouraging in soft tones. The same angel held her as she rose to relieve herself and guided her back to bed when her legs buckled. She knew she would not have the energy otherwise.

"Let her sleep," she heard a muffled voice say. "She must process and remember everything. She will recover fully and regain her strength."

It was not just fatigue. Dina's lifeless face, blood trickling from her eyes, nose, and mouth, haunted her dreams. When semiconscious, her thoughts went to Sa'gola. She had killed the Purple Lady's mentor, the venerable partner of Shadona, founder of the Order. She knew how devastated she would be if Sa'gola was fatally hurt, and could only imagine how it felt after apprenticing with someone for decades.

Her times awake were mercifully short and scattered. When she was able to get past the image of Dina dead, she returned in her mind under the lake and recalled the transformational ceremony that she had claimed for herself. She regretted not taking a weapon. Her father had claimed his Win Dao swords there. She wondered what weapon Dina had chosen. But the Room of Words was where Mharina spent most of her dreamtime. She read and reread the words, testing herself, perfecting the intonations, absorbing the power behind the words.

Finally, the day came when she woke and rose by herself. Maugwen led her to the baths and helped her wash. She gasped when she saw her reflection and ran her hands through her Wycaan white hair, such a contrast to her dark skin. They ate their next meal at the table, and Mharina was suddenly ravenous. Maugwen put a hand out and stopped her.

"Take it easy. Your body must get used to food again. You don't stuff yourself after a moon cycle drinking only liquids."

"A complete moon cycle! Is that why I can barely stand?"

"In part," Maugwen said. "But you must also adjust to your body. I massaged your arms and legs twice a day to keep them supple. Your snowy hair is only a part of what's changed. All your muscles have expanded, and you are impressively toned for one who only sleeps. You are thinner, but your chest is, well...."

Mharina stared down at her body. She wore only a flimsy night-shirt and gasped, feeling the tips of her ears burn. Maugwen burst out laughing, and it was a lovely sound.

"Hey," Maugwen said when she had stopped laughing. "Take it from the dumpy girl: you look great. You'll get used to it."

"How is Sa'gola?"

Maugwen sighed. "She left once she knew you were in no danger. Dina was like a mother to her, and quite possibly the only person she ever really trusted. She took it hard and needed her own space to mourn. But she returned two days ago, and we quickened your recovery. As soon as you're ready to leave, we'll depart."

"I would like to see her."

"Then let's get you back on your feet, okay?"

Sa'gola did not ride out with them. After crossing the lake, they were escorted by two armed women in black leather. Neither spoke to Mharina, but she caught them sneaking surreptitious glances. At the mouth of the cave, they stopped and took their time adjusting to the light, even though it was gray and overcast. Their horses waited, grazing nearby. They looked groomed and cared for, and their saddles were already in place, the bags full. One guard pointed to the path on their left and nodded. Then both guards turned and silently retreated back into the cave.

Mharina led the way, and they allowed the horses to set a comfortable pace. She filled her lungs with fresh air. After a full moon cycle underground, the scent of grass and animal was pungent and distinct. When they turned a bend, they saw Sa'gola mounting her horse to take the lead. No words were exchanged, and this filled Mharina with anxiety. Could Sa'gola forgive her, or was she destined to leave and return to Odessiya? Though she desperately wanted to see her mother and siblings, she knew now wasn't the time. She had to learn how to wield the Wycaan magic and balance it with the sorcery.

But beyond the practical need, she was simply not ready to leave her teacher. Yes, she killed Dina, but the old woman had instructed her to do so. She began to feel indignant and glared at Sa'gola's diminutive form in front of her. But a stubborn pride prevented her from saying anything. She was the apprentice. She could wait. Her thoughts turned to Maugwen, who had come hoping for some breakthrough in her own mysterious magic, but it seemed she had done nothing but tend to Mharina.

Mharina was very fond of Maugwen, enjoying her sharp wit and appreciating her dedication to healing. Maugwen came from a poor family. Her father had evaded taxes, spending everything he had on herbs for her ailing mother. They arrested Maugwen for her father's crimes when she was only a young girl and threw her in jail with

Ilana, Shayth, and Rhoddan in Galbrieth. When Mharina's *ahdahr* rescued the others, Maugwen joined them.

Shayth had apparently been somewhat cruel to her, and Rhoddan ambivalent, but her *ahdahr* saw the young woman's potential. Before coming to Grogin, she served in the prince's court and grew very close to Shayth. Even Mharina's mother on Wycaan Island had heard the rumors and wondered about Maugwen's future. Shayth was required to marry a princess, or at least the daughter of a great house. Was his affection for Maugwen the reason he never seemed to settle down?

Deep in such thoughts, Mharina almost rode into her teacher. Her horse whinnied, and she pulled too sharply on her reins, causing another complaint that elicited a glare from Sa'gola.

"We will stay in that entrance tonight," Sa'gola said, pointing to a cave in the jagged hill. "There is a hot water pool there, and I think we all need it."

Mharina almost snapped something regrettably sarcastic back, but Maugwen, as ever, was quick to pick up on the dynamics.

"Sounds great," she chirped.

Sa'gola peered at her, a mystified look on her face. Then she looked at Mharina and, in an uncharacteristically soft voice, added: "It will be an apt place to discuss what happened."

Mharina's anger melted away. "Thank you," she said, and meant it.

Chapter 69

They quickly unsaddled the horses and brushed them down, leaving them loosely tethered to graze comfortably. No one was in a hurry to eat, so they walked into the cave and down a dark corridor. Sa'gola lit a small, purple ball of fire, which flickered eerily on the walls. The path forked, and Sa'gola led them down to the soothing, if somewhat hot, water. It was more metallic than previous pools and, because of the temperature, they alternated between submerging their bodies and perching on the edge.

Mharina began to wonder whether she should begin, but she wasn't sure how. She caught Maugwen casting furtive glances at her and Sa'gola. When their eyes met, Maugwen silently nodded.

"Sa'gola. I'm sorry for your loss. It was never my intention..."

"No, but I think it was hers."

"She coached me before the Testing." Mharina pressed on. "She came and helped me prepare and strategize. She said that if an opportunity arose, I should take everything, because that is what my opponent would do without hesitation."

"Did you know she was the one who would test you?"

"She told me, but only after she imparted what I needed to do."

"I should have guessed. She has been fascinated ever since I first took interest in you. She urged me to take you for my apprentice."

"Did you know she was Wycaan?" Mharina asked.

Sa'gola did not answer immediately, but finally said, "There are secrets between teacher and apprentice. I—"

"I've been inside her head, touched her very essence. I know more than I ever should about her." Mharina regretted the harshness of her tone.

"And that was a sacred journey," her teacher snapped back. "You should never reveal—"

"She's de—"

"I KNOW SHE'S DEAD," Sa'gola cried, and the water bubbled furiously and spurted up in a majestic, hot fountain of pain.

Maugwen gasped, and Mharina lowered her head in her hands. Sobs erupted and echoed throughout the cave. Then Mharina felt herself being guided into the water and her teacher's embrace. She clung to the older woman.

"I'm so sorry," Mharina cried. "I would never do anything to...h-hurt you. I harbored no malice for D-Dina...but it was so unexpected, s-so...To find out that I, t-too...am a Wycaan. She gave me... her rite of passage...She gave me the words, the experience. She...s-sacrificed everything so d-dear to herself, and I took it all. I took her last breath. I k-killed her!"

She continued to cry and shake. Maugwen was behind her now, also hugging her. The waves of grief gradually began to subside, and the three disentangled, seeking relief from the hot water. Perched on the rocks, they sat in brooding silence for a long time. Then Sa'gola spoke, her voice once again composed.

"I'm not sure she woke the Wycaan inside of you, my dear. If it was there, I believe the Wycaans at Grogin would have sensed it. If not them, then certainly the Master. Your father, too, must have been seeking it in you. Why did no one find it? How did it wake?"

Mharina thought for a moment. She allowed herself to sift through the painful confrontation. "She was frustrated and angry at my father for wasting his potential with the *Iyzun*. She vented and hurled insults at him and the Emperor, too. She was so desperate to find something that might stop Ithea, but what she said was so harsh.

"I guess it kind of erupted out of me in an uncontrollable rage. I just kept hearing Dina's advice earlier to take whatever I could from my adversary. So I did..."

As tears welled up again, she paused and took a deep breath. Sa'gola sat silently for a while. Finally she leaned over, and when she spoke, there was awe in her voice.

"I think you took her Wycaan essence. It wasn't your father's legacy, but Dina's. I've never heard of anything like this, but the Wycaan inside of you is Dina's, and she knew exactly what she was doing. She possessed both the male and female powers, but could never bring them both to bear. She must have been so frustrated and then she met you. She set you up to seize the male power inside of her and claim the *Iyzun*. In a sense, Dina lives on inside of you. Take comfort in that, my child. I know I will."

Sa'gola pushed them harder now, eager to return and help Mharina fuse the Wycaan and sorceress energy. Until this was achieved, nothing could be taken for granted. Mharina, for her part, was just as anxious. She wanted to use the Anwar to see if her family was well and, while she would not seek him out with the ancient stone, she wanted to know where Ithea was.

As they rode on, her thoughts turned to the Mushroom Man. She wanted to see him, as well. She wondered if he had found anything out about her family and if he was okay. A wave of guilt rose as she pondered whether something could have happened to him as a consequence of her request. Watching Sa'gola ride in front of her, she wondered what her teacher knew about him. She had clearly had contact with the man. He had alluded to this, himself. Had there been something romantic between them? Was that why Sa'gola had taken such exception?

But Mharina's mind returned to herself. She had changed in these past few months. It wasn't just her Wycaan awakening, but something else. She saw all of her teaching with more clarity. It was all coming together; the elements were becoming a part of her, rather than something she was trying to control. She felt the urge to practice, to summon the fire and water and air. She wanted to feel it coursing through her body again and fuse it with her Wycaan power. She realized that it had become an integral part of her.

Now she understood Sa'gola's sense of urgency. She had to stop herself from pushing her horse forward.

Chapter 70

They had been back at Sa'gola's cottage for three days before Mharina ventured out into the swamp. Since returning, their time had been spent resting and gently exercising. Sa'gola was often found late at night bent over a book, a dusty tome, or a scroll. She was searching for clues on how to fuse the two magics and settled in for a long period of study.

It was on the fourth day that Mharina, returning from bathing in the lake, felt an intuitive urge to check the perimeter. She left her washed clothes on the porch and peered through the window. Sa'gola was hunched at her table, engrossed in a scroll. Maugwen was passing her a mug of tea. Mharina would not be missed. She made her way to the swamp with considerable trepidation. Unlike last time, she was fully focused on the task at hand, barely noticing the two farmers and their cart when they passed. There was no playing with water and mist. She wanted to leave a sign for her Mushroom Man and return.

But as she approached, she sensed he was already waiting. She stopped to see if he was alone. He had his back to her and sat on a log, tending a fire. She saw his straw hat and red cloak, and his wicker basket sat next to him. She stood and watched, intrigued at how his fingers delicately touched his prizes as he checked them for damage and wrapped them in burlap.

Mharina stepped through the barrier, feeling the tingling

sensation move through her body. Quiet so as not to disturb him, she circled to get a better view of his face. She silently folded air around her, disappearing, becoming part of the forest. She was about twenty paces in front of him now, with the fire between them. He had more growth on his face, and his clothes looked more disheveled than before. She wondered if he was hurt, but all she saw suggested a long journey and nothing more. He looked up in her direction, and she froze. His expression went from inquisitiveness to fear. He stumbled cautiously around the fire and stood a dozen paces from her.

"Sa'gola? I can feel your presence. Show yourself. I came back to complete a task. I must speak with Mharina, and soon. I know you don't like me foraging around here, but I promised her."

He paused for a moment, but recorded no response. "Don't be angry with her. You and I can't understand the pull of a family. We don't know the bonds of blood, only loyalty. It's my fault. I cannot refuse her, nor can I get her out of my mind. I have never felt like this about a—"

"Stop," Mharina blurted. "It's me, not Sa'gola."

"Really?" There was a hint of embarrassment in his voice, but it softened. "The Purple Lady trains you well. Will you show yourself? You have me at a disadvantage."

Mharina grounded the elements and offered a genuine warm smile. "It's so good to see..."

She couldn't finish the sentence. The look of horror on his face was...horrendous, destroying the romantic scenarios she had dreamed of.

"What has she done to you?"

Mharina was shocked as he approached cautiously. He stared at her hair and reached out to touch it.

"What happened?" he whispered. "Did she—"

"It's not like that," she protested. "I went...I was tested. I cannot tell you more, only that I am okay and more powerful than even

I dreamed I could be. But it's still me, the silly elfe who laughs at your stories and helps to distribute cookies to your adoring young audience."

He again extended his hand to stroke her hair. She sighed as his hand moved down the side of her head before nestling her cheek in his palm.

"Yes," he said, his voice wavering a bit. "It is still you."

The Mushroom Man stroked her cheek for a few moments and then remembered where he was. He withdrew his hand, half embarrassed, half reluctant to relinquish her skin. He laughed nervously and then invited her to sit on the log with him. He carefully wrapped a yellow mushroom and returned it to the basket with great care. Then he sipped from his wine skin and passed it to Mharina. The wine was rich and fruity. When she handed it back to him, the Mushroom Man tried to smile, but worry furrowed his face.

"I went to Grogin as you suggested, my lady. Along the way, I saw traces of many taragusii marching in all directions. The sorcerer, Ithea, now controls the beasts and has them on a search. They had captured a huge elf warrior and his mate."

"Rhoddan and Pyre?"

"I don't know their names, but she is dark, thin, and beautiful, with a haunted expression and long, black hair. I'm told she fights with a staff."

Mharina frowned. That didn't describe Pyre, and now she was not sure if the elf was Rhoddan.

"What else?" she asked, hoping there was no more.

"Describe your mother to me."

"Why?" She felt her body tense.

"I heard something from someone I don't trust, so I have to make sure."

Mharina described her mother, and the Mushroom Man smiled as she talked. Her description was rich and poignant.

"She sounds as beautiful as her daughter," he said.

"No. She is far more beautiful." She frowned. "And we no longer share the same hair color," she finished quietly.

"If this scum is to be believed, then Ithea has your mother, brother, and sister. But I want to stress that I would be suspicious of anything that spews from his mouth."

He hesitated. "There's more. He spoke of a human couple—a pale woman with dark hair. She has a mate with curly blond hair and a legendary sword."

Mharina wept quietly. "I'm not ready," she mumbled. "I need more time to fuse my magic." Suddenly, a dam burst and the sorrow poured out. "I'm not ready for this. I need...I need...my *ahdahr.*"

She fell into the Mushroom Man's arms, and he held her as she cried, pulling her tighter when another wave took her. They stood like this for ages, and then she looked up at him through swollen, tear-filled eyes.

"I must look a mess," she sniffed.

Mushroom Man looked down at her and smiled. Then he kissed her—not the restrained peck as he had previously, but a full, passionate kiss—and Mharina kissed him back.

CHAPTER 71

T he Prince of Odessiya stood on the battlements the dwarves had hastily erected. There were hints of an approaching dawn through clouds pregnant with snow. A slight breeze succeeded in finding its way under his furs, but he did not pull his cloak tighter. Two guards stood about fifty paces to either side of him. They furtively glanced his way. Shayth had stood here for some time, alone with his thoughts. He needed the space away from his commanders and advisors, none of whom had any idea what they were facing or how to deal with it.

The second army had left Shindellia, but messengers arrived with news of slow progress, Rhoddan's capture, and Pyre's new traveling companion. Shayth couldn't sleep. Rhoddan was imprisoned at Grogin, and Pyre was wandering around with Ahad. *Ahad*! Shayth sighed. After his parents were murdered, General Tarlach and his family had taken in Shayth, including his son, Ahad. Their relationship turned hostile as Shayth spiraled into his violent escapades.

After Shayth killed the older Tarlach, Ahad trained to become a Master Assassin. They had almost confronted each other, but Seanchai convinced Ahad not to fight and, after he killed the Crown Prince, Ahad disappeared. Shayth feared him. He would be a fool not to. Ahad could find and kill him whenever he wanted. Assassins were very effective at their jobs, the Master Assassins almost flawless.

Now he had teamed up with the only Wycaan Shayth could count on for support, and the message at this point became confusing. The messenger claimed to have met a wounded but alive Seanchai, who would not come to help Shayth. In addition, Pyre was not coming to help Shayth because of her loyalty to the Wycaan.

Shayth didn't believe this was true. He could accept that Seanchai was dead far more easily than that he would deliberately disobey Shayth and refuse to come to his aid. Seanchai was far from perfect—none of them were—but he would not betray his friends or his duty. It couldn't be Seanchai; he simply wouldn't act like this.

He heard a familiar whine from behind him and turned. "Here, Azura," he called, slapping his side.

The puppy ran clumsily to him, wagging both its tail and its behind. Shayth bent down and scratched her behind the ears. Azura tried simultaneously to extend her head to allow more scratching and lick her owner's hand. It was easy to name her in this white world when she looked at him with those cold, blue eyes. She followed him everywhere, often getting stuck in the deep snow with her little legs. He was growing to love the pup, despite her eyes constantly reminding him of the impending battle.

It had been nearly a month since he returned from meeting the Ashen Elves. He knew the assault would come soon, and he had no idea how to deal with it. He had, in fact, sent his cavalry south. They were his most impressive asset, but they had nothing to contribute in this terrain. The second army that had set out from Shindellia was still a week away. He should not complain about the wait.

A second line of defense was being established beneath the snow line; Shayth had to hold on long enough to allow the cavalry and the other army to set up defenses before he retreated. And he knew that he would be forced to retreat. The waiting was getting him down, and his men sensed an impending battle and worried leader. He needed to talk to Umnesilk, the reinstated First Boar of the Pictorians, who was resistant to sacrificing their homeland and joining the retreat.

Shayth found a piece of wood and picked it up. "Fetch, Azura," he said, and threw it. The dog watched it rise, fall, and land, then let out a yip of approval and sat down, eagerly waiting for another one.

"Go fetch," Shayth said, ushering her with his hands.

The dog yipped again and wagged her tail, but did not offer the stick more than a cursory glance. Shayth walked over, picked it up, and threw it again. Same result.

"You must train it hard. Samoyed very smart, but need clear instruction."

Shayth turned slowly. He already recognized the voice and this time did not wait for permission to look upon the big Ashen Elf towering over him. He was a powerful specimen, despite his lined face and graying hair. Shayth made a conscious effort to conceal any surprise he felt.

"Welcome," he said, glancing around to see if there were others. "I did not expect another visit."

"Why not? Mage gave you choice, and you not answered her. It only right I sent to hear answer."

Shayth moved closer. The Ashen Elf wore dark armor that paled his skin even more and, at the same time, enhanced the red jewel around his neck. There was no armored protection there.

"What is your name?" Shayth asked, determined to keep the initiative on his own home ground.

"Always strange questions. Why does it matter, not-King?"

"It matters," Shayth replied, "just like it matters to you *not* to call me by my name. I think it makes it easier for you to justify murdering innocent people."

The Ashen Elf frowned. "I fail to see point. We driven by need for revenge. It simple."

"I don't think so. You aren't driven by revenge; otherwise, you wouldn't vent your wrath on innocent races. You feel inferior after being defeated and vanquished, dependent on my uncle to free you.

And now, without his help, you lash out at the nearest victim in the hope of vanquishing such inferiority. Your people act like petulant bullies."

Shayth expected to be ridiculed, but the Ashen Elf just turned, his ice blue eyes staring out into the snowy tundra.

"No," he said at last, his voice measured. "I think you over-simplify. Certainly, trauma of generational incarceration cannot be underestimated, but it more than that. Odessiya ignored and eventually forgot us is the ultimate insult. That is why you all fall to our blades."

"Listen to yourself," Shayth interjected. "You are so intelligent. How can you not see past the barbarian thirst for blood?"

The stone-faced elf slowly smiled. "Surely you, of all people, understand how trauma leads to culture of violence. But I not come to banter with you, not-King. I come to deliver message: give us the elves, and we spare rest of your people."

"You know I cannot do that," Shayth replied. "I told your Mage. I serve and protect all my people, regardless of race."

The Ashen Elf slowly nodded. "Yes, you did, and she understands. The mural is finished. Die well then, not-King. I have enjoyed meeting and talking with you."

"That's it?" Shayth exclaimed. "Just like that? One moment talking and the next, massacring anyone who gets in your way?"

"It is so. We will attack in morning." The Ashen Elf turned to go, but stopped. He turned back, and when Shayth looked into his blue eyes, he thought he saw hesitation. "My name is Criantol, Prince Shayth Shindell."

Then he bowed his head, turned, and disappeared.

Chapter 72

Shayth hugged the mug of hot broth as he sipped it. Dawn was breaking, and his troops were in position. He had slept little since returning to his tent, already summoning the battle rage. He knew from experience that it would keep him going beyond the limits of normal physical exhaustion. When he finished drinking, he moved among the soldiers. He could easily see who was fearful and who wasn't. Most stood stoically, moving only to warm stiff muscles, but a few fidgeted and looked around, seeking solace from those more experienced.

He stopped beside two soldiers who were fervently whispering to each other. When they saw him, they stiffened, as if caught in some mischievous act.

"What do you speak of?" Shayth asked.

The men glanced at each other.

"Answer me," he ordered.

"We made a pact, milord," the older said, not looking Shayth in the eyes. "If one of us gets out of this alive, he'll take care of the other's family."

"Me wife just 'ad our first, milord," the younger said. "I only gotta 'old 'im once."

"What is your family name?" Shayth asked.

"Jewel, milord. Me son is called Shayth, too. 'Ope yeh don't mind."

Shayth smiled. "I am honored, and I will join your pact. If I get out and you don't, Jewel, I will see your wife and son steady."

"Thank yeh, milord." The man smiled. "It's the waitin' that's the worst."

Shayth nodded and patted the man on the shoulder, but he had nothing to add and moved on. Behind him, Azura padded along, careful not to fall under a soldier's boot. The men rubbed her thick fur and played with her. They complimented her piercing eyes, and Shayth wondered whether they would be so affectionate once they saw the similarity with their enemy's eyes.

A horn blew, and Shayth moved quickly to the central ramparts. Through the gloom of the dawn, he began to make out figures approaching. There were not many, he thought—perhaps five hundred. Was this an initial skirmish to assess their adversary's strengths? The Ashen Elves did not hurry, shout, or even seem excited. In the first light of day, they looked eerie and almost surreal, and he felt the unease of his soldiers.

"Steady, men," he shouted. "Archers, prepare and fire on my mark."

He waited, remembering his Weapons Master telling them to refrain from firing until they could see the whites of their enemy's eyes. There would be no whites—only the disconcerting blue—and Shayth would rather spare his men such a sight for as long as possible.

"No one shoots without my order." he called out. Then he turned to the man he had summoned, one of his best archers. "We need to see if our arrows will have any effect," he said quietly. "Choose one and shoot when you know your aim will be true."

The archer drew an arrow and noched it. His movement was smooth and unhurried as he took aim and let fly. The arrow stuck in the elf's armor and quivered from the impact. It was a heavy ash arrow, and the elf staggered back a step, peered at the arrow, wrenched it out, and continued to advance.

"See the elf two to his right?" Shayth asked. "Shoot him, but aim for the throat."

The archer noched again and took aim. He waited a few more moments, and Shayth could now see the elf's blue eyes. The arrow shot up, arched, and fell true. The elf moved his hands to his throat and fell to his knees. He did not rise.

Suddenly, the archer gasped and fell forward, a serrated blade through his chest. Shayth whirled, and his broadsword decapitated the Ashen Elf who stood before him, his head rolling onto the churned snow. It was Criantol, the messenger, and his head rolled to Shayth's feet. The prince felt a pang of grief for the elf, but seeing his best archer staring lifeless, the sentiment swiftly passed.

"On my mark," he cried. "Aim for their throats. Fire."

The whoosh of a hundred arrows cut through the icy morning air, and their trajectory was coordinated and true. Dozens of elves fell to their knees or staggered backwards, but many rose and continued their grim advance.

Shayth grabbed the bow and quiver of his fallen champion and began shooting fluidly. He watched carefully as some Ashen Elves fell and recovered while others lay still. He could not determine why this was and wanted to examine the bodies, but more elves were coming out of the mist. A horn blew and the elves retreated, slowly and almost nonchalantly. There was a feeling of relief among his warriors, but Shayth knew better than to think this would last.

The sun had risen and the mist dissipated when the elves attacked again. This time, they approached behind a wall of huge, interlocking shields. Their movement was disciplined, and there were very few opportunities to shoot through gaps. When they succeeded, the advance barely faltered, and Shayth knew that hand-to-hand combat was imminent.

Huge javelin spears were thrown from within the advance, and Shayth heard groans from his men's first wave of casualties. As the elves reached the walls, Shayth gave the order, and rocks and burning oil were dropped upon them. Fire arrows lit up the advance, and the Ashen Elves' formation was broken. Shorn of their defensive shields and only a few paces from the wall, the archers made short work of those left standing. Cheers went up as an elven horn blew the retreat once more. A few elves managed to grab shields, and the retreat was again organized and without panic. Shayth turned and called to three soldiers.

"Get down there and retrieve the red stones they wear around their necks."

The men scampered down ropes and went to three bodies. Shayth was already giving further instruction to others when he heard the screams. He turned and watched with horror as each man turned gray and crumbled into dust before his eyes, the red stones falling onto the white snow.

Chapter 73

The next assault proved more cautious. As the sun reached its zenith, Shayth began to hear heavy machinery rumbling. Over the ridge in front of them came catapults and other siege weapons. They were pulled by particularly large Samoyed and pushed by elves. It was slow moving them through the snow, but they made steady and unhurried progress. Shayth called his generals to him to confer. Some counseled to attack the machines before they could inflict damage, but most were reluctant to engage the elves in open battle. Umnesilk spoke up.

"Prince, let me take few pictorian warriors and archers with fire arrows. We try first with fire, then if not work, pictorians fight for short time."

Shayth nodded. "But do we need to send in our First Boar?"

"Must," Umnesilk replied, his voice firm, and Shayth recalled how he'd offended Arad'gug by refusing to let him lead a foray.

He looked at Umnesilk's grim expression. "Okay, but name your successor should you fall. He will rule until the end of hostilities without challenges. Clear?"

Umnesilk nodded and turned away, already gathering troops as he walked. Shayth selected his archers, choosing younger men who could run faster. He sent them to change their arrows to the heavier, pitch-laden ones. When they were ready, he and a small group of human and pictorian troops climbed down in front of the wall.

They moved off to the north of the battlefield as a diversion while Umnesilk led his party in a wide loop to the south.

Standing on a ridge, Shayth had his troop change formation every once in a while to keep the elves watching him. When they had exhausted this, he and a pictorian pretended to fight. They moved relatively slowly, and he fended off the boar easily. However, Shayth had failed to mount adequate guards, and suddenly, a man's scream alerted them to an attack by a dozen Ashen Elves.

Shayth and the boar he was sparring with were the first to respond, and the two parties fought desperately. The pictorians' axes were as heavy as the elves', and they stood their ground. The men, however, had a harder time, with even the stronger and more experienced barely able to parry the elves.

Shayth called for them to slowly retreat, but the pictorians either did not hear or disobeyed. He realized that the humans could not retreat alone, and he reluctantly charged back into the fight. Flanked by two of his best guards, Shayth pushed the elves back, killing three. With a gap forming, he called again for the pictorians to close around him and retreat. This time they heeded him, and the fight slowly moved toward the wall.

Once within range, his archers were able to dispose of the remaining Ashen Elves. Shayth saw one's red stone pale as he died. As Shayth climbed the rampart, he determined this was surely the key to something important. Safe on the rampart, he looked over to where smoke rose from two of the catapults. There were still several elves standing, and he could see Umnesilk and his boars in organized retreat, protecting the archers.

More Ashen Elves appeared beside the siege machines, and a horn blow signaled their advance. They moved forward slowly, negotiating the terrain with great deliberation. But they steadily approached, and Shayth could not decide how to meet this new challenge. He had the distinct feeling that the Ashen Elves were simply testing him. This bigger force making a more strategic approach perhaps signaled that the Mage felt she had learned enough.

When the machines stopped and elves began to crank them back to hurl boulders, five archers jumped over the wall, ran to within shooting range, and loosened fire arrows. Shayth watched, wondering who had given the order. It had not been him.

The archers managed to launch one volley of fire arrows, setting two siege machines on fire, before a swarm of javelins flew out to meet them. One machine caught, but the other was extinguished. All five archers lay lifeless, pierced multiple times. It was too high a price to send more, and Shayth called out as five more archers prepared to go. Judging by their expressions, the men were relieved.

"Prepare for an assault," he cried. "This is the first time we engage the Ashen Elves. We will face them with bravery and yield no quarter, because behind us are our families, our wives, and our children, a free people, and we will give everything we have to keep them free. Our enemy is strong and well trained, but we have faced such adversaries before. Be brave and disciplined. They will not breach the wall. We will hold—"

He stopped as the first boulder hurled through the air. The wind whistled its acquiescence to the greater weight and all eyes followed the rock's trajectory. It went over the wall and landed harmlessly behind them, crushing an unoccupied tent.

"That's where mah barrels of ale was!" Ballendir cried in a disgusted tone, and laughter spread along the wall.

Azura whined, but no one went to pet her.

That projectile had been meant to measure distance. Shayth turned back to see several more hurtling through the sky.

"Watch yourselves," he cried as men and pictorians scampered out of the way. All the rocks but one landed on or near the ramparts, but none hit the wall itself. One lone rock fell short, close to where Shayth stood. He glared down at the huge boulder. Where had they come from? Surely, the Ashen Elves had not transported them across the tundra.

The red stones. He had to get hold of one and find out what their magic was. It was the key to everything. The Ashen Elves had not yet unleashed their magic on his army. What were they waiting for? Why were they playing with him?

CHAPTER 74

"Was he there?" Sa'gola asked without looking up from the book she was studying.

Mharina took some tea from the pot and came to sit opposite her teacher. She didn't answer until Sa'gola peeled her eyes from the heavy tome. Seeing her student's distress, she leaned forward.

"You heard bad news? What did your beloved discover? Another woman?"

Mharina ignored the jibe. "Ithea has Rhoddan and an elfe."

"Pyre?" Maugwen asked, coming quickly to join them.

"It doesn't sound like her," Maugwen replied, "but there's more. He thinks Ithea might have my mother and the twins."

"Thinks? Might?" Sa'gola accompanied this with an arched eyebrow.

"He doesn't trust his source, but the man described my mother and some companions."

"Who else?" Maugwen asked.

"Montclair and Riona."

Sa'gola nodded and turned to Mharina. "Listen carefully. You have the potential to change everything. You are one of only two living beings to balance *Iyzun*, except you haven't learned to control it yet."

She turned to Maugwen. "I only know this elf warrior, Rhoddan, by reputation. If he could speak to Mharina, what would he say?"

Maugwen winced. "Rhoddan would tell her not to come and rescue him until she was ready."

"As I thought."

"But," Maugwen continued, "it isn't just Rhoddan. The twins change everything."

"Why?"

"They're my family," Mharina answered with the same terseness. "Isn't that enough?"

Sa'gola glared at her, but Maugwen cut in.

"You sensed that Senzia has great power, and that probably means Ilan does, too. You said their power made Seanchai dispensable." Maugwen glanced apologetically at Mharina for revealing that.

Sa'gola sighed deeply. When she spoke next, her voice was soft. "Everything I told you about your father is true. I did not go with intent to kill him. I was under orders to bring him to Grogin."

Mharina felt the tears welling up, but she needed to stay strong and focused. "If he was here," she said, her voice quivering, "he would know what to do to help me. Then he would go save his family, because family means everything to him, as it does to me."

"It also made him careless and vulnerable, and he is now dead for it." Sa'gola took a deep breath, looking at her hands entwined on the table in front of her. When she next spoke, her voice was again soft, almost pleading. "Don't make the same mistakes he did. I cannot face Ithea until I know we have an advantage, until I know we can win. Right now, that depends on these scrolls." She smacked her hand on the one that was open, and a cloud of dust floated up. Perhaps you should be helping me." She thrust a heavy, leather-bound book at Mharina.

"What are we looking for?" Mharina asked.

Sa'gola stared at her and, for the first time, Mharina saw fear in her teacher's eyes.

"You don't know, do you?" Mharina couldn't hide her shock. "You have no idea where to go with this, or what to seek. You're grasping for straws." She felt a wave of nausea as the reality hit her. "Sa'gola! I need to hear that you have some idea what you are looking for."

Sa'gola just stared back. Mharina looked to Maugwen, usually so composed but now pale as she also stared at their teacher.

"Sa'gola," Mharina ventured, her heart thumping in her ears. "Who can help me? Is there anyone in the Order?"

Sa'gola shook her head slowly. "Only those who are dead could help us."

"Can we get in touch with them?" Maugwen asked, completely serious.

Sa'gola again shook her head. "We don't mix with the dead, and the wisdom they take to the grave is closed to us, as their knowledge is too unwieldy."

"Perhaps I can help," Maugwen said. "When I lived in the monastery as a healer, I assisted in a few of their ceremonies. I know it's not the same, but it might help."

They stood before the fire, three women wrapped in black cloaks, their faces buried deep in their cowls. The fire hissed and crackled, an angry, wild animal, untamed and proud. Mharina could not make out the words that tumbled from Maugwen's mouth, but the bitter herbal concoction she had ingested was taking its effect. Sa'gola's hands moved in a blur, conjuring up a thickening veil of air. There was a sizzling vibrancy around her. Mharina built her own cone of power, the colors surrounding her becoming muted.

Then Sa'gola was no longer there, and Maugwen's words were a distant echo. Mharina walked in a stone cave, following a path that gently descended. She saw symbols she did not recognize on the walls, and she shivered as it became increasingly cold. She created a small ball of fire to give herself both warmth and light to see her way. She wore only her black training vest beneath her cloak, and she rubbed herself with her free hand. Thick, cold air puffed in front of her as she exhaled. The cold pierced her bones, and she directed more energy into the fireball.

In front of her, the path ended at an arched stone entrance with the head of a lion carved on one side and a dragon's on the other. As she approached, mist rose and began to take form. By the time she reached the entrance, a heavyset old man, his skin almost translucent, stood before her, holding a staff of blackened wood with an orange gem at either end. Mharina could not take her eyes off the staff. It had marks all the way up, symbols that she did not recognize—runes, maybe.

The man glared at her. "Who dares disturb the sleep of the dead? Speak now and make every word count, for the dead stand in judgment of the living, and you won't leave if your reasons are frivolous."

CHAPTER 75

M harina could feel a rich power emanating through the staff. "Who are you?" she asked, trying to keep her voice steady.

"If you do not know, then you should not be here. You tread on thin ice, child."

Child! "I am Mharina, eldest *calhei* of Seanchai, the Wycaan Master. I must speak with him."

"Must?" The old man scratched his grizzled face. "A child comes here because she misses her dead father? Do you think every child should traverse the bridge between dead and living because they miss their parent? Leave fast, child, for already my anger stirs."

Mharina felt her own anger rising. "I care little for your anger or your objections. The land of Odessiya is in danger, its people again on the brink of slavery."

"The dead care not for the trials and tribulations of the living. You waste your time and mine. Now leave me while I still—"

"My father will care. He won't turn his back on me or his people."

"He is no longer your father, child. He won't care. This is the last time I tell you. Turn around."

"My father," Mharina hissed, her voice firm. "Now."

She felt the power being summoned as the staff began to glow, symbol by symbol, lit up with a familiar orange. She stared at it, mesmerized.

"Where did you get that staff?" she demanded.

"I do not answer to the likes of you," the doorman said. "I will not suffer—"

Orange fire erupted out of her hand and fused with the staff, crackling and hissing streams of bright orange fire. The earth shook, and sparks bounced off the walls. She heard other voices, but could not tell who they were.

"You will suffer me, for the need of my people is great," Mharina roared, her voice riding her power. "Summon my father."

"Break your fire," he yelled back, and Mharina did so, whispering the word *Alye* under her breath.

When the fire was grounded, the staff was in her hand, warm and glowing. The old man looked stunned, and there was fear in his eyes.

"It is not possible," he whispered. "You have both?"

"Yes," she boomed, the power surging through her. "Now, my father!"

Three figures appeared behind the old man, though Mharina only recognized one of them.

"Dina?" she said. "I'm so sorry."

"Hello, sweet thing. Do not be sorry. I was always the master of my own destiny. What brings you to wake the dead? Why do you fight the Keeper of the Keys?"

"And by what rights do you take my staff?" another woman said, and Mharina saw she and Dina held hands, fingers interlocked.

"Shadona?" Mharina whispered.

"Isn't it obvious?" the third said to her friend as she removed her hood to reveal Wycaan-white hair and round ears. "You no longer have need of it, Shadona."

Shadona stepped forward and approached Mharina. Even dead, she cut an imposing figure. "Did you come seeking a weapon, child?"

"No," Mharina said, her voice a quiet tremor. "And I am a *calhei* no more. I seek my father. I need to learn to fuse my sorceress and Wycaan magic."

"Your father has not reached us," the human answered, "or I would know it."

"Are you Ilana?"

"No, dear. Ilana was an elfe like you, though she does walk among us. I was your father's first teacher, and I am honored that you are named after me."

"Mhari," Mharina gulped.

"Your father is not among us," Mhari repeated. "But you stand before the three of us. Shadona was an *Iyzun*, and Dina held the potential inside of her. Ask, then, for what you need."

"I must fuse the energy I received from Dina with that awakened in my studies with Sa'gola."

"I think you already have, judging by how you disarmed the Keeper of the Keys," Mhari said, and the three laughed while the doorkeeper scowled.

Shadona extended her hand. "My staff, please."

Mharina hesitated. The staff's energy hummed through her. "Why was I able to feel *Iyzun* with your staff?"

"Why, indeed?" Shadona asked, keeping her hand extended. "You tell me."

"You were *Iyzun*, and your magic flows through the staff," Mharina answered, gripping it tighter.

"Give me my staff, Mharina," the woman said, a cold edge in her voice.

"No," the young elfe said. "Please. Give it to me with your blessing. I can fuse the magics through your experience and imprint in the staff."

"And then you will use it to try and kill my son?" Shadona was closing cautiously now, her body braced to attack.

"He wants to kill me and Sa'gola. He has my mother and siblings. You know what he turned out to be," Mharina said. "I must confront him, and I cannot lose."

"He is my son."

"And he killed you while you fought to defeat him."

"Perhaps I did not try hard enough," Shadona snarled.

"You created this monster, hid him, and watched as he killed so many of your Order. Let me right your wrong."

"My staff!" Shadona flicked a hand, and the staff began to move to her.

"*Alye,*" Mharina responded, mustering all the authority she could. The staff froze in midair, halfway between them. The staff lit up, one rune after another, as fire sizzled along its length. "Shadona. Will the staff help me? Tell the truth."

"He is my son," Shadona cried as tears ran down her cheeks.

Suddenly, Shadona was inside Mharina's head. *He is my son. How can I—*

Because you know it to be the right thing. Mharina pushed back and felt herself extending through the staff and into Shadona. *Because you know it must be done, and maybe I am the only one standing between Ithea and his terrible vision.*

You will not prevail. He is experienced with Iyzun. All you possess is untried and muddled.

But your staff will give me your clarity.

Mharina struggled to advance into the woman's head, but Shadona resisted.

"Don't force me to take it from you," Mharina cried. "Please. I did it to Dina. I don't want to—"

Then you have not heeded Dina's sacrifice, and you will fail. I will not give—

"I WILL NOT BE DENIED," Mharina screamed, and her inner fire ignited.

Riding its burning drive, she advanced deep inside Shadona's head, and the woman's memories and words flew into her. The world was two shades of orange, but as Mharina advanced, the lighter one paled and she drew more strength, more power, and then the staff was in her hands. She clenched it tightly, and her knuckles paled with the strain.

"I WILL TAKE MY FATHER'S PLACE," she roared. "I WILL PROTECT SA'GOLA AND MY FAMILY, AND I WILL SERVE ODESSIYA IN HIS PLACE."

"Swear it!" Mhari roared.

"ASHBAR!" Mharina cried, and the world exploded into a bright orange ball. Then everything went dark.

Chapter 76

When she woke, Mharina had a blinding headache and a charred staff with orange stones at each end. She grimaced from the former and clutched the latter with all her strength. She was blindfolded. She heard Sa'gola's soothing voice but could not distinguish the words. Warmth emanated from Sa'gola's hands as they pressed gently on her face. Then she fell asleep and woke only when hunger roused her. She was still wearing the blindfold, but the intense pain had been replaced by a dull ache. Maugwen spoke to her as she helped her rise and sit against a rock.

"Drink some broth," Maugwen said, placing a spoon in her hands.

The soup was warm and smooth. The mushrooms that flavored the soup filled her with images of her Mushroom Man. He had left to return to the town and offload his harvest. Then he would join her, he had promised.

"Sa'gola?"

"She left. She was in a great hurry after she saw your staff. Pretty neat. What happened?"

Mharina started to answer, but yawned and was immediately dismissed to sleep. When next she woke, Sa'gola was back. They were eating, and Maugwen removed Mharina's blindfold. It was night, and she felt only the slightest ache. Sitting against a tree trunk, she sipped her soup and waited for it to take effect. Sa'gola had brought some bread, and they dipped it into their bowls.

"I know that staff. It was generous of Shadona to give it to you, especially considering it is her son who will feel its wrath."

"She didn't actually give it to me," Mharina replied, fearing Sa'gola's reaction.

"You took it by force? How?"

Mharina chewed her top lip.

"You could not have...unless...Mharina. What happened? Was it the same as with Dina?"

Mharina nodded as she felt the tears well up. "I couldn't help it. Once she knew I had the *Iyzun*, she became protective of it because she realized I posed a challenge to Ithea. She tried to enter me, and I repelled her."

"You did more than repel her. You learned from Dina to show no mercy and take what you need. Am I correct?"

Mharina nodded and clutched the staff as if her teacher was about to take it away from her, like a parent confiscating a toy wrongly wrestled from another kid.

"I want to hear more," Sa'gola said, and there was awe in her voice.

"There is more," Mharina said, "but it does not concern Shadona. It concerns my father."

Sa'gola stiffened. "What did he say? Remember, people sometimes change when they pass over."

"It's not what he said," Mharina replied. "It's that he wasn't there to say anything. I met the teacher I'm named after. She said she would know if he was there."

Sa'gola sighed and reached out to stroke Mharina's arm. "I can't explain why he wouldn't see you. I don't understand the ways of the dead. But maybe he felt he couldn't face you so soon after...He failed you and the twins, Mharina, and I am sure that cuts deeper than the fire I sent into him."

"You would like that to be the explanation, wouldn't you?" Mharina snapped, ignoring the flash of anger in Sa'gola's eyes. "But there is another option. Perhaps—"

"NO!" Sa'gola yelled, then swallowed hard. "No, Mharina, there is no other option. No man can survive the pure white fire, not even a Wycaan Master, not even your father. Please don't walk down such a hopeless path. It is long and dark."

Mharina stared at her but said nothing, and the dark night enfolded each of them.

They returned to the cottage in the night. It was easier on Mharina's eyes, and she fell on her cot as soon as they arrived. She woke to shuffling in the kitchen. It was dark outside, and she was pretty sure it was still a long time until dawn. Again, there was a noise of feet and then cups scraping. A small purple flame ignited, and a pot was put to boil. There was a heavy sigh and a gasp of frustration.

Mharina rose and wrapped her blanket around herself. Barefoot, she moved silently across the floor, the cold stone waking her up. Sa'gola sat hunched at the table, seemingly asleep, an empty cup in her hands. Mharina took the cup from her, and she jerked awake.

"Thank you," Sa'gola mumbled when Mharina returned her cup, now filled and steaming.

Sa'gola looked awfully disheveled and, as Mharina eased into the chair opposite her, she felt a wave of concern.

"What happened?" she asked at last. "Where did you go?"

"Grogin."

"Did he sense you?"

"Yes."

"Are you hurt?"

"No. Just exhausted. It's harder each time to elude him. And now he knows that we know."

"Know what?" Mharina asked.

"He has your mother, brother and sister, the big elf and his mate, and several others I recognized."

There was a long silence as both stared into their hot drinks. Maugwen joined them.

"Sa'gola," Mharina said, her voice soft and apprehensive. "You know I must go. My family is everything to me."

Sa'gola nodded but still stared into her cup.

"I won't ask you to come with me," Mharina continued. "I don't want you to face Ithea and risk what he did to you in the past."

"You are my apprentice," Sa'gola said, and yawned. "We made a commitment to each other. Would you stay behind and let me go face him alone?"

Mharina shook her head without hesitation, and Sa'gola reached across the table and took her hands. They fell into an intimate silence.

"We should sleep," Sa'gola said at last. "We will prepare tomorrow and then have a good night's sleep. The day after, we ride for Grogin."

"Thank you," Mharina whispered, and squeezed her teacher's hand.

CHAPTER 77

T he Wycaan stood in meditation, as he did for hours now when they weren't traveling. It was the only time he looked serene, but Pyre could tell it was different than in the past, because she had watched him reverently so many times. He came to the great Forest of Markwin to study with the Elves of the West, but had, in turn, taught them a vital lesson. He won the support of the greatest teachers and students, not because of his physical prowess, but because of his values and spirit.

He moved into the fifth position, his hands by his side and palms facing down. He sighed deeply, and she felt his pain. But most of all, she knew his spirit was defeated. What happened to him? He said he had no recollection of his defeat by the Purple Lady. Was he guilty about the massacre of his students on Wycaan Island or that he had failed his family?

Pyre frowned to herself as Seanchai transitioned into the first position, his palms now facing his sides. He had no memory of any of these things. He would not recognize Sellia or his children if they walked up to him. Something else was holding him back, and Pyre became certain that this needed to be unlocked before he could recover.

"Wycaan!" she cried impulsively. "Draw your swords!"

He opened his eyes, momentarily annoyed at being disturbed, but then his expression became curious. Pyre approached, drawing her Win Dao swords, and he instinctively drew his. She leaped at him, swinging first one sword and then the other in a slow but deliberate motion. He responded smoothly, if unenthusiastically. She attacked with both swords in a graceful combination of overcuts and side-swipes. His reactions were not as fluent as hers, but his body recalled long-practiced regimes.

She began to incrementally speed up, switching forms and adding undercuts and feints. He met her moves, but made no attempt to counter or try to unbalance her. She even allowed him a couple of openings, and he did not take them. Feeling her anger rising, Pyre led him to defend on his left, abruptly swinging a side kick with her boot, which connected to his ribs. He snorted and glared at her.

"Got a problem?" she sneered, but he just rolled his eyes.

She did it again moments later, ducking and twisting to hit him in the back with the hilt of one of her swords. He staggered forward, but then just turned and raised his swords. His lack of expression in-furiated her, and she launched a fast combination that ended with her ducking under his guard and elbowing him hard in the jaw. This sent him reeling to the ground, and when he rose, blood trickled from the corner of his mouth. He touched the blood with his forearm and stared at the wet, red mark on his skin. Then he resumed his stance.

"What's wrong with you?" she hissed.

"Everything," he replied. "Maybe you can beat it out of me. It's the Wycaan way, no?"

"You have no idea. You might be a pathetic mess, but the Wycaan way is a noble path, and you forged and raised it to new heights."

"That was in another lifetime."

"No, it was in this one. You just lost your spine. That's fine, but don't belittle what you achieved. Many wonderful people stood by you and helped you achieve it. They paid a high cost and did so with pride. You have not lost what they did. You did not suffer as they did. You are alive and whole. You have a wonderful mate and *calhei*, amazing *calhei* who worship you and will one day take the torch from you, the torch you lit and brandished with pride. You have entire races of elves and dwarves all thankful that you set them free.

"You can do what you like now, but don't cheapen the Wycaan Master I followed when I was a *calhei*, the one I left my home and family for to help realize a crazy dream. Don't diminish the elf I dedicated my life to. Don't taint his memory—not for me or Sellia, not for Mharina or Senzia or Ilan."

He stared at her, and she felt pain rising up through her body.

"Your teachers are looking down on you: Mhari and Master Oxnyei and the Weapons Master. The dreamwalker, Denalion, who gave his life for Sellia and me; they are all wondering when you became such a selfish, sorry elf."

She was shouting now but couldn't stop. "In two days, we will arrive at Grogin. I will face the taragusii and Ithea, and I will die trying to rescue your best friend. I don't mind dying for my friends or for freedom or to stop evil, but do you know what makes me sad about it? Knowing that the elf I followed and believed in gave up because he didn't have the backbone to carry on, because he felt sorry for himself despite the riches he accrued and I didn't.

"He became a Wycaan Master and I didn't. He fell in love and I didn't. He had beautiful *calhei* and I didn't. He fulfilled his dreams and freed his people. I just followed him into battle and then discovered he wasn't there. And I will pay for that with my life. I will die with grace, but what pains me is knowing that you just gave up on those who taught you, sacrificed for you, and loved you."

She turned and walked to a rock overlooking a valley. She didn't want him to see her cry. She didn't want him to know how much she cared and how hurt she was. But then she was sobbing, and her whole body was racked with grief. Her swords clattered to the ground as he pulled her into his huge chest and held her.

"Don't give up on the Wycaan yet," Seanchai whispered. "Maybe he's still inside somewhere."

CHAPTER 78

"There it is," Ahad said as the three of them stared across the valley at the looming fortress of Grogin. "I guess now is as good a time as any to come up with a plan."

It really was an impressive sight, black volcanic rock, smooth and shining where it met the mountain. A sparsely populated valley was nestled in front of it, an agricultural hub fed by a river that wound through the center.

"We tried to use an entrance off to the side," Pyre said. "That way, I think."

"What happened when you got through?"

"We didn't. They had set a trap for us."

"That's encouraging," Ahad grimaced.

"They knew we were coming. This time is different. We'll wait for dark."

Pyre led them to a small cave, where they rested. It was the cave she, Sellia, Montclair, and Riona had used. She found the black polish Montclair used to blacken their weapons and buckles, and she wondered how he and Riona were faring. Were they still together? Were they even still alive?

A few hours later, with blackened weapons and faces, she led them out of the cave and down into the valley. The fields they passed were dark and, if there were dwellings, they were invisible in the night. She led them parallel to the path that hugged the walls. She wasn't exactly sure where the cave entrance was, and she recalled that last time, there were taragusii patrols. But they encountered no one.

They crouched at the entrance to the cave, straining to see if there were guards. Finally, Ahad took a rock and threw it further along the path. No one came out to inspect, and he stood up and signaled for them to proceed. Pyre led them up to this point, but no one knew what was waiting inside, so Ahad took the lead. They came upon a small, closed, wooden door, and he stared at the hinges. Then he took a small vial of oil from his cloak and dabbed it on them and the door handle. He cautiously opened the door and nodded, satisfied by its silence.

They passed through, and Ahad closed it with the same care he'd opened it with. It took a few moments to adjust to the darkness, but they were soon ready to move. Pyre grabbed Ahad's shoulder and leaned him into her.

"I think this path leads to the kitchens," she whispered, and he nodded his acknowledgement.

They soon began to hear voices and the bustle of labor. An aromatic cacophony of smells tantalized them as they drew closer. Ahad signaled for them to wait, and he moved forward by himself. This was his territory, though he had never stepped foot in this castle. As a Master Assassin, he knew how to extract information silently and persuasively.

Lurking in a dark corridor, he soundlessly dragged a young woman into the dark, holding his hand over her mouth. "I'm a Master Assassin and can kill you right now in over two hundred and sixty ways. I have no intention of hurting you as long as you do not shout, scream, or in any way give me away. Nod if you understand."

It took a few moments before she complied. Ahad slowly removed his hand but kept her in front of him.

"You are going to lead me to the dungeons. Do you know where they are?"

"Y-yes," she whispered. "I'm about to take food to the prisoners, but there will be two of us."

"That's fine. I'll follow. Neither of you will know I'm there. Which corridor will you go down?"

She pointed to the one adjacent to where Pyre and Seanchai hid.

"Good," he said. "No one will get hurt if you just go about your business, then. Understand? But know I'll be watching."

She nodded, and he gave her a gentle push. It was a little while before she and another kitchen maid carried a large bucket between them into the corridor to the dungeon. Ahad followed closely while Pyre and Seanchai crept a dozen paces behind. The passage led downward and curved. It was getting hotter, and Ahad was already sweating. Finally, the women entered a cavern and spoke to the guards, who poked fun at their hats and uniform, not-so-subtly insinuating that they would be better off without such clothes. When the women passed back through with two other empty buckets, they wore relieved expressions.

As they approached, Ahad knelt close to the ground and covered himself with his cloak. They never saw him or the Wycaans. Still crouching, Ahad peered into the cavern. He counted six guards: four hovering around a small fire contained in a metal bowl and two others standing several paces away. He signaled to Pyre that he wanted them to take out the four, and then made his way silently around the cavern. When he stood just a few paces from the two men, he shot one with a dart from a blow tube and the other with his small, one-handed crossbow. Both darts were tipped with a paralyzing poison, and the guards slumped slowly to the ground. He turned to the other four just in time to see Pyre step up to them.

"Hello, boys," she said sweetly before cutting all four down with two strokes from each of her Win Dao swords.

Ahad rummaged around the bodies, searching for keys. Finding what he wanted, he led Pyre into the cavern. They passed quickly between cells until they found Rhoddan and Troja. But they were not alone.

"Montclair!" Pyre exclaimed, earning an angry hiss from Ahad. When she next spoke, it was in a whisper. "Ahad, this is Montclair and Riona. What are you doing here?"

"Ithea caught us on our way west," Riona whispered. "He has Sellia and the twins, but I think they have quarters somewhere."

Rhoddan stepped forward, his body stiff and his cheeks puffy, but when he spoke, his voice was calm. "Is it just the two of you?"

Before Pyre could answer, Ahad jumped in. "Yes," he said, his tone firm.

Pyre turned and stared behind her. There was no one else there.

Chapter 79

He followed the serving girls back through a maze of stone corridors. Though he was a huge elf, he walked silently, his hood drawn over his head. He did not use any special stealth technique or Wycaan magic; he wouldn't know how. He just followed the women and soon joined other men and taragusii, all hungry and more intent on food than conversation.

The eating hall was large, with long wooden tables and benches. A series of stone blocks held mounds of food. He followed the line and filled a tray. Beyond the food table was a smaller hall, and Seanchai stopped and stared at the back of an elfe and two *calhei* sitting opposite facing him. One of the *calhei*, an elfe with white hair, stared over at him for a moment and frowned.

A fortune sword pushed the elf impatiently, and he resumed taking food. With his plate laden, he searched for a seat that would offer a view into the smaller hall. He found one at the end of a table of taragusii. He could feel their furtive glances on him and realized that the humans and taragusii sat at separate tables. He ignored them, appearing to stare into his food, and they let him be.

The hall went abruptly silent, and Seanchai saw all eyes move toward the entrance of the hall behind him. He allowed himself a cursory glance and saw a tall, pale figure, bald and with piercing red eyes, glide through the hall. He ignored the greetings of the fortune swords and barely glanced at the taragusii, who lowered their own gazes as he passed. The man, if that was what he truly was, emanated a power that felt vaguely familiar.

Ithea, Pyre had called him. He ignored the table of food and went to sit with the elves in the other room. The taragusii and fortune swords returned to their eating, and the hum of conversation resumed. Seanchai watched Ithea stand and address the elves. The older elfe rose and turned to face him. She was a dark-skinned elfe, beautiful, with long, dark, curly hair. She wore a thin, sleeveless vest, and her muscles were toned. She stared up at Ithea, her expression defiant and hard.

Whatever he said seemed first to give her hope, but then she slumped back into her seat. Ithea drew a chair next to her and continued to talk, both to her and the *calhei*. Seanchai desperately wanted to hear what was being said, and the word *keshev* formed and left his mouth.

"They, too, will be here soon," Ithea rasped. "It seems that everyone wants to rescue you. That's nice, but a fool's task. I'm surprised that Sa'gola would fall for this. I think your daughter is making her soft."

"Perhaps they are simply ready to confront you," the female *calhei* said, her voice defiant as she hooked a white strand of hair behind a pointed ear.

"They will never be ready," Ithea replied. "You, on the other hand, Senzia, could become that threat. I feel it in you. But to defeat me, you will need to be the best, and to be the best, you must learn from the very best...and that would be me."

"Why would you teach me if I was then going to use it against you?" Senzia asked.

"It is a strange desire to take on an apprentice and train them even at such inherent risk. Look at your sister. Her teacher murdered your father when she was only told to bring him here. Yet your sister shuffles after her like a pathetic puppy. Do you think Sa'gola has not considered that she might try to take revenge for your father's murder? Yet she takes the risk in the hope that the strong bonds between master and apprentice will prevail."

"My *calhei* will be trained by Wycaan Masters," the older elfe snapped.

Ithea just smiled. "How did that work for Mharina? Did you lovingly consent that she go and study with the murderer of your mate?" He turned again to Senzia. "The choice is yours as long as my offer remains open. I am, luckily for you, a very patient man."

Senzia did not answer, and this seemed to agitate her mother. Ithea rose, laughing at the discord he had sown. "Join me in the council hall when you finish eating. I think we shall greet our guests there."

"Do you think I'll study with you if you kill my sister?" Senzia blurted out.

Ithea stopped and slowly turned around. "It will make your decision more difficult, but you need to think strategically, my young elfe. When I've finished with her and the witch, there will be no one left to fight me. You will be the only one with any potential." He glanced at her brother, who looked away. "And backbone."

Seanchai couldn't see clearly, as Ithea had his back to him, but there was some kind of nonverbal interaction between Senzia and the male *calhei*.

"Make your choices strategically, not emotionally, Senzia. Maybe I will train your brother, but he's different than you, despite your bond. Don't make the same mistake your father did or that Sa'gola is making now."

With that, he turned and walked out. Seanchai focused on his plate again as Ithea strolled out of the hall. The elf's breath caught in his chest. His family sat a few dozen paces away, despondent and without hope. He could just stand and walk over and sweep them up in his arms. He felt a flood of emotions that did not need to feed on non-existent memories. This was his family, and he had to rescue them.

He watched them stand and leave the hall. Again, Senzia glanced over at him, but he remained motionless until they were past him. Then he rose and carefully followed them.

Chapter 80

T he Mushroom Man was waiting for them in the mining town. Mharina found him showing different mushrooms to an enthralled group of children. She leaned against a pillar and felt a wave of love as she saw the creases on his face disappear. She had argued fiercely with Sa'gola about whether or not to take him with them. Sa'gola refused to impart any information, but she clearly did not trust him. Mharina was infuriated that her teacher was holding something back.

"If it is so important that it might harm me, then why not tell me?" she implored.

"Because I swore not to. Only he can reveal his past to you, and he is too afraid to do so."

"Why?"

"Because he will lose you if you have any sense still left in your head."

They glared at each other while Maugwen stepped carefully around them, packing a few extra salves and ointments into her bag.

"Mharina," Sa'gola said at last. "There is one condition by which he can join us. If he turns on you, me, or Maugwen, or if I suspect he endangers us in any way, I will kill him. And you must accept my judgment, because it's likely there'll be no time for discussion."

Mharina stared at her teacher, her jaw dropping open. "You would not do that lightly?"

"No. If I wanted him dead, he would be already, a long time ago. Is my condition clear?"

Mharina nodded.

"Good," the Purple Lady said. "If we have finished with the topic, please close your mouth."

Now, Mharina watched him and once again wondered about the past he shared with Sa'gola. There had been no option but to agree. Sa'gola had not hesitated in coming with Mharina, facing her worst fear by confronting Ithea.

A child stood in front of Mharina, holding up half a cookie. "This is for you," she lisped through gaps in her teeth. "Will you marry the Mushroom Man? I think you will. You're the only grown up that he shares his cookies with. You must be very special."

Mharina took the cookie and bent down to give the girl a hug.

"Your hair smells so good, and I love that it's white and your skin's black."

"Thank you," Mharina said, not sure how to respond.

The little girl ran back to the other children, and soon the Mushroom Man stood next to Mharina.

"I need to collect my bags and sleeping roll," he said as they walked through the market. "It will be a difficult goodbye for my grandparents, but I want them to meet you. Then they'll understand why I must go."

The old man and woman were waiting and hugged her, exclaiming how beautiful she was, though Mharina was sure her appearance mystified them. The old woman had packed a third bag full of food, which the Mushroom Man was loath to take, but did.

"This is food they need for themselves," he said, and as they walked away, Mharina saw tears in his eyes. She hooked her hand around his arm and squeezed.

"I don't think I'll ever see them again," he said solemnly. "I always thought I'd be here to ease them through to the next world. They've been together since they were your age."

Mharina wondered, not for the first time, how old he was.

"How did you persuade the Purple Lady to let me come along?" he asked.

Mharina grimaced. "Err. It wasn't easy."

"Did she tell you anything about me?"

"No. She said it was for you to tell me when you are ready."

"That's very nice of her. Did she also tell you she'd kill me if I endanger any of you?"

Mharina didn't answer, but she was pretty sure the tips of her ears were glowing red. The Mushroom Man released an easy laugh.

"I'm sure she did. I bet it was a condition." When Mharina reluctantly nodded, he turned to her and his face went serious. "Mharina, I want you to promise me something, too. If I do endanger either of you or your family, then don't wait for her to strike me down. You do it."

"What are you talking about?" She tried to laugh, but it came out a half-strangled squeak.

"Sa'gola sets her conditions for good reason. Promise you won't let me cause your demise. It's really important to me. I'm coming with you mainly because I…I think about you all the time, and no one has ever made me feel like that. But part of what drives me is that you have a family and are willing to risk it all for them. I never had such an opportunity. Promise you won't let me ruin it for you."

"Okay," she replied hesitantly, her unease growing.

They walked on in silence, and only when they saw Sa'gola, Maugwen, and a half-dozen horses waiting did something occur to her.

"You didn't bring your basket."

He laughed. "I feel almost naked without it, but I don't think I'll have much time to forage mushrooms where we're going," He turned to Sa'gola and bowed his head. "A horse? I thought you'd make me run behind you."

Sa'gola cocked her head. "If you don't behave yourself, I might still."

He laughed as he attached his bags to one of the geldings, and Mharina again was left wondering about their relationship. She sighed as she mounted a gray horse and patted the side of its neck. The horse, a mare, shook its mane, and its body quivered as it adjusted to her weight. Mharina adjusted the staff across her back, now concealed in a hastily sewn burlap sack.

"We'll ride fast," Sa'gola announced, "and take some shortcuts. There are still taragusii patrols everywhere, and we don't want to announce our arrival." She turned to Mharina. "You ride with your hood up during the day and show your talents only if there's no other choice. Your staff remains covered at all times. If Ithea finds out about it, he will begin to piece things together. I know how he thinks. Our one chance lies in the surprise you have for him. Don't give it away. To Grogin."

Then she turned her horse and led them out of the mining town.

Chapter 81

A dark, threatening storm finally broke toward the end of the day and forced them to seek cover. Sa'gola had been trying to reach a small hamlet, but several bolts of lightning made the horses so jittery that they sought shelter in the barn of a small farm. They had not even unsaddled the horses when three men entered. The oldest of the three had a white beard and brandished a pitchfork. The two younger men behind him each held cudgels, rivulets of rain dripping off them.

"Who be you?" the old man snarled. "This be my barn."

Sa'gola signaled for the others to stay back and approached the farmer. He was only a little taller than she was, but his farmhands loomed over her. Nonetheless, she moved with ease, though Mharina saw her free up both hands.

"I apologize," she said. "In our haste to escape the storm, we came straight to the barn. I should have sought permission. We will take nothing, and I can pay for the hay our horses eat."

The man glared at her but seemed to understand that there was something different about this woman. It unnerved him that she was totally unafraid of him and his men. He looked from her to the Mushroom Man to Maugwen and Mharina.

"Someone is ill?" Sa'gola asked. "Is it your wife?"

"How be you knowing?" The man blanched.

"I can smell the ointment you're using. Let me see her. I am skilled at healing."

"Can't pay you," the man said.

"I think it will suffice if you allow us to use your barn. Maugwen. Bring your bag. You two stay here and brush the horses down."

Soon, only Mharina and the Mushroom Man were left in the barn. The rain battered the roof. Silently, they stripped the horses of bags, saddles, and blankets and set about brushing them and cleaning their hooves. A clap of thunder made the walls shudder, but the barn stood firm. They were dry, and the animals emanated heat. Mharina suddenly looked up.

"I don't know your name," she exclaimed.

"I'm the Mushroom Man," he replied without looking up.

"Your mother wanted to impress upon you early what trade you would have?"

He straightened up now, a heavy expression on his face. "I never knew my mother. I never had the opportunity to ask."

"I'm sorry," Mharina replied and, flustered, returned to her work.

A flash of lightning lit up the gaps in the barn roof, and Mharina quickly moved away from the horse she was working on as a second roll of thunder boomed, shaking the walls.

"Ouch!" The Mushroom Man staggered, holding the arm his horse had kicked.

"What happened? You should have moved away from—"

"Thanks for the advice. Next time, perhaps offer it beforehand."

She was rather affronted by his tone. "Thought you would know something like that," she muttered, and returned to the horse she was tending.

When she finished with the horses, Mharina lit a fire in a metal can. She put water on to boil and rummaged for vegetables and meat.

"I have some buttons we can add," the Mushroom Man suggested.

"I don't want your mushrooms," she snapped, and then felt her face flush.

The Mushroom Man gently took her arm and lifted her so that they were both standing.

"I'm sorry," he said, his voice soft. "I was in pain from the horse kicking me and reacted badly."

"And I should have warned you," Mharina conceded. "I'm sorry, too."

He took her into his arms and embraced her in a calm, yet strangely familiar way. It was intimate and comforting, and Mharina was reluctant to pull away.

"Still haven't told me your name," she said, stirring the soup, a mischievous grin on her face.

"No, I haven't," he said, raising an eyebrow. "Do you want my buttons?"

"Sure," she laughed. "But you will wash and cut them."

When he had done so, he settled down next to her. The fire illuminated his fair curls, and Mharina noted a few wrinkles. She also realized he was looking back at her and felt the heat return to the tips of her ears.

"I'm afraid of magic, Mharina. I've seen it at work for good and bad, but mostly bad. I avoid it and anything to do with it."

"But not me?"

"No, not you. But if I harbor any doubts about our future, aside from confronting the most powerful sorcerer in the world, it's that you possess magic. I hate it. Even seeing you appear in the forest before my eyes was hard."

"So why come with me now? Surely you know this is going to be settled by magic."

He stared into the fire and sighed. "I really don't know, beyond that I care strongly for you and I know what this is demanding from Sa'gola."

"You care about her, too."

He laughed. "Yes. I love and hate her, but I also owe her." He didn't say for what.

They went silent, listening to the crackle of wood and occasionally stirring the soup. The rain pounded on the roof, and darkness began to press in on them. Mharina shuffled over, and the Mushroom Man put an arm around her.

"A name has power," he suddenly said, and his voice sounded alien in the gathering night. "I share mine with no one. Only two living people know it, and I fear them both. I'm not ready to share it with you. Please forgive me and be patient. Letting someone in, trusting them, is a big and scary step for me."

They lay down together and wrapped themselves in their blankets. Mharina had almost fallen asleep when she smelled burning mushrooms. She abruptly sat up and removed the pot from the fire. The Mushroom Man joined her, and they sipped the charred soup. Sa'gola returned and took the rest of the soup, though she couldn't hide her grimace when she tasted it. She looked warily at the two and then returned to the house.

Mharina lay down again, facing the glowing embers of the fire. The Mushroom Man settled down behind her, wrapping his blanket around them both.

But Mharina couldn't sleep; there was something bothering her. "Do I know the two people who know your name?"

She felt him stiffen and move slightly away from her. She regretted breaking the intimacy, but something about this felt important.

When he finally answered her, his voice shook. "Yes. Sa'gola is one, and the other is…Ithea."

Chapter 82

The Mushroom Man turned away from her and, whether he slept or not, never spoke again that night. She turned and draped an arm around him, but exhaustion took over, and when she woke, he was already up preparing the horses. She was relieved he had not left.

The rain had stopped, but it was still cold and damp. The path they followed was soft, and they pushed the horses forward as fast as they could. They broke for lunch and the Mushroom Man and Mharina switched horses, riding those who had thus far carried the supplies. As the sun set behind sharp mountain peaks, they made camp in a cave. Mharina wished for a thermal pool, but there was none here.

Cradling a bowl of steaming soup, Sa'gola spoke up. "In the morning, we will enter Grogin. There is a shortcut nearby. We will leave the horses and supplies here. But we need to decide our approach. Do we try and sneak in or go through the front gate?"

No one offered an answer. Finally, Mharina asked, "Is there any way Ithea won't detect our presence? Surely, he has placed wards specific to you."

"He does lay such traps," Sa'gola replied. "I can often evade them if I'm alone, but I can't react quickly enough to divert him for all of us."

"Perhaps just you and I go," Mharina suggested. "He isn't interested in the other two."

She did not miss the glance between her Mushroom Man and Sa'gola. But then Maugwen spoke. "I'm going. If it helps, I'll go alone, but I'm not staying out of Grogin."

There was considerable determination behind her words, and they all stared at her. Sa'gola frowned. "Why did you come with me?"

"I need to find out what I am, what potential I have. You know that."

"And…?"

Maugwen just stared at her, and no one spoke for a while.

"Thank you," Mharina said at last.

"Who instructed you to do so?" Sa'gola's voice was sharp, but Maugwen did not wither.

"No one. It was my way to pay tribute to a dear friend, keeping an eye on his daughter. I have done nothing wrong."

"No, you haven't," Sa'gola conceded after a heavy moment of silence. She turned to Mharina. "Whatever his shortcomings, your father had a gift for attracting great friends."

"Let's focus on Ithea," Mharina snapped. "If our goal is to keep him from knowing what I have become for as long as possible, perhaps the three of you walk through the front gate and I join you once you're inside."

"How?" Sa'gola asked. "If you fold air, then he might discover you."

"Not if you're distracting him."

"I won't be able to buy you much time, but I can try." Sa'gola turned to the Mushroom Man. "You don't have to come."

He nodded and stared at the mushroom knife he was absently cleaning. "I do," he said. "You know I do."

Sa'gola took a deep breath as they crossed the bridge and began the final ascent to the gates at Grogin. The smooth, black rocks that formed the outer walls shimmered in the bright sunlight, and her thoughts went to the man she had served here for years. While her relationship with the Master was one of mutual respect, the fact that he had died at her hands had not seemed totally surprising. They had always danced a strange dance of submission and independence. He had a strategic subtlety that Ithea, for all his knowledge, totally lacked.

She heard the rushing water as the locks on the gate turned. Though taragusii patrolled the walls, they had clearly been instructed not to impede. The gate creaked open majestically. Sa'gola smiled to herself at how proud the Master had been of this. Water running uphill from the stream to open the gates had been a powerful statement to whoever was smart enough to understand. She remembered how Ilan had immediately comprehended and how his young eyes bulged in amazement.

When they passed through the second gate, First Scale, in his white toga and purple sash, slowly descended the stairs from the Great Hall. He had always been old, but now he seemed withered and feeble. A younger taragus hovered close to him.

"Mistresss," he beamed. "It isss good to sssee you."

"And you, First Scale. What news?"

"Massster Ithea requestsss your presence in the Great Hall." He stared at the Mushroom Man and frowned. "Welcome, sssire," he said at last, "and you, Missstress. Oh, my apologiesss. I missstook you for sssomeone elssse."

Maugwen had been wearing her cloak hood up, attempting to pass as Mharina. It had worked up until now, but perhaps this taragus knew Mharina's scent. She just nodded. First Scale turned slowly, his brow furrowed, and led them with considerable effort up the stairs.

"Next time I visit, First Scale, please meet me at the top of the stairs," Sa'gola said.

"Ah, Mistresss, I look forward to it."

They moved slowly through the black marble anteroom and on to the Great Hall. Sa'gola glanced up the stairs to the council room, the scene of her final confrontation with the Emperor. Clearly, Ithea did not want to face her there. Two huge taragusii stood guard outside dark wood doors with elegant bronze carvings that rose up the wood and gleamed in the sunlight. Abruptly, more taragusii ran in from Sa'gola's right. She braced herself to fight, but they ran past her group, and she heard sounds of a confrontation from the corridor to her left.

"What's happening?" she demanded from the guards, fearing that Mharina had been discovered.

The guards did not respond, but the doors opened, seemingly of their own volition.

"Do come in," a familiar voice said, and Sa'gola could not prevent a shiver of fear.

Chapter 83

P yre led the assault on the palace guard. They had not met an organized force since they left the dungeons. Ahad had led the way, silently dispensing of any guard unfortunate enough to be in the wrong place at the wrong time. This worked for the few they encountered. But now they faced about twenty taragusii in a narrow corridor. It prevented the big taragusii from pressing their numbers, but was wide enough for Pyre to use both Win Dao swords. Perhaps realizing this, the guard retreated to the anteroom and spread out.

Rhoddan and Montclair fanned out on either side of her, each brandishing broadswords taken from fallen soldiers. Riona held a short sword, awkward compared to her curved knife, and Troja followed with an unfamiliar halberd she was clearly uncomfortable with. Rhoddan had charged the healer with looking after the elfe while he took the vanguard. Taragusii fell without engaging as Ahad continued to wreak havoc from the periphery. A barked order sent the guard retreating into the Great Hall, where they took their place in the ranks of over eighty taragusii and fortune swords.

Everyone stopped. Ithea sat in the grand chair on the dais with Sellia and the twins on the bench by his feet. The sorcerer seemed unperturbed by their entry, and Pyre saw that his attention was on Sa'gola and the two figures with her, both hooded, one clearly female.

"This is between you and me, Ithea," Sa'gola said. "Why don't we enjoy a private audience, just the two of us?"

Ithea laughed. "I have indeed waited for such an occasion to again have you curled on the ground writhing under my whip. But now it is at hand, I rather have you at an even greater disadvantage."

He pointed to the cloaked figure. "Is this the she-elf who almost killed me? My goodness. It must be my birthday. I assume you've trained her enough to die well at my hands." He pointed to Maugwen, and his voice went cold. "If you attack me, I'll kill your mother and maybe your brother and sister, though I recognize they have considerably more potential than you."

He laughed again and turned to Pyre. "You interest me, too, she-elf. Are you an incomplete Wycaan? Precious. You have a lot to gain from siding with me."

"If you recognize me as a true Wycaan, then you know I would never join you," Pyre said.

"Fair enough." He shrugged. "But you may change your mind later when you realize how few options are open to you."

He flicked a finger at her, and Pyre flew into a stone pillar and crumpled to the ground. She moaned and did not rise. The lead taragus barked for silence as a disturbance at the back of their ranks broke out. When it did not subside, the taragusii turned. A fight had broken out, and the instigator fled into the adjacent room. The taragusii broke ranks and charged, stumbling over a dozen of their fallen comrades. Rhoddan cried out and charged the guard, and Montclair followed. Riona grabbed Troja and moved behind the column.

Ithea, momentarily surprised, raised his arms to send fire at Rhoddan. As he did, a powerful orange light flashed and smoke rose, spiraling all around them. Ithea cried out, and the smoke dissipated as fast as it had come.

"Nice try, Sa'gola. But orange really isn't your color."

Sa'gola smiled. She had not coordinated with Mharina, but now she was impressed and proud. "I did say I prefer to finish this without too many others in the room."

Ithea looked around and realized why the Purple Lady was smiling. He stared down at the empty bench and howled his fury.

"Where did you take them?" he roared as he stood and lifted his hands.

Sa'gola just laughed, and this infuriated him even more. He sent tendrils from his whip sizzling and crackling at Sa'gola. The Purple Lady braced her defenses, but the cords deflected to her right without her doing this.

Ithea stopped, puzzled, and stepped down from the dais. "She has no sorceress' magic," he growled, staring at the covered form of Maugwen. "Who is she?"

Maugwen didn't move, and Sa'gola positioned herself in front of the healer. But then the taller figure stepped aside and withdrew his hood. Ithea's eyes widened.

"You?"

"Yes, my dear brother," the Mushroom Man said.

"Why? You have no part in this fight. You collect fungus in the forest. Have you come to protect the harlot who sheltered you?" When the Mushroom Man shuffled uneasily, Ithea frowned. "No, she isn't the reason. Why are you here? It must be very important to you."

The fighting in the other room subsided and, with the last few grunts, a hooded figure entered the Great Hall with a beaming Rhoddan and a flushed Montclair flanking him.

"Did you just kill eighty taragusii and fortune swords?" Ithea said. "Impressive. Please introduce yourself."

The figure did not move, and Sa'gola felt the need to take the initiative. "We have you, Ithea. Let's end this."

"I prefer your previous offer," he said. "Let's keep this just the two of us."

His whips flared, and a wall of magical heat expanded out.

"Get out!" Sa'gola cried as she tried to slow it.

The fire flashed purple and then orange before it abruptly dissipated. Now only five remained in the room: Ithea, Sa'gola, and two hooded figures. The Mushroom Man shrank against the wall, eyes wide and chest heaving.

Then a hand protruded from the center figure's cloak, fingers flicked, and all three sets of doors slammed shut. "Yes," the young, female voice said slowly. "This is how it should be."

"Ah, Mharina." Ithea shrugged. "So you learned a few tricks from your teacher. They won't be enough to save you."

"I agree," Mharina said, removing her hood and letting her cloak fall to the ground. "But that is not all I have."

Ithea gasped…and so did the hooded man.

Chapter 84

"Wycaan! When?" Ithea snapped. "How?"

"It's of no significance," Mharina replied. "Do you still intend to take on both of us?"

Ithea shrugged and instantly released two fiery whips, but these were different than his usual fare. Each whip transformed into a huge snake, and the one closest to Sa'gola coiled itself around her body before she could raise her ward. It was unable to penetrate and crush her, but it held her in place, trapped in her own cone of power.

Mharina fared better as she pulled her staff in front of her, its runes igniting. Orange light flared from both ends to the snake, which halted its advance abruptly, hissing and withering in retreat.

"The staff: where did you get it?"

"I claimed it for my own," Mharina said. "Do you recognize it?"

"Pup," Ithea hissed. "It should be mine, and you know it. You didn't steal it from her tomb, for I know it wasn't there."

Mharina laughed. "Plundering your own mother's grave? Low even by your standards, Ithea."

"It takes more than a stick to balance the male and female energies, pup. My mother's staff won't help you. It didn't help her."

He unleashed a dozen strands of his fiery whip. Some attacked her sorceress's defenses, others her Wycaan ones. Snakes, vultures, dragons, wolves, all glowing with the red of his eyes, roared up to assail her. Mharina saw the sorcerer's own eyes shine with greater intensity than she could have ever imagined. She retreated, sending her fire out in defense by instinct. She sweated, and her staff felt increasingly hot to hold. As panic rose in her stomach, she called wordlessly to Sa'gola.

To her right, purple flames exploded and Sa'gola twisted into the air, free of her bonds. But she landed awkwardly and too near Ithea. He shot red fire into her, and her wards barely repelled it. Suddenly, he stopped, and, without the pushing force, she staggered forward toward him. From a sheath on his back, Ithea drew a huge, gleaming, red broadsword and swung it through her weakening wards, cutting through her defenses and her neck.

Mharina screamed and, letting down her own wards, charged Ithea with her staff. He met her attack, magic for magic, and swung his sword. Sword clashed with staff, and a pink fusion of his red and her orange energy exploded and disappeared. Then it was a simple staff-against-broadsword fight, and Mharina blocked only one strike before he sent her sprawling with a vicious sidekick. She heard her ribs crack with a sickening crunch. Panting and almost fainting from pain, she raised the staff, but it shook. Ithea laughed and approached her, his sword making elegant arcs and swishing sounds that echoed against the stone walls.

"How sad," he jabbed, "that the only other person to balance the *Iyzun* is so weak and pathetic. You weren't ready, she-elf. Your impulsiveness will be your death. You share your father's weakness for family. Time to join him and your teacher, little she-elf. Give my regards to my dear mother. Thank her for sending me her staff."

As his sword made its way to her neck, Mharina sobbed at her failure. But the swing never made it. A thin, blue sword deflected Ithea's broadsword, and a boot sent Ithea staggering back. He turned to face the remaining hooded figure.

"Who are you?" he hissed.

"One who lives and balances *Iyzun* and an impulsive love for family," Seanchai said, and his cloak dropped to the ground. He leapt at Ithea, Win Dao swords arcing in majestic formation.

"*Ahdahr*," Mharina panted, trying to rise. Despite the physical pain, her spirit soared.

"You're supposed to be dead," Ithea panted, stunned into retreat, though his sword moved as fast as his opponent's to fend off the attack.

"I was, in a way," Seanchai murmured. "And yet, strangely, you and your evil have brought me back to life."

Ithea twisted and sprung back twenty paces with incredible grace. He stared at Seanchai and released a ball of red fire. Seanchai hacked it away, and then Ithea advanced, sending ball after ball at him with increasing speed. A smile crept across his face.

"Use your magic, Wycaan. Show me what you have beyond the swords."

Seanchai retreated, his swords working at great speed, and Mharina suddenly realized he had nothing else to offer—not even Wycaan magic. She crawled to gather her staff. Ithea was laughing now, his attention focused only on Seanchai.

"It will take more than physical prowess, Wycaan. How did the Master not see it? Did you truly fight him twice and not use magic? Or have you lost it? Well, either way, it ends now for you."

He raised his hands to summon his whips of power and sent them hurtling at Seanchai. Mharina used all her remaining strength to meet his whips with her fire, and the orange and red again locked around each other. But Mharina felt her magic draining.

"*Ahdahr*," she cried. "Do something. I can't…"

But she didn't have to look to know that he was helpless. At least they would die together.

Then a voice cried out from within Ithea's body. His lips were still, and there was terror in his deep red eyes as they bulged in fear and surprise.

"Seanchai!" Denalion roared. "Remember your other self."

"You are dead!" Ithea screamed, clutching his head. "I took your body."

"Yes," Denalion replied, his old voice powerful and confident, "but you neglected my soul. Did you think you alone knew how to move between bodies? Did you think you could take mine so easily? I am Denalion, Dreamwalker of the Elves of the West, and I walk either side of the veil. My magic goes back to the World of Faded Memory and is more ancient than anything even you have experienced. I stand as one with the wolf, the eagle, the dragon, and the great grizzly." His voice thundered across the room. "Seanchai! The great grizzly! I summon you!"

As Ithea twisted, frantic to release the voice and spirit in his head, the grizzly roared its anger and the hall shook.

"No!" Ithea screamed as he turned inside himself to find the dreamwalker. "You are dead!"

"Never is a bear fiercer than when defending its young," Denalion cried, and the grizzly leapt on the sorcerer, its mighty jaws clamping onto the man's neck. Ithea's head ripped back, and his spine snapped. Blood spurted across the room as the great grizzly roared with rage.

Moments later, there was only heavy silence broken by the gasps of the bloody-mouthed, white-haired Wycaan. Mharina crawled over to her father, sprawled naked on the ground, his body heaving from exertion. She winced with every movement as she dragged her broken body.

"*Ahdahr*," she wheezed.

He just stared at her, his blue eyes glazed with tears, and extended a shaking arm to pull her to him.

"Denalion?" she asked.

"I think he died with Ithea," Seanchai whispered. "His spirit cannot live in a dead body. He surely rests with the greatest heroes of our time."

Mharina pulled herself up and turned to stare at her teacher. Her neck was almost severed and blood spread down her chest, staining her purple dress in dark finality. The Mushroom Man leaned over her, cradling her body. He stared at Mharina, and she saw only terror in his eyes.

He rose slowly and backed away. "I can't," he said quietly. "I saw you like her, like him. I can't."

"No," Mharina cried. "I'm not like Ithea. It's over. It's finished."

He shook his head, his blond curls falling over his face. "It's magic," he said, stumbling as he backed away. "It's never finished. It consumed them, and it will consume you, too. I've seen it with all those I love. It's never over."

He turned and staggered out of the Great Hall.

Chapter 85

Shayth stared across the ramparts, wondering. Why had the Ashen Elves not unleashed their magic? The sky filled with boulders that landed progressively closer to the wall. The first boulder hit the wall directly to Shayth's right, and the loud crack of hastily assembled timbers proved that the structure would not stand the assault. He had discussed with his officers how to retreat in a way that would prevent chaos and minimize fatalities. The pictorians were adamant that they would stand and fight here and not immediately abandon their homes. But this pride would prove costly for all if they tried to hold out for too long.

The only chance Shayth thought they had was to unleash his cavalry, and that meant retreating and engaging the Ashen Elves beneath the snow line on level ground. But they would have to draw them down there. The more he thought about it, the more impossible that seemed. Should he have forced the issue with the pictorians, or should he leave them to hold the tundra for as long as they could?

He sent a messenger for Umnesilk as more rocks crashed into the wall. Already, hundreds of Ashen Elves advanced with ladders, but the intensity of the barrage had Shayth wondering if there would be any ramparts left standing to warrant the ladders. Umnesilk lumbered over, the tips of his horns glistening in the bright sunshine. Two boars ran on either side of him. One was Dar'thuk, the boar who had guided Shayth's to Horn's Point.

"We ready to fight," Umnesilk declared. "What you need?"

"Can we talk alone?"

"Yes, but these boars replace me if I fall. Best they hear your commands so to lead if I dead."

Shayth nodded. "Only a few of my men can stand against the Ashen Elves. Our enemy has the speed and agility of elves and the strength of pictorians. Humans are no match, so this cannot be a long fight. I need your boars to stand and allow us to retreat to the second line."

Umnesilk nodded. "We ready. Know you stay only for our wishes. We drive them back some and then retreat. You go."

"Not yet. I need to know: has any boar ever touched the red stones that hang around their necks?"

Umnesilk grunted. "Not pictorian, maybe elf? They share same magic, no?"

"I don't know. Take positions. I will see if I can find an elf to... Azura!"

"What?"

"Azura, my dog. I think she might be able to pick it up. Return to your positions."

He turned and called Ballendir. "We won't deploy the dwarves. We'll need to retreat quickly."

"Yeh not gonna let mah miss all the fun, laddie."

"We aren't going to win this one," Shayth replied. "I'll need your troops at the next line, when we make a genuine stand."

Ballendir began to argue, but Shayth cut him short and turned away. He felt a growing fear that staying here was a terrible mistake, and that too many men would pay for him not ordering the pictorians to retreat.

He sent a guard to bring Azura, who was ecstatic when she saw Shayth. The prince hugged his dog, who was growing fast, and told the guard what he wanted. Once the Samoyed had two stones,

she was to drop them into a tourniquet, and the man would tie
the material to the dog's neck without touching the stones. Then
he would take the dog and stones to Shindellia. There, the scholars
might find a way to understand and counter the Ashen Elves' magic.
One of the stones was to be sent to the Elves of the West.

With everything in place, Shayth turned his attention back to the
battlefield. Three more waves of boulders had been unleashed, and
the wall was breached in several places. Umnesilk had placed pictorians at each of these places, and humans manned the walls that were
still standing. The Ashen Elves advanced behind an interlaced shield
wall, making them difficult targets for the archers. Their main force
soon massed at the foot of the wall.

"Stand strong!" Shayth cried. "Stand for your families! Fight for
your people! Fight for freedom!"

A ladder scraped against the wall and, together with two other
men, Shayth threw it back. At other points, men poured burning oil
down the wooden structures and set them alight, but more and more
elves and ladders approached. The first Ashen Elves engaged the pictorians, and the cries of battle were particularly loud in the barren,
thin air. Javelins were thrown up onto the ramparts to hinder those
trying to push the ladders away.

Then gray elves scaled the ladders, carrying long pikes that
pushed the men on the walls back. Shayth twisted inside the pike's
range and hacked at its shaft, cutting it on the third stroke. Other men
followed his lead and, for a few moments, it looked like they might
repel the assault.

Shayth noticed that those climbing up the ladders did not wear
the red stones around their necks. It might explain why there was

nothing beyond physical fighting. Perhaps only a few possessed the magic, he thought. Before this thought finished, he heard cries from soldiers in the rear. He turned and gasped. Ashen Elves appeared and charged toward the wall. These all wore the red stones, and Shayth cried to his men.

"Front line, stand firm against the ladders. Rear guard, to me. To me!"

And, broadsword in front of him, Prince Shayth Shindell led his men into the fray. The battle for Odessiya had officially begun.

Chapter 86

S hayth killed two Ashen Elves as they appeared in front of him. They did not resist, and he realized they needed a few moments after they appeared before they could begin to move and fight. He cried out to his men.

"Kill them as they appear. Don't hesitate. They're vulnerable."

This revelation enabled Shayth's men to hold their ground and inflict fatalities. More men ran to help, emboldened by the news. For a while, it looked as though they might actually gain ascendency, but the pictorians were soon being pushed back and the wall was relinquished, allowing the Ashen Elves to come through unencumbered.

Hacking his way through the gray elves with the red stones, Shayth watched the guard he had sent to bring Azura return with the dog under his arm. Azura was not wagging her tail, but staring around in bewilderment. Her ears were pinned back, and her blue eyes wide with fear.

Shayth called his personal guard to him, and the seven men circled the guard who held Azura. Shayth directed them to the prone body of a gray elf and then entered the circle to help with his dog. He drew a knife from his boot, stooped to a corpse, and cut the chain, allowing the stone to slide off the dead elf's neck and into a burlap bag the guard had brought. They did this a second time, and then Shayth carefully tied the parcel around Azura's neck. The dog yipped and shook to free herself from the weight, but soon settled as Shayth bribed her with some dried meat.

"Prince Shayth," one of the guards called, his voice wavering.

Shayth rose. The Ashen Elves had stopped fighting, and all had turned to look at him. As one, they began to move toward him, ignoring everyone else.

"Kill them!" Shayth screamed, his voice raw, and his men jumped upon their adversaries. "Get Azura out of here," he cried to the guard. "Move!"

The man turned and ran as the Ashen Elves gave chase.

"Stop them," Shayth yelled. "Protect his passage."

Even as he spoke, two pictorians gliding adroitly on long, smooth planks picked up the man holding Azura and hurtled away. Shayth, his mouth open in amazement, looked over to Umnesilk. For the first time in so long, the First Boar actually smiled.

The Ashen Elves were retreating now. Something had fundamentally changed, and Shayth hesitated about whether to press their advantage.

"Do we give chase?" he asked Umnesilk.

"Want to, but soon dark," Umnesilk replied. "They live in dark. Will be too dangerous. Must set secure camp for night. Not sure we sleep through dark."

They retreated to the camp, and Shayth briefed his officers. He wanted torches to be kept lit in case the elves breached their camp during the night. He ordered the men who weren't set to guard to eat and go to sleep.

"Wear your boots and keep your blades close. This might be a very short night," he warned. Then he retired, himself. Exhausted, he fell into a deep sleep.

"You fought well today," the Mage said.

Shayth was immediately awake, the dirk from under his pillow extended in front of him as he rose to his feet. He had to resist the temptation to rub his eyes in disbelief. The old elfe stood before him in a haze, her edges shimmering and crackling.

"I am not as brave as you, not-King. I would not come into your camp alone."

"What do you want?" he asked.

"You did well. Your tactics were solid, and you reacted quickly to whatever we threw at you. I believe I compliment you."

Shayth snorted. "That's why you came? To compliment me?"

"And warn you."

"The stones?"

"It is an ancient and powerful magic. You do not know what you meddle with."

"I do not," Shayth conceded. "But I have people who might."

"Return the stones."

"What are you offering?"

"To spare you, the pictorians, and the little ones."

"They're called dwarves," Shayth replied. "What about the elves?"

"For the fair elves, there can be no compromise," the Mage replied, her tone as cold as her eyes.

"Then you offer me nothing new."

"I offer you life. What transpired today was but a taste. Tomorrow I will unleash the full extent of my force. Bring me the stones before dawn, or you will not live to see the sun set again."

"I never thanked you for Azura," Shayth quipped.

"What?"

"My dog. She proved a valuable gift."

The Mage snorted, and it seemed as if the energy around her sizzled even more. "You named your Samoyed?" She shook her head and slowly faded away.

Shayth hesitated for a few moments, and then returned the dirk back under his pillow. He returned to bed, but sleep evaded him as he replayed what the Mage had said. He whistled softly for Azura before remembering that the dog wasn't there.

His thoughts went to his friends—to Rhoddan and Sellia and Maugwen and finally to Seanchai. Could he really still be alive and refusing to come to their aid? What had happened that could so fundamentally change him? Shayth refused to believe it was possible. The messenger had been wrong or the message garbled as it moved from one man to the next.

But what if he *was* alive? If Seanchai truly refused to aid his prince, his friend, then Shayth would have to deal with this and try Seanchai for treason. He felt an old, familiar rage well up inside of him. How could Seanchai have turned his back on him after all they had been through together? He felt his hand move under the pillow and grasp the dirk, his knuckles squeezing the hilt.

Failing to fall asleep and feeling increasingly angry, Shayth rose and went to the central tent. He poured himself some hot broth and glanced around at the few men for whom sleep also proved elusive. He walked out to talk with the guards, but bumped into Umnesilk, Narasilk, and Dar'thuk.

"Why aren't you sleeping?" Shayth asked.

"Could ask same question," Umnesilk replied.

"I had a visitor." Shayth told them of the conversation.

"Stone means something," Narasilk said, and the others nodded, except Dar'thuk, who just scowled.

"What is it?" Shayth asked.

Dar'thuk turned away.

"Prince ask, you answer," Umnesilk growled.

"Think wrong to be here," Dar'thuk said. "This camp is...is known. Too easy to attack."

Shayth stared at him and frowned. "Maybe you're right," he said, mulling over again what the Mage had said. *Bring the stone before dawn...*

The sky was beginning to light up with false dawn as the Ashen Elves silently entered the camp. They snorted derision at the lack of guards and spread out so that gray elves with axes drawn stood at each tent. A swift whistle sent them inside the tents, hacking at the sleeping mounds. All that could be heard was guttural exertion as the elves ran between the beds.

So intent were they that they failed to notice the burning arrows arching out of the night. Tents soaked in flammable liquids blazed up with Ashen Elves inside. Those who escaped the fire were hacked down by waiting pictorians. The battle was swift and vicious. Intermittently, a burning body ran from the camp, screaming in agony. The tents began to collapse and, as the sun rose, Shayth's army, situated on a hill above the camp, cheered into the new day.

Only Shayth refrained from joining the celebration. He was looking north, to where organized lines of Ashen Elves advanced. This was the real army, and it was on the move.

Chapter 87

They pulled back past the pictorian villages. Shayth watched Umnesilk offer a cursory glance to his old hearth, destroyed by Arad'gug. He wondered what his friend was thinking. As usual, the pictorian was stoic and silent. A unit of archers had stayed behind. They were not only accurate bowmen, but also trained to harry opponents on the run. Shayth strained his ears to hear the distant cries as they engaged the enemy. Now it would be a chase, as the Ashen Elves were anxious to retrieve the red stones he had taken. It was not clear if they understood that he had already sent them on to the capital.

Once past the pictorian villages, they began to descend through narrower gorges. Shayth knew there was a problem as soon as his advance exited the first gorge. He heard shouts and exhorted those in front of him to move faster. Exiting into a wide valley, he saw his men pointing up at the mountain to their east. Shayth could make out a mass of figures on its summit, but nothing else. He wished he had an elf with him, and his thoughts immediately went to Seanchai. His rage erupted once more at the inexplicable betrayal.

He turned and called for those behind him to hurry and exit the gorge. They formed up, with the pictorians taking the flank nearest the mountain. As they did, those on the mountain began to descend on boards and in Samoyed-drawn sleighs. Shayth ordered his archers to take positions. "Take out the dogs," he ordered, though he regretted having to give the order. "Sorry, Azura," he whispered beneath his breath, wondering if the puppy's parents would be among the victims.

The skiers did not ride in long, graceful loops, but instead hurtled straight on. It was a cavalry charge, and Shayth knew how effective this could be. He began to run toward Umnesilk, but it was clear he would not get to him in time, much less affect a change in formation.

He stopped, helpless, as the Ashen Elves descended upon the pictorians and human soldiers. The pictorians seemed more prepared, rolling out of range at the last moment in what was clearly a practiced move. But his soldiers were not so organized, and the Ashen Elves cut through them with horrific efficiency. The sleighs were less effective as Shayth's archers cut down the dogs, sending many sleighs spiraling out of control. A few crashed into each other and took out several unfortunate elves riding snow boards.

Shayth turned to help those on the western side deal with the elves that had passed through on their boards. He didn't figure there were more than forty or fifty, but when he turned, he gasped. Hundreds of elves advanced from already-close quarters. Those attacking from the mountain had been little more than a diversion.

Shayth cursed and called his troops to face the main offensive. He realized that not only were they caught by surprise, but the pictorians, best suited to fight the Ashen Elves, were also on the wrong side. Letting out a lung-busting battle cry, Shayth launched himself into the mass of elves. His soldiers, seeing him charge, were quick to rally to his side, but they did not advance far. The gray elves approached in terrifyingly coordinated formation, and the men were soon halted and retreating.

Shayth turned and saw Umnesilk trying to bring the pictorians around to help, but it was slow and difficult, and they were not able to hold any formation. More gray elves appeared behind those already fighting, where they could safely take the seconds they needed to recover from their transformation. The prince was at a loss for how to turn this around. They had been caught in the open and were outnumbered and outmaneuvered. There was nothing to do but fight, and Shayth launched himself into the thick of the fray, his heavy broadsword cutting through elves considerably stronger and faster than him.

Shayth had fought many times, and the battle rage flowed through him. He heard himself cry out to his men, but his voice sounded alien and distant. As he focused upon the long, gray, pointed ears, his rage flowed into hate for these elves and for the Elves of the West, who had ignored his call for help and yet represented the very race he was defending. As his anger reached new heights, he saw Seanchai in every Ashen Elf, and his sword movements blurred as he charged into the point of their offense. His men, newly inspired by their prince's courage, rallied again.

The casualties grew on both sides. Shayth was aware of the pictorians finally entering the fray. He saw Narasilk take the position of two fallen royal bodyguards and Dar'thuk lead a group of Ice Clan pictorians. Still, where Ashen Elves fell, more appeared, and Shayth's advance soon became a retreat. He called his troops into formation, a rough triangle that only allowed one elf to attack one man. Still, they were pushed back.

Then, as his strength began to desert him and he felt a wave of hopelessness rise, there came the blast of a deep horn, and the dwarves, led by Ballendir, swarmed over a ridge and slammed into the backs of the elves. Now, dwarf axes cut down the newly appearing Ashen Elves, and the enemy fell into momentary confusion. But it lasted only a short while, as those at the back turned and descended upon the dwarves. Taller and faster, the elves routed their smaller opponents.

Shayth pressed forward now, determined to protect those who had come to his aid, but their advance was slow, as the Ashen Elves matched their ferocity. The battle raged as the sun began its descent, making it difficult to see what was happening. Gradually, it seemed that fewer elves confronted them, but also that only Shayth, a few of his bodyguards, and pictorians remained.

When the fighting became sporadic, the prince began to search for any dwarves still fighting. He found that only a small group stood encircled. Shayth cried out to nearby Dar'thuk, and the huge boar changed his direction. Together with a dozen boars, Shayth launched himself between the last fighting gray elves and the few surviving dwarves. Panting from exhaustion, he stopped and stared at the final confrontations, and then all that remained were the moans of the wounded and dying. Shayth made his way over to where the dwarves gathered. In the center, lying on the ground, was Ballendir, blood leaking from too many wounds. A dwarf was trying to get his leader to drink from a pewter flask. When Shayth leaned over, Ballendir managed a strained smile.

"That was a glorious fight, mah friend," he said. "Thank yeh for sharing it."

"Why did you hang back?" Shayth took in his friend's wounds. "This is why I sent you on."

Balllendir coughed. "We saw the ambush and couldn't let yeh have all the fun," he said, trying to laugh, but only coughing and wincing.

"Hang in there, my friend. I'll get a healer."

Shayth began to rise, but a dwarf grabbed his sleeve. Ballendir was beckoning him to come close, and Shayth knelt down again.

"We were a great team...yeh, mah, Rhoddan, Sellia, and Seanchai. Don't let it fall apart now I'm gone. If Seanchai lives...yeh find and help him...If he did neh come to help, there must be a reason. I know yeh rage, Shayth...hear him first before yeh judge."

Shayth swallowed hard and nodded.

"Yeh a stubborn pup," Ballendir coughed again and winced as

even more as blood dribbled down his chin. "Promise mah. I wanna hear yeh."

"I'll hear him first, my friend, in honor of the friendship between you and me. But he'll have to answer now not only for failing to come, but also for your death."

"Noo! Yeh cheapen…mah death." Ballendir coughed and sputtered. "I died…by the axe…of an Ashen Elf…in battle…the way it should be. No one can take it away from mah…not even mah king."

"I'm no—"

"Yes, yeh are, laddie…now more than ever…Odessiya needs a king. Do what must be done. Long live the…king…"

"Ballendir is dead," a dwarf cried. "His last words were 'Long live the king!'"

The surviving soldiers took up the cry. "Long live the king! Long live the king!" Then the pictorians joined in, and the sound echoed back from the mountains as though the dead all around him had taken up the chant.

Shayth stared down at the dead dwarf. He leaned over and closed Ballendir's eyes but did not adjust the smile on his brave friend's face.

Epilogue

The Mage of the Ashen Elves stared down from the mountain at the thousands of strewn bodies lying lifeless on the snow. She saw dark bodies and pools of bright blood contrast vividly with the white terrain. The gray elves had lost more soldiers today than they had in any other battle, and she felt remorse for their loss. But they had equipped themselves bravely in their first real test, and those who had fallen had done so more due to the young prince's creative tactics. She would be better prepared next time they engaged.

Her hand reached down to absently scratch behind the ear of the tall Samoyed that sat nobly by her side. Her mind went back to her meeting with the young Shindell, and she begrudgingly acknowledged her admiration for him. He had been calm in battle and remarkably astute. His discovery that her stone-carriers needed a few seconds before they could move had been critical and costly. She would not be able to employ them so close to their enemy again.

She fingered her own red stone around her neck. He possessed one now, and that was her greatest fear. Should he discover what the stones did or succeed in replicating the magic, the Ashen Elves' advantage would be seriously compromised.

The Emperor was dead, and now perhaps his successor, too. She had felt something dramatic rock the web of magic that connected the earth. For now, nothing stood in the way of her gray warriors, and they would advance as she had always planned.

She strained her eyes and watched as the prince left a group crowded around a fallen dwarf. He moved onto a nearby ridge with an elf soldier, who pointed in her direction.

She doubted the prince could see her at such a distance, but he could hear her if she wanted. She muttered a few words and stroked her stone. Then she whispered just loud enough to catch his ears alone.

Look well upon your losses, not-King. They are heavy and will get heavier. All Odessiya will fall like these brave soldiers. We will slaughter your humans, dwarves, pictorians, and especially your elves. We will show no mercy for your mates and children. None shall stand as the Ashen Elves take back what is rightly theirs.

It has only just begun.

THE END

Author's Note:

Dear Friend,

Let me begin by thanking you for staying with me on this roll-ercoaster journey. In this novel, some have been forced to grow up fast while others fell by the way. Those who emerged as leaders and flawed heroes really excite me. *From Ashes They Rose* seemed to write itself as the newer characters stood up and established themselves. I welcome them into the family. Yet I remain deeply fearful for them.

The next book shall, I assume, offer closure to so many and I feel a driving need to get behind my keyboard and let the story fulfill its destiny.

The world of epic fantasy is thriving, and there are many great authors producing fine novels to choose from. I thank you for taking the time to read *From Ashes They Rose* and the Wycaan Master series.

Once more, if we meet upon the road or at a tavern, let us meet as companions and tell tales of old times: of battles won, love lost, and alliances formed. Let us speak with pride of those who died along the way and weep with bitter joy that we had a chance to share their path.

If we do not meet, feel free to contact me at anelfwriter@gmail. com or sign up for my weekly blog post at http://www.elfwriter. com. I also tweet at @elfwriter. Please consider leaving a brief review of this book online wherever you bought it and on Goodreads –it really helps the book garner attention!

Thank you again,

Alon
http://www.alonshalev.com

NON-FANTASY NOVELS BY
ALON SHALEV:

Unwanted Heroes (Three Clover Press, 2012)

A Gardener's Tale (Three Clover Press, 2011)

The Accidental Activist (Three Clover Press, 2010)